The Spirit in Washington Square

Also by Mary Kay Remick:

SEARCHING FOR BLANCHE

SWEET AND SOUR

The Spirit in Washington Square

A Novel By

Mary Kay Remick

Pen Oak Press

Published by PEN OAK PRESS, P.O. Box 187, Hollywood, Alabama, 35752-0187
Fax: 256-228-9665

Library of Congress Control Number: 2003099033

ISBN 0-9667128-3-8

10 9 8 7 6 5 4 3 2 1

Printed in the United States of America

January, 2004

First Edition

Cover Art by Liz Morgan
Cover design by Liz Morgan
Author photograph by Jo Stafford

For my last born daughter, Lisa Wheeler Perkins

(March 21, 1961—December 21, 1978)

ACKNOWLEDGMENTS

It has been my good fortune to have a wide net of friends and supporters. I am nothing if not greedy – once you're caught in my net you're considered keepers, and no matter how hard you may try to break the line, I hold fast.

Among those tangled in my net are a group of fellow writers loosely known as the "Tennessee Mafia." I met these girls back in 1982 at a week-long writers' conference in St. Simons, Georgia, and we've been supporting, critiquing, encouraging, and loving each other ever since: Pat Boatner, Connie Green, Pat Hope, Joy Margrave, Jo Stafford, and Sue Ellen Hudson. (On October 4, 1997 our much-loved head cheerleader, Sue Ellen, succumbed to cancer. We all miss you, sweet Sue!)

The ever-expanding net has caught still more writer friends: Donna Ash, Donna Bond, Jan Brown, Vicki Brumback, Helen Friese, Jane Hicks, Elizabeth Howard, Dixie Huthmaker, Lou Kassem, Gay Martin, Denise May, Nelle McFather, Cathie Pelletier, Sue Orr, Mona Raridon, Betty Roe, Mike Roe, Brenda Rollins, Dot Senn, Ruth Smalley, and Denise Stafford. A special thanks goes to Jan Brown for her fine editorial skills.

Also snared in my net and lending continuous support despite their entrapment are: Connie Albright, Linda Bourgeois, Millie Barrilleaux, Patricia Bancer, Joan Brandt, Sue Freeman, Myrtle Green, Brenda and Johnny Crabtree, Ann Sims, Garry Hudson, Dick Green, Nancine and Sam DeHaan, Cheryl and Paul Wilson, Maggie Garrett, Tana Broadbent, Bruce Mitchell, Peggy Swanger, Stanley Joyce, Juanita and Art Snure, Barbara and John Day, Joan and Bob MacCullum, Sunny and Bruce MacDonald, Helen Thomas, Judy and Jack Hayward, Shirley Robinson, Donna Rivest, Marilyn Masters-Lawrence, Dave and Barbara Roberts; Delores, Marie, and Nancy of the Scottsboro Public Library, Barbara Jacobs, Arlene Grede, Sarah Betty Ingram, Ella Ruth Lamberth, and the Scottsboro chapter of the American Association of University Women.

My family doesn't have a chance of breaking free–I need them and love them too much: To first my adult children: Kathy Perkins, John Perkins, Elizabeth Morgan, and Shon Remich. Then to the rest of the catch: Dee Perkins, Elaine Perkins, Betty Wheeler, Rose and Sam Remich, Dave Remich, Ron Remich, Paula Guenther, and of course the grandchildren: Jeremy and Jessica Perkins; Stephen, Benjamin, and Joshua Remich. And to my future granddaughter-in-law, Lindsey Marshall.

Best and last on the list is my loving husband Jack, for his enduring patience. He is truly a jack of all trades.

For Cliff,
It was great fun having you spend time with us in Alabama. Hope we didn't traumatize you too much.
Laissez les bons temps rouler!

The Spirit

Love,

in

Mary Kay
05/16/04

Washington Square

One

The shiny Checker cab sailed through the intersection of Rampart Street and Elysian Fields like a giant yellow butterfly. Unseasonably warm air for February flowed through the open windows, the sound of Judy Garland's voice floated out.

"When You're Smiling," Judy sang from the tape deck.

Behind the wheel, Art noticed the usual cluster of punks hanging around Rampart's southwest corner. They looked up from whatever they were dealing, their pierced ears picking up the vibes coming from the cab. Art wanted to shout: *That's what real music sounds like, you dopes*! Instead he flashed them a toothy grin and the peace sign. The punks stared after him, their bristly jaws agape.

Art snorted a laugh. That was the most fun he'd had all day. Come to think of it, it was the most fun he'd had all weekend–the thought of which wiped the grin off his face. If he and Belle couldn't take a simple overnight trip to Mississippi without it wearing him down to a nub, how in the hell would they make it all the way to California?

Judy sang on. Art could hear the little tremble in her voice that made him want to cry even though she was singing a happy song. No other singer had ever moved him as deeply as Judy, God rest her soul.

Beside him, in the passenger's seat, Belle was busy conducting the orchestra, arms flailing, blue eyes shining, golden hair flying in the breeze. Every now and then she'd sing along, but quietly so as not to take anything away from Judy. Ordinarily, Art would have joined in. Singing made him feel like a kid again, like the choir boy he once was back in Jersey, but today he didn't have it in him. Truth was, he wasn't feeling so good.

With only a slight pause for breath, Judy started belting out the words to "This Can't Be Love." Putting the cab on automatic pilot, Art let the tune wash over him. Nobody wrote songs like that anymore; nowadays, all the so-called music blasting out of car stereos and boom boxes sounded like gibberish screamed from the mouths of monkeys gone mad.

It wasn't the hour that made him so achy and groggy–it was still daylight, though dusk was creeping in fast–it was everything that had and hadn't happened over the past two days.

Today had been particularly nerve-wracking. After striking out in Laurel, Mississippi–where they'd hoped to find Blanche–he'd decided Belle needed a diversion, so they'd headed down to Biloxi. What happened there provided a distraction all right. It turned Belle's world, and no doubt his as well, upside down. At the time, all Art could think about was getting them out of town, which he'd tried to do by constantly reminding Belle of her six o'clock curfew. Did she listen? Not a chance.

First she'd insisted on buying souvenirs for Mammy and Marge and all the girls, and then she'd wanted to stop at every thrift shop and yard sale they passed. He'd made more U-turns than a hyperactive boomerang.

By the time they hit the road, Sunday traffic was bumper-to-bumper. Near Slidell it came to a complete halt. Art figured a construction crew was working overtime. He'd been wrong. A bad wreck had shut down two lanes. Though they couldn't tell exactly what had happened, it looked like a big rig had rear-ended a pickup, sending it across the median and into the path of a utility van. When a cop finally flagged them by–squad cars, fire trucks, and ambulance crews all over the place–Belle burst into tears, certain that everyone involved in the crash had been killed. Art had no choice but to let her cry it out. Once Belle turned on the waterworks the pipes had to drain dry, which they did when the skyline of New Orleans came into view.

By then they both needed a little cheering, so he'd plugged the Garland tape into the slot. Nothing like a little toe-tapping music to perk a body up. Trouble was, Art's toes had gone numb.

Judy segued into, "Just You, Just Me."

Because Art hoped that someday he and Belle would be "just us, just we," he made a promise to himself: No more rehashing the day's events. No more blaming Belle for all the delays. They were going to make it back in time. All he had to do now was coast.

No sooner had he started to relax, slumped down in his seat, hands loose on the wheel, than Belle let out a squeal. He jerked upright, heart thumping, eyes darting between Belle and the side-and rearview mirrors.

Judy sang on. He punched the off button and the tape popped out.

"What? What?" he asked, thinking he must have run over something–a bird, a squirrel, maybe even a kitten.

"Hallelujah!" Belle cried. "We're almost there!"

Art's eyes glazed over. "You mean I didn't hit nothing?"

"What are you talking about?" she said. "Slow down. We're here."

Squinting through the windshield, Art saw that she was right. There, three houses down, stood the blue and white house known as Hope Haven.

"Hell's bells," he said, "you almost gave me a heart attack."

"Hush," she said. "You're always saying that, and it scares me to death."

"I'm always saying it because it's true. Your little piggy squeals drive me nuts." He eased the Checker up to the curb and braked in his usual spot.

"Everything drives you nuts," she said, giggling and starting to gather her stuff.

"Not so fast," Art said. He pretended to check the meter, which hadn't been turned on in days, then flipped his right hand palm side up and held it out to her. "Okay, lady, two grand oughta do it."

She slapped at his hand. "Don't be silly."

He frowned. "Hey, lady, you trying to stiff me, or what?"

"What," she said. She scooted over to his side, flung her arms around his neck and proceeded to cover the right side of his face with kisses.

"Cut it out," Art said, half-heartedly trying to push her off him. "You're getting lipstick all over me."

She pulled her head back and studied him. "You could use a little color," she said. "Here, let me do the other side." She raised up, leaned over him and started kissing the left side of his face.

"Getouttahere," he said, pushing her more forcefully. "You got four minutes to get your scrawny butt in the house."

"Oh pooh," Belle said, plopping down in her seat. "You're no fun at all."

"Yeah, I know. If I was you I'd trade me in on a new model. Hey, now that you're rolling in dough you probably will. Coupla months from now you'll be tooling around in some dude's–"

She pressed two fingers against his lips to shush him. "Don't even think such a thing. You're stuck with me, Art Barkoff, whether you like it or not."

"Oh yeah? Well, Mammy Daisy ain't gonna like either one of us if you don't make curfew." For the past five months he'd had Belle back to Hope Haven by six o'clock and he wasn't about to screw up now.

"Yes, I know, but–"

"No buts, kiddo." He held out his wristwatch and stabbed a finger at the dial. "Two minutes. Go. Scat. Vamoose."

"Alright, already," she said, mimicking his oft-used phrase. She scrambled out of the cab and hurried up the walk. Midway to the front stoop, she turned around and headed back.

"Now what?" Art asked when the open window framed her face.

"I forgot my overnight case. It's in the trunk."

"Not to worry. I'll bring it in."

"Don't forget the souvenirs."

"I won't."

"Well?" Belle said. "What are you waiting for?"

Art made a swatting motion, as if at a pesky fly. "Gimme a minute, will ya?"

She didn't budge, just kept looking at him.

"What?" Art said. "You think I'm gonna leave you alone with all those money-grubbing hussies? Soon's they get wind of you winning that jackpot they'll be begging for a hand out."

A troubled look came over her face, and before Art could stop her she climbed back inside.

"Aw, come on, Belle. You know I was only kidding."

When she didn't respond, Art ran a hand through his curly mass of salt-and-pepper hair. Times like these tied his stomach in knots. It was a wonder he didn't have ulcers. Come to think of it, maybe he did. He'd been popping a lot of Tums lately.

After a long minute, Belle turned to him. "I'm not going to tell them about winning the jackpot."

"What! You jacked your jaws for a solid hour about how you couldn't wait to tell 'em, and now you're telling me you're not gonna tell 'em? What's your problem?"

"I'm afraid of how they'll react. What if they turn against me? What if they hate me? I couldn't bear it."

"Hate you?" He thumped his forehead with the heel of a hand. "No way could they hate you. Those girls are crazy about you. They'll be turning cartwheels soon's they hear the news. They won't have their hands out neither."

"Do you really think so?"

"I know so. Have I ever steered you wrong?"

"No. Not yet anyway."

"Lissen, Belle, those girls have been around. When one of their own strikes it lucky, it gives them hope they're next. You get what I'm saying?"

"It was luck, wasn't it?" she said as though the possibility hadn't occurred to her.

Yeah, Art thought, like everybody who drops a silver dollar in a slot machine wins a jackpot. "You betcha it was luck," he said. "Take my word for it, those girls'll be jumping for joy."

"Oh, I hope you're right."

"'Course I'm right. Now getouttahere."

"I can't. It just doesn't seem fair. Gloria needs money for school clothes, Janette needs work clothes, Boots needs–"

"Forget all that *fair* crap," Art said. "Those girls'll make out just fine. Now you ... that's a different story. Your old man dumped you when you was just starting treatment. Filed for divorce without saying goodbye, so long, it's been nice to know you. Was that fair? Hell, no. And that daughter of yours ... you ask me, she's been nothing but a pain in the ass. But despite all that, you stuck it out here at Hope Haven. You made a whole new life for yourself. A helluva better life. So fair ain't got nothing to do with it. Now get in the house. Trouble with Mammy we don't need."

Belle hunkered down in her seat. "I can't go in until I've decided what to do. Maybe I should share my winnings. I could divide the total by seven. Nine, if I include Mammy Daisy and Marge. Oh, and I'd better set some aside in case Darleen comes back. What do you think?"

"What do I think? I think you're crazy. Don't you get it? You're flat broke. Busted. You're gonna need every cent of that dough to get your business going. You're a professional mural painter, remember?"

She heaved a sigh. "I suppose you're right. But I still feel guilty."

Art shook his head. "She feels guilty. Jesus, what am I gonna do with you?"

Her sudden smile caught him by surprise. "Be my business manager, that's what."

"Now you're talking," he said. "Okay, lissen up. The first rule of business is, you don't loan money and you sure don't give it away unless you're a banker or a millionaire. Which you ain't. The second rule of business is, do everything your manager tells you to do, and right now he's telling you to get out of his cab and go in the house. We can work out a plan later."

Still smiling, she gave a little salute. "Yes, sir." Then she added, "But I'm not going to tell them until you're standing by my side. So hurry up, you old poop."

Art watched her steady progress up the walk, willing her to keep going. At last she disappeared into the house. Groaning with relief, he sagged back against the seat. After two days and a night with Belle, hunting for someone who might or might not exist, he was convinced her search for Blanche would be the death of him yet. Every journey they'd made over the last six months, up and down the roads of Louisiana and now Mississippi, seemed to have added a year to his life. Yet Belle, at forty, kept bouncing along like a six-year-old, her hopes of finding Blanche, though sometimes wavering, never ceasing.

The clock on the dash showed the time as 6:06. He'd give Belle a few more minutes to do the huggy-kissy thing with Mammy and the girls and then he'd carry her things in. After that he'd call it a night. Forget dinner. Every one of his fifty-two years were tugging at him like hundred pound weights. All he wanted was a hot shower followed by eight hours of uninterrupted sleep.

At 6:10, Art opened his door and tried to swing his legs out, but for some reason they wouldn't cooperate. What the hell was going on? He pondered the question for a moment, then decided the old arthritis was acting up again. To ease the stiffness in his lower limbs, he lifted his left leg with both hands and planted it on the road. He did the same with his right. Then he grabbed hold of the door frame and tried to pull himself up. Stars danced before his eyes as he struggled for balance. This was more than stiffness, he thought. This was a sign his blood pressure had dropped way below normal. Had he taken his pills that morning? He couldn't remember.

The blast of a horn jarred him into a rigid standing position. He pulled the cab's door tight against him just as a tour bus rumbled by, missing him by inches. He blinked, amazed he was still in one piece. Fearing another close call, he slammed his door shut and walked around to the trunk, where he collected Belle's overnight case and the shopping bag full of souvenirs.

The rush of fear-driven adrenaline that had given him the strength to get out of the street faded the moment he stepped over the curb. From there the front walk seemed a mile long. Every time he stopped to catch his breath he thought his lungs might burst. Sure, he'd felt lousy on the road home but this was ridiculous.

Finally he stood before the front door, his breath coming in short, ragged gasps; beads of sweat coating his upper lip and brow. Setting Belle's things on the porch floor, he dug a handkerchief out of his back pocket and used it to wipe his face. For two cents he'd take off right now. Leave the overnight case and shopping bag for Belle to find in the morning. So she'd pepper him with questions, so what. Naw, it wasn't worth it. He tucked the handkerchief back in his pocket, worked up enough saliva to swallow, and opened the door.

The girls swooped down on him like a greedy flock of jays, their claw-like fingers clutching and grasping, wing-like arms encircling, beaked lips smacking. Art tried his best to fend them off, but it took every ounce of strength he had to keep from falling down.

"Jeez, Louise," he said, his face and ears turning beet red, "you'd think we'd been gone a year."

"Don't you wish," Gloria said with a sly wink.

From out of the corner of his eye, he saw Mammy Daisy hanging back from the others. He tipped his head to her. She returned the greeting in kind. No way would Mammy join the group hug. Not because she didn't like him, but because such displays were beneath her dignity. She was Hope Haven's housemother, after all. Mother, guardian, counselor and friend to the eight women who lived here.

"Hey, what about me?" said a familiar voice.

Art peered over the tops of the girls' heads to see who'd spoken.

A slim, long-legged girl in skin-tight black leather pants and a hot pink T-shirt stood off to one side.

"Well, I'll be darned," Art said, forcing strength into his voice and a grin onto his face. "If it ain't my old pal. Couldn't take life on the road, eh?"

Darleen sashayed up to him with an exaggerated swing of her hips. "I'll have you know I love being on the road. Just wait till you see Roger's rig. You'll be trading that old cab of yours in for one just like it."

"Ha," he snorted. "That'll be the day." Bought new in 1971 and now considered a classic, the Checker was his most prized possession.

"So, how're you doing?" he asked her. "This guy Roger, is he good to you?"

"He's the best. Just like you." She put her arms around him, hugged him tight, and planted a kiss on his cheek.

Thrown off balance by her embrace, Art swayed in place for a moment. Darleen didn't seem to notice.

Of all the girls, Darleen had been his favorite. Back in the days when he was hoping to get a glimpse of Belle during her no-visitors stint, Darleen always blew him a kiss. Later on, just as he'd gotten to know her, she'd run off with a trucker. Not for sex, dope, or rock 'n' roll, she'd said, but for love. Now, seeing the happy glow on her face, Art guessed she'd told the truth.

"So, when do I get to meet this guy?" he asked.

"As soon as the French Market crew unloads the rig. Oh, and the good news is, Roger got a contract to haul produce from Texas to Mobile, so we can come by here more often. Isn't that great?"

Mammy Daisy stepped forward, wagging a finger at her. "Girl, don't you be thinking you can pop in here any old time. We got rules and regulations in this house. And I ain't having you bringing no man by here lessen I say so."

"Yes, ma'am," said Darleen, her cheeks turning as pink as her shirt.

"Oh, Mammy," Belle said, "you know Darleen wouldn't break the rules."

"Humph," Mammy grunted. "She done broke number one when she took outta here without our blessing."

"But she was in love!" Belle exclaimed.

Mammy made a face and muttered,"She shoulda said goodbye."

Gloria changed the subject. "Belle, if you don't tell us what happened in Mississippi, I am going to wring your neck. That goes for you too, Art."

Art looked at Belle, saw her face cloud over, and stepped to her side. "Y'know," he said, "I think we all oughta sit down." Before I fall down, he added to himself.

"Amen, brother," said Mammy. "My corns is killing me." She turned and shuffled towards the kitchen, her terry cloth scuffs slapping against her heels.

Heavy sighs and murmurs came from the girls as they tagged along behind her.

Linking arms, Art and Belle followed the flock.

At the door to the kitchen, he leaned her way and said, "If you don't tell 'em, I will."

Two

Before sitting down in the head chair, Mammy Daisy put a pan of brownies still warm from the oven, a pitcher of milk, a stack of paper napkins, and a tray of drinking glasses on the table.

While the girls passed the milk and brownies, Art dragged an extra chair from the corner of the room and wedged it between Belle's and Mammy's. Weak and panting by the time he sat down, he straddled the table leg, pressing his knees against it to keep them from shaking. Hang on, he told himself, he'd be out of there in fifteen minutes max. All he needed was a hot shower and a good night's sleep. Tomorrow he'd feel like a new man.

"Hey, Art," Darleen said, "I hear you sprang for this dining set. It sure beats that old picnic table we used to crowd around."

"Ain't that the truth," said Mammy. "Don't know what we'd do without our main man here." She reached over and gave Art's arm a motherly pat.

Art blushed but said nothing. The dining set had been his Christmas gift to the house. An oblong walnut table with two leaves, armchairs at each end, and six side chairs, it had cost him a month's wages, but it was worth it. He'd wanted to burn the ratty old picnic table they'd been using, but the girls moved it to the backyard and refused to let him torch it.

"Isn't this wonderful," Belle said, beaming a wide smile around the table, her eyes lighting briefly on Gloria, Janette, Darleen, Boots, Gracie, Fran, Millie, and Mammy Daisy. "Here we are, Hope Haven's finest, together again."

Though Hope Haven was officially known as a halfway house for recovering substance abusers, a way station for addicted females to shed their past and embrace their future, to Belle it was home.

"Yeah, yeah, it's terrific," Janette said drily. "Now tell us about Mississippi."

Belle's smile dissolved. She cast a worried glance at Art, then cleared her throat and said, "You will never believe it."

"You found Blanche," Gloria stated flatly.

"No, sad to say, I did not find Blanche. Or Stella or Stanley, or the old plantation."

"Ohhhnoooo," the girls lamented as one.

"But that doesn't mean they weren't there," Belle said. "It's just that everything in Laurel had closed so the townspeople could go to the mayor's funeral. Apparently, he'd taken his son out to a target range and the boy accidentally shot him. Imagine how awful that poor boy must feel. Shooting his own daddy like that. That will haunt him for the rest of his life. I can't–"

"Belle," Janette said, "please get to the point."

"The point? Oh, well, everything was closed. The courthouse, the chamber of commerce, the library, the museum, even the drug stores. I did get to talk to a few people on the street, but none of them had ever heard of the DuBois family. Or the Kowalskis. Isn't that strange? How could those people live in Laurel and never hear of Blanche and Stella? They were born and raised there, for heaven's sakes, and the play Mister Tennessee wrote about them made them famous. Laurel, too. Either the people I talked to were playing dumb or they were from some other place. And to top it all off, they kept giving me these funny looks."

"What were you wearing?" Gloria asked.

"My very best outfit," she said, meaning what she considered the best of her collection of vintage clothing from the 1940s. "The pale yellow dress with the big floppy sleeves."

"That explains it," Gloria said. "We used to look at you funny, too, didn't we, girls?"

"Unnhuhh."

"Yeah, I thought you looked really weird in those fancy duds," said Janette, whose fashion statement consisted of a snake tattoo running the length of her left arm. "But that was before I got to know you."

"I tried to get her to ditch the hat," Art said, "but you know Belle." He reached for the pitcher to pour himself a glass of milk. When his hand began to shake he changed his mind.

"Which hat?" Gracie wanted to know.

"The cream-colored organdy that matches my pumps," Belle said. "And of course I wore my pearls. Blanche just adores pearls."

"So do I," said Boots.

"Who cares," snapped Janette. "What I wanna know is, what won't we believe?"

When Belle turned a blank look on her, Janette rolled her eyes. "You said we'd never believe what happened, so *something* must've happened."

"Oh, it did, it did."

"Then tell us what, for gawd's sakes."

"Well, since we couldn't find Blanche, Art thought we needed a change of scenery. So we drove down to Biloxi. We planned to walk on the beach, listen to the sound of the surf, feed the–"

"Dammit, Belle," Janette said. "We don't need to know every little detail. Just tell us what happened."

"Girl, you better watch your mouth," warned Mammy Daisy.

"Yes, ma'am," said Janette.

Art nudged Belle with an elbow. "Go on," he urged, "tell 'em the news."

"Oh, *that* news. I won a jackpot."

Mouths popped open and eyes bugged out. Several girls rose halfway out of their chairs. "What kind of jackpot?"

"A slot machine jackpot."

Before the girls could react, Mammy Daisy zeroed in on Art. "You let that child gamble?" she asked, her voice low and threatening.

"Well, I ... ah ..." Art lost his train of thought. A sudden spell of dizziness, like the one he'd had when he climbed out of the cab, made his brain spin.

A voice sounded, as if from a great distance. It was coming from Belle and she was sitting right next to him! Was he going deaf? He tried to concentrate on what she was saying, but all he caught were snatches.

"... bad storm ... out of the rain ... wasn't his idea ... didn't want ... casino ..."

Now Mammy was talking. Art had no idea who to, but she was looking straight at him. "... done us wrong ... trusted you ... care of her ... take her ... house of Satan!"

Then everyone started yammering at once. Art shook his head, hoping to clear it, but that only made him dizzier.

"Y'all hush!" Mammy ordered.

Art heard that loud and clear.

Mammy went on. "You better do some fast talking, Mister Man, else you done seen the last of this welcome mat."

Art felt his features pinch together. Did she mean him? With the back of a hand gone clammy he took a swipe at his brow. He could feel the sweat from his chest and underarms bleeding into the fabric of his shirt. How did it get so blasted hot in here?

"Art," Belle whispered in his ear, "are you all right?"

He could feel his head swelling, like a balloon being blown up. He could picture it bursting, his brains splattering everywhere. That is if he had any. He tried to laugh. Couldn't.

"Hot," he croaked, his tongue as thick as twisted hemp. "Thirsty." Had anyone heard him?

Her face flushed with alarm, Belle looked to Mammy.

The girls squirmed in their seats, their eyes darting from Belle to Art to Mammy and back again.

"Give the man some air," Mammy said. "Open the back door, Janette. Gloria, you get him a glass of water." She leaned in Art's direction and laid a hand on his forearm. "Art? Can you hear me?"

The numbness started at his toes and worked its way up to the top of his skull. Then everything went black.

. . .

Belle watched in horror as Art keeled over, the right side of his face thudding against the table, his cheek mashing her brownie, her drinking glass gushing milk as it tumbled onto its side. She jumped up, her mouth wide open and not a sound coming out.

Mammy Daisy clasped her hands to her breast. "Lord'a'mercy. I done scared the life outta this here good man."

"Omigod!" someone screeched. "Is he dead?"

"I'll call 911," Gloria called. She ran to the wall phone and snatched up the receiver. Holding it in her left hand, her right index finger flew over the dial.

Darleen wiped up the spilt milk with paper napkins. Janette came whipping around the table. She pushed Belle aside and put two fingers against a spot on Art's neck. "He's still breathing," she said. "Gloria, tell them to hurry. I think he's had a stroke."

Belle rushed to the sink, ran cold water over a clean dish cloth and brought it back. She laid the cloth across Art's forehead. He never stirred. His skin had an ashen cast. Drool leaked from the corner of his mouth, forming a dark circle on the table. His eyes were slightly open, like someone half asleep.

Belle stroked the hair back from his face. "Now you listen to me, Art Barkoff. You've got to hold on. You know I'll make a mess of things if you don't handle my affairs. Besides that, I love you, Art. I truly do." She kissed his exposed temple, then laid her hand on the wet cloth and kept it there.

"Please don't take him, Lord," Mammy prayed. "He's a good man and we needs him."

"Someone go outside and wait for the ambulance," Janette said.

"I'll go," the others cried as one. Chair legs scraped the floor as they stood en masse and headed for the front door, leaving Belle, Janette, Gloria, and Mammy to tend to Art.

"Belle, does he have a regular doctor?" Gloria asked from her station by the phone.

"Yes, but I can't think of his name. Jensen, Jackson, something like that."

With the finesse of an expert pickpocket, Janette lifted Art's wallet and riffled through the business cards. "Here it is," she said. "His name is Jennings. Clark Jennings. He's a cardiologist. His number is 576-9223. Did you get that, Gloria? Five-seven-six-nine-two-two-three. Oh, and Art's got Blue Cross."

Seconds later, Gloria was giving the information to whoever was on the other end of the line. She paused, then asked, "What hospital will they take him to?" Silence. Then, "Okay. Thank you very much." She hung up and faced the women.

"That was the doctor's answering service. The lady said he's not on call tonight, but she'll try to reach him. Oh, and she said they'll take him to Charity."

"Charity!" Belle wailed. "But he has insurance."

"I know, but that's what she said. Maybe it's closer. Maybe they have the best emergency room."

Janette grimaced. "Let's hope so."

"Dear Lord," Mammy prayed, "give that doctor the wisdom to heal our man, and give Art the strength of all your angels. Thank you, Lord, and Amen."

Belle looked at Janette. "Shouldn't we be doing something? I feel so helpless just standing here."

"I know. I wish I could think of something. He's still breathing, so I'm afraid to do CPR. I guess we could try to lay him down somewhere and loosen his clothes." She looked around as though searching for a likely spot.

"Put him on my bed," said Mammy, pushing her heavy frame up and out of her chair with unusual vigor. She moved towards her room, just off the kitchen.

Belle, Gloria, and Janette hovered around Art, fretting over the best way to move him. He was a large man, well over six feet tall and close to two-hundred pounds.

A siren sounded in the distance.

"Don't get your hopes up," Gloria said. "It's probably a fire truck or a cop car."

Still, the women stood stiff and silent, each of them listening as hard as they could.

The scream of the siren grew closer.

A collective gasp went up when Darleen appeared in the doorway. "Roger's here," she said, her eyes cutting past the girls to Art. "We could carry him to the hospital. We've got a bed behind the cab."

Janette looked at Belle. "What do you think?"

Belle cupped a hand to her ear. "Listen," she said.

The siren gave one last piercing scream and then stopped altogether. It sounded as though it had come from in front of the house.

"That must be them!" Janette whooped. To Darleen, she said, "Go tell the medics where we are."

"Praise the Lord!" Mammy cried, her eyes gazing upwards.

Belle bent over Art, "It's going to be all right, sweetheart. Help is on the way. You hold on, or I'll never forgive you."

. . .

Gloria turned to Belle. "Do you want anything from the canteen?"

Belle shook her head. "No, thanks."

"I'm going out for a smoke," Roger said. He got to his feet. "You coming?" he asked Darleen.

Darleen looked at Belle, as though seeking her permission. When Belle continued to stare straight ahead, she looked at Janette. "We'll be back in a minute."

"Take your time," Janette said. "Nobody seems to be in a hurry around here."

Neither Belle nor Gloria said a word.

They had all arrived together in Roger's truck; Belle, Janette, and Gloria back in the sleeper section, Darleen up front with Roger. Fortunately, he'd left the trailer at the French Market's loading dock. Without the full rig they'd almost caught up with the ambulance. Little good it had done them. They'd been waiting for word for nearly three hours, passing the time by either talking to each other in hospital voices–hushed tones and whispers–or sitting silently. Every now and then someone would step outside for a smoke, or visit the canteen.

Aside from worrying and wondering, what bothered them the most was they weren't even waiting in the area where Art had been taken. They were where the accident victims were treated. Art was on the other side of the security station that separated the two emergency rooms. He was in a place reserved for serious cases.

Belle broke the heavy silence. "Roger seems like a nice man."

"You think everybody's nice," Janette said.

"Well, one thing's for sure," said Gloria, "Darleen thinks he's nice."

"Yeah," Janette said, "let's see what she thinks six months from now."

"I'm sure she'll think he's even nicer," Belle said.

At that, the three of them lapsed into another heavy silence. Again, Belle was the first to speak. "Mammy thinks what happened to Art is all her fault, but it isn't, it's mine. I shouldn't have dragged him all over creation."

Gloria put an arm around her shoulders. Janette, who was sitting on Belle's other side, patted her knee. "Stop blaming yourself," Gloria said. "You didn't drag him anywhere he didn't want to go."

"Oh, but I did. He wanted to head back early, but after I won the jackpot I just *had* to go shopping. And then I just *had* to stop at all the yard sales and thrift shops we passed. If only I'd listened to him, but no. He didn't want to take me into the casino, either. We were out on the beach when a storm blew up out of nowhere. Art wanted to take cover in a restaurant, but I coaxed him into the casino. I wasn't thinking about gambling or anything, I just wanted to see what it looked like. Poor Art. He's always saying I'm going to give him a heart attack, and now look what's happened." Tears streamed down her cheeks in a steady flow.

"That's just it," Gloria said, brushing the tears away with her fingertips. "We don't *know* what happened. Maybe it was something he ate."

"But I ate the same things he did!"

"Sshhh," Gloria whispered. "We've got to be quiet or they'll kick us out of here."

Belle sniffed her nose, then hiccupped. "And another thing ... when we finally made it back to the house, he wanted me to hurry inside so I wouldn't get him in trouble with Mammy. Did I listen? No, not me. I'm such a selfish brat."

"Stop that kind of talk right now," Gloria hissed. "You are the most unselfish person I know. Isn't that right, Janette?"

"Right. Remember when Mammy Daisy said I had to go to church with her because I'd been cussing a blue streak? Well, even though I'd been real mean to you, you offered to give me your best dress to wear." She paused, then added, "Not that I would've worn it, but it was nice of you all the same."

Belle looked at her, a faint smile creasing her face. "I remember that. You didn't own a dress back then and all your shirts were sleeveless, and you were afraid that someone would recognize your tattoo and make fun of you for going to church. I offered my dress because it had long sleeves."

"See?" Gloria said. "I can think of a thousand generous things you've done, so don't ever let me hear you call yourself selfish again, you hear?"

"I hear," Belle said, sounding unconvinced.

Several seconds passed before Janette said, "Belle, this may not be the time or the place, but you never did tell us how much money you won."

"I didn't?"

"No."

"Oh. Well, it was one hundred and thirteen thousand dollars."

"Wow," said Janette, barely audible.

"Double wow," said Gloria.

"I don't care about the money," Belle said. "If I lose Art, I'll give it all away. Without him, it doesn't matter."

"You're not going to lose Art," Janette said. "I know I'm not a doctor, but I worked in a nursing home once. If Art had a stroke he may have some paralysis, but physical therapy can take care of that."

"But we don't know that he had a stroke," Gloria said, flashing warning signals to Janette with her eyes. "We don't know anything."

Janette stood up. "You're right. I've got to go to the bathroom."

"And I'm going to get a cup of coffee," said Gloria. "Belle? Are you sure you don't want anything?"

"No, thank you. You two go ahead."

"Will you be all right?"

"I'll be fine. Maybe I'll know something by the time you get back."

"Let's hope so." The two girls took off.

Left alone, Belle's mind turned to practical matters. If something bad happened to Art, should she be the one to call his wife in New Jersey? Even though she'd never met Lil, she felt like she knew her. She felt like she knew his daughter, Sandy, and Artie, his son. Of course she had no idea where Artie was–even Art didn't know that–but maybe Lil or Sandy would know. She would hate for any of them to hear bad news from a stranger.

The problem was, she didn't know Lil's phone number. Surely Art had it written down somewhere, probably in an address book at home. She'd hate to go snooping around his house, though, especially if something bad happened. It'd be better to call information. Then again, maybe the doctor should make the call.

Would either Lil or Sandy make the trip down here? She supposed it would depend on Art's condition. If one or the other or both of them came down, where would they stay? At Art's house? Probably not. According to Art, Lil hated the house. She also hated New Orleans. That, supposedly, was why she'd moved back to New Jersey.

That reminded Belle of another problem. Her time at Hope Haven was almost up. She was supposed to move in with Art next weekend. She'd planned to start packing her things tomorrow. Not that she had that much to pack. She'd leave the bright touches she'd added to hers and Gloria's room for Gloria to enjoy. When she came right down to it, everything she owned would fit in the steamer trunk Art had given her for Christmas.

What if he wasn't out of the hospital by Friday? What if he was incapacitated? No, he'd be fine. He had to be. Everything would go as planned. If they couldn't fit her trunk into the cab, they could borrow Mr. Sidney's trailer. She had painted a mural of a choo-choo train on the Sidneys' living room wall, and the mister was so happy he'd be glad to help them out.

Thinking of the choo-choo reminded her of Art's cab and that reminded her of his driver's license. Janette had given it and his insurance card to the medic in the ambulance. Belle hoped they hadn't gotten lost, especially Art's license. Losing it would be the worst thing that could happen to him. *Oh no it wasn't.*

Don't think about it, Belle told herself. Think of something else.

The nurse at the reception desk looked bored. What a difference a few hours had made. When they'd first arrived, the place had not only been packed with people of all ages, sizes, and colors, it had reverberated with sounds–moans, cries, groans, shouts, curses. And the commingling of body odors had been overwhelming–sweet deodorants laced with sweat, strong aftershaves, cheap perfumes. These had come from the family members who waited. Now that all but a few people had been treated and released only a faint antiseptic smell lingered, and it was quiet. Too quiet. Belle wished the phone would ring, that it would be Art's doctor on the line. Better yet, she wished the doctor would come striding through the door and talk to her directly.

She fought the temptation to go to the reception desk. Early on, she'd made a scene when the nurse wouldn't let her go next door to be with Art. She'd attempted to go anyway but had been stopped by the security guard. Since then she'd sat, with the others, in a far corner of the room, ashamed of her behavior but at the same time frustrated and more than a little angry.

Maybe if she'd told them she was Art's wife they would have treated her with more respect. Been more understanding. Maybe she would know something by now.

Friends. That's all the nurse and the guard thought they were to each other. Well, it wasn't too late to tell the nurse otherwise. A little fib couldn't hurt.

The nurse wore an ID tag that gave her name as Yvonne Collins. "I still haven't heard anything," she said as Belle approached.

Belle put on her most pleasant face. "I understand, Ms. Collins. I'm sure you would have let me know. By the way, Yvonne is a lovely name. Are you named after someone in your family?"

"No. My mother read it in a book."

"A book. How interesting. Do you remember the title of the book?"

"No."

"Oh, that's too bad. If I'd been named after a character in a book I'd want to read all about her."

The nurse made a sour face. "Knowing my mother, I probably wouldn't like her."

"Ah," said Belle, feeling a twinge of empathy. Her own mother was still upset because she'd changed her name from Kathleen Mallory to Belle Reve. "I gave you a perfectly good Christian name, Kathleen, and I expect you to use it," Edith had said. But Belle wasn't about to use it–that name belonged to another person, another life.

"Well, anyway," she said to Yvonne Collins, "I wanted to apologize for my outburst. You see, Mister Barkoff means the world to me. He's my hero and soon to be my husband. The others–"she glanced over her shoulder at the still-empty chairs–"are good friends of his, but I'm his fiancee. That's why I got so upset when you wouldn't let me see him. I'm sure you'd feel the same way if you were me. The not knowing worries you to death. Not that the others ... his friends, aren't worried. Of course they are. They love him dearly. Everyone loves Art. It's just that I will die right here on this spot if anything happens to him. Couldn't you please, oh pretty please, call over there and see how he's doing?"

Ms. Collins didn't answer right away. Then she picked up the phone and punched a number. Presently, she said, "Barkoff, Arthur. B-A-R-K-O-F-F."

What seemed like an eternity passed before Ms. Collins hung up the phone. She looked at Belle and said, "He's ready to go."

"Go?" Belle gasped. "Go where?"

"Home."

Three

"Where you been?" Art wanted to know. "I was starting to think you'd run out on me."

Incapable of speech, all Belle could do was stare at him. Fully dressed and sitting on the side of a narrow bed in a curtained cubicle, he looked perfectly normal.

"What're you looking at?" he asked, eyes narrowing. "It's me. Your old pal, Art."

Belle finally found her voice. She leaned in close to him and whispered, "I told them I was your fiancee, so don't give me away."

Art cracked a grin. "My fiancee, eh? I like that. It's got a nice ring to it."

"If I hadn't told them that I'd still be sitting over there, waiting to hear if you were dead or alive."

"Over where? Why weren't you in here keeping an eye on things?"

"They wouldn't let me. I begged and I pleaded, I even threw a fit, but they made us wait on the other side of the hall. Oh, Art, are you really all right?" She peered deep into his eyes as though the answer lay buried there.

"Yeah, I'm tiptop." He slid off the bed and took hold of her arm.

"Let's get outta here."

Belle stood her ground. That he was free to leave still hadn't sunk in. "But I don't understand," she said. "Janette told us you had a stroke. We all thought you were dying."

"Ha, that shows how much Janette knows. I just had a little problem with my blood sugar." He shrugged. "So I passed out. No big deal. C'mon, let's go."

Belle wasn't about to go anywhere until she got some answers. She looked around for a doctor or a nurse, someone who could tell her what was wrong with him, but the unit seemed more like a morgue than an emergency room. What sounded like heavy breathing and the beeping of machines came from behind one of the curtained areas, but not a soul was in sight.

"What're you waiting for?" Art grumbled. "Christmas?"

A deep but mellow voice answered. "I been trying to get my hands on this here set of wheels. Folks 'round here just leave these things any old where, and then I gots to go hunt me one up." A young man the color of coal came toward them pushing a wheelchair. Dressed in whites, his ID tag gave his name as Clarence Frawley.

He positioned the chair behind Art. "Here you go, Mister Barkoff. You just hop in my sleigh here, and we'll go find me a chimney to get stuck in." He gave a hearty laugh and then bellowed, "Ho, ho, ho!"

Hoping the noise hadn't startled the person–if it was a person–behind the curtains, Belle put a hand to her mouth to stifle a giggle.

Art was not amused. "I don't need that thing," he said, sneering at the chair. "I can walk outta here on my own steam, thanks."

"Oh-oh," the orderly said, "we got us another hero. Hey, man, you trying to get me fired?"

Art thought it over. Then, grumbling to himself, he sat down in the wheelchair.

"That's my man," the orderly said. Once Art's feet were braced on the footrests, he looked at Belle. "Ma'am? You got a car waiting outside?"

"No. Ah, I mean yes. Well, sort of. It's a truck. A big one. But first I want to know what's wrong with him." She inclined her head toward Art.

"You'll have to ask his doctor, ma'am."

"Fine. Where is his doctor?"

"Long gone. Mister Barkoff here is ready to go."

"See?" Art said. "What'd I tell you?"

"And I'm telling you we're not going anywhere until you tell me what this blood sugar problem is all about."

"Nosy, stubborn broad," he muttered. "Okay, here's the poop. I got diabetes. It ain't the serious kind. I don't hafta take shots or nothing. I just have to watch what I eat and check in with the doc every now and then. Can we hit the road now? Nothing personal," he said, looking up at the orderly, "but I've had it with this place."

The orderly grinned. "You ain't the only one."

Belle eyed Art suspiciously. She knew he'd had a heart attack several years ago, she knew he took medication for high blood pressure, and she knew he'd been steadily losing weight. But diabetes? She didn't know that much about the disease, but how could a person appear to be near death and then look and act so normal four hours later?

She looked at the orderly. "Mister Frawley, is what he said true?"

"Sorry, ma'am. Nobody tells me nothing. He could have leprosy or shingles for all I know."

"Perish the thought." Her gaze shifted back to Art. "Did you know you had diabetes?"

"What? You think I'm stupid? You think I'd stuff my gut with all that junk food if I'd'a known? We must'a stopped at a hundred fast food joints and eaten a ton of greasy fries, and all because you kept having to go to the bathroom."

"It didn't seem right to use their facilities and not buy something," she explained to Clarence Frawley, hardly able to meet the man's eyes.

He nodded. "My wife feels the same way."

"She's not my wife," Art said out of the corner of his mouth. "Not yet, anyway."

Belle threw herself at him, jolting the chair, Art, and the orderly. She buried her face in his shoulder, her hands squeezing his sides. "Oh, thank God you're all right. I just knew I'd lost you."

He stroked her hair and breathed in her lilac scent. "Not a chance. I gotta stick around to make sure you don't get into trouble."

"Ha," she said, pulling back. "You're the one causing all the trouble."

"Uh, ma'am," the orderly said, "if I don't get upstairs, they'll be sending the dogs after me."

Belle gave him her special smile. "My apologies, kind sir. I'll go find the others." She took off in a swirl of skirt.

"What others?" Art called.

She didn't answer, just kept going.

Art slowly shook his head. "Women."

"Ain't it the truth," said the orderly.

. . .

Outside the hospital, with everyone brought up to date on Art's condition, they stood in the parking lot arguing over who should sit where. All except Roger. He'd climbed in the driver's seat and sat drumming his fingers on the steering wheel.

The orderly hadn't wanted to leave his patient standing there, but since Art wouldn't stay in the wheelchair, he'd wished him luck and gone back inside the hospital.

The biggest obstacle to making a decision came when Belle wanted Art to lie down in back. No matter how much she pleaded, he firmly refused. Around and around they went until Art threatened to call a cab for himself. As far as he was concerned, the rest of them could argue till doomsday.

The four women settled in the sleeper section, which was more like a small studio apartment, and Art sat up in the passenger's seat. The drape that separated the two areas was left open so they could see and hear one another. A small brass wall light above a cabinet in the sleeper gave off a dim yellow glow, enough to see by yet not enough to distract Roger from seeing the road.

"This is some kinda rig," Art said once they were rolling. "Where's the rest of it?"

"Back at the market," Roger said. "I gotta haul outta here at four o'clock."

"In the morning?" Belle asked from her spot behind Art.

"Yep," Roger said.

"Oh dear, and here we've kept you up half the night."

He shrugged. "I'm used to it."

"You are, but I'm not," Darleen said. "The long hours are the only bad thing about trucking. That and sitting on your fanny all day."

"Listen to her," Roger said with a chuckle. "She sleeps while I do all the work."

"I sleep because I get sick of watching TV."

"What about reading?" Belle asked. "There's nothing like a good book to make the time fly."

"She reads trashy stuff," Roger said. "Like those tabloids you get at check-out counters. Stories about aliens getting women pregnant, junk like that."

Belle's heart gave a lurch. Nine years ago, she'd been unloading her cart at the local supermarket when she'd caught a glimpse of one of those tabloids. Its cover featured a picture of Siamese twins, supposedly spawned by the devil. The next thing she knew she could hardly breath; she couldn't move or speak, she felt cold and clammy, and then she was peeing on herself.

The doctor said her reaction was due to postpartum depression. Seeing the picture, he explained, brought back the trauma she'd suffered when her own twins died–her precious newborn sons.

Though born prematurely, the boys each weighed over three pounds and seemed perfectly formed. Until their tiny lungs failed to expand.

The doctor's diagnosis of postpartum depression, though understandable, had been flawed. A few days later she had a similar attack while at the post office, a place she'd always felt safe and secure because her father was the postmaster. Another attack occurred outside the local pharmacy, then another, all happening in familiar locales and without any reminders of the twins.

It would take nine long years and a chance encounter with her therapist Marge before she learned the true nature of her condition: agoraphobia, commonly known as a fear of the marketplace, or any open place.

"Belle? Oh, Belle, where are you?" someone sang out.

She looked all around, became aware of her surroundings, and said, "Oh, I must have dozed off."

"Well, wake up, girl," Janette said. "You still haven't told us how you won the jackpot, and you need to do it before we get back to the house."

Art looked over his shoulder. "What's with the house?"

"We don't want Mammy Daisy to hear," Darleen said. "And Roger, you'd better watch your language when you're around Mammy. One bad word and she'll wash your mouth out with soap."

"That's a fact," Art said. Then, "Am I missing something? Did Mammy get hot about the jackpot?"

"Hot?" Gloria said, "She was boiling. Don't you remember?"

"Naw, I was out of it."

Janette picked up where Gloria left off. "Mammy was furious because you took Belle to a casino. She called it an evil place, a house of Satan. Spit was actually coming out of the sides of her mouth she was so mad."

"Jesus," Art said, "and Belle was worried about you guys."

"Why?"

If Belle could have reached him she would have slapped a hand over his mouth. As it was, she tried to hide in the shadows.

"She thought you'd turn against her 'cause she won the jackpot and you didn't."

The girls fastened their eyes on Belle, disbelief showing on their faces.

"How could you think such a thing?" Gloria asked.

Belle was slow to answer. "Well, I know how much you all need money."

That got the three girls talking at once, about how she needed money too and how happy they were for her and on and on they went.

"Enough already," Art said. "You convinced her, right Belle?"

"Yes," she said, swallowing the lump in her throat, "and I love you all for being so kind."

"We love you too, okay?" Janette said. "Now tell us all about it."

Belle hesitated. "Art? Do you feel up to telling them?"

"Sure, no problem." He twisted around in his seat and looked back at the girls.

"Like Belle said, after we bummed out in Laurel we headed down to Biloxi. I'm thinking it'll cheer her up to see the beach. Try to spot one of those pelicans she's always talking about. So we get to the beach, plow through the sand toward the Gulf, and a storm blows up. I wanna duck in the first beer joint I see, but Belle's heading straight for the casino. Big mistake. I shoulda yanked her sideways into the cab, 'cause once she gets a load of all the lights and the ding-dongs and stuff she's hooked. So I give her five silver dollars to play the slots. I figure she'll lose them in two seconds flat and we can get outta there. She puts the first dollar in and comes up with nada. Same thing happens with the second and the third. I'm already putting on my walking shoes. Then she drops the fourth dollar in the slot. The doohickeys go round and round, and all of a sudden the machine lights up, the bells start clanging, and silver dollars start raining all over the place. People crowd around, trying to see how much she won. 'Course Belle's screaming and jumping up and down. You want numbers? How does one hundred and thirteen thousand clams sound? Jesus, I still can't believe it."

"Man," Roger said, "that's one for the books."

Art faced forward. “Yeah, over a hundred G’s on a four dollar bet. ‘Course the fun didn’t last long. They had a tax man right there and he made sure we didn’t go nowhere till he got his.”

“You mean you had to pay out right there?”

“On the spot. They took us into this office, asked Belle a buncha questions, then started punching away on one of them whatchama-callits.”

“A calculator,” Gloria said.

“Yeah, one a them. Anyway, they come up with a number and take it outta her winnings. Now she’s gotta file here in Louisiana. She’ll get credit for what she paid out in Mississippi, and being single with no income puts her in a lower bracket, so it could be worse.”

“How much will she have left?” Janette asked.

“I dunno. You got your state and federal taxes ... I figure she’ll end up with about sixty-five grand.”

“Is that all?” Janette said.

“Man, that sucks,” said Roger.

“Ain’t it the truth. But it’s more than she started with.”

“Right on,” Gloria said.

“I know what I’d do with that kind of dough,” Roger said. “I’d pay off my rig and buy Darleen the biggest diamond I could find. She’d have to wear her arm in a sling just to carry it around.”

Darleen whooped. “Oh, Roger, that’s so sweet.”

Janette said, “First thing I’d do is have my tattoo burned off. Then I’d take a Caribbean cruise. After that I’d get my own apartment and go to nursing school. And then–”

“I thought you wanted to be a dental hygienist,” Gloria said.

“No, it’s Marge who wants me to be a hygienist. The thought of digging around in people’s mouths doesn’t exactly thrill me.”

“Yes, but look at it this way. Marge has already got the job lined up. You work for the dentist, save your money, and then ....”

Belle shut her ears. Because she wanted all the girls dreams to come true, listening to the discussion made her sad. She wished she’d never won the money. Sudden riches could be a curse. She’d read about people whose lives were ruined after winning a lottery. Their families, friends, people they didn't even know, hounded them to distraction. Some even had to move to a secret location and start their lives all over again. She'd give the money away before she'd let that happen. Her new life was just beginning. She couldn't bear it if things changed. Most of all, it would break her heart if the girls began to treat her differently.

Twenty years ago, after she married Lin and moved into the grand old estate he'd inherited, her own mother, though never loving or affectionate, had begun to treat her either with cold indifference or blatant disapproval, as though she were unworthy of such finery.

Edith loved nothing better than to pop by the house and set about rearranging all of the priceless objects Lin's family had collected over the years. That done, she would move on to the kitchen.

"It would make more sense to put this here and that over there," she'd say and then start in on all the cabinets, cupboards, drawers, and, lastly, the refrigerator and freezer.

Because Edith wanted Lin to think her daughter well-bred, she always made sure to finish her tasks before he came home from the office. "There now," she'd say with smug satisfaction, "try real hard to keep things in order this time. We don't want Lin thinking you're some hick that doesn't know any better."

In lieu of a birthday or a Christmas gift, Edith made a point of telling her she'd made an extra donation to the church. "You don't need a single thing," she'd say. "You have far too much as it is. Tsk, tsk, such a dreadful waste." Belle had wanted to tell her mother that what she wanted more than anything was a simple hug and a kind word.

If it hadn't been for her father's love and devotion, she would have felt like an orphan. Jesse, now retired, had been the postmaster in Stone Mountain, Georgia, where Belle grew up. Throughout her youth, she spent all of her free time at the post office in order to be near her father. It was there, when she was a junior in college, that she met Linwood Mallory, III.

Nudged by someone's foot, Belle started. "What? What is it?"

"We've been spending all your money," Gloria said, "but the real question is, what are *you* going to do with it?"

Belle didn't want to talk about her winnings. She didn't want to hear about it, she didn't even want to think about it, but there seemed to be no escaping the subject.

"You'll have to ask my business manager," she said. "Art?"

As though he were just waiting for the chance to lay out his plan, Art started talking. "First thing she's gotta do is open up a bank account and learn how to write a check. Then, if she's gonna make it in the mural painting business, she's gotta buy a decent set of wheels. A van big enough to haul all her stuff, but not too big. 'Course that means she's gotta have insurance, tags, a business license, all'a that. Then there's ..."

Back in the shadows, Belle listened while Art mapped out her immediate future in fixed terms. Little did he know she had a few plans of her own.

Four

It was long past the designated hour for lights out before Mammy Daisy and the residents of Hope Haven settled down for the night. At least they were supposed to be settled. Belle didn't know about the others, but she and Gloria were still awake, lying sideways on their beds facing each other.

As on most nights, a shaft of light thrown by the house next door spotlighted a portion of the first mural Belle ever painted. It was a picture of Art's Checker cab crossing the Ponchartrain Causeway. When Art first laid eyes on it he'd wanted Belle to paint an exact replica on his bedroom wall. Much to his disappointment, she'd turned him down. Not because she didn't have the time, but because she didn't feel comfortable working in such an intimate setting. It was foolish, perhaps, but she made it a condition of all the jobs she took. She would paint a mural in a living room, a dining room, a kitchen, a den, even a bathroom, but not in someone's bedroom, unless the room belonged to a child.

Now, as she gazed beyond Gloria's prone figure, she wished she could transport the mural intact to Art's bedroom wall. On this night of all nights, the sight of it might bring him comfort, a reminder of better times.

What a glorious day that had been, the day they crossed the Ponchartrain Causeway. Blessed with ideal weather and a sense of adventure, Belle had been so inspired by the view she'd sketched the outline for the mural on scraps of paper torn from Art's receipt book.

They'd been on their way to Mandeville, expecting to find Blanche at the mental hospital there. Because it was Blanche's birthday, Belle had taken the special gift she'd brought all the way from Atlanta. Unfortunately, she still had the gift, tucked in the bottom of her trunk, still waiting to be presented.

"My, but that seems so long ago," she mused out loud.

Gloria raised up, her elbow digging into the mattress, head propped in her hand. "What does?"

Belle gestured toward the mural. "The day we crossed the causeway. September fifteenth of last year. Blanche's birthday."

"Do you think you'll ever find her?" Gloria asked.

"Oh yes, I'm sure of it."

Gloria didn't respond right away.

"You know, Belle ... me and some of the girls were talking, and, un ... well, have you ever thought she might be dead?"

"Yes, I've thought of that. But don't you see? I can't go on wondering, I have to *know.* That's why I have to keep searching."

"Well, just so you're prepared."

"I am. At least I think I am."

"Good," Gloria said. "We don't want you freaking out, especially now that you're ready to move in with Art."

Belle rolled onto her back and stretched out full length. "It's Art I'm worried about. I don't like the idea of him being alone tonight. What if he passes out again?"

"He's not going to pass out. They wouldn't let him leave the hospital if they didn't think he'd be all right."

"I don't know about that. You read all the time about someone being sent home too soon and then having a relapse. I'd feel a lot better if I could have talked to his doctor."

Art said he had an appointment to see him in the morning. You can talk to him then."

"No, I can't. Art won't let me go with him. He says he's a big boy and can take care of himself."

"You know what I'd do if I were you? I'd show up anyway."

Belle turned her head in Gloria's direction. "That's a good idea. I could take the bus."

"Right. Oh, I can just see the look on Art's face when you waltz in."

"He'll be furious."

"He'll get over it. It's the only way you're going to get the real story."

"I know. And I should be back in plenty of time to keep my one o'clock with Marge."

"Marge," Gloria said. "Lord, I'd forgotten all about her. Oh, how I wish I could be a fly on the wall when you tell her about winning the jackpot."

"I may not tell her."

"If you don't, Mammy Daisy will."

"That's fine with me. I really don't want to talk about it. Especially to Marge."

"You know what she's going to say, don't you?"

"Yes, the same thing she's been saying. She's going to try to talk me out of moving in with Art."

"Right. And now that you've got all that money, she'll say you can afford your own place."

"Not if I'm going to buy a van and go into business. Not yet, anyway. I just wish Marge could accept that. It's not like I'm going to live with Art forever."

"Wanna bet?" Gloria said.

"You can think what you want, sweetie. I'm going to sleep, and I suggest you do the same. Good night." Belle burrowed her head in her pillow, tucked her hands under her chin and closed her eyes.

The only sound in the room came from the ticking of the old-fashioned alarm clock.

Then Gloria said, "Belle? You don't have to tell me, but I've got to ask. Did you and Art do it?"

"Do what?" Belle asked, opening one bleary eye.

"You know. *It*."

"No, I don't know. We did a lot of things."

"Honestly, Belle, you are so out of it. I'm talking about sex. Did you and Art have sex?"

Belle's head came up off the pillow. "Of course not."

"Did you want to?"

"No. Now go to sleep."

The light from next door blinked out. Grateful for the darkness, Belle lay back down and pulled the covers up to her neck.

"I'll bet Art wanted to."

"Gloria, if you don't hush I'm going to move to Darleen's old bed."

"But you love Art. I heard you tell him so myself. At the table tonight, when you thought he was dying. We all heard you."

"Just because you love someone doesn't mean you want to *make* love to him."

"Well, what about when you move in with him? Will you sleep with him then?"

"Gloria, I've already told you, I'll have my own room. I'll be a boarder and a friend, nothing more. Good night. I'll see you in the morning."

"Okay, okay. But I'll tell you one thing. Art's dying to make love to you."

Belle heaved a weary sigh and closed her eyes. She rolled onto her left side, bedsprings creaking, and tried to settle down.

Should she tell Gloria the truth? That Lin had stopped making love to her after the twins died. Nine years without sex, and now the mere thought of it scared her to death. No. She'd never told anyone, not even Marge.

Despite her best efforts, sleep eluded her for a very long time.

. . .

Art was leafing through an issue of *Sports Illustrated* when Belle breezed into the waiting room. Out of breath from rushing to get there, she plopped down beside him on a chintz-covered couch.

"Whew," she said, fanning her face. "I was afraid I wouldn't get here in time. How are you feeling?"

Art did a double-take. "What're *you* doing here?"

"I'm here to see about you, silly."

"Okay, you've seen me. Now get outta here." He slapped the pages of the magazine together and tossed it aside.

"Listen to you. I took two buses and walked half a mile to get here, and I am not about to leave, so there."

"Well you ain't going with me to see the doc."

"I most certainly am."

"You try and I swear I'll walk outta here."

She knew he meant it. "I'll wait out here on one condition. You have to promise to tell me everything he says."

"You are one nosy broad," he groused.

Belle ignored him. She was plotting a way to hear firsthand what the doctor had to say. She'd have to slip past the receptionist and then hope the attending nurses were too busy to notice her. Once she found the examining room she could stand outside and press her ear to the door. If someone questioned her she could say she was looking for a bathroom. She'd bluffed her way through prickly situations before, she could do it again.

"What're you up to?" Art asked, his eyes narrowing.

"Me? Nothing." She crossed her legs and adjusted the crease in her trousers so the fabric over her knees wouldn't bulge when she stood up. Doe-colored with flared legs, the pants were made of rayon twill. Into them she'd tucked a white blouse with tatting around the collar, over which she wore a pale yellow cardigan with pearl buttons. The outfit, found in a vintage clothing store, made her feel like a young Katharine Hepburn.

"Were you able to get any sleep?" she asked.

"Tell you the truth, I conked out so fast I don't even remember climbing into bed."

"Good. You needed it."

"It was a rough day alright. All that running around, you winning the jackpot, the drive back from Biloxi ... then I had to go and get sick. Jesus, I thought I'd never get home."

"Thank goodness for Roger. I knew you'd have a fit if we drove your precious Checker to the hospital. If Roger hadn't shown up when he did I don't know what we would have done."

"Yeah, Roger's okay. Y'know, that rig of his is really something. If I was thirty years younger I might think about driving a truck."

"Thank goodness you're not," she said. "If you drove a truck I wouldn't have met you, and even if I had, you would have been too young for me. Which reminds me, I wonder how Darleen and Roger met. She never did say and I forgot to ask. They seem very happy, don't you think?"

"Yeah. Funny how things work out."

"It certainly is."

When Darleen left Hope Haven before she'd completed the program, most people thought she'd be back on the streets within a week, doing tricks for drugs. Belle never believed it. She'd had the same faith in Darleen that she'd had in Gloria. On that awful November day when Gloria snuck away from classes at rehab without a word to anyone, Janette and the others predicted she'd never be seen again, that she'd be swallowed up and spit out of the scene. Thankfully, they'd been wrong. Unable to bear her old way of life, Gloria, more determined than ever to start anew, had come back to the fold.

"Take you and me," Art said. "Six months ago I couldn't wait to dump you off at six-thirty-two Elysian Fields and head home to watch the ball game. Who woulda thought we'd end up living together?"

"We're not living together, yet," Belle said.

He shot her a look. "You ain't changed your mind, have you?"

"Arthur Barkoff," a female voice called. They both looked toward the sound. A nurse holding a manila folder beckoned to Art from a doorway.

He pushed himself up from the couch. “Don’t try nothing,” he warned and started off.

“Please let me go with you,” Belle said, trying to catch hold of his arm.

“Not a chance.” He kept walking.

Belle waited until he was out of sight then checked her watch. She’d been to enough doctors to know the usual routine, which meant she needed to wait about fifteen minutes before making her move. If she went too soon, the doctor would catch her in the hall on his way to Art’s room.

That decided, she looked at the people around her. On the love seat across the room a young couple huddled together talking quietly. Attractive and neatly-dressed, they looked like newlyweds. Belle prayed nothing serious was wrong with either one of them.

Three seats down sat an older woman with a crown of silver hair. Impeccably done up from head to toe, she reminded Belle of someone but she couldn’t think who. Even though she knew it was terribly rude, she stared at the woman in hopes a name would come to her.

The woman glanced her way, smiled, then lowered her eyes. Belle forced herself to stop staring. She hated it when people stared at her.

A wide picture window set into the far wall looked out on a magnificent live oak tree. It looked like one she’d seen in Laurel. Laurel! Her heart fluttered wildly. Blanche! Could this woman possibly be Blanche? Had she found her at last? Here in this doctor’s office? She closed her eyes and opened them. The woman was still there! She hadn’t been hallucinating.

Her pulse racing, Belle moved to sit at the woman’s side. “Excuse me,” she said, hardly able to contain herself, “would you happen to be Blanche DuBois?”

The woman’s eyes crinkled when she laughed. “Do I look like Blanche DuBois?”

“Yes, yes, you do. And if you are Blanche, I’m going to fall right off this chair.”

"Well then," the woman said, a soft drawl dripping off her tongue, "I'd better tell you my name is Iris Mason. But I appreciate the compliment. Blanche DuBois is one of my favorite characters."

In a way, Belle was relieved. This wasn't the time or the place to meet Blanche. Especially since she, Belle, wasn't dressed in her finest. She wasn't even wearing a hat, for goodness sakes. But Iris Mason knew who Blanche was and that was really something. Most people didn't have the foggiest notion.

"Blanche is my idol," Belle said. "In fact, she's why I'm here. Not here in the doctor's office, here in New Orleans. You see, her birthday was last September, and I brought her a gift all the way from Atlanta, Georgia. It's a red satin kimono, exactly like the one she wore when she stayed at Stella and Stanley's. But I haven't been able to give it to her because I can't find her. I've looked everywhere. I can't find Stella and Stanley either. Sometimes I think they're hiding from me, but of course that can't be true. They don't even know I'm looking for them. Anyway, when I saw you, I couldn't believe it. You look exactly like I pictured Blanche would look. I should have known it was too good to be true. But it's nice to meet you all the same. You're a beautiful woman, and I'm so glad you're fond of Blanche."

A look of confusion deepened the fine web of wrinkles on Iris Mason's face. "My dear girl," she said, "I'm afraid your search has been in vain. Blanche and Stella are characters in a play written by Tennessee Williams. All of his plays were based on fictional characters. They simply don't exist as real people."

Belle sighed. How many times must she hear this very same denial? Would no one ever believe her? "Oh, but they are real," she said. "Blanche and Stella and Stanley, Mitch and Pablo and all the others are as real as we are. I don't know about his other plays, but *A Streetcar Named Desire* was based on facts. You see, Mister Tennessee had a sister named Rose, and Rose knew Blanche and Stella. So when Rose told her brother their sad, sad story, he felt so bad he was compelled to write about them."

"Really?" Iris Mason said.

Belle bobbed her head up and down."Yes, really." She babbled on and on, all about Stanley selling the old house on Elysian Fields to a group of lawyers, how they'd fixed it up so you'd never recognize it, about going to the mental institutions in Mandeville and Jackson in search of Blanche, the recent trip to Laurel ... She was almost finished when she was interrupted.

"Mrs. Mason, the doctor will see you now."

"Oh, dear," Belle said, realizing where she was. Iris Mason was a patient. She could be seriously ill. "I hope I didn't wear you out. Sometimes I get carried away. Please forgive me."

Iris Mason gave her a warm smile. "Don't fret, my dear. I'm sure if you keep searching you *will* find Blanche." She rose and turned toward the waiting nurse.

Heartsick, despite Iris Mason's departing words, Belle sank back against her chair. The only way she could prove that Blanche existed was to find her–or her grave. How long would she have to search? How long before Art felt up to making a return trip to Laurel?

Art! She looked at her watch. No matter how hard she tried she couldn't remember how long he'd been gone. Clutching her handbag, she got up and headed for the door through which he'd passed, careful to avert her face from the receptionist so as not to draw attention to herself.

She'd almost made it when the door swung open.

Art took one look at her and said, "Where d'ya think you're going?"

Startled, Belle gasped and put a hand to her throat. "Un, I, ... there was this woman–"

"Sure there was. Let's get outta here before you start something I hafta finish." He headed for the exit.

"Wait," Belle said. "What did the doctor say?"

Art held up a booklet and waved it at her. "You can read all about it."

The book acted like a magnet and out they went. But not before Belle called, "Good luck!" to the young couple on the love seat.

Five

Engrossed in reading all about diabetes, Belle barely looked up when Art parked in front of a pharmacy on Rampart Street.

"I gotta get some stuff," he said. "Be right back."

"Hmmm," she murmured, eyes fixed on the page.

Art climbed out of the cab and onto the curb. From the sidewalk, he glanced back at Belle. Knowing how much she loved reading about stuff, he figured she'd be too busy to get in any trouble.

Trouble. The word came back to him as he waited for the pharmacist to fill his prescription. Was that the same thing as stress? The doc had asked him if he'd experienced any major changes in his life. Like a divorce, a death in the family, or the loss of a job. Art had told him about Lil going back to New Jersey, but that it hadn't bothered him one bit. Fact was, he needed the peace and quiet. Anything else, the doc asked. Art lied and said no, that was it. Then the doc told him to avoid stress. Art started to ask what that meant, but he didn't want to sound like an ignoramus. And he wasn't about to ask Belle.

When the pharmacist returned to the counter, Art said, "Hey, Burt, you got a dictionary?" He'd been buying his blood pressure pills from the guy and they'd hit it off.

"What kind of dictionary?" Burt asked.

"You mean there's more'n one?"

"Sure is," Burt said. "It would help if you told me what you want to look up."

Art hedged. "A word."

"Come on, Art. I haven't got all day. What word?"

"Stress," Art mumbled.

"What? I can't hear you." Burt was grinning and that pissed Art off.

"Forget about it."

"Must be a dirty word. Is that it, Art? You ashamed to tell me?"

Cursing himself for bringing it up, Art looked behind him to see if anyone was listening. Satisfied he wasn't been heard, he turned back to Burt and said, "Okay, wise guy, the word is *stress.*"

The grin left Burt's face. "My apologies, Art. Diabetes is no laughing matter, and stress is to be avoided at all costs. That means getting rid of all the disturbing influences in your life. The people and situations that upset you. The main thing is to try to stay calm. Like the song says, 'Don't worry. Be happy'."

"Great. Then gimme something to help me stay calm."

"No can do, Art. Not without a 'script from your doctor."

"Damn," Art said under his breath.

"Just do what I do. Remember that life is too short to sweat the small stuff."

"Yeah, but what about the big stuff?" Like Art Junior being a drug addict, a thief, and a liar. Like Lil slipping Artie *his* hard-earned dough when she knew damn well he was gonna go out and score some dope. Like his daughter Sandy and her three kids being on the dole and always asking him for another handout. Jesus, the big stuff never ended. And now he had this damn disease to worry about.

"Take my advice, Art. Go back to Jennings and have an honest talk with him. He's a good man and a good doctor. You can trust him. If he gives you a prescription, bring it here."

Art mulled it over while Burt put his stuff in a white paper bag.

After handing the bag over, Burt said, "Listen, Art, I know Jenning's nurse already showed you how to use the home monitoring kit, but take my advice and read the directions till you get used to it. Just remember, keeping track of your glucose level can save your life. If you have any side effects from the Micronase, be sure to call Jennings right away. He may need to switch you to something else." Burt gave him the once-over and asked, "Are you going to be okay?"

"Yeah, sure. No problem. Hey, and thanks, Burt. I'll be seeing ya."

Burt laughed. "Not if I see you first."

"That's funny, Burt. Real funny."

On his way out of the pharmacy, Art stopped by the candy counter and picked out some Necco wafers and a box of Black Crows for Belle. She loved the things and for some reason they were hard to find.

Glad to see she was still reading, Art opened the trunk, slipped the pharmacy bag inside, then pressed both palms on the lid till he heard the click of the lock. That done, he climbed behind the wheel of the cab and tossed the bag of candy in Belle's lap.

"Oh," she said, jerking her head his way. "I didn't hear you coming."

"I wonder why. You finished the book yet?"

"Almost. Which type of diabetes do you have?"

"Number two."

"Thank goodness. Type one is far more serious."

"Huh," he said. "Guess I'm pretty lucky, eh?"

"I wish you didn't have diabetes at all."

"You can say that again." He started the cab, checked for on-coming traffic and pulled into the street. "I got you something. It's there in your lap."

Belle looked down, picked up the bag and opened it. "Oh goodie," she squealed. "My favorites." She leaned way over and kissed him on the cheek. "Thank you, thank you, thank you."

"You better watch that kissin' business. You might catch what

I got."

"It's not contagious, silly."

"I know that. Whaddaya think I am, stupid?"

"Never mind what I think. Where are we going?"

"I'm gonna drop you off at the house and then I'm gonna grab some breakfast. They wouldn't let me eat this morning 'cause they had to take blood."

"What about me? I'm starving. I was in such a hurry, I grabbed one of Mammy's biscuits on the way out of the house and then I dropped it when I got on the bus."

It pleased Art no end that she'd taken two buses and walked half a mile to get to a place she'd never been. And to think she couldn't even walk the four blocks to Schwegmann's Supermarket just two months ago. Hell, five months ago she couldn't make it out of Hope Haven. All because of those panic attacks, where she'd freeze up and not be able to move. But she'd licked her problem and he could damn sure lick his.

"Hey, I know this diner near here," he said. "They got the best ham and cheese omelets in town."

"Are you supposed to eat omelets?"

He gave her a look. "What are you, my mother? Lissen, I know what I can and can't eat, so don't start bugging me."

"Yes, but–"

"You want I should take you to the house?"

"No, but–"

"Then zip your lip already."

Belle flipped through the pages of the booklet to see what it said about nutrition. She knew Art was supposed to get plenty of exercise, monitor his blood glucose level, and take medication, but she hadn't gotten to the part about diet. She found the section at the back of the book and read it twice.

She looked at Art and said, "At the risk of upsetting you, Mister Barkoff, I must tell you that eating healthy foods is a must. You need to focus on cutting the fat in your diet, especially saturated fat and cholesterol, and if I remember correctly, omelets are full of both. So, if you insist on eating one, you can take me back to Hope Haven, because I'd throw up the second you took your first bite."

"Alright, already," he groused.

Five minutes later, he ordered a bowl of shredded wheat, a carton of skim milk, a grapefruit, and a glass of V8 juice. Proud of him, Belle ordered the same.

Midway through their meal, Art said, "Y'know, I used to eat this stuff when I was a kid." He raised a spoonful of wheat squares. "One time I saved enough box tops to send away for a Dick Tracy watch. Every day, I'd run home from school to see if it'd come yet. Come to think of it, maybe it was Wheaties or some other cereal. Whatever, the thing finally came, and it was nothing like the real Dick Tracy watch. Hell, it didn't even tell time. What a ripoff."

"Well," Belle said, "at least you were building strong bones."

"Ha. That prob'ly ain't true neither."

"My mother used to feed me nothing but oatmeal for breakfast. I got so I couldn't stand the sight of it, and even though Mother nagged me about it, I couldn't bring myself to feed it to Mandy."

"Yeah, I know what you mean. I felt the same way about castor oil. When Lil tried to give it to the kids, I poured it down the drain."

"Ugh," Belle said. "My mother used to mix it with orange juice, but that didn't help one bit. I used to close my eyes and pinch my nose shut."

"Hey, sounds like we've got lots in common."

Belle gave him a playful smile. "I guess that's why we get along so well."

He sobered. "Lissen, I know I can be an old grouch, but I want you to know ... well, I'll try to do better."

She feigned interest in her grapefruit. After chewing and swallowing a bite, she took a sip of V8 juice. Unable to hold it in any longer, she looked at Art and said, "We need to talk about something. Promise me you won't get upset."

"I ain't promising nothing till I hear what you got to say."

"It's about my moving in with you."

He cocked his head to one side and lifted an eyebrow. "Yeah? What about it?"

"The book says you need to avoid stress, and I have to wonder if my disrupting your routine would be in your best interest." She held up a hand when he opened his mouth to speak. "You can have your say when I'm finished. Now, the thing is, you know how impulsive and unpredictable I am. I never know what I'm going to do next or who I'm going to do it with. And you know what a mother hen I can be. I'd be wanting to make sure you ate right and got enough exercise. All in all, I'd drive you crazy. And if I tried to tippy-toe around and not bother you, I'd drive myself crazy. I think it would be better for both of us if we lived apart for a while. See how things go. Back when I was painting the choo-choo for the Sidneys, they told me I could move into their garage apartment anytime I wanted to. Nothing would change between you and me. We'd still see each other all the time, but we'd have our own space. What do you think?" She held her breath, afraid he'd blow up at her.

Art hunched over the table and looked her straight in the eye. "Hey, I don't blame you for not wanting to hook up with me. 'Specially now that I got this disease. But I'll tell you what. Why don't we try living together for ... say, three months. That oughta give us time to figure out how we're doing. If it don't work out, no hard feelings. How about it?"

She gave him her special smile. "Mister Barkoff, do you have any idea how smart you are?"

"Smart? Ha, that's a good one."

"But you are smart. Oh, I know you don't have a college degree, but you've got common sense, which, as far as I'm concerned, is worth ten degrees."

"Does that mean you're gonna give us a chance?"

"That's precisely what it means." She glanced at her watch. Eleven-twenty-two. Her appointment with Marge wasn't until one o'clock. "And, since I'm going to be moving in this Friday, how about showing me my new home?"

Art flashed a grin. "Let's go."

. . .

A thick mist of drizzling rain and fog met them as they stepped outside the diner. Earlier, the sun had shown bright through a cloudless blue sky, giving no hint that rain was on the way. Belle had gotten used to the changeable weather, and in fact rather liked the cozy feel of rain-laced fog. The fresh smell cleared her sinuses and seemed to make her brain expand, like when steam rose from her bath water.

"Go back inside and I'll get the umbrella outta the cab," Art said.

"That's not necessary," Belle replied. She skipped down the three steps to the cracked asphalt parking lot, then threw her head back and lifted her arms to the heavens. "Oh, isn't it glorious?" she cried. "I can feel the mist seeping into my pores."

"Whaddaya, nuts?" Art said, approaching her from the rear. "Get in the cab before you get soaked."

"Oh, pooh," she said, acquiescing.

When both of them were tucked inside the cab, Art looked at her and shook his head. "You beat all I ever seen."

She returned his look. "Sometimes you have too much common sense. Instead of worrying about getting wet think of all the benefits of rain. It's nourishing the flowers and the trees and making it easier for the birds to dig for worms."

"You won't be caring 'bout no worms when you come down with pneumonia."

"Don't be silly. I'm as healthy as a horse." The instant the words were out of her mouth she wanted to take them back. Bragging about her good health to Art was like pouring alcohol into an open wound.

"That was very insensitive of me, Art. From now on, I'll try to behave."

"You? Behave? Don't make me laugh." He started the cab and

off they went, windshield wipers flapping back and forth, headlights illuminating the gloom.

As they made the turn off Rampart onto Esplanade, Belle said, "I forget which side of the street it's on, and how far down."

"It's on the left, just past Royal."

Belle strained forward in her seat, trying to see through the fog to get a feel for the neighborhood. Last September, on her third day in town, they had driven down this same street on the way back to her hotel. Art had pointed out his place to her, but by the time she turned to look they had passed it.

As was the case on most of the old streets in or near the French Quarter, the houses ranged from small single-story dwellings to three-story mansions. Painted mostly in pastels and built of brick, wood, or stucco, some had wide wraparound galleries and some had narrow balconies. Some butted up to the sidewalk or a gated brick wall, some had front yards. All had extra large drainpipes set into the ground, and most had chimneys. Few lacked shutters. Beds of tulips, iris, geraniums and begonias added splashes of color to the landscape.

A For Sale sign in front of a three-story house painted a pale green prompted Belle to muse aloud. "I wonder how much that one costs."

Guessing which house she meant, Art thought she might be thinking of buying it with her jackpot money. Ha, he had news for her. "At least a mil or two," he said.

She gaped at him. "A million *dollars*?"

"You got it. Places around here don't come cheap."

"I had no idea," she said, resuming her study of the houses with a new appreciation. She wondered how Art had been able to afford to buy in the area, but to ask would insult him, so she didn't.

He pulled a left on Chartres Street, then another left onto the opposite side of Esplanade, which was divided by a broad, grassy median. As he made the turn the rain stopped and the fog began to lift.

"How 'bout that?" he said, flipping off the windshield wipers and the headlights. "Just in time."

Belle said nothing. She was too busy looking. On the corner lot an old church had apparently been converted into apartments. Next came a three-story yellow house followed by a three-story beige. A pink hotel came next. They'd almost reached Royal when Art parked in front of a neat stucco bungalow painted a deep lavender. Sandwiched between a three-story frame dwelling and a two-story brick, the bungalow had a bluish-gray slate roof that extended over a porch that ran the width of the house. On the porch sat two white wicker rocking chairs separated by a matching table.

The front door, which was the same bluish-gray as the roof, featured an oval inset of opaque glass with an elaborate design of tangled vines. Glossy white paint covered the wood trim and the four sets of shutters that flanked tall, multi-paned windows. A brick walkway separated equal halves of a small but well-tended yard. A narrow driveway on the right side of the house led up to an attached gate made of white wooden slats. An identical gate blocked the left side.

"This is it," Art said. "They call it a Creole Cottage. Whaddaya think?"

Unexpected tears stung Belle's eyes as she gazed at the house. She'd expected to see a drab brown building without an ounce of charm, but this ... this looked like an adult-sized version of a doll house.

"Oh, Art, it's adorable. It's the prettiest house I've ever seen."

"Yeah? Prettier than that castle you left in Georgia?"

She laughed. "It wasn't a castle, silly. And even if it had been, I'd much rather have your cottage."

Art beamed with pride. "You shoulda seen it before I bought it. The real estate guy called it a 'fixer-upper'. It needed fixing alright. The roof was about to cave in, the stucco looked like it'd been rammed by a Mack truck, some of the shutters were missing, the rest of 'em were eaten up with termites, and the inside was a joke."

"Oh my. What did Lil think of it?"

"She thought it was a dump. 'Course nothing we looked at suited Lil. Okay, so the place was a dump, but it had potential and the price was right. Plus, time was running out. We'd sold the house in Jersey and the new owners wanted to move in. So I made a deal with Lil. I'd stay here and keep looking and she'd go back to Jersey and start packing. I put her on a plane and headed straight for this place. Got hold of the real estate guy and looked it over from top to bottom. Long story short, I put a down payment on it and started fixing it up." He made a move to open his door. "C'mon, let's go."

"Wait. What did Lil say when you told her you'd bought it?"

He grinned a wicked grin. "She hollered bloody murder. Threatened to move in with her sister. Then I told her what all I was gonna do to fix it up and that she could buy new furniture, and that's all it took to get her down here."

"Do you have a picture of the house before you fixed it up?" she asked.

"I got a bunch of 'em."

"Good," she said. "Okay, I'm ready." She opened her door and climbed out of the cab.

On the porch, she rocked to and fro on the balls of her feet while waiting for Art to unlock the door. Once it was opened and he motioned her inside, she hesitated, uneasy about intruding on someone else's territory. This was a home Art had shared with Lil, and even though Lil no longer lived here, Belle could feel her presence.

"What're you waiting for?" Art asked. "Nothing's gonna jump out and bite you."

"I know. It's just that I ... well, it's my first time here and I'm a little nervous."

"What's to be nervous about? This is gonna be your new home."

"But it's your home. Yours and Lil's."

"So that's what's eating you. Lissen, Lil's the kinda person that won't let herself be happy. Even when we got the place all fixed up the way she wanted, she always found something to gripe about. The pipes rattled, it was too hot or too cold, the floors creaked ... hell, she said the same thing about the house in Newark. Fact, it was her idea to move down here. Told the folks she was gonna sit on the porch and sip Mint Juleps all day. Ha, whatta crock. Those folks in Jersey? The kids, the grandkids, her brothers and sisters? She missed 'em. So when I wouldn't sell this place and move back with her, she left. End of story."

"Hmmm," Belle murmured, still torn between wanting to go inside and feeling awkward about it. Art was standing so close she could feel the heat coming off his body. His aftershave smelled like a freshly peeled orange. What to do, what to do? She took a deep breath and stepped into a whole new world.

Art heaved a sigh and closed the door. "It's about time. I'll be swatting flies all night."

Belle paid no attention. She was feasting her eyes on an eclectic mix of furnishings: an oak hall tree; an overstuffed sofa upholstered in a floral design featuring blues, moss green, pink and magenta on a cream-colored background; carved end tables, each bearing a Tiffany lamp; a Shaker-style rocking chair; a Windsor chair and a roll top desk. An off-white wool rug with a border of grapes and ivy covered a large portion of the hardwood floor; in its center a magnificent peacock showed off his long tail feathers. The walls were painted a bold sky blue; the high ceilings, woodwork, and interior shutters a glossy white. Over it all drifted the pleasant aroma of lemon-scented furniture polish.

"Oh my word," Belle said. "How could Lil bear to leave these beautiful things behind?"

"She didn't," he said. "I bought this stuff a piece at a time. Started the day Lil left. There's this guy, James, that lives a coupla doors down. He hunts for old stuff and makes it look like new. His brother, Henry, does the upholstering. I got a ways to go but I'm getting there."

Belle shook her head in slow motion. "I must be dreaming. Never in a million years did I expect you, of all people, to be a collector of fine furniture."

"Whaddaya mean?" he said, obviously insulted. "Just 'cause I drive a cab and talk like a dope don't mean I ain't got taste."

"You have excellent taste, Arthur Barkoff. But why have you kept it a secret? All these months and you've never said a word."

He shrugged. "I wanted to surprise you."

"Well, you certainly accomplished that. I'm not only surprised, I'm stunned."

"C'mon," he said. "This here's where I flop." He crossed through an arched opening in the far wall and into the next room. "It's 'spose to be a dining room, but I wanted a den."

Joining him, she looked all around. "It's wonderful. Such rich colors, and so cozy." A plum-colored leather sofa and matching easy chair faced a console complete with a large-screen TV, a VCR, and a CD player. An old-fashioned cherry-wood smoker's stand stood next to the chair, a coffee table made of pine and cane with metal legs served the sofa. Extra large floor pillows in various designs were piled between the console and a glider rocker with an ottoman.

"I got my eye on this oak chest to go next to the bookcase," Art said, jerking his head toward the other side of the room. "James's working on it now. Says it's from the seventeenth century. Who knows?"

Belle was disappointed that the bookcase, though it held a collection of old bottles and other treasures, didn't contain any family photos.

Art moved on. "Back here's the kitchen. I hope you like it."

"Like it? I love it," Belle said from the threshold. Large and airy, with whitewashed walls and with windows on either side of a back door, the room contained an oak trestle table with six cane-bottomed chairs, a chopping block, a Hoosier cabinet, and a punched-tin pie safe. The usual complement of cupboards and drawers surrounded a porcelain sink, gas stove, and a modern side-by-side refrigerator. An old cheese grater, a warming pan, a corn shucker, a washboard, and other odds and ends dangled from wooden pegs in the walls.

Belle felt a lump in her throat. It was all too much to take in. She didn't know which was worse, to not have known that Art was a collector of fine old things, or to imagine living among them. When she left Lin's home in Georgia, she'd vowed to never be a caretaker of someone else's possessions again. Not that she didn't like keeping house. She'd liked it so much she'd talked Lin into letting his long-time, live-in maid go. But after the twins died, when Lin started to treat her the same way he'd treated the maid, she'd lost interest.

"Whaddaya think?" Art asked.

She swallowed hard and said, "I have a problem."

He frowned. "You're not gonna bring up Lil again, are you?"

"No. It's this house. Everything about it is perfect ... too perfect. Are you always this neat?"

His brows shot up. "You gotta be kidding. I been keeping the place up 'cause I knew you was coming."

"You knew I was coming today?"

Shrugging, he said, "Today, tomorrow, what's the difference? I knew it'd be sometime this week."

"So you're usually more at home?"

"Truth is, I'm a slob."

"Oh, I can't believe that."

"Aw, I'm not as bad as I used to be, but the dust and the cobwebs can get pretty thick around here."

She put a hand to her chest. "Thank goodness. You had me worried. When I first moved in with Gloria she accused me of being a neat freak, and I was beginning to think the same thing about you."

He laughed. "Not to worry. C'mon, I'll show you the rest of the place." He crossed to an interior door a few feet down from where Belle stood. "This hallway goes to the bedrooms and the bathroom. At the end of the hall there's a door goes into the living room. I had 'em cut that one in so I wouldn't have to go around the world to get to my room." He stepped into the hall, still talking about the layout.

She made as though to follow then faltered when a sudden rush of panic gripped her in a stranglehold. Heart pounding, limbs tingling, throat tightening, she could see herself having an all-out attack–unable to move or speak, urine running down her leg. No! She would not give in to it! She had to get out of there. Breathe fresh air.

Art came looking for her. "Hey, what's the matter?" he asked, heading her way.

Holding her hands out, as though to ward him off, she inched her way backwards, towards the den.

Art kept coming. "Belle? Tell me what's wrong. Is it the house? Something I said? What?"

She was closing in on the front door.

Hey," he said, "you need to go somewhere, I'll drive you."

Whirling around, she cleared the door, letting it bang shut behind her.

By the time Art reached the front edge of the porch, she was halfway down the block.

Six

Once inside the Chartres Mental Health Center, Belle went straight to the receptionist. "Connie," she gasped through labored breaths, "I have to see Marge."

With her usual calm demeanor, Connie said, "You're early, Belle. Marge just went to lunch."

"But I have to see her," Belle said, gripping the edge of the counter so hard her knuckles turned white.

Connie rose from her chair and came around the end of the counter. "It's all right, Belle," she said, gently laying a hand on her shoulder. "I'll walk you to Marge's office. You can wait there while I tell her you're here."

"But I don't understand," Belle said. "She's here in the building?"

"Yes. She's having lunch in the staff lounge."

"Thank goodness," Belle murmured. She pulled a tissue out of her trouser pocket and dabbed at her face. She'd walked, run, and jogged all the way from Art's and her entire body felt wet and clammy.

"Could I have a cup of water?" she asked as Connie led her to Marge's office.

"Certainly. I'll get it as soon as you're settled."

Belle sank into her usual chair. A few moments later, Connie handed her a paper cup filled with water. Belle gulped it down as though she were dying of thirst. For the first time in months she wished the cup contained vodka.

"Would you like more?" Connie asked, taking the empty cup from her. "I could get you a Coke."

Belle looked up."No, thanks. I'm fine."

Connie's eyes expressed doubt. "Well, just try to relax. Marge should be with you soon." She left the door ajar, her footsteps echoing down the hall.

Too agitated to sit, Belle got up and started pacing, her hands in constant motion: running shaky fingers through her wind-blown hair, straightening her collar, tucking in her blouse, drawing her cardigan together, taking it off and draping it over the back of her chair, pulling it back on when she felt a chill. Though her calves ached from running and the back of her neck burned with tension, she kept moving.

Marge's office was as plain and unadorned as the woman herself. Dull gray metal desk, swivel chair with worn black padding on the seat, mud-brown filing cabinet, two maple visitor's chairs with nicks and scratches. A musty odor lingered, like that of a room seldom aired. There were no framed photographs, mementos, or certificates. The only bright spot in the entire room was a sampler of the Serenity Prayer hanging on the wall behind the desk. Once, when Belle had remarked on it, Marge told her it was a gift from a client.

Gifts! She stopped pacing and let out a groan. What with all that had happened to Art last night she'd forgotten about the souvenirs she'd brought from Biloxi. She didn't even know where they were.

"What is it?" Marge asked as she came striding through the door.

Belle took one look at her, buried her face in her hands and burst into tears.

Marge crossed to her desk and plucked several tissues from a box of Kleenex. She went to Belle, forced her hands down and stuck the wad of tissues into one of them. "Blow," she said.

Belle's sobs subsided to sniffles and hiccups. She wiped her eyes and blew her nose. "I didn't mean to do that," she said. "It's just that I ..."

"It's all right, Belle," Marge said. "Take your seat and we'll get started."

Marge settled behind her desk, laced her fingers together and held them over her midriff. "Belle," she said, "look at me."

Belle, who'd been studying her lap, lifted her chin and looked across the desk. Her eyes were puffy and moist, her features pinched.

"Good," Marge said. "Now listen to me. You are to start your breathing exercises. Do you understand?"

Belle nodded. She closed her eyes and tried to concentrate on inhaling and exhaling. One, one thousand, two, one thousand, three, one ...

Marge sat silently watching, her gaze never leaving her client's face. Except for the sound of Belle's breathing, all was quiet.

At the count of twenty, Belle opened her eyes.

"Feeling better?" Marge asked.

"Yes."

Marge unlaced her fingers and scooted her chair closer to her desk. "Did you stop by the house before you came here?"

"No. I ... ah ... all I could think about was getting here. Is Mammy Daisy looking for me?"

"Yes. She's very worried. I'll let her know you're okay." She reached for the phone.

While Marge made the call, Belle scolded herself for not calling Mammy when she first got to Art's. She ought to have known Mammy would be worried. She had told her she'd be back in an hour or so and that had been over three hours ago.

Still on the phone but cupping a hand over the mouthpiece, Marge looked at her and said, "Mammy wants to know how Art is doing."

Belle had to stop and think. After running out on him without a word, she had no idea how he was.

"Belle?"

"Um, Art ... well, he has type two diabetes."

"And?" Marge said.

Belle spoke as though reading from a text. "He has to take medicine, monitor his glucose level, exercise, and watch his diet."

Marge held her hand over the mouthpiece a second longer. When it was clear that Belle had nothing to add, she repeated the information to Mammy. A pause, then, "Yes, I'll tell her. Talk to you later." She replaced the receiver in its niche, leaned back and said, "You're to go straight to Hope Haven when you leave here."

"I should have called her," Belle said.

"Yes, you should have. Just because you're ready to move out doesn't mean you can come and go as you please."

"But that's just it!" Belle cried, straining forward in her seat. "I'm not ready! I have to stay at least another month! Please, oh please, don't make me go out there."

Marge's expression remained neutral. "What brought this on?"

"I don't know ... I just know I'm not ready." She started plucking at the wadded ball of tissues in her hand.

"You were ready last week," Marge said.

Belle looked at her, pleading with her eyes. "Yes, but everything's changed. Nothing's what I expected it would be. And today I almost had an attack." She shuddered.

"You either had an attack or you didn't. Which is it?"

"Well, I guess it wasn't a real attack. But I felt like one was coming on."

"In other words, you panicked. Where were you at the time?"

Belle looked down at the mess she'd made. She'd shredded most of the tissues. Bits and pieces stuck to her trousers, a few had fluttered to the floor. She bent over and picked them up.

"Where were you?" Marge repeated.

Belle blurted it out. "At Art's."

"What were you doing there?"

"He was showing me his house."

"And?"

"It wasn't what I expected."

"What were you expecting?"

"Um ... I'm ashamed to say."

"All right, then. What was it like?"

"It was a doll house. Perfect in every way. All of the furnishings, the decor ... everything so neat and clean. It was like being in a model home. You know, the kind that people look at but no one actually lives in."

"And that frightened you?"

"Well, yes, in a way. It was overwhelming." She tilted her head to one side and gave Marge a curious look. "Doesn't it surprise you to know that Art collects antiques?"

"Not really. His Checker cab is a classic. That in itself tells me he appreciates old things. Besides, you never know what special qualities lie beneath a person's surface."

Guilt pricked Belle's conscience. "You're right, of course. Art's been so good to me, the best friend a person could ever have, and I ..." Her voice trailed off.

"Don't be so hard on yourself," Marge said. "We all tend to make unwarranted assumptions. But enough of that. I want to get back to the panic you felt. Close your eyes and visualize yourself entering Art's house. What did you see, how did you feel? Where were you and what were you doing when you began to have symptoms?"

"I don't have to visualize it. I was nervous from the start. First, because I felt like an intruder. After all, Art once shared the house with Lil. Then, as we walked through the rooms, the thought of living in a model home reminded me of my last years with Lin, when all I did was scrub and polish."

"You were thinking Art wanted you to be his housekeeper?"

"No, not exactly."

Marge studied her. "All right. We'll move on. When did you first feel you were on the verge of an attack?"

"When Art wanted to show me the bedrooms," she said, her voice barely audible.

"What was it about those rooms that frightened you?"

"I don't know."

"I think you do."

Belle felt the familiar flush coloring her cheeks. "I ... um, it's hard to explain."

"So what happened next?"

"I ran out on him. I didn't even tell him goodbye. I didn't ask about his medicine or his home monitoring kit, I just ran."

The room fell silent. Belle studied her hands. Marge appeared deep in thought.

"Tell me," Marge said. "When you and Art spent the night in Mississippi, did you share a room?"

Belle's head jerked up. "No, of course not."

"You're not lovers?"

"Absolutely not. Why would you even think that?" She remembered that Gloria had thought the same thing. Did everyone?

For the first time that day, Marge smiled. "For a lot of reasons, but mainly because the two of you have been so close."

Belle shifted in her seat. "Not that close."

Marge persisted. "Because you don't want Art as a lover? Or because you have a fear of intimacy?"

A nervous tic played at the corner of Belle's mouth. "Why are we talking about this? What has it got to do with anything?"

Marge spoke in her same steady voice. "Among other things, it has to do with why you became frightened. It has to do with your plans to move in with Art. And, if you do, whether or not you're ready to confront your fears."

Belle shook her head. "I don't understand. Are you saying I *should* move in with Art? That it may be scary at first, but that if I confront my fears I'll eventually get used to it?"

"More or less."

"But I didn't think you wanted me to live with Art."

"I don't. But it wouldn't be the worst thing that could happen."

"What would?"

"Having you move back to Georgia."

"But you know I have no intention of doing that."

Marge took a deep breath and let it out. "Your ex-husband called me this morning."

Belle's jaw dropped open. "Lin called you?"

Marge nodded. "He wanted to know when you were being discharged. He said your mother told him you were almost ready to leave. She's under the impression that you plan to come home."

Belle's mouth went dry. "Home?" To her ears the word sounded like a strangled cry for help.

"Yes."

"Darn!" Belle said, slamming the chair arm with a fist. "My mother never listens to a word I say. And what business is it of Lin's what I do? We're divorced, for heaven sakes."

"Bravo," Marge said. "Your reaction gives me hope. Belle, I've told you this before, but it's worth repeating. You are not responsible for what other people say or do. The only person you're responsible for is yourself."

"But why does everything have to get so complicated?" She heard the whine in her voice and hated herself for it.

"Learning how to *un*complicate things is all a part of growing up."

Belle slumped down in her chair. "Then I guess I'm still a child."

"In many ways, you are," Marge said. "You've led a very sheltered life. Been dominated by your mother and your ex. It's only natural that you're just beginning to come into your own. Bearing that in mind, I agree that you're not quite ready to leave Hope Haven." She consulted her desk calendar. "We'll set a moving date for March first. That's two weeks from this Friday."

Belle sat up straight and pressed her palms together. "Oh, thank you, thank you, thank you."

Marge continued. “Do you have any jobs lined up?”

Belle’s head bobbed up and down. “I’m working on one now and I’ve promised to do three more.” Following the open house in December, she’d had so many requests for murals she hadn’t been able to handle them all. The larger, more detailed works took an inordinate amount of time, especially since she had other obligations as a resident of Hope Haven.

“You can continue to work in your free time,” Marge said. “But you’re not to go anywhere without telling Mammy where you’re going and when you plan to be back. If you see that you can’t make it on time, you’re to call her right away. I’ll meet with you three times a week, more if I feel it’s necessary. We’ve got a lot of work to do.”

Belle was practically bouncing up and down in her seat. “Oh, Marge, I can’t tell you how grateful I am. And I promise to be good. Honest, I will. Oh, and I intend to pay you in full for all of my sessions. Mammy Daisy told you about me winning the jackpot, didn’t she? I also plan on using some of the money to spruce up Hope Haven. We need new furniture in the parlor and all of the mattresses need replacing. Oh, and a matching set of dishes would be nice, and we really need more flatware.” Breathless now, she gave a little laugh and said, “But I guess you don’t want to hear about that.”

“You guessed right,” Marge said. “I’m well aware of Hope Haven’s shortcomings. But here’s something you’re not aware of, so listen carefully.” She paused, waiting for Belle to settle down. Then she went on.

“Arrangements have already been made for your sessions to be paid in full. Also, a sizable donation to the house is on its way. Personally, I’d prefer not to accept the money–it’s coming from your ex–but our finance manager doesn’t agree with me.”

Belle blinked. “Lin is paying for my treatment?”

“That is correct. But remember, it’s not what happens to you, it’s how you react. That’s a major part of keeping life from getting complicated. You have no control over what Lin Mallory does or doesn’t do. I have no idea what his motives are, but I suspect it has something to do with a guilty conscience."

"But I don't want him to pay my bills. I don't want anything from him. I thought I made that clear when I signed the divorce papers."

Marge hunched her shoulders in a shrug. "Apparently your ex has other ideas. The best thing for you to do is to accept the things you cannot change and go on about your business. As for your jackpot winnings, I have mixed feelings about that. On the one hand I'm happy for you. It will make a nice nest egg. On the other hand it could cause problems. But we'll discuss that later. Where is the money now?"

Thoughts of Lin flew out of Belle's head as she tried to remember what she'd done with her winnings. Except for the five-hundred dollars she'd requested in cash, the man at the casino had given her a check. She'd tucked it into her handbag. The same handbag she'd taken with her today!

"Oh no. I must have left it at Art's."

Marge glanced at her watch, then pushed back from the desk and stood up. "My two o'clock isn't due for another forty-five minutes. I suggest we go get the check and put it in a bank."

Uncomprehending, Belle remained seated. "You mean you're taking me to Art's?"

"That's exactly what I mean. After what you've told me, I'd like to see his house."

"But what about Mammy Daisy? What about your lunch?"

"We'll stop by Hope Haven on our way to Art's. Mammy's bound to have some kind of leftovers we can munch on."

Belle popped up from her chair. "Oh goodie, I can give you your souvenirs." She laughed and said, "If I can find them." She paused, then added, "And I can apologize to Art and make sure he's all right."

Poor Art, she thought as they headed out the door. She had a lot of making up to do.

Seven

After trying to figure out what to do with himself, Art ended up in bed, lying flat on his back, hands clasped behind his head. He'd tried to sleep but his mind kept working overtime. He'd thought about going to work, but figured he needed to stick around in case Belle showed up. Nothing on TV was worth watching, so he lay there, blankly staring up at the ceiling.

Not for the first time, he wondered what he'd said to make Belle run off like that. Maybe it wasn't him, maybe it was the house. Too perfect, she'd said. Too neat and clean. He should've tossed dirty laundry around, left last night's dishes sitting out. Hell, he should've made as big a mess of the place as he could.

Would it have mattered? Probably not. She'd taken off because of something else. She'd had that trapped look in her eyes, as if he was going to lock her up and throw away the key. Yeah, he bet that was it. She'd been wishy-washy about moving in with him all along. He shouldn't have pushed her, shouldn't have made that deal about trying it for three months.

For all he knew, he might be the one wanting out. This past weekend in Mississippi was no picnic in the park. Trying to budge Belle when she had her mind set on something was like trying to budge an elephant. Maybe her moving into the Sidneys' apartment would be the best thing that could happen. More aggravation he didn't need. He'd had enough of that with Lil.

'Course Belle was nothing like Lil. Belle appreciated the things he did for her. She was always calling him her hero, her prince, her gallant squire. She'd even told him he had beautiful teeth. Just this morning she'd said he was smart. Ha, that was a joke. If he was so smart why was he lying here like a dummy?

Another thing about Belle. She wasn't a picky eater like Lil. Belle, she'd scarf down anything you put in front of her. And she liked going places, doing different things. He'd never once heard her complain. She never had anything bad to say about anyone. She had even made friends with that pimp Tyrone. Let the dude come to Hope Haven and take pictures of the murals. 'Course she wouldn't believe he was a pimp–hell, she probably didn't even know what the word meant. And she loved her pain-in-the-ass mother and that spoiled rotten daughter even though they treated her like shit. Yeah, Belle was special. He'd never known anyone like her. Kind-hearted, generous to a fault, affectionate–not to mention beautiful. So she acted like a nutcase now and then, so what?

Now that he thought about it, she'd okayed the three-month deal. Even seemed happy about it. So what made her run off? Something came to him. She'd gotten scared when he wanted to show her the bedrooms. Was that it? Did she think he was gonna crawl in her bed one night? Try to make out with her? Jesus, if she only knew. Lil had cut him off after Sandy was born. Said she didn't want to risk getting pregnant again. He'd told her he'd wear a rubber, but being a good Catholic she'd said that would be committing a sin against the Church. As far as he was concerned, cutting him off was a worse sin. Sandy was twenty-four years old, for crissakes.

Okay, so he'd had a few one-night stands since then, mostly to prove he still had it in him, but he hadn't had sex in a long time. Fact, he couldn't remember the last time. And now that he had this disease, along with his bad heart, having sex would probably kill–if he could even get it up. Maybe he ought to ask the doc about that. Just in case.

All in all, it'd be better for both of them if Belle got her own place. It'd give her a chance to see if she liked living alone, and it'd give him a chance to see how his medicine was going to work. For all he knew it might give him the runs. Nothing like having the runs with a woman in the house.'Specially with only one bathroom.

Which reminded him. He needed to take a leak. Then he needed to go get his stuff out of the trunk so he could check his glucose. What a helluva deal that was. Sticking his finger every day. Well, as Belle said, he was lucky to get away with not having to give himself shots. Better to stick his finger than shoot a needle into his hip, or wherever. How his son shot dope into his veins every chance he got boggled Art's mind. What did the kid get out of it, besides pain and bruises? Maybe the kid would wise up one of these days. Belle had told him to never give up on Artie. Sandy either. And after he'd seen Gloria turn from a smartass punk into a regular girl, he had to believe anything was possible.

He rolled to the side of the bed and pushed himself up. Whoa. He sat back down when a dizzy spell made his head spin. While sitting there, trying to get his bearings, his stomach growled. No wonder he was dizzy. He hadn't eaten anything since breakfast. Some breakfast, he thought–a lousy bowl of cereal and half a grapefruit. He got up, steadied himself against the side of the bed, then padded into the bathroom.

After relieving himself, he headed for the kitchen. He'd fix a sandwich and then go get his stuff out of the trunk. He opened the fridge and stared inside, wondering what would be good for him. Ham and cheese? Corned beef? He needed to read that book the doc gave him. If Belle was here, she'd know what he should eat, but Belle wasn't here, so he pulled out a package of sliced turkey meat, mustard instead of mayo, a chunk of lettuce, and a jar of dill pickles.

His sandwich made, he stood at the sink and gobbled it down, surprised that it didn't taste all that bad. When he finished, his stomach still felt empty so he made another. What the hell, he could stand to gain a few pounds. Besides, this stuff couldn't be that fattening. Not like ham and cheese with butter and mayo.

Thirsty for a beer, he opened the fridge again and pulled out a bottle of Jax. He started to uncap it, then stopped. What did the book say about booze? Maybe he should drink water for now. He put the bottle back, sighed and ran tap water into a glass.

He's just finished drinking when the doorbell rang. He looked over his shoulder, through the den and the living room to the front door, wondering who it could be. Maybe it was James. Maybe the chest he'd had his eye on was ready to go. Or maybe James wanted to show him a new piece of furniture he'd found in somebody's attic. Yeah, he bet it was James.

Still in his socks and undershirt, his slacks rumpled, he plodded towards the door. The bell rang again when he was almost there. "Hold your horses!" he hollered.

Reaching the door, he opened it. There stood Belle and Marge.

Was he seeing things? "What the hell?" he said out loud.

"Hello, Art," Marge said, as though they came calling every day.

Flustered and feeling naked in his undershirt, his eyes cut from Belle to Marge and back again. "What're you guys doing here? Am I in some kinda trouble?"

Belle gave a nervous giggle. "No, silly. I'm the one who's in trouble. I don't know what came over me, Art, I just–"

Marge cut her off. "She left her handbag here. It has the check in it, so we thought we'd better pick it up and take it to a bank."

When Art just stood there, Marge went on. "Do you mind if we come in? Belle has told me you have a fine collection of furnishings. I'm something of a collector myself, mostly old bottles."

Art ran a hand through his mop of hair and backed away from the door. "Sure. Make yourself at home."

Belle's eyes roamed over his face. "If it's inconvenient ..."

"Naw, naw, come on in. Take a look around. I'll be back in a jiff." He made a beeline for the door that led to the bedrooms and disappeared behind it.

From his room, he could hear murmurs of conversation. So they'd come for Belle's purse, eh? Funny, he didn't remember her carrying one in. If there was a purse sitting around someplace, why was Marge taking her to the bank? He'd planned on doing that. Did this mean Belle was turning her affairs over to Marge? Was she getting ready to dump him?

In the bathroom, he splashed cold water on his face and brushed his teeth. After combing his hair he donned a fresh shirt and put on his shoes. Instead of retracing his steps, he went down the hall and through the door that led into the kitchen. Noticing his lunch makings sitting on the counter, he decided to leave them there. Let Belle see he was no neat freak.

He started for the den. Before he could make it, Belle came rushing up to him, looking frantic. "I can't find my purse anywhere. Did you put it away?"

"Haven't seen it," he said. "Fact, I don't think you brought one in."

"Then I must have left it in the cab." She spun around and headed back the way she'd come, passing Marge, who was inspecting the colonial bottles on the top shelf of the bookcase.

"Wait up," Art called. "I'm coming."

"What's going on?" Marge asked as he hurried past her. She'd been distracted by the bottles.

"Out to the cab," he said without looking back. "She thinks her bag's in there."

"Did you lock the cab?"

"No." He slammed out the door.

"I found it!" Belle exclaimed, waving her straw bag in the air. "I found these, too." She held up the white paper bag containing the Necco wafers and the box of Black Crows.

Art caught up with her, his heart thumping in his ears. "Jesus, what were you thinking? Running around town with all that dough. Don't you know a cashier's check is the same as cash? Hell, anybody could've signed your name to it and been in like Flynn."

She looked down at the ground and drew a long breath. "It was pretty careless of me, wasn't it?"

"Careless? It was downright stupid."

She looked up at him, her chin quivering. "Oh, Art, I don't blame you for being angry. I'd be mad at me, too. First I run away without saying goodbye, then Marge and I barge in on you, and now this ... oh my gosh, I can't believe I could be so dumb."

Art glared at her, a belligerent set to his jaw. For two cents he'd take off in the cab and leave her standing there, just as she'd left him.

"Did you find it?" Marge asked from the porch.

Belle made a half-turn and held up the purse for Marge to see. Then she faced Art and spoke in an undertone. "I need to talk to you. It's very important. If Mammy will let me, can I come back later?"

That caught him off guard. "You wanna come here?"

"If it's all right with you." She gave him a playful smile. "I still haven't seen the rest of the house."

"I have," said Marge, joining them. "And it's lovely, both inside and out." She gave Art a look of admiration. "Congratulations on a splendid job."

He squinted at her. "You wouldn't kid an old kidder, would you?"

Marge drew herself up to full height. "Certainly not. And if you ever think of selling any of your bottles, please let me know."

Convinced she was serious, Art warmed to the subject. "Tell you what, Marge. I got most of 'em at that little shop this side of the Gallier House on Royal. You know the one I'm talking about? It looks like they got nothing but junk, but you dig deep enough and they got some good stuff."

"Thanks for the tip," Marge said.

"Think nothing of it. There's another shop on Chartres. It's up a coupla blocks from the French Market."

"I'll find it," she said, then looked at Belle. "Speaking of finding things, we'd better get that check to the bank."

"Good idea," said Art, suddenly feeling expansive and a little cocky. After all these months of Marge giving him tips, he'd finally gotten the chance to dish one out. And all because of some old bottles he'd picked up. Who woulda thought?

• • •

Two hours later, Art was sitting at one end of the leather sofa in his den with Belle at the other. They'd been talking about this and that, mostly about his health and Belle's need to stay at Hope Haven a while longer. Their exchanges had been polite but slightly strained, like that of two people who didn't know each other very well.

"Oh, I almost forgot," she said. "If you start getting mail for me it's because I used your address on my bank account."

He shot her a look. "Why'd you do that?"

"Because it seemed like the logical thing to do. After all, I'll be living here as of March first, won't I?"

"Will you?"

"Art? What is it? Didn't we agree to try it for at least three months?"

"Yeah, but I figured you'd changed your mind."

"Why would you think that?"

"Why wouldn't I? You weren't too happy with the place the last time you was here."

"Well, I'm happy now," she said. "Don't I look happy?" She gave him an exaggerated grin that showed a lot of teeth.

"Getouttahere," he said.

She giggled, then took a sip of the iced tea he'd made especially for her. Early Frank Sinatra tunes played in the background. A vanilla-scented candle flickered from the top of the stereo, spilling its fragrance about the room. Belle had forgotten what it felt like to snuggle up on a comfy sofa with mellow music floating in the air. It was so cozy and dreamy she wanted to stay there forever.

"So," Art said, "you made up your mind for sure?"

"Yes. I'll be moving in two weeks from Friday."

"Marge said it was okay?"

"Yes. We talked about it on the way to the bank. She thinks it will help me confront my fears."

Art tensed. "What kinda fears?"

She took another sip of tea and set the glass back on the coffee table. "Oh, you know ... different things."

Art thought about what she said and decided to lay it out for her. "Lissen, Belle, you got nothing to worry about. I got bad sugar and a bad ticker. My rutting instincts are long gone."

"Thank heavens," she blurted. Then, quickly, she added, "I didn't mean that the way it sounded. It's just that ... well, I didn't know what to expect."

"You can expect nothing and nothing's what you'll get," Art said, harsher than he'd intended.

"Okay," she said in a tiny voice.

"That settles that," Art said.

"Yes," she said. "You can be my big brother and I'll be your little sister."

"Right," said Art.

"I never had a brother or a sister, did you?"

"Yeah. My brother died in Nam."

"Oh, how awful."

"You got that right. Paulie was a great kid."

"Was he younger or older than you?"

"Younger. I still miss the little twerp."

"I'm sure you do. It must have been devastating."

Art pushed up from the sofa. "I need a brew. You want more tea?"

She looked up as he passed in front of her. "No, thank you. Are you supposed to drink beer?"

"Don't start," he warned. Then, knowing he was acting like a jerk, he did an about face and marched back to his end of the sofa. In the background, Sinatra crooned the words to, "I've Got You Under My Skin."

Seated, Art set his right ankle on his left knee and jiggled his foot, wanting to kick himself with it. All he'd meant to do was put her at ease. He didn't have to tell her he was washed up, for crissakes. They'd live like brother and sister, she said. What a crock that was. And then he'd had to go and tell her about Paulie. What did that have to do with anything? Not a damn thing.

"Maybe I should go," she said, making a move to get up.

His foot hit the floor as he put out a hand to stop her. "Don't," he said. "You were right about the beer. But I sure do want one."

"I understand," she said. "I felt the same way about Mister Vodka."

Mister Vodka had been her best friend and constant companion. If it hadn't been for him she would never have had the courage to leave Georgia. He'd seen her safely on the train, stayed with her throughout the long journey, calmed her when she felt anxious, kept her sane. But once she entered treatment at Hope Haven she'd had to give him up.

"Y'know," Art said, looking at her with a renewed sense of kinship, "I still got that plastic bottle you kept your vodka in. It's in the kitchen cabinet to the right of the sink."

She gazed at him in wonder. "I can't believe you kept it."

He shrugged. "Hey, you never know when an empty bottle might come in handy. 'Specially one named 'Mister Vodka.'" He paused. "What I wanna know is, do you ever think about taking a drink?"

"I thought about it just this morning," she said, "while I was waiting for Marge. Connie brought me a cup of water and I was wishing it was vodka. That doesn't happen very often. But I still thank my lucky stars for Mister Vodka and all he did for me."

Art sat back and slung his left arm across the top of the sofa. "I guess we're just a coupla old teetotalers. Who woulda believed it? Not me."

"Oh, I don't know," she said. "If we're real good, maybe we can have a glass of wine now and then. But first you'll have to ask the doctor."

He looked at her. "You wouldn't get hooked again?"

"To be perfectly honest, no. I've gotten a lot out of the AA meetings, and I like all the people who come to them, but I never believed I was an alcoholic. Oh, I indulged a bit too much at times, but the panic attacks, the agoraphobia, started long before I began keeping company with Mister Vodka. Like Marge said, he was my safety net, my crutch. A nice crutch, but a crutch all the same."

"Yeah, I remember when you wouldn't go out of your hotel room unless you had that bottle stashed somewhere handy. And then that one night you forgot it and you had that attack at Galatoire's. I got all hot and bothered hunting for the bottle, but you was happy-go-lucky 'cause you had a new safety net. Namely, yours truly."

She giggled. "I can still see you down on your knees, turning my purse upside down on the sidewalk, trying to find the bottle."

"Yeah," said Art, "we sure had some crazy old times." His brain perking now, he snapped his fingers. "Hey, Mardi Gras's coming up. You wanna go? I guarantee you'd get a charge outta it."

Her expression turned wistful. "I've always dreamed of going to Mardi Gras. All those costumes hanging on the walls at Ralph and Kakoo's make me yearn to dress up in something exotic." She sighed. "The problem is, Mammy Daisy won't let us go."

"Why not?"

"She says it's a drunken orgy full of naked women and nasty men. She said some of the men even go tinkle in the street. Is that true?"

Art snorted a laugh. Only Belle would say *tinkle* instead of *piss.* "Things can get pretty wild," he admitted, "but there's lotsa good stuff too. It depends on when and where you go. Take St. Charles Avenue. It's not near as raunchy as Bourbon Street. You'll see lotsa families on St. Charles. Grandmas, grandpas, little kids. I'm telling you, Belle, those floats are really something. But hey, if Mammy won't let you go it's no big deal. We can wait till next year."

Her face brightened. "We can, can't we?"

"You betcha." Next year! Would he and Belle still be living together? Hell, would he still be breathing?

With the last note of Sinatra's "Fly Me To The Moon" ringing in her ears, Belle swung her legs over the edge of the sofa and slipped her feet into her moccasins.

"This has been wonderful," she said, "but alas, it's time for me to go."

"Already? Seems like you just got here."

She smiled at him. "It seems that way to me, too, but Mammy gave me strict orders to be home by five." She stood up and stretched her arms over her head. Then she picked up what remained of her iced tea and carried it into the kitchen.

Tagging along behind her, Art felt as self-conscious as he had earlier. Should he ask if she wanted to see her room? Naw, that might set her off again. Better to let her pick the time. At least now she knew he wasn't gonna be sniffing around, trying to catch a peep of her in her undies.

"I love this room," Belle said from where she stood with her back to the sink. "Maybe after I get settled, we could have a dinner party. I'd do all the cooking and the cleaning up. We could invite Marge and Mammy and the girls. Oh, and we could ask your friend James and his brother Henry. What do you think?"

Art could see it now. Pots and pans boiling over on every burner, smoke pouring out of the oven, dishes crashing to the floor, people roaming all over the house, poking their noses where they didn't belong.

He grinned and said, "I think it sounds swell."

"Oh, goodie. Now, if you don't mind, I'd like to see my room."

His grin widened. "No problem."

Eight

With the dishes cleared and the aroma of beef stew lingering in the air, Belle went around the dining table depositing a shiny gold gift bag on each placemat. "Don't open them until I say it's okay," she told the group at large. Excited murmurs and whisperings followed in her wake.

After collecting her winnings in Biloxi, she'd tried to find a different gift for each girl, something that reflected the individual's taste and personality, but with Art hurrying her along she'd gotten so confused she'd ended up buying everyone the same thing: snow globes that showed pelicans flying over the Gulf; chunky silver charm bracelets featuring various kinds of seashells, and baby air plants set in delicate pieces of driftwood.

As soon as she was seated and gave the go-ahead, the ripping and tearing sounds of paper soon gave way to oohhs and aahhs. Belle took it all in, trying to gauge reactions.

"I know it's not much," she said above the buzz. "If only I'd had more time to shop."

"Bless you, child," Mammy Daisy said as she fastened the bracelet around her wrist. "I'm still mad 'bout you goin' in that evil place, but you done real good by us. I ain't never gonna take this here pretty thing off." The seashell charms clinked together as she held her arm out and twisted her wrist this way and that.

Belle laughed. "I hope it doesn't turn your skin green. It's supposed to be sterling silver, but you never know."

"Excuse my ignorance, but what is this?" Janette asked, holding up her piece of driftwood.

"Yeah," Boots chimed in. "I've seen these at the French Market. What do you do with them?"

"They're air plants," Gloria answered. "They're called that because they live on the moisture in the air. You can hang it on your wall, stand it on your dresser, or sit it on your windowsill. Then all you do is spritz them with water every two weeks or so."

"Don't you be spraying no water on my walls," Mammy warned. "And I don't wanna see no nails sticking out of 'em neither."

"Why don't we put them out on the picnic table," Millie said. "We could write our initials on the driftwood so we'd know which one was ours."

"I want to keep mine in my room," Janette said. "I've never had a plant and I want to watch it grow."

"Me, too." said Boots.

And so it went around the table.

Belle sat back in her chair, content to listen. Which hadn't always been the case. Back when she was a newcomer to the house, the girls were constantly sniping at each other, saying mean, spiteful things that made it hard for her to draw an easy breath. Someone was always getting in trouble for using gutter talk, as Mammy Daisy called it. Depending on the offense, the resident was either sent to her room or denied a pass. One time, when Janette couldn't seem to stop spewing curses, Mammy made her go to church, which to Janette's way of thinking was the worst punishment of all.

Back then, the jokes the girls told and the slang they used sounded to Belle like a foreign language. She'd had to take her cues from the group: laugh when they did even though she had no idea what was funny. All that started to change when she began helping them study for the GED exam. Gloria, whose vocabulary had been liberally sprinkled with four-letter words whenever Mammy wasn't around, was the first to become aware of her pattern of speech. She stopped using profanity, and when she misused a simple word or phrase she either corrected herself or looked to Belle for the answer. Eventually, the others followed her example. Even after the girls earned their GED, they continued to improve themselves, not only in the way they talked but in their appearance and manner as well. They were indeed Hope Haven's finest.

"Belle?" Gloria said. "What did you get Art?"

"Nothing."

"Nothing!" the girls exclaimed as one.

"I couldn't," she said. "He wouldn't give me a minute to myself. I've decided to get him something for his house." She was planning to go to the shops he'd told Marge about or talk to his friend James. She wanted to buy him an antique clock, one that chimed on the quarter hour.

"What's his house like?" Janette asked.

For the next half hour or so the conversation centered around Art, his home and his health. It ended with Belle telling them about the dinner party they planned to have.

"Oh, and I have one more bit of news," she said. "Some of you already know this, but I'm not moving out until March first."

That brought on another round of dialogue. Without divulging anything of a personal nature, she was able to convince the skeptics that it was not because Marge ordered her to stay but because she'd requested an extension.

"Well, I'm thrilled," Gloria said. "Our room would have been the worst kind of empty without you."

"Thank you, sweetheart," Belle said, blowing her a kiss.

"You know," Boots said, "I've been thinking maybe I should stay awhile. My mother *says* she wants me to come home, but what she says and what she thinks are two different things. Besides, I like New Orleans. There's a heck of a lot more to do here than in Brownwood,

Texas."

"Yeah, and there's a lot more trouble here too," said Gracie.

"Girl, if you is lookin' for Mister Trouble you can find him anywhere," Mammy Daisy said.

"Amen to that," said Millie. "I had nothing but trouble back in Stillwater."

"Honey," Janette said, "the only place you haven't had trouble is right here in Hope Haven."

The sound of laughter followed.

Still thinking about what Boots said, Belle addressed her. "Have you told Marge how you feel about going home?"

"I don't dare. She's already arranged for my bus ticket."

"That don't mean a thing," said Mammy. "You best talk to Marge. Nobody's wanting you to go home lessen you wants to, y'hear?"

"Yes, ma'am."

"See that you talk to her tomorrow." She looked around the table. "Anybody else got the jitters 'bout leaving?"

Glances were exchanged around the table but no one said a word.

Mammy Daisy pushed her heavy bulk out of her chair. "Then y'all run along and get ready. We got us a meeting here tonight."

Moans and groans came from several of the girls. Even Belle, who enjoyed the AA meetings, would have preferred to unwind from the day's events in her room.

As usual, four of the residents ducked out the back door to smoke cigarettes. Since smoking wasn't allowed in the house, a makeshift ashtray consisting of a large can filled with sand sat on the picnic table. Neither Mammy Daisy nor Marge harassed the girls about smoking. Their motto was: "One addiction at a time."

The ones who had never taken up the habit–Belle, Gloria, and Janette–headed up the stairs to freshen up before the meeting.

At the upper landing, Janette tapped Belle on the arm. "I need to talk to you."

"I'll join you in a few minutes," Belle told Gloria. She followed

Janette into the room the girl shared with Gracie.

Closing the door behind her, Belle moved to sit on the bed opposite Janette's. "What is it?" she asked.

"It's about Amber."

Belle's heart gave a lurch. Other than Mammy, she was the only one in the house who knew Janette had a daughter in foster care. "Is she all right?"

Janette winced. "That's just the problem. She's doing so well her foster parents want to adopt her."

"What? I don't understand. How can they adopt her when she already has a mother?"

"It's simple," Janette said. "If I agree to give Amber up, anyone social services approves of can adopt her." She started to rock to and fro, her features twisted into a mask of despair. "Oh, Belle, I don't know what to do. I want the best for my little girl. I want her to have all the things I never had. A good home, a loving family ... I'm afraid if I don't sign the papers I'll ruin her chances."

Belle moved to sit beside her. "What does Marge say?"

Janette expelled a long breath. "She says it's up to me. But the social worker is pressuring me to let Amber go."

"But why is all this happening now? I thought you had a year to prove you could make a home for Amber."

"That's what her foster parents are worried about. They're afraid I'll take her back. That's why they want to adopt her now. They're good people, Belle. I've met them at visitations. They're crazy about Amber, and she seems to love them, too." A tremor came into her voice. "She even calls them Mommy and Daddy."

"Oh, honey," Belle said, for want of anything better. With her right hand she began to rub Janette's back in a circular motion. She'd done the exact same thing the first time she heard about Amber. About how Amber's father had deserted them soon after the baby was born; how Janette then fell into a sordid life of drugs, often ignoring Amber's needs, leaving her alone for hours at a time, sometimes overnight.

Finally, and most horribly, how surgeons had to suture multiple wounds on the baby's arms and legs because rats got into her crib.

It was a clear case of neglect that was promptly reported to Child Welfare Services. That department, under the auspices of the Office of Community Services, or OCS, took over the care of the child. Amber was soon placed in a foster home.

It took two more years of self-destructive behavior before Janette was willing to commit herself to Hope Haven for treatment. Now, after ten months, she was ready to move into a supervised boarding-house and go to work for a local dentist. If she stayed off drugs and made progress in her work, in one year's time she would be allowed full custody of Amber, who would then be five years old.

Belle wished Janette had never confided in her. The girl didn't know that she, Belle, had lost her precious twins. Nor did she know how desperately Belle had wanted to adopt. But this wasn't about her. It was about Janette, and she had to try to look at the girl's dilemma objectively.

She knew that some would say Janette didn't deserve a second chance at raising her daughter, that for all intents and purposes she'd given Amber away the first time she'd left her alone. Perhaps they'd be right. But Belle hadn't known that Janette, she only knew the girl sitting next to her. This Janette had undergone a dramatic transformation. She'd worked hard to regain her self-respect. What would it do to her to lose her child? What would it do to the child to stay with her mother?

"When do you have to decide?"

"Whenever I'm ready," Janette said. She turned to Belle, a feverish look in her eyes. "But I can't stand the pressure much longer. What would you do if you were me?"

Belle shook her head. "It's impossible for me to answer that. I can't imagine giving up my child. Yet, if the foster parents love her and she loves them, perhaps it would be for the best. Oh, Janette, there's just so much to consider. It's a wonder you can sleep nights."

"I can't!" the girl cried. "I have horrible dreams. I see those rats in Amber's crib, only she's not there. I look everywhere for her, I'm still looking when I wake up. Other times I see cops hauling me away in handcuffs and locking me in a dark cage. I see Amber dressed like an angel, her foster parents showing her off to all their relatives. I even saw God once. His face was a fiery red and he was shaking a fist at me. I swear I'll go crazy if I don't decide soon."

Belle's insides churned. How, under such pressure, could Janette possibly make a rational decision? And if she did decide to give Amber up, would it threaten her sobriety?

"You know," Belle said at last, "if I were you I'd talk to Mammy Daisy. Marge is a great therapist, but Mammy has a lot of common sense. She must know of other girls who have faced the same quandary. After all, she's been here a long time. She's seen a lot of girls come and go."

The door to the room suddenly swung open. "Oh," said Gracie, a startled look on her face. "Am I interrupting something?"

Belle answered the question with one of her own. "Is it time for the meeting?"

"We've got five minutes."

"Then I'd better go." To Janette, she whispered, "Talk to Mammy."

When Janette nodded, Belle gave her a pat on the back and stood up.

Still lingering at the door, Gracie didn't seem to know what to do with herself..

"Janette's not feeling very well," Belle said to her. "She's going to skip tonight's meeting." She looked back at Janette. "See if Mammy's got something to help settle your stomach."

Choking back tears, Belle brushed past Gracie and closed the door behind her.

"What's wrong with Janette?" Gloria asked the moment she entered their room.

"Oh, she's just worried about her future."

"Aren't we all," said Gloria.

Gloria's comment stayed with Belle throughout the AA meeting. It was true. Every single one of the girls was concerned about her future. Was it always that way when a person was preparing to leave the safety of a halfway house? Darleen came to mind. From all indications, Darleen seemed content to be riding the highways and byways with Roger. But what if she'd never met Roger? What if she was still a resident of Hope Haven?

Belle had read about convicts who, after their release, committed crimes in order to be sent back to prison. According to the experts, when a person couldn't function in the outside world they had become *institutionalized.* They needed confinement, rules and regulations. Had that happened to her? To the others as well? It was a worrisome thought.

The people in the room were stirring, some standing up. She looked all around. The meeting had ended without her knowing it. Instead of mingling with the group as she usually did, having one of Mammy's homemade cookies and a cup of coffee, she made a dash for the stairs, anxious to check on Janette.

"Who is it?" Janette asked in response to Belle's knock.

"It's me, Belle."

"Come in. I've been waiting for you."

Belle entered the room. No sooner had she taken her seat on Gracie's bed than Janette started in.

"You were right about Mammy knowing other girls with the same problem as me. One had two kids, one had three, one had a little girl about Amber's age, and one had a nine-month old baby. The one with the baby was only fifteen. She'd run away from home because her step-father raped her. When she tried to tell her mother, the mother slapped her and called her a liar. The girl wandered all over the place, hitching rides, living in junked cars ... hobo jungles. She didn't even know she was pregnant till she got picked up for possession. Anyway, she had the baby in jail and social service placed him in foster care. A few months later the judge sent the girl here to serve out the rest of her time. Mammy said she did well for about three months. Then one night she took off. No one has seen or heard from her since. She signed the adoption papers the day before she left."

Belle bowed her head and clasped her hands tightly. All she could think about was the missing girl. More than anything, she wanted to clasp the poor darling to her breast and tell her she believed her.

"Belle? Are you all right?"

Belle's eyes slipped closed and then opened. "Janette, I don't think I can bear to hear anymore. It's just so sad."

"Oh," Janette said with an angry toss of her head. "Well, I'm sorry if I upset you. I keep forgetting you're not like the rest of us."

The words stung. "Oh, but I am. No, I've never felt the pain and terror of being raped. I've never had to live in an alley or sell my body f or drugs. But there are other kinds of suffering, Janette, and I wouldn't be here if I hadn't had my share of hurt."

"But you're such a lady. The rest of us ... we're nothing but a bunch of tramps."

"Don't ever say that!" Belle cried. "Don't even think it. Yes, we were born into different worlds, yes, we've lived different lives. But we've got one thing in common. We are survivors."

Janette seemed to ponder that for a moment and her expression lightened. "We are, aren't we?"

"Yes, we are. We've each been given a new start in life, and this time we're all going to make the most of it."

"Belle?" Janette said.

"Yes?"

"Can I tell you what happened to the other mothers?"

"If it will help you to talk about it." She steeled herself for what was to come.

"Two of them, the one with the little girl and the one with three kids, signed the adoption papers within three months of leaving Hope Haven. Mammy said the strain of trying to hold down their jobs and take care of their children was too much for them. One of them got so depressed she cried all the time. The other one missed so many days of work she got fired. I guess they ran the social worker ragged. But she finally persuaded them to sign the papers. The third one still has custody of her boys They're nine and seven. She works in the cafeteria at their school, and so far so good. Anyway, Mammy gave me a lot to think about."

Relieved that no harm had come to any of the children, Belle asked, "How is the girl who was so depressed doing now?"

"Mammy says she's much better. So is the one who got fired from her first job. And guess what? They're both living in the same boardinghouse that I'm moving into. Isn't that terrific?"

"Yes, it is," Belle said, hoping it would be.

The two of them talked awhile longer. Janette came to the conclusion that she needed time to adjust to her new home and job before making a decision. Meanwhile, she would pay special attention to her daughter's interaction with her foster parents during visitations. Adults usually showed only their good side when trying to make an impression, but a child of four normally lacked the ability to deceive. She might try, but if you watched closely, the child's eyes would eventually give her away.

Feeling more positive about life in general, Janette declared she was hungry. At that, the two women embraced, then parted ways.

Belle went straight to her room, expecting Gloria to pepper her with questions. But Gloria hadn't come upstairs yet. Grateful for a moment of privacy, Belle collapsed on her bed.

The relative comfort of lying down provided no relief from the scorching images that darkened her mind: fathers raping children, mothers turning their backs on the truth, the innocent babies born into such a world.

Turning onto her stomach, Belle mashed her face into the chenille bedspread and beat the mattress with her fists. Tears leaked from her eyes and mucus filled her nose. A dull ache at the back of her skull began to throb.

"What on earth are you doing?" Gloria asked from the doorway.

Belle became perfectly still. Then she rolled onto her side. "Tell me,"she said. "What was life like on the streets?"

Gloria gave a harsh laugh. "Believe me, Belle, you don't want to know."

Belle thought it over. "You're right, I don't." Plucking a tissue from the box on the bedside table, she dried her eyes and blew her nose. Then she scrambled to the head of the bed and propped herself up with her pillow.

Settled, she smiled at Gloria and said, "Tell me a bedtime story. And make sure it has a happy ending."

Nine

For the next few days Belle buried herself in her work. It was the perfect antidote to her growing list of concerns. Except for doing her chores at Hope Haven and meeting with Marge, she spent every possible moment working on a mural for a couple who lived on Kerlerec Street. A block and a half from Art's house on Esplanade, Kerlerec was one of those streets that tested one's homing instincts–it started, stopped, started, and stopped. The couple were both employed by the city, he as a building inspector and she as a court reporter. They'd given Belle a key to the house so she could come and go according to her schedule.

The job had come about through word of mouth, the way most of them had. Following the open house in December, when AA members, mental health and rehab staff, and people from all over the neighborhood came to see the murals she'd painted at Hope Haven, the requests just kept coming in, some from people who hadn't even been to the house. Because she didn't want to depend on Art for daily transportation she made it clear that she'd have to leave her equipment at the customer's house until she finished the job. No one complained because, in the beginning she didn't charge for her time, only for her supplies.

Art had a fit when he found out. She was running a business, he said, her time was worth at least twenty-five dollars an hour. "Hell's bells, plumbers get twice that just for making a house call." But Belle didn't care what other people charged, she didn't want to feel like she had to rush through a job in order to save the customer money. After a lengthy, rather heated discussion, she finally agreed to charge ten dollars an hour. Even though her customers thought that a bargain, she still felt uncomfortable about taking their money. To prove to them and to herself that the final amount was correct, she kept a meticulous record of the hours she worked.

She loved her current job. With her customers away at work, she was free to create without distraction, especially without someone looking over her shoulder as so many of her retired customers were wont to do. How peaceful it was to have no TV or radio blasting in her ear, no caged birds trying to peck their way to freedom, no cats or dogs treading on her drop-cloth or threatening to dip a nose or a paw in a can of paint, and best of all, no comments or questions that required a response.

Belle also loved the scene the couple had chosen, though she thought it would look better in their den than in the living room, where they'd hung framed posters of Mardi Gras scenes on all the other walls. She hoped that once the project was finished they would remove the posters so as not to detract from the mural–a night view of Algiers as seen from the French Quarter's Moon Walk, a gathering place on the banks of the Mississippi River. Both the husband and wife had been raised in Algiers, and sitting hand in hand on a bench on the Moon Walk was a favorite pastime. When Belle heard the story she wondered if she and Art had sat near them a time or two.

Though the preparation of the wall was tedious–filling cracks and holes, sanding, scrubbing, applying a primer and then the background coat–it was vital to the finished product.

Once she started painting the mural itself she entered another realm, much like a conductor directing a symphony orchestra, she imagined. Or a writer lost in the minds of her characters. It was as if she were standing outside herself watching this other person wave a magic wand. Only instead of a wand it was a paint brush, a sponge, a powder puff, a rag, a feather duster, whatever object it took to create the right effect.

Even though she always intended to follow the sketches she'd drawn beforehand, had them laid out on the floor to consult, she rarely looked at them; instead, she let her imagination take flight.

For Belle, night scenes, such as this one, required more thought than, say, a daytime scene of Jackson Square. Too little shading and sprinkling of city lights would make it too dark, yet too much would make it look fake.

On Thursday afternoon, when the alarm clock she always brought with her buzzed at four o'clock, she groaned out loud. This had been one of those marvelous days when her creative juices flowed from her brain to her hand in a steady stream. Left up to her she could have worked all night, but Mammy Daisy was expecting her home by four-thirty to help prepare the evening meal.

Standing back, she surveyed the scene. Pleased with what she saw, she retrieved her log book and recorded her time. Then came the bothersome task of cleaning up her mess. It wasn't the actual task she disliked, it was the fact that she was through for the day whether she wanted to be or not. Of course that would change once she moved in with Art. With no deadlines to meet, she would be able to paint as long as her heart desired.

• • •

Several mornings later, a sleepy-eyed Gloria raised her head off her pillow. "What's your hurry?" she asked.

Belle had been up for almost an hour. She'd made her bed, tidied the room, taken a shower, gotten dressed, and was now watering her plants. "If I get an early start I think I can finish the Bardets' mural today," she said.

"Oh. Then what will you do?"

"Soak in the tub for an hour or two," she said with a laugh. "What's on your agenda?"

"The usual."

Belle added the last drops of water to her Schefflera, one of the many plants sitting around the room. She placed the empty watering can on the floor of her closet, then went to stand at the foot of Gloria's bed.

"How is it going?" she asked. Gloria had been preparing for her college admission test, its sole purpose to determine whether or not she needed to take any remedial classes.

Gloria made a face. "Can't you see that I'm dying of boredom? I need you to make it interesting."

"Don't you and Millie study together?"

"No way. She's turned into a real nerd."

"What does that mean?"

"You don't know what a nerd is?"

"No," Belle said with a smile, "but I'm sure you're going to tell me."

Gloria turned up her pert little nose and looked out the window. "Ask Millie."

Belle laughed. "You can be such a brat." She picked up the shopping bag that contained her painter's smock, the alarm clock, a pair of vinyl gloves, and a bandana to wrap around her head.

"A nerd is a brain," Gloria said. "Someone who studies all the time."

Ready to go, Belle headed for the door. At the threshold, she looked back. "Why don't you try being a nerd? Who knows, you might like it." She blew Gloria a kiss and sashayed into the hall.

"You're the brat!" Gloria called after her.

The aroma of fresh-baked biscuits and sizzling bacon drew Belle into the kitchen. Standing at the sink, Mammy Daisy was whisking eggs for scrambling. Two glass pitchers, one full of orange juice, the other containing milk, stood on the serving counter. Out of necessity, breakfast was served buffet-style. With only two bathrooms for eight women, the residents drifted downstairs singly or in pairs. Late arrivals heated their meals in the microwave.

Belle set her bag on the table, went to Mammy and gave her a peck on the cheek. “Good morning,” she said.

Mammy added a splash of milk to the eggs and went back to her whisking. “Child, what you doin’ down here? Breakfast ain’t ready yet.”

“I’m off to work. Do you want me to turn the bacon?”

“If it needs turnin’ turn it.”

The bacon was popping and spitting hot grease. Belle pushed the sleeve of her sweater up to her elbow and used tongs to turn each strip. Finished, she turned the heat down a notch and stepped away from the stove.

“Well, I’d better be going,” she said, eyeing the crisp strips of bacon longingly. “Marge has to be out of town today, so I’ll be working straight through. What time should I be home?”

“You ain’t goin’ nowhere till you gets you something to eat,” Mammy said. “Slice you some ham off that butt in the fridge and stick it ‘tween a coupla biscuits. You be home in time for supper.”

Belle gave her another peck on the cheek. “Thanks, Mammy. What will I do without you?”

“Humph,” Mammy grunted.

Minutes later, with the shopping bag in one hand and a brown paper sack in the other, Belle sailed out the front door. She made it no farther than the sidewalk before hunger pangs drove her to retrieve one of the ham biscuits and gobble it down. She would save the other one for lunch.

Noon came and went, and the other biscuit was still wrapped in foil. If someone had asked Belle the day, the month, or the year, she wouldn’t have had the foggiest notion–if she heard the question at all. Up on the platform she’d built out of planks and cable spools, she was putting the finishing touches on a harvest moon when the phone rang. Startled, the hand holding the brush jerked past the moon’s surface and into the night sky.

"Darn," she muttered. Her work had been going so well.

The phone jangled again. Belle glared at it, willing it to stop. But it didn't, and she made no move to answer it. This wasn't the first time a phone had disrupted her concentration. She could repair the damage done to the mural but doubted if she could get her rhythm back. Once a phone rang a part of her brain kept expecting it to ring again.

The answering machine finally clicked on and a robot-like voice told the caller to please leave a message. Not a sound could be heard. Thinking that whoever placed the call had hung up, Belle turned back to the mural.

While assessing the damage, she was reminded of her very first day at Hope Haven. She'd been sitting in the bedroom Mammy had assigned her, waiting for the other residents to come home from rehab. Nervous about meeting them, she'd looked for something to do. Having bought a sketch book the day before, she'd immersed herself in drawing the scene that would eventually become the mural of the Checker cab crossing the Ponchartrain Causeway.

Lost in thought, she hadn't noticed the girl standing in the doorway until the girl spoke. The suddenness of her appearance had caused Belle's hand to shoot across the page, ruining her sketch. But that was nothing compared to the girl's hostile attitude at finding Belle in her room. The girl, who had spiked orange hair, silver studs running up each earlobe, and who wore enough makeup to cover the faces of ten women, had been the old Gloria.

Now, as she continued to assess the damage to the current mural, Belle smiled to think of the new Gloria–a carbon copy of Dorothy, straight out of *The Wizard of Oz.* The smile vanished when the phone rang again.

Belle tried to ignore it, but the persistent ringing made her anxious. She climbed off the platform and snatched up the phone.

"Hello?"

Mammy Daisy's voice came over the line. "Child, you best get yo'self together. Your ex-husband's headin' your way."

Unable to believe what she'd heard, Belle croaked, "What did you say?"

"I said you best get yo'self together. Your ex-husband's headin' your way. Gloria done give him the address."

Struck dumb, Belle held the receiver away from her ear and stared at it as though she'd never seen one before. No, it couldn't be. Lin couldn't possibly be here in town. Mammy had made a mistake. Either that or it was some kind of sick joke.

She started to question Mammy as to who had put her up to this, then realized the line had gone dead. Which was just as well, she thought. Mammy wouldn't tell her such a thing if it weren't true.

A terrifying thought swept through her mind. Something must have happened to Mandy. Lin had come to tell her their daughter had been in a serious accident, that her injuries were life-threatening and the doctors held out little hope for her recovery.

Mandy had gotten numerous tickets for speeding and reckless driving. Lin had always laughed it off as "kid stuff." But it wasn't kid stuff, it was dangerous. Yet if something had happened to Mandy, why would Lin be here? Why wouldn't he be there, tending to her care? No, it couldn't be Mandy.

Maybe it was her parents who had been in an accident. Possibly killed! At the open house, her mother had complained about her father's failing eyesight. Edith said it had gotten worse, that Jesse was always taking the wrong road, getting all turned around, and she hoped they'd make it home in one piece. They had made it home, but that was then and this was now.

Sour bile rose in her throat as bloody images overlaid with medical whites swirled through her brain. Swallowing repeatedly, she clutched her stomach and squeezed her eyes shut. What to do, what to do, her mind screamed.

Marge's voice whispered in her ear: *Start your breathing exercises.* Yes, yes. Thank God for Marge.

Several moments later, with elaborate calm, she pulled off her vinyl gloves, her smock, and the bandana. After draping the items on one end of the platform, she sought out the bathroom, where she used the commode and washed her hands. One look at the wraith-like image in the mirror and she knew she'd have to do something she would never have thought herself capable of doing. She borrowed Mrs. Bardet's hair brush to fluff her curls and applied a touch of the lady's lipstick and blush.

Checking herself over in the full-length mirror on the back of the bathroom door, her yellow sweater looked as clean as when she'd put it on. Not so for the tan cargo pants she used for work and her once-white sneakers. Both were speckled with multiple shades of paint. But now, as she turned from one side to the other, she rather fancied the look of herself as a working woman.

Still feeling an amazing sense of calm, she returned to the living room and started lining up her paint cans and replacing the lids, all the while telling herself that Mammy had made a mistake. It hadn't been Lin at the door, it had been someone else. Perhaps an old boyfriend. None of the relationships, and there hadn't been many, had been serious, but the partings had been amicable. Of course none of her old friends, male or female, had written, called or visited during the past six months, but that didn't mean it couldn't happen. Friends had a way of popping up when you least expected them.

Despite her theory she flinched when the doorbell rang. Instead of Marge's voice whispering in her ear, this time she heard Art: *Take it easy, kiddo, just take it easy.* So she did. Ever so slowly, as though her legs might break if she moved too fast, she walked to the door and opened it.

Blinded by a broad beam of sunlight that hit her full in the face, she shielded her eyes with a hand and squinted hard at the hazy figure before her.

"Hello, Kathleen," said an all too familiar voice.

"Quick!" she said, her heart thudding against her chest. "Tell me what's wrong. Is it Mandy? Is it my parents?"

Lin gave her a queer, searching look. "Nothing's wrong. Mandy's doing exceedingly well, and Edith and Jesse send their love."

Faint with relief, Belle put a hand to her brow. "But I thought .... I, ah .... Are you sure nothing's wrong?"

"I'm certain, Kathleen. I know I should have called you–"

Possessed by a sudden flash of fury it took every ounce of strength she had to keep from hitting him. Clenching and unclenching her fists, she wanted to pound on his chest, slap the smirk off his face, kick him in the shin.

"Damn you, Lin Mallory. How could you do this to me. Popping in like this ... without a word ... scaring me half to death. I just knew you'd come to give me horrible news."

"I'm sorry, Kathleen. I–"

"You're not one bit sorry! And stop calling me Kathleen. My name is Belle. Belle Reve." She stepped back, prepared to slam the door in his face.

He held out his hands like a supplicant. "Please don't. I had to see you." His hands fell to his sides. "Would you have seen me if I had called first?"

For an answer, she compressed her lips into a tight, thin line.

Lin shifted from one foot to the other. "I didn't think so. Kath–" He stopped mid-word and started over. "You have no idea how difficult this is. I drove around for hours before I had the nerve to go to that house. And when I did, you weren't even there. What are you doing here? Isn't this the day of your discharge?"

Again, she refused to answer. That she'd requested an extended stay was no concern of his.

He looked behind him and to both sides, then back at her. "May I come in? We need to talk."

She almost laughed. "*We* need to talk? It's a little late for that, don't you think? Nine years too late, to be exact."

He looked up at the sky and held his gaze there. It was then that she noticed how much he had aged. How could that happen in only six months? Maybe it hadn't, maybe he'd started aging long before she left. Since he'd rarely been at home, and had avoided her when he was, she hadn't had an opportunity to take a good look at him. Now she did. The athletic frame he'd been so proud of had turned flabby. A small potbelly protruded from above his belt, his jowls had begun to sag, and wiry wisps of gray hair sprouted from his temples. Maybe he'd been ill. Maybe he still was.

Lin turned bloodshot eyes on her. "Please," he said. "Can we go somewhere? Have a cup of coffee? Talk like reasonable adults?"

Reasonable adults. Would Marge say she was being unreasonable if she refused to talk to him? More than likely. Learning how to handle complicated situations was a part of growing up, Marge had said. *It's not what happens to you, it's how you react.*

"Give me five minutes," she said. She closed the door and turned the dead bolt.

. . .

After dropping off a fare at the U.S. Mint, Art decided to take a detour past the house on Kerlerec before heading home. With any luck, Belle would be taking a breather out on the front stoop. She did that sometimes, to escape the paint fumes, she said.

It had been a busy morning, lots of folks coming to town for the weekend, and Art hadn't had lunch yet. He was supposed to eat four or five small meals a day to keep his blood sugar in the normal range, but that was hard to do when you drove a cab for a living. You never knew where a fare would want to go, which meant you never knew how long it would take to get there. He could've knocked off a couple of hours ago, but the extra dough would come in handy. Furnishing the house had cost more than he'd bargained for and he wasn't through yet. He guessed he needed to start taking snacks with him to tide him over. He needed to rake in the bucks while he could because he didn't figure he'd get much work done after Belle moved in. Knowing her, she'd want to go back to Mississippi to hunt for Blanche.

They'd be on a different kind of hunt tomorrow. Because it was Saturday and Belle had a day pass, they could check out all the leads he'd gotten on used vans. She didn't need a big van, just one large enough to hold a six-foot ladder and the rest of her supplies. The main thing was to find a sturdy, dependable vehicle she could handle. Driving in New Orleans was tough enough without having some balky beast to maneuver.

That got Art to wondering what kind of driver she was. She'd said her ex took away her car keys after she had her first attack. If someone had done that to him, he would've jumped off the nearest bridge. Yes sir, life wouldn't be worth living without a set of wheels under him. He remembered the first car he'd ever owned, a 1949 Mercury coupe with fender skirts, fiesta hubcaps, and dual exhausts with glass-packs. Man, cruising the old neighborhood, with that low, deep-throated rumble announcing his comings and goings, had made him the happiest dude on the planet. Yeah, those were the days.

Belle told him she'd finally figured out what she'd been missing soon after she took up with 'Mister Vodka.' She'd swiped her daughter's key to the family station wagon–the kid drove a BMW, the old man a Corvette–had a copy made, then snuck out of the house every chance she got. Mostly to search for Blanche's birthday gift. Her ex still didn't know she'd been driving all over town.

What an asshole the guy had to be. Art didn't know what all had happened before Belle came to New Orleans, but he knew the jerk filed for divorce because she wanted to stay here and get help for her problems. Hell, back then her biggest problem was *him*. Him, her nag of a mother and her spoiled rotten daughter. Being away from them probably helped her more than all of Marge's counseling sessions put together. Whatever, Art knew one thing for sure. If he ever met up with the bum, he would punch him in the nose.

With that thought in mind, he began humming a cheerful tune. After making a right onto Chartres, he turned left onto Kelerec. As soon as he straightened the wheel he started looking for the house. If Belle wasn't taking a breather outside he had no choice but to drive on by. She was a stickler for following rules, which banned him from visiting her at a customer's house.

The hum died in his throat when he caught sight of the car parked in front of the Bardet's house. What was it doing there? Who was the guy sitting in the driver's seat? The owner of the house? Naw, the tag showed the car to be a rental. Straining to get a better look, Art slowed to a crawl. He could tell the guy was big, at least as big as he was, from the way he took up the seat. So who was he? And why was he sitting outside the house? Waiting for someone? Belle? Or someone he'd dropped off?

Art had to make a decision. He either had to pass the car or pull up to the curb and park behind it. The last choice didn't exactly appeal to him. If Belle came out and saw him sitting there she'd accuse him of spying on her. He'd been known to do that, back when she first started living at Hope Haven and wasn't allowed to see anyone from the outside. He shuddered to think of how pissed she'd been when she caught him in the act. This time he didn't have to be hit over the head with a ball-peen hammer to know he'd better mind his own business.

He gave the rental car a wide berth and went on his way. He'd grab a bite of lunch and go back to work. Tomorrow was soon enough to find out about the mystery guy.

Ten

Lin was sitting in a car Belle didn't recognize, a sleek black Lincoln. Arms folded across her chest, she stood on the sidewalk in front of the house waiting for him to notice her. What on earth was he doing? she wondered. Had he dozed off? Or was he plotting some kind of strategy? For what she didn't know. Still, she would have to watch herself. A successful lawyer, Lin excelled in manipulation.

Standing there doing nothing made her feel naked and exposed. She looked up and down the street to see if anyone was watching. Thankfully, no one was in sight. Of course someone could be looking out a window. Darn him. Why didn't he make a move? She'd made a special effort to not keep him waiting. Had cleaned her brushes in a hurry, gathered all her tools, and made a quick call to Mammy to let her know what was happening. And now nothing was happening, nothing at all. If he was waiting for her to come to him he would have a very long wait.

She was about to go back inside when he tossed a glance in her direction. She gave a little wave. He gave a nod of acknowledgment, climbed out of the car and hastened around to open the passenger door.

"No, thank you," she called from her spot on the sidewalk. "I prefer to walk."

"As you wish," he said and closed the door.

Joining her, he appraised her with a keen eye. Expecting him to make a disparaging remark about her paint-stained pants, she was taken aback when he said, "You look wonderful. As young and as beautiful as the day I met you."

"It's the climate," she said, secretly pleased by the compliment, his first in many years.

"How's your health, Lin?" she asked. "Have you been ill?"

He barked a mirthless laugh. "I know I look like hell. That's what comes from living the so-called good life."

Ah, yes, she thought, the 'good life'. Which, for Lin, meant being the first to arrive and the last to leave every party. Parties she'd stopped going to a long time ago.

"Well," he said, rocking back on his heels, "since I'm the stranger in town, you'll have to lead the way."

"Aren't you going to lock the car?"she asked.

He shrugged. "Why bother? It's only a rental."

She shook her head. "That is so typical."

"Of what? Me?"

"Yes. If it was your car you'd lock it."

With a twitch of irritation only she would notice, he went around to the driver's side of the Lincoln and locked the door. His looks had changed but his style of casual dress remained the same. Except for the burgundy-colored ascot at his neck, he was a study in grays. Gray tweed sport coat, gray shirt, gray slacks. The color did nothing for his complexion, which bore a sickly, greenish cast.

Belle started walking when he was but a few steps away. In order to avoid most of the congestion on Decatur Street, she decided to cut across Chartres and down to the Café Du Monde by way of St. Ann. Now that she knew Mandy and her parents were alive and well, she could enjoy the truly glorious day. Warm and sunny, a balmy breeze caressed elegant ferns, flowing masses of bougainvillea, and the beds of iris, jonquils, and lilies that graced the landscape. Having inhaled paint fumes all morning, she drew each breath deep into her lungs. The day, the sweet air, and the flowers helped her forget about the man walking beside her. Until he spoke.

"I thought you'd given up painting."

"I did. But once I got down here I started in again." She paused. "Unlike you and my mother, the people here think I have talent."

"That's not fair, Kathleen. I might not have taken you seriously, but I don't believe I ever said you didn't have talent."

She let his use of her old name slide. "You didn't have to. But never mind all that. It's water over the bridge."

"Under," he said.

She looked at him. "What?"

"It's water *under* the bridge."

"Whatever," she said, one of Art's favorite expressions. "Painting murals is a business. It's how I plan to make a living. I also happen to love doing it."

"A business, eh? Pardon me for asking, but what do you know about running a business?"

"Not much," she admitted. "But I'm learning." She started to tell him about Art being her business manager, and about winning the jackpot, then decided it was none of his concern.

"Is this part of your treatment?" he asked.

"No." She sidestepped a gaping hole in the sidewalk caused by a bulging tree root. "Marge, my therapist, wanted me to go back to school and get my teacher's certificate. But then I started painting murals and one thing led to another."

"What kind of murals?"

"I specialize in scenes of New Orleans. Mostly in the French Quarter. But I painted a train once, and another time I did some nursery rhyme characters."

"Like the ones in our nursery?"

She glanced at him, feeling that old, rusty pain stab at her heart. "Yes."

He said nothing. He didn't have to.

When she was pregnant with Mandy, she had wanted to prepare the nursery herself, but Lin insisted on hiring an interior decorator. Belle never cared for the end result. To her, the room lacked imagination and vitality. When, after years of trying, she became pregnant for the second time, she worked on the new nursery when Lin wasn't home. Though the challenge of switching from painting on canvas to painting on a wall was daunting, she persevered, knowing she could cover up any mess she made by hanging wallpaper over it. When she'd completed the job, her characters looked more like caricatures, but they made her laugh. Certain they would delight Lin's fancy as well, she'd been astonished by his reaction. How dare she risk climbing up and down a ladder, he'd shouted. She could have fallen and hurt herself. Worse, she could have lost the baby. And what about the fumes? They couldn't possibly be good for a growing fetus–that she was carrying twins was an unknown at the time.

From then on she'd worried that what Lin said about the fumes might be true. And when the doctor had told them their precious twin boys had died, it was the first thing she had thought of. She had killed them, damaged their tiny lungs. Perhaps it was the first thing Lin thought of, too. She'd had no way of knowing what he thought, because following the doctor's pronouncement, he'd walked out of the hospital and quietly removed himself from their life together.

Days later, when she was done weeping, she'd asked the doctor if the fumes had been to blame. He assured her they had not. The nursery had been well-ventilated–summer breezes blowing through the open windows and the ceiling fan turned on. No, he said, the twins died from *hyaline membrane disease,* a lung disease more likely to strike premature infants delivered by Caesarean section. By the time she understood and sorrowfully accepted the doctor's explanation, she'd not only lost her sons, she'd lost her husband as well.

In a desperate attempt to push the past to the back of her mind, she found herself pointing out various landmarks and places of interest. Lin listened attentively, as though every word she uttered was of major importance. His attention fed her self-esteem and she rattled on and on.

At one point, Lin said, "Well, you certainly know your way around."

Though she was fairly bursting with pride, she gave him a shy look and said. "I walk a lot."

By the time they reached Decatur, she felt a rush of well-being. While the side streets had been relatively quiet and uncrowded, here a mass of humanity thronged the sidewalks and bumper-to-bumper traffic lined the streets. Horns honked, brakes squealed, tour buses spewed clouds of exhaust, hard rock music blasted from car stereos, the blues wailed from a nearby bar and grill, and from Jackson Square came the sounds of Dixieland jazz, which inspired young black boys to tap-dance a little faster for the coins passersby tossed into the cardboard boxes at their feet.

Standing on the corner, she embraced the scene with arms flung wide. "Isn't it incredible?" she cried. Without waiting for a response, she darted into the street. Threading her way between idling cars, she made it to the other side, turned and looked back. Lin was still standing where she'd left him. Stifling a giggle, she motioned for him to follow. He held up a hand, then made his way to the crosswalk, where he and a host of other people waited for the light to change.

Reaching her at last, he let out a puff of air, something he did when exasperated. Beads of sweat dotted his upper lip. "Is it always like this?" he asked

"Oh, this is nothing," she said gaily. "It'll be even busier tomorrow."

He grimaced. "Is there a quiet place around here? A place where we can talk?"

"We're here," she replied, turning to face a sea of umbrella tables, all of which appeared to be filled.

"This wasn't what I had in mind," he said, obviously dismayed by the crowd.

"You'll love it," she chirped. "This is Café Du Monde. Famous for their café au lait and beignets. You can tell how popular it is by how crowded it is, and it's always like this. We need to be fast on our feet when a table becomes empty."

Her eyes roamed from chair to chair, looking for the slightest hint that a party might be leaving.

Lin said, "I see several empty tables inside."

"Oh, you don't want to sit in there. It's much nicer out here."

He made no further comment as they waited, but she could feel impatience seeping from his pores.

A foursome caught her attention. Cameras hung from the necks of the men while the women wore layers of brightly colored Mardi Gras beads, marking them as tourists. They were all talking at once, as though discussing where to go next. Belle made her way to their table zigzag fashion to keep from bumping into someone or tripping over an outstretched leg.

As if on cue, the group stood up the moment she reached them. "Excuse me," she said. "Do you mind if I claim this table?"

Again, everyone started talking. Belle wished she understood their language–German?–but their gestures indicated she should sit down. "Thank you," she said. She pulled out a chair facing Jackson Square and settled into it. "Enjoy your stay," she said to the departing tourists. Still talking, they smiled and nodded and went on their way.

She looked around for Lin. Apparently he'd been skirting the area's outer edges, probably trying not to be seen, for he was approaching her from the left. Cafés, whether indoors or outdoors, were not his style; he preferred the intimacy of fine dining rooms.

"There you are," she said.

"Yes, here I am," he said, clearly disgruntled. He pulled out a chair and started to sit down.

She stopped him. "If you want fast service you'll need to go inside and order from the counter."

When his jaw tightened, she put a hand to her mouth to smother another giggle. He was a man so used to being waited on, she knew he'd rather lose a case in court than to have to go inside and carry their order back on a tray.

"If you want me to go you'll have to give me some money," she said. "I didn't bring my wallet."

He squared his shoulders as though gearing up for battle. "I'll go," he said. "What would you like?"

"Black coffee and a beignet, please."

He left the table and took the long way around, keeping his head down all the way.

As soon as he was inside, Belle let the giggles erupt. Whatever he'd come to talk to her about, he certainly hadn't counted on having to do it in the midst of a horde of people.

Her laughter spent, she sat back and enjoyed the view, never tiring of the circus-like atmosphere of Jackson Square on a sunny day. Pedestrians, young and old, gawked at street artists, fortune tellers, mimes, jugglers, tap dancers, magicians .... donkey-driven carriages queued at the curb waited to take tourists on a tour of the Quarter. Beyond the sculptured garden, with its winding walkways and magnificent statue of Andrew Jackson on his horse, rose the lofty spires of St. Louis Cathedral, the oldest active cathedral in the nation.

To her left stood Jax Brewery, once the home of Jax beer and now a five-story shopping mall. Above and beyond the hill and the train tracks behind her lay the Moon Walk on the banks of the mighty Mississippi. On her right, down a block or two from where she sat, was the famous French Market, a sprawling mass of stalls that offered everything from artichokes to wood-carved zebras. That she actually lived in this exciting city never ceased to amaze her.

She thought it sad that Lin didn't appreciate the scene. Take him away from his suite of offices, his private clubs, his favorite golf course, and his cronies, and he was lost. Which meant it hadn't been easy for him to come here.

Belle had known that she would have to deal with seeing him eventually. Time after time she'd imagined what they would say to one another. The content of their conversation changed depending on the situation, but it had always taken place at some future date, and

Mandy had always been in the picture: Her graduation from college, her wedding day, the birth of the first grandchild, and so on.

More often than not, she'd pictured Lin with a new wife at his side. She, Belle, would graciously offer her best wishes to put the new Mrs. Mallory at ease. She would conduct herself with the poise and self-assurance that comes from finding one's niche in the world.

Edith and Jesse would then join the group and the talk would flow as easily as a lazy mountain stream. They'd act like old friends, gathered together to celebrate some mutual occasion.

Throughout the celebration, Lin would appraise her with frank admiration. He would finally understand that she had made the right decision by choosing to remain in New Orleans. Later, he would tell her so. In kind, she would tell him she was indebted to him for not interfering with her treatment and subsequent plans. That she felt no bitterness over the divorce, that by formally ending what was already over, they were both free to make new lives for themselves. From then on, they would maintain a distant but cordial relationship.

Lin returned to the table with two coffees and one beignet.

"Thank you," she said.

"You're welcome," he replied.

Expecting him to sit across from her, she was somewhat disconcerted when he chose the chair to her right. Then again, the proximity would make it easier to be heard above the din.

Still linked to her daydream of seeing him at some future date, she looked at him and said, "Why did you have to come here now? I'm not ready for you."

His eyes roamed over her face for a long moment. He licked his lips and said, "I had to see you. I've missed you, Kathleen."

"Missed me?" She laughed. "Oh, Lin, surely you jest." She took a sip of her coffee.

"I mean it, Kathleen. I've never been more serious in my life."

It's not what happens to you, it's how you react. "Relax, Lin," she said, spreading a paper napkin over her lap. "Sit back and enjoy the view." Suddenly starving, she took greedy bites of her beignet.

When it was gone, she wished for another but wasn't about to ask for one. Crumbs and sprinkles of powdered sugar littered her lap. She swept them to the ground for the birds to find.

Glancing sideways, she saw that Lin had taken her advice. Though she doubted he was enjoying the view, he was sitting back in his chair sipping his coffee. Had Marge been right? Had his motivation for paying her debt to the mental health center and making a donation to Hope Haven been prompted by a guilty conscience? Maybe so. But that didn't explain what he was doing here. Or why all this nonsense about missing her.

The lengthening silence began to wear on her nerves. She tried to think of something to say, a neutral topic that wouldn't rattle any skeletons.

If she and Art were sitting there they'd be discussing her plans to move in with him, which was only a week away. Or they might be searching the want ads for used vans. It was hard to believe she'd soon have her own source of transportation. And, without having to abide by the rules of Hope Haven, she'd be able to come and go as she pleased. What a thrill that would be. Of course she'd miss Mammy and Gloria and the rest of the girls, but it wasn't as though she were leaving town; they'd only be four blocks away, neighbors instead of housemates.

Lin stirred in his seat. Thinking he meant to start mouthing more marlarky, she looked at him and said the first thing that popped into her head. "How are Jerry and Martha doing?"

He didn't answer right away. "I have no idea. I haven't seen them in months."

"But you see Jerry every day."

He cleared his throat, clearly uncomfortable with the subject. "I see him, but I'm afraid we're not on very good terms."

"Oh dear," she said, unable to imagine what could have caused a rift between them. Lin and Jerry had been best friends since college. They'd been law partners for the past fifteen years.

"How are the rest of the staff? Do you still have the same

secretary?" The smirky redhead, she added to herself. "What was her name? Faye?"

He cocked an eyebrow. "Why do you ask?"

She held his gaze. "I don't know. It just seemed like the natural thing to say."

He was the first to look away. Then, without any warning, he moved his chair close to hers and twisted around so his left knee was pressing against the edge of her chair. "I'm prepared to make a full confession, Kathleen. I know you suspected this, and, well, it's true about me and Faye. It didn't mean anything. She was just ... there. I shouldn't have done it. It certainly wasn't fair to you, and it created bad feelings in the firm." He drew in a long, shaky breath and let it out. "But it's over. And I am sincerely sorry."

"Well!" she said brightly. "You are just full of surprises. But guess what, Lin? I don't care about you and Faye. Oh, I did at one time, and I care that it damaged your friendship with Jerry, but, as you say, that's water *under* the bridge."

He regarded her solemnly. "But you do care, Kathleen. I know you."

"You're wrong about that. You *used* to know me. A long time ago. And my name's not Kathleen, it's Belle. Belle Reve."

He lowered his voice to a snarl. "It's Kathleen Mallory and it always will be."

"For heavens sakes, Lin. What has gotten into you?" She put the back of her right hand to his cheek. "You must be feverish."

In a sudden movement that caught her unaware, he grabbed hold of her hand. Wrenching it away from his face, he held her wrist in a vise-like grip. "Listen to me, Kathleen. I came here to claim what's mine. I came to take you home. Do you understand?"

She tried to pull free of him. "You're hurting me, Lin. Let go."

"Not until you've heard me out."

"All right, all right," she said, feeling a twinge of panic. She couldn't have an attack! Not here! Not now!

He relaxed his grip but kept a steady hold on her. "You're still

Kathleen Mallory because you're still my wife."

Her lungs felt compressed, as though someone had squeezed the air out of them. Several seconds passed before she could catch her breath. "I can't be your wife. We're divorced. I signed the papers."

"But I didn't." He laid his left hand palm-side down on the table. The gold wedding band she'd slipped on his ring finger some twenty years ago glittered in the sunlight.

He went on. "Every time I held the pen in my hand and looked down at the dotted line, I saw you standing in the post office the first time we met. I knew then, just as I know now, that we're meant to be together as man and wife."

She cringed. "No, no, you must be mad."

He tightened his grip and leaned closer. She could feel his hot breath on her cheeks. "The house has been like a tomb without you. More than anything, I miss the sound of your laughter. Remember how you and Mandy used to play hide-and-seek? Remember how we used to go dancing at the club? Remember the pool parties we used to have? Oh, God, Kathleen, everywhere I look I see your smiling face. It can be that way again. I–"

She rared back, trying to break his hold on her. "Let go of me. Please let go."

He went on. "I went a little crazy after the twins died. It was like I died, too. My insides just shriveled up. There you were, grieving your heart out, and I didn't feel a thing. Then you had that attack ..."

A giant fist was squeezing the blood out of her heart, sending it rushing to her brain. For a moment she thought she might faint. Making a conscious effort to control her breathing, she practiced her exercises. One, one thousand, two, one thousand ... Lin was still talking. It was more than his words that frightened her, it was the unearthly quality of his tone.

"... I thought you were faking the attacks to get my attention. Playing on my sympathy. It made me angry, Kathleen, very angry. I blamed you for ruining our lives. But it wasn't you, it was me. Now that I see that, I can make it all up to you. Our life will be just like it used to be. You'll see, Kathleen, you'll see. I *need* you."

She could see that he needed professional help. But for now all she could do was remain calm. "I'd better be getting back to work," she said softly. "Mammy Daisy will be calling the house. If I'm not there she'll be worried." She tried to rise from her chair.

He held her down, his jaw set in a stubborn line, his eyes glinting like cold steel. "You are my wife and you are coming home with me."

Afraid he'd break her wrist, afraid she'd never paint again, she turned meek. "All right, Lin. But I'd like to pack my things first."

"Your *things* are at home."

"But I–"

"Just think, Kathleen. Now that you're cured we can start entertaining again. I know what we'll do. We'll have a big party. Invite everyone we know. Mandy would love it. So would Jerry and Martha. It would be fun. Just like old times."

A faint golden glimmer caught a corner of her eye. It was cruising down Decatur, growing bigger and brighter as it came. That it was Art's Checker was too much to hope for, but just the thought gave her the courage to go on.

"A party," she said, her eyes shifting between Lin and the road. "What a lovely idea. Can we invite my parents?"

"If you like," he said, his fingers slowly loosening their grip on her wrist. Then, with a shudder that shook him from head to toe, he released her.

She drew her hand back and rubbed the hurt. Neither of them spoke for several seconds.

The hurt easing, Belle glanced up and down the road. The golden glimmer had faded from sight. But the Checker was out there somewhere.

With as much dignity as she could muster, Belle rose from her chair and looked down. "I want to thank you for coming here, Lin," she said, regarding him with genuine fondness and more than a little pity. "I've listened to everything you've had to say, and now I have one very important request."

He cocked his head to one side, a look of indulgence on his face now that he thought she'd surrendered. "What is it, Kathleen?"

"Sign the divorce papers, Lin."

Then she was off, skipping past tables and around knots of people until she was lost in the crowd.

Eleven

After securing the dead bolt to the house on Kerlerec and closing the mini-blinds, she reported to Mammy Daisy. Next she turned her attention to the mural. She would repair the damage to the moon and sprinkle the night sky with stars, trusting that whatever came next would flow naturally. She would not worry about whether Lin could find his way back to his rental car or what he might do when he did She would not, repeat *not*, answer the door or peek out the window–she would think about nothing but her work.

Minutes later, wearing her smock, bandana, and vinyl gloves, she was physically up on the platform with brush in hand. Mentally, she was sitting on the Moonwalk gazing across the river at a night-time view of the city of Algiers.

She climbed down from the platform at 3:57, noted the hour in her log book and began the final cleanup. Not once did she pause to look at the mural. The time for that had passed. Once she had finished a project to her satisfaction, had written "The End," so to speak, it was over. The only mural she'd ever truly looked at once it was done was the Checker cab crossing the Ponchartrain Causeway, and that because it evoked such pleasant and personal memories.

She left the Bardets a note. She would return with Art the next day, present them with an invoice, and remove her belongings from their house. That done, she picked up her shopping bag and set out for Hope Haven.

She'd almost reached the sidewalk before she noticed that the Lincoln was gone. What Lincoln, she asked herself. It had all been a dream, a very bad dream.

By the time she reached Elysian Fields she'd thought of a design for her business cards. She'd put off ordering them because she hadn't known what address to use. Now that she'd decided to move in with Art she could use his. She wanted a standard size card with *Scenes by Belle* written in bold gold script on a purple background. Art would probably think it too flashy, but never mind what Art thought. After all, this was New Orleans–gold and purple were Mardi Gras colors.

Cheered by the thought, and the prospect of shopping for a car tomorrow, she all but skipped the rest of the way home.

Her gait faltered when she saw Gloria waiting on the stoop. Remembering that Gloria was the one who had told Lin where she was, she treaded carefully. A foot from where Gloria sat, she put out a hand as a sign of caution.

"Please don't mention him," she said. "I finished the mural, I'm in a good mood and I don't want to spoil it."

Wearing a pained expression, Gloria sighed and said, "I have to. He's waiting for you."

Belle sucked in her breath. "Where?"

"At the airport. He said he'd be expecting you no later than six." She jumped up from the stoop, a frantic look on her face. "You're not going, are you?"

"Of course not."

"He acted very strange, Belle. I didn't want to tell him where you were, but I was scared not to. Mammy had a hissy fit when she found out. She's afraid he'll cause trouble."

Belle winced. "He already has."

"She's afraid if you don't meet him he'll come back for you. She thinks maybe you should go to Art's."

Deciding to make light of it, Belle chucked Gloria under the chin. "Listen, sweetie, I've done enough hiding for one day. Right now I need a long, hot soak in the tub. If you're a good girl I might even let you wash my back."

"But what about him?"

"Never mind about him. If he gives us any trouble we'll call the police."

"The cops! But I hate cops! We all hate cops!"

"Correction. You *used* to hate cops, back when you were walking the streets and doing drugs, but now you like them. Cops can be your best friends. In fact, you might even end up marrying one."

Gloria made a sour face. "Very funny."

They climbed the steps and entered the house.

The aroma of onions and garlic filled the air. Having eaten nothing but a ham biscuit and the beignet, Belle's mouth watered. She looked at Gloria. "Please tell me we're having spaghetti with meat balls."

"I could tell you that, but I'd be lying. We're having chili."

Belle thought it over. "Chili's good. Chili's great." She gave a loud whoop and cried, "I love chili!"

That brought Mammy Daisy flapping into the foyer like a hen escaping a hungry man's hatchet. "Child, what you doing here? I done told Gloria to send you directly to Art's."

Belle approached her calmly. "It's okay, Mammy. Everything is under control."

Mammy squinted at her. "How you know?"

"Well, let's just say I'm pretty sure."

"*Pretty* sure don't count. That man looked like he 'bout ready to set fire to the house."

"As a matter of fact, that man made a donation to the house. Marge said we might be able to use some of it for new mattresses."

"Sure 'nuf?"

Belle nodded.

"Humph," Mammy said. "I reckon the man's got more money than sense."

Belle had to laugh. "He can be very generous when he wants to be. He's just going through a difficult time right now." She glanced at her watch. "I'd better hurry if I'm going to take a bath before supper."

Mammy made her usual comment. "Don't you be usin' all the hot water, y'hear?"

Belle waited till she reached the staircase before making her usual reply. "I'll try not to."

"Humph," Mammy said and flapped her way back to the kitchen.

• • •

Refreshed from her bath and dressed in clean, paint-free clothes, Belle headed downstairs for supper. Having taken an extra long bath, an unexpected luxury since normally one or more of the girls would be pounding on the door, she was running a few minutes late. Midway down the stairs, excited chatter rose up to meet her. No doubt the girls were discussing the events of their day. Eager to join them, and more than ready to start feasting on chili, Belle picked up her pace.

Bounding into the room, she said, "Hi, y'all," and took her seat.

Dead silence fell over the table. No one responded and not one single girl looked at her.

Oblivious to the hushed tension surrounding her, Belle rattled on. "Mmmm, this smells so good. I am absolutely famished. Mammy, have you said the blessing? Can we start?"

Still no one spoke.

Finally aware that something was amiss, Belle scanned the group for clues. "What's wrong? Did we get bad news today? Did something happen to Marge? Darlene?" She waited.

"Gloria," Mammy said, giving the girl a meaningful look, then cutting her eyes Belle's way.

Gloria fiddled with her spoon, her hair, her napkin. At last she turned to Belle and said, "We, ah ... we took a vote. We ... we think you should move in with Art."

"Is that all?"Belle said. "Well, I'm glad everyone agrees, because that's exactly what I plan to do."

Gloria stopped fidgeting. "No, you don't understand. We think you should move in with him tomorrow."

"Tomorrow! I can't. We're going shopping for cars tomorrow. Besides, Marge gave me permission to stay till the first of March. I thought you were happy about that."

Janette took over. "Marge is out of town. She doesn't know the latest."

"The latest?"

"Belle, don't be so damn dense," Millie said. "Marge doesn't know about your ex coming to town."

Belle leaned back in her chair. So that's what this was all about. The girls hadn't been discussing their day, they'd been discussing *hers.*

"Listen up, Belle," Janette said, hunching over the table. "We don't want to hurt your feelings, and we don't want you to leave, but we also don't want any trouble. Remember how the neighbors used to feel about having us here? They tried to close us down. Why? Because they thought we'd be doping and tricking and corrupting their kids. But thanks to you and the murals, they like us now. They actually respect us. But if the cops start coming around ... well, they wouldn't like that at all."

"Good heavens," Belle said, "I had no idea you felt this way. I–"

Janette cut her off. "It's not just for Hope Haven, Belle, it's for you. We love you. We want you to be safe. There's no telling what your ex might do. From what Gloria said he wants you bad."

Belle's pulse was racing as fast and hard as her mind. "What time is it?" she asked though she was wearing her watch.

"Five-thirty-five," Gracie said.

Belle looked at Gloria. "What time did he say for me to be at the airport?"

"No later than six."

She pushed up from the table and made for the stairs. "If I hurry I can make it. Call Art. Tell him I need him. If he's not there, call me a cab."

Chair legs scraped across the linoleum as five of the girls jumped up and went after her. Catching up with her on the bottom landing, they surrounded her on all sides. "You're not going anywhere," Janette said. "Not until tomorrow."

Belle tried to push past them. "But you said–"

"Stop!" Fran ordered. Because Fran, an introverted slip of a girl, rarely spoke, the girls froze in place. Fran took hold of Belle's hand and led her back to the table.

"Sit," Fran said.

Belle sat.

Fran filled a soup bowl with chili and set it before her. "Eat."

As soon as Belle dipped her spoon into the mixture, Fran took her seat and the rest of the girls drifted back to the table.

Soup bowls were filled and a pie tin of cornbread was passed. Soon, the subtle sounds of slurping and lip-smacking could be heard.

Though not so much as an "uh-huh" or an "un-un" was uttered, Belle knew the girls were silently communicating with one another. All it took was a look here, a glance there, a nod, a shake. They'd done this before, when, for one reason or another, speech was prohibited. In the past, she had never understood what they were "talking" about, but this time she knew they were discussing her situation and the pros and cons of their vote. Though it was difficult to swallow, she continued to eat, awaiting the verdict.

It came with dessert, a heaping dish of peach cobbler.

"Okay," Janette said, taking the role of official spokeswoman, "here's the deal. Go shopping tomorrow as planned. Stay gone all day. Meanwhile, we'll play dumb if your ex comes looking for you. Then on Sunday we'll help you move your stuff to Art's."

Seven pairs of eyes fastened on her. She gave them a reassuring smile and said, "That sounds like a good plan."

Cheers, whistles, and hand claps followed.

"Except I think it'd be a bit overwhelming for all of us to invade Art's space, so while I appreciate the offer of help I'd rather do it myself."

Glances and nods were exchanged and then everyone started in again.

"That's fine with me," said Janette.

"Me, too,"said Millie.

"I can live with that," said Gloria

And on it went.

"Soon's I get home from church," said Mammy, "I'll fix us a fine Sunday dinner. Fry us some chicken, fix us a mess of greens, some pinto beans, and slaw. You be sure to tell Art, y'hear. He loves my fried chicken."

"I'd like to make my special potato salad," said Gracie.

"I'd like to bake a chocolate cake," said Millie.

"Whoooeee," Mammy cried, "we'll have us a party."

"No cake and no party, thank you." Belle said. "It's going to be hard enough to say goodbye as it is."

"Who said the party's for you?" said Boots. "I'm heading for Texas come Sunday evening."

That was news to Belle. "You've decided to go home?"

"I decided to see how it goes. If it goes okay, I'll stay. If it doesn't, I'll come back to New Orleans."

"Excellent plan," said Belle.

"I'm starting my new job on Monday," said Janette.

"Good for you," Belle said.

"Yes, and Gloria and I are taking our college admission's test on Monday," said Millie.

"What about me?" Fran said. "I've got a job interview Monday."

That caught everyone by surprise. "Sure 'nuf?" asked Mammy.

Never one to offer more than what was asked, Fran merely nodded.

"What kind of job?" Janette wanted to know.

"Where?" asked Gracie.

"Doing what?" said Millie

"Waitressing at Trailways."

"The bus station?"

"Uh-huh. They've got a real nice coffee shop there."

"You want to do that?" Gracie asked.

"Very much so."

"Why?"

"Because a bus station is the most exciting place on earth."

At that, all eyes shifted to Belle.

"What were you saying about no cake and no party?" Janette asked.

Belle feigned innocence. "Did I say that? We're going to have the biggest dang party this house has ever seen."

High-fives were slapped and laughter shook the walls.

• • •

"Alright, already," Art said. "I got one more place to look and then we can break for lunch. Do me a favor, will'ya? Try not to be so damn picky."

They'd been shopping all morning, had scoured five used car lots and met with two individuals, but Belle had yet to find a van she liked. It was the same thing over and over again: the color didn't suit her, they were too big, sat up too high, too hard to get in and out of, didn't handle well. Never mind that they were mechanically sound. Aesthetically, according to her, they had no pizzazz.

"Maybe we should eat now and look later," she said glumly. She'd had such high expectations when they first started out, had thought she'd find the perfect van the first place they went to, but now she'd almost given up hope. Besides, Art was getting grumpy. He needed to eat, and neither of them had thought to bring a snack.

"Naw," he said, "this place is right around the corner."

And so it was. Another dreary lot loaded with cars, trucks, and vans.

Art steered the cab toward the showroom. "A mechanic I know told me about this place. He said to ask for old man Wallace, that he'd give you a square deal." He braked and shoved the gear into park. "You wait here. I'm gonna see if the old man's around."

The moment the showroom door closed behind him, Belle climbed out of the cab. Wallace or no Wallace, if she didn't see a van she liked she wasn't buying, no matter how good a deal he gave her.

Bypassing the trucks, she headed back to the vans. On her way to the rear of the lot she noticed a motley mix of old cars sitting off to one side. Intrigued, she wandered that way.

There, in the back row, protected from its neighbors–two old wrecks with battered chassis and rusted fenders–by an aluminum carport, sat her dream car. She gave a joyous whoop, whirled around and went running to find Art.

"Hey, hey, take it easy, will'ya!" Art called, trying to slow her down.

She'd met up with him as he came out of the showroom, babbling like a fool about finding the perfect car. Then she'd taken off. He'd had no choice but to follow. Old man Wallace was trailing along somewhere behind him. How far did they have to go, for crissakes? All the way to Metairie? He trudged on.

Finally he saw her. She was waving her arms and jumping up and down beside an old woody wagon.

"This is it! This is it!" she squealed, still bouncing around like a jack-in-the-box. "Oh, Art, don't you just love it?"

He stopped dead in his tracks. "What? That old thing?"

She stopped bouncing, set her hands on her hips and glared at him. "*Old thing*! What a terrible thing to say. Tell her you didn't mean it. Tell her right now."

Art shoved his hands in his pockets and muttered something under his breath.

Taking it as an apology, Belle babbled on. "Isn't she the most beautiful thing you ever saw?" She ran around the car, pausing now and then to run a hand over a door panel, the roof, the hood. "Just look at her wood. It looks like she came straight from the factory. Oh, and she's even got whitewalls. Best of all, just look at her paint job. I adore this shade of yellow. Look," she said, bending over the hood, "it almost matches my hair." Then she was opening the driver's door.

"Oh my," she gasped, "I can't believe it. The upholstery looks exactly like the bottom of my granddaddy's cane chair. And look, the steering wheel is bright red."

"Well, now," said a booming voice.

Belle swung around to see a portly man wearing red suspenders over a white dress shirt.

He stepped forward and offered a hand. "Clyde Wallace, ma'am. Pleased to make your acquaintance. You've picked yourself a beaut, young lady, a real beaut."

Belle smoothed imaginary wrinkles out of her skirt then shook the man's hand. "Hello, Mr. Wallace. I'm Belle Reve." She glanced at Art. "I suppose you've met Mr. Barkoff."

"I sure did," he boomed. He hooked his thumbs under his suspenders and proceeded to strut around the car. "This here vehicle's a 1951 Ford, one of the best models ever made. Original wood and interior, new paint, new tires, new chrome, and new headliners. All that and she purrs like a kitten. Only thirty-seven thousand miles on a flathead V8. She's got overdrive and a tilt wheel. Want to take her out for a spin?"

"Oh my," Belle said, so excited she could hardly breathe, "could I?"

"Well of course you can. You wait here while I fetch the keys. Look her over Art. Lift her hood, poke around, kick a tire or two. You won't find no finer vehicle on this whole lot."

"How much?" Art said.

Clyde Wallace beamed a broad smile. "That, sir, is negotiable."

No sooner was he out of earshot than Art started in. "Whaddaya, crazy? You don't haul stuff in this automobile. You need a utility van.

This baby's for show."

"What do you mean?"

"Just what I said. This baby's in mint condition. You gonna load her down with platforms and paint cans? You gonna shove a ladder up her rear?"

She gave him her special smile and said, "I don't think she'd mind."

Twelve

Art parted the drape and peered out the window. She was still there, sitting in one of the white wicker rocking chairs. Turning his back to the window, he faced the living room and the kitchen beyond. He was hungry, but he couldn't say for what. He'd eaten more than he should have at the party, little of it good for him, but he was a sucker for Mammy's home cooking, especially her fried chicken, collard greens with a splash of vinegar and hot sauce, and pintos. Just thinking about the spread she'd put out made him feel full. Still, a gnawing hunger remained.

For the past couple of hours he'd been staring at the TV, not really watching it but not knowing what else to do. It was bad enough having Belle move in early, shooting down his plans to work overtime all next week; it was worse not knowing why. She'd given him some mumbo jumbo about the time being right, whatever that meant, and when he'd cornered a few of the girls at Hope Haven, they'd turned flighty.

"You look thirsty, Art," Gloria said. "Let me get you a glass of water."

"Oh, I just remembered," said Janette. "I have to spritz my air plant. I'll be right back."

Trouble was, no matter what excuse they gave him, none of them came back to him, which had made it all the more obvious they were keeping something from him. Then, when the party was over and it came time for Belle to leave, they'd acted as though she was being shipped off to the gallows. Such weeping and wailing he'd never heard, although he had to hand it to Belle, she'd kept her cool. In fact, she'd seemed glad to get out of there. But ever since she had moved in, instead of making herself at home she'd been hiding out on the porch. Her trunk was still sitting at the foot of her bed and she didn't seem to be in any hurry to unpack. Which made him wonder if she was having second thoughts.

He turned on his heels, opened the front door and stepped out on the porch. "You gonna stay out here all night?" he asked.

"I might," she replied, looking up at him. "Why don't you join me?"

"Don't mind if I do," he said, taking a seat in the other rocker.

Moments later, as though by mutual agreement, they started rocking in tandem. Clear and mild, it was a perfect night to be outdoors. A three-quarter moon and a forest of stars winked in the night sky. In the distance, a pool of pale yellow light cast by the gas lamps at Jackson Square shimmered like an oasis. Except for the occasional passing car and the creak of their chairs, all was quiet. The birds had retired for the night and the droning cicadas and pesky mosquitoes of summer lay dormant.

"You worried about the car?" Art asked. "Trust me, she ain't going nowhere."

"Please. Her name is Tallulah. After the late, great actress, Tallulah Bankhead." Earlier that day, with Art, Mammy, and Hope Haven's finest as witnesses, she'd christened the woody wagon with a bottle of ginger ale. Now tucked between the side of the house and the next door neighbor's wooden fence, with the Checker protecting her flanks, Tallulah was resting peacefully.

"Did you know she was an Alabama girl?" Belle asked.

"Who?"

"Tallulah. She was born in Huntsville, Alabama. But rather than being a happy occasion it was all very sad. Her poor mother, Adelaide, died shortly after giving birth. Legend has it that Tallulah was baptized beside her mother's casket. That may or may not be true. But her father went on to serve in Congress. He was the Speaker of the House when he died."

"Huh," Art said. "So the kid became an actress."

Belle looked at him with disbelief. "You really don't remember her?" It didn't seem possible that Art, a true movie buff who'd idolized the late Frances Farmer, had never heard of Tallulah Bankhead.

"Can't say that I do."

"Think, Art, think. She had this real low voice and she was famous for calling everyone *darling*, only she pronounced it *dah*ling. 'Hello, dahling! Dahling, how are you'! She played on Broadway for years, and her best known movie was *Lifeboat.* From what I've read she could be pretty wild, kind of like your Frances."

Art had been slouching in his seat. Now he sat upright, the rocking chair coming to a sudden halt. "Hey, don't be bad-mouthing Frances. Sure, she got in her share of scrapes, but she didn't take no guff from anyone. She told it like it was, and for that they locked her in an asylum and cut out part of her brain."

The thought made Belle's stomach churn. She gulped a big breath of air and expelled it. "You know," she said, "I've had the strangest feeling that's what happened to Blanche. Maybe that's why they don't have any record of her up at the hospital in Jackson. They turned her into a vegetable, and she ... she just withered away. Oh, Art, I can't bear to think about it."

Art shook his head. With Belle, every road they took always led back to Blanche. "Now you know how I feel," he said.

"Oh, I do, I truly do. It's just that ... well, you *know* Frances is dead and buried, but I don't know what happened to Blanche. It's the not knowing that drives me crazy. Maybe I should hire a private investigator."

Art looked at her. "Aw, you don't wanna do that."

"Why not? *We* certainly aren't getting anywhere."

"That's 'cause we haven't had a break. But that don't mean we oughta give up."

"But where else can we look? We've searched all over New Orleans; we've been to the mental hospitals in Mandeville and Jackson; we've even gone to Laurel, Mississippi, where Blanche and Stella were born, and no one has ever heard of them. Well, a few people have, but they don't count because they think Blanche and Stella are just characters in a play. You know, as much as I dislike Stanley, I wish I knew where he came from so I could go there next."

"Sounds like he came straight from Hell," Art said.

"That's not funny, Art ... even if he is a bully and a brute."

"Alright, alright, lemme think for a minute, will'ya?"

The creak-creak of the wicker and the soft thuds of the rockers started up again.

Time passed. Then Art leaned forward and snapped his fingers. "I got it," he said. "That couple you just finished painting the mural for? The ones on Kerlerec? Didn't you say the lady worked at the courthouse?"

"I think both of them do."

"Yeah, so, isn't that where they keep all the records? Births, deaths, all'a that stuff?"

"I think so."

"So ask the lady to see if Blanche is listed in the dead file."

"But if Blanche died in Jackson, she'd be listed up there."

"Well, can't the lady find out?"

"I suppose so."

"There you go," he said. "If Blanche ain't dead, we keep looking for her."

"What if there's more than one Blanche DuBois? What then?"

"We cross that bridge when we get to it."

She drew in a sharp breath. It was his use of the word *bridge* that jolted her. Though it was the last thing she wanted to deal with on this night of all nights, their first together in his home, she had to tell him. She'd been remiss in not telling him sooner.

"Art?"

"Yeah?"

"Remember last fall, when I said you were keeping company with a divorced woman?"

"Yeah. You made a big deal outta it because I was still married. We were having pizza at that place in Jax Brewery. The one with the terrace overlooking the river. You was wearing that whatchamacallit. That thing you called a cycling outfit."

"My," she said, "you do remember. Everything."

He snorted. "It comes and goes, mostly goes."

"Well, it seems I was mistaken."

"About what?"

"About being divorced."

"Whaddaya talkin'?"

"Apparently, I'm still married."

He stopped rocking. "Who says?"

"My husband."

"Whaddaya mean?"

"Lin came to town last Friday. He–"

Art jumped up from his chair and stood looking down at her. "That Lincoln was *his* rental?" he all but shouted. "And you didn't tell me?" He thumped his forehead with the heel of a hand. "I'm not believing this." He twisted around and looked up and down the street. "Where is he? Where'd the bum go?"

"He went home to Georgia."

Art turned to face her. "You better tell me what's going on."

"I will. As soon as you sit down."

"I don't wanna sit. Start talking."

She began with what Marge had told her about Lin paying her bills and ended with the decision made by the community of Hope Haven for her to hasten her departure from the house. During the telling she skipped over certain details: Lin's extra-marital affair; his violent insistence that she return home with him, how she'd fled from the scene. That kind of information could serve no useful purpose. All Art needed to know, at least for now, was that she was here and Lin wasn't.

"So," Art said, "everybody had a say in this but me."

"I'm afraid so. Do you want me to leave?"

"No, I don't want you to leave. I just want–oh hell, I'm going to bed." With that, he went inside, the door banging shut behind him.

Belle fixed her gaze on the golden pool of light shimmering above Jackson Square. It was a perfect night for strolling, perfect for strolling arm in arm with one's companion. Like she and Art used to do when they first starting going out together. Up and down Bourbon Street they'd go, then down one of the side streets to the Square, and from there to the Moon Walk. How long had it been since they'd done that? A sob rose in her throat. She buried her face in her hands, prepared to weep, but the tears wouldn't come.

Her head came up when the door banged open. There stood Art wearing a sleeveless undershirt and a pair of pajamas bottoms. His feet were bare.

"Lissen," he said, "if we're gonna live together we gotta get one thing straight. No more secrets. Something happens to you, I don't care what it is, you gotta tell me. Same goes for me. *Capisce*?"

"Yes, I understand. No more secrets. I promise."

"Okay then, that settles it. Now, 'less you got something else to say, I'm going to bed."

She rose from the chair and took a tentative step in his direction. "There's just one more thing."

"What?"

"I could use a hug."

"Yeah? That's funny. So could I."

. . .

Over the next several weeks they settled into a workable routine.

Belle started on a new mural, a Louisiana plantation scene, which was the most detailed work she'd done. She particularly liked painting the live oak trees draped in Spanish moss. Left to herself, she could easily have painted nothing but trees with an old cemetery in the background. Painting a cemetery would not have appealed to her had Mrs. Bardet, her previous customer, not checked the courthouse records and found no listing among the deceased for Blanche DuBois. To celebrate the news, she and Art had gotten all dressed up and had dinner at Galatoire's. This time the bright lights didn't unnerve her and it turned out to be a most happy occasion. They'd even shared a bottle of white wine with no ill effects.

While Belle painted Art drove his cab, picking up and dropping off fares all over town. Because he liked to shower in the mornings, Belle took her bath at night. While he was showering, she made breakfast–either eggs and grits or oat cereal with bananas. She also prepared various fruits and raw vegetables for him to snack on throughout the day. He took his medication and tested his blood glucose level at the same time every morning and she recorded the results. Lingering long at the kitchen table was reserved for weekends. On Sundays, after reading *The Times-Picayune*, they treated themselves to the jazz brunch at the Court of Two Sisters.

Since Belle didn't want to arrive at her customers' house before they left for work, Art was the first to leave. That gave her time to tidy up, finish dressing, gather the tools of her trade and load them into Tallulah. They both arrived home somewhere between four and five o'clock. Regardless of who got home first, they took turns cooking dinner. Coming from a long line of Italians, Art specialized in pasta dishes. Belle cooked a little of this and a little of that, always keeping Art's diet in mind. On Tuesday and Thursday nights, she attended AA meetings at Hope Haven while he watched some kind of sport on TV. Friday nights were spent watching old movies. The other nights they took walks and sat on the porch.

It was on such a night toward the end of March that Belle said, "I used to love sitting on the porch when I was a child. We were living on the outskirts of Macon then, and the house had a wide wrap-around porch with an old-fashioned glider. It also had a porch swing, but the chains were so rusty they squeaked real bad and Mother wouldn't let me sit there. Anyway, I used to sit on the glider and draw in my coloring book. After it got dark, my dad would come out and watch me catch lightning bugs. I'd put one in a jar, watch it light up, and then set it free." She laughed. "I probably caught the same firefly over and over again, but Daddy always carried on like I'd caught the moon. I think every house should have a front porch, don't you?"

"I guess," he said. "When I was growing up in Jersey we lived in a four-family flat. All the flats had porches, but they weren't open like this one, they all had brick walls around them. They made the best hideaways. You could crouch down, throw a rock at somebody and then duck so nobody'd know where it came from."

"Arthur Barkoff. Shame on you for throwing rocks."

"Aw, all the kids did it."

"Not the girls, I'll bet."

"You'd be surprised. There was this tomboy lived down the street. The girl could throw like Mickey Mantle. Kids would cross to the other side of the street before they got to her flat and she'd still nail you."

"Heavens."

"Yeah, we were all wishing we had an arm like that. If she'd'a been a guy she could've pitched for the Yankees."

"I was never very good at sports. I tried, oh how I tried, but I could never get the hang of it. I could do all kinds of tricks with a jump rope, though. Oh, and Daddy used to take me fishing. He'd row us out to the middle of what looked like a swamp and we'd sit there for hours and hours. I can't tell you how awful it was. The place gave me the creeps. I used to think the hanging moss on the trees were snakes, ready to fall in our boat. And the mosquitoes ... lord! You never saw such hungry little boogers, and they just loved me to death. But I never let on to Daddy. It would've crushed him to know how I felt. He always thought I was having the time of my life. Too bad he didn't have a son."

"Huh," said Art. "What makes you think a boy woulda liked sitting in the middle of a swamp any better than you did. Jesse prob'ly didn't like it either. The way I got it figured, he went out there to get away from your old lady."

"Arthur Barkoff. What a terrible thing to say."

"It's the truth and you know it. The old bat doesn't give him a minute's worth of peace. 'Member at the open house? Me and him had a blast at Pat O'Brien's, but the minute we got back to the house Edith came down on him like a ton of bricks."

Belle couldn't deny it. "Poor Daddy," she said, "I wish he'd get a part-time job or take up golf or something. He's been at loose ends ever since he retired."

"You ask me, men with nagging wives should never retire. They oughta get dressed in the morning and pretend they're going to work. Hang out somewhere. Look what happened to me. I get this thing with my heart, so the doc tells me to cut down on my hours. But Lil don't want me hanging around the house, so the marriage busts up. Not that there was that much to bust."

Belle turned pensive. "It's sad, isn't it. You and Lil. Me and Lin. Mother and Daddy. If only couples would learn how to compromise."

He eyed her. "You heard anything from the bastard?"

She knew he meant Lin. "No, not a word. I'll tell you if I do."

"You sure about that?"

"Positive."

"Yeah, well, it seems kinda strange to me. He comes down here, tells you you're still married and he wants you to go home with him, and then he slinks away like the snake that he is and you don't hear nothing else."

"It seems strange to me, too, Art. But I'm not about to call him. I told him to sign the papers and all I can do now is hope that he does."

"What if he don't?"

"Like you always say: We'll cross that bridge when we come to it."

Thirteen

A few nights later, they were out on the porch discussing Art's longtime dream of taking a road trip to California. He had the route all mapped out, the states they would cross, and the stops they would make along the way. Once they traversed the coastline from San Diego to Eureka, they would take a different way home, across the Rockies and the prairies.

Caught up in Art's dream of touring the west, Belle jumped when the jangle of a telephone cut into his words. At first she thought it might be a neighbor's phone–the night was balmy enough for windows to be left open–but then Art got up from his chair.

"I'll get it," he said. "Whaddaya wanna bet it's Sandy wanting another handout."

"Oh, Art," she said, hating to hear him speak about his daughter that way. Although they'd never met, Belle had a soft spot for Sandy, a troubled single mother with three young boys.

Moments later Art was back. "It's for you."

"Which one is it?" she asked, thinking it must be one of the girls.

"The one that never has much to say."

"Fran?"

"That's the one."

"Then this won't take long." True to her word, she returned to the porch, happy to be the bearer of good news. "She got the job."

"At the bus station?" Art asked.

"Yes. You should have heard her. She's so excited she could hardly talk. Of course she doesn't get much practice," she added with a giggle. "At talking, that is. Anyway, she was fitted for her uniform today and thinks it's the most beautiful outfit she's ever owned. Oh, I am so proud of her."

"You ask me, all'a girls are doing pretty good."

"Yes, they are. Janette likes her new job at the dentist's office a lot better than she thought she would, and she's making friends at the boardinghouse. Gloria and Millie start school in two weeks, and neither one of them has to take any remedial courses. I just wish we'd hear from Boots. I know she hasn't been gone that long, and she warned us she was bad about writing, but I worry about her all the same."

Art grunted and said, "You worry about everything and everybody. What's Gracie up to?"

"Nothing much. She can't seem to decide what she wants to do. Between you and me, I think she'd like to live at Hope Haven forever. As a sort of assistant to Mammy."

"Huh," said Art.

"I thought we'd be seeing more of Darleen. Didn't she say she and Roger would be coming to town more often?"

"Yeah. Wonder what happened."

"Maybe they haven't had time. Or maybe Mammy scared them off with her talk about rules and regulations. I think she hurt Darleen's feelings."

"Could be," Art said. "Mammy's got a sharp tongue on her."

"Yes, she certainly has," Belle said. "But I love her to death." She paused then said, "You know, Art. With our help, Sandy could accomplish as much as the girls have, if not more."

As usual, Art jumped on the defensive. "What's this *our* business? I send her money every month. What have you done for her lately?"

"That's just it. I haven't done anything because you won't let me. As for you sending her money, that helps pay her rent but it doesn't do a thing to change her circumstances."

"So whaddaya want from me? You want I should bring her and the kids down here? Get her into Hope Haven while you and me babysit the boys? Not a chance."

"Oh, Art, how many times do we have to have this argument? Yes, at one time I did suggest that you bring Sandy and the boys down here. But that was unrealistic. At least for the immediate future. What I meant by *our* help was to let me talk to Marge. See if she can refer Sandy to someone up there. Someone who would not only counsel her but also get her involved with vocational rehabilitation. Now tell me, what could that hurt?"

"Alright, already. So talk to Marge."

"Really?"

"Yeah, really. Like you said, it couldn't hurt."

Though she wanted to go hug his neck, she restrained herself, knowing if she made too big a fuss he might change his mind. "I'll talk to Marge as soon as she gets back."

"She still up at her mother's?"

"Yes. According to Mammy, her mother has taken a turn for the worse."

"Cancer?"

"Yes, and it's spread."

"That's rough."

She started to respond when the phone jangled again. "Do you want me to get it?" she asked.

"Naw, I'll go. It's gotta be Sandy this time around."

"Be nice, Art."

"Ha. Easy for you to say."

But it wasn't easy, Belle thought as the door closed behind him. Here she was, trying to get Art to forge a new relationship with his daughter while her own daughter grew ever more distant. Over the past six months she'd written Mandy an average of one letter a week, and in all that time she'd received two notes, the first expressing anger at Belle's decision to remain in New Orleans, the other a brief summary of college life. As Gloria had said, the latter was the kind of note one would write to a rarely seen aunt.

Marge had counseled her to keep the lines of communication open despite Mandy's unwillingness to reciprocate, and she had, but it took more of an effort now that she was living with Art. Even though Mandy had never met him, Belle knew her daughter would not approve of Art, primarily because he drove a cab for a living. Mandy's world consisted of white-collar professionals–attorneys, doctors, engineers, stock brokers, business executives .... Anyone who labored for a living was beneath her. Belle imagined that included her.

Thoughts of Mandy leaped to the back of her mind when she heard Art's approaching footsteps. She watched as he returned to his chair. "Was it Sandy?" she asked.

"Nope, it's for you. It's Jesse."

"Daddy?" she asked, feeling a sense of unease. She couldn't remember her father ever calling her; they usually exchanged letters. Edith was of the opinion that long distance phone calls should be reserved to announce births and deaths.

"Yeah," Art said. "Lucky for you it's not your old lady."

"Hush." she said on her way into the house.

Reaching the wall phone in the kitchen, Belle lifted the dangling receiver and said, "Hi, Daddy. Is something wrong?"

"Hi, honey. You and Art getting along alright?"

"We're doing fine, Daddy. How about you?"

"I reckon I'm okay, for an old geezer."

"Is Mother all right?"

"She's down to the church. Organizing a prayer vigil."

A fluttering sensation began in the pit of Belle's stomach and worked its way up to her heart. "For who, Daddy?"

"For Lin."

Her hand tightened around the receiver. "What's wrong with him, Daddy?"

"I reckon he had a heart attack. Leastways, that's what they say."

"When did it happen?"

"I don't rightly know. Mandy, she called here 'bout an hour ago. Said they got him in a special unit at Emory."

"What else did Mandy say?"

"Nothin' much. She was callin' from one of them newfangled phones. I couldn't hardly hear her."

"Did she tell you to call me?"

"No. Your mama told me. Don't tell her, but I'd already thought of it. I reckon you best skedaddle on home, honey."

"I'll have to give that some thought, Daddy."

"Okay, honey. Just don't take too long. Lin ... well, I reckon he's a mighty sick man."

"I'll call you tomorrow morning, okay? Oh, and Daddy, thanks for telling me. I love you, Daddy. 'Bye 'bye."

Her hand was shaking as she punched out the numbers for Lin's house. She doubted that Mandy was there, but she had to try.

The answering machine clicked on at the end of the fourth ring. Belle waited for the beep. "Mandy, sweetheart, it's me, your mother. I just wanted you to know I'm thinking of you and praying for your father's recovery. If you feel up to it, please call me back. I'll understand if you don't, but please try. I love you very much, sweetheart. Goodbye for now."

She headed straight for the cupboard. Art said he'd put the plastic bottle in the one to the right of the sink. She looked inside. There he was–Mister Vodka. With trembling fingers she pulled him out of his niche, uncapped him and held him to her lips. The taste was still there, on the rim. But he was empty. Thank God. She put him back in the cupboard and closed the door. Then she went out to the porch.

"What'd he have to say?" Art asked.

"Promise you won't make any disparaging remarks."

"About your old lady?"

"No. About Lin. He's had a heart attack."

"Well I'll be damned."

Belle went on, the words getting stuck in her throat. "I have no idea how bad it is. Daddy tends to get confused. Then again, Mother wouldn't be organizing a prayer vigil unless it was serious. Oh, Art, I don't know what to do. Daddy talked like they were expecting me to come right away, but I don't want to go. Not unless ... unless Mandy wants me to."

"Call her."

"I did. I left a message on the answering machine. I'm sure she's at the hospital."

"Which one?"

"Emory."

"Then call her there."

Belle looked at him. "I could, couldn't I?"

"Yeah."

"But what if she doesn't want to talk to me? I'd hate to upset her any more than she already is."

"Only one way to find out."

"I can't."

"Marge always says *can't* means *won't.*"

"All right, I won't. If Mandy wants to talk to me she'll call."

"Have it your way."

"It's not my way, it's *her* way."

. . .

The call came shortly before dawn the next morning.

Having lain awake for hours waiting for the phone to ring, Belle had finally drifted off into a deep, dreamless sleep. She was so sound asleep she didn't hear the phone. It was Art, nudging her shoulder and calling her name that finally brought her to full consciousness.

Without asking who the caller was, she popped out of bed and ran to the wall phone. "Yes? Hello?" she said and then held her breath.

"Mommy," a tiny voice cried across the miles.

"Yes, sweetheart, I'm here."

"Daddy's dead, Mommy. Daddy's dead and I'm all alone. Tell me what to do, Mommy. I don't know what to do."

"Call Grandma and Grandpa. Tell them you need them. Tell them I'm on my way."

"Okay, Mommy. Hurry."

"I will, baby, I will."

By seven-thirty that morning, Belle and Art were on their way to Stone Mountain, Georgia.

Fourteen

Because they hit Atlanta at the height of rush-hour it took well over an hour to get across town. Once on Memorial Drive, a busy thoroughfare in the best of times, traffic slowed to a crawl. By then it was full dark. Headlights, taillights, and stop lights winked and blinked from all directions.

During the day an unexpected cold front had swept down from Canada. Though the Checker's heater was pumping out warm air, neither of them could stop shivering. Along with the temperature a rise in humidity made it seem even colder, and their manner of dress didn't help matters. Belle was wearing what she called her Katherine Hepburn outfit, a pair of dressy dove-gray slacks with a silk magenta-colored blouse, flat gray pumps, and her pearls. At the last minute she'd grabbed a gray bulky knit sweater, which she huddled in now. When she left Mallory House last September, she'd left a whole closet full of clothes behind. No doubt they were still there, but she knew she wouldn't wear them, wouldn't even look at them. In fact, she planned to ask her mother to box them up and take them to the church's clothing store.

Art wore an argyle sweater vest over a tan shirt with olive-drab trousers. He'd tossed a brown suede jacket into the back seat but had forgotten about it. Packing had been such a hit-and-miss affair neither one of them could remember what they'd brought. If worst came to worst, they'd decided, they could always go shopping.

The other problem was where to stay once they got there. Art was all for getting a motel room, figuring the less seen of him the better. But Belle knew her parents wanted them to stay at their house. She couldn't imagine sleeping under Lin's roof, and of course Art wouldn't hear of it, though Mallory House was where they were headed.

"Turn right!" Belle exclaimed. "There by the church!"

"Jesus," Art muttered, veering sharply to the right without signaling, causing an irate driver to issue a protesting blast from his horn. Regaining control of the wheel, he glanced in the rearview mirror, expecting to see a ten-ton truck bearing down on him, ready to smash the Checker into next Sunday, but the vehicle behind him was at least a car's length away.

Pure dumb luck, Art thought, not for the first time. What with Belle making split-second decisions, it was a wonder they weren't lying in a ditch somewhere.

More than the mission itself, the traffic and the sudden turns, it was being in unfamiliar territory that kept Art on edge. If there was one thing a taxi driver hated it was not knowing where he was or where he was going. On top of that, he was having to depend on Belle's sense of direction–a high-strung woman on her way to her dead husband's funeral.

"How far?" he asked for the umpteenth time.

"I'm not sure. I've never gone this way."

"What! What're you, crazy?"

"Please don't shout. It hurts my head. Daddy said to take Rockbridge Road to Devon Street. He said it's a short cut." She'd called her parents before leaving the house to make sure Mandy had let them know they were coming.

They drove a little farther, Belle straining to see the street signs. "Oh, I wish it was still light out. It would make it so much easier for me to get my bearings."

"You? What about me?" Art groused.

"At least it's not raining,"she said, hoping to appease him.

"Or foggy."

"True. But I'll swear if feels like it's going to snow."

"Don't even think about it,"Art said.

"I can't help it, I'm freezing." She burrowed deeper into her seat wishing she'd brought a blanket.

"Turn up the heat," Art said.

"It's up as high as it will go."

A two-lane stretch of road, Rockbridge wound up and down and all around. Denuded trees, their spindly arms sticking out at all angles, stood side by side with lanky evergreens. Roof-tops wearing coats of frost glistened in light thrown by porch lights. Coming from a New Orleans spring to the bleakness of winter was a shock to the system.

"How's about trying to get some news," Art said. They'd been listening to the radio off and on all day. That's how they'd known about the cold front.

Belle played with the dial, trying to get something besides music stations and preachers spouting the gospel. All she got for her efforts was static. "I give up," she said, switching the radio off. "We'll know what the weather's like when we step outside."

"That's what I'm afraid of."

"Whoops!" she cried, twisting around in her seat to look back. "We just passed Devon."

Art thumped the wheel with the heel of a hand and muttered a curse.

"I couldn't help it!" she cried. "I can't keep my eyes on the road and be searching the airwaves at the same time. Why don't you try reading the signs for a change."

"Alright, already. So we missed another turn. So we don't get there till midnight, so what." He kept looking for a place to pull off, but was blinded by the headlights and taillights that lined both sides of the road. Worse, the jerk driving behind him was hot on his tail.

Belle said, "If I'd driven Tallulah we would have been there by now."

"Ha. You'd'a been lucky to find your way outta town."

"Stop the car," she demanded. "I'll walk the rest of the way, thank you."

"Over my dead body."

He realized what he'd said when she gasped. After all, they were on their way to her husband's funeral.

"Aw, shit," he said. Then, "Lissen, we gotta take it easy. We're tired, we're hungry and we're freezing, but we gotta keep our cool, okay?"

"Okay," she said, bundling the sweater around her so it bunched in the middle. "Other than being tired and hungry, are you feeling okay?"

"Yeah," he said. "I feel terrific."

"Liar. I should have packed more snacks."

"Forget about it. Be looking for a place I can turn around."

Turning her attention to the world outside the window, she saw from the bank of lights up ahead that they were nearing the heart of Stone Mountain. Soon, familiar landmarks came into view. "Slow down," she said. "There's a clearing up ahead."

Art flipped on the turn signal and tapped on the brake in staccato-like bursts. After making the turn he headed back the way they had come. "What'd you say the name of the street was?"

"Devon. We'll make a left."

"Well, at least traffic's not as bad going this way."

"That's because we're heading away from town."

"What town?"

"Stone Mountain."

"Ain't that where we're 'spose to be going?"

"Not exactly. Mallory House is away from town."

"Mallory House," he repeated. "Sounds like some fancy hotel."

"It does, doesn't it. It'd make a wonderful bed-and-breakfast."

She paused, then added, "Or a halfway house."

Art's head swivelled sideways. "Don't tell me," he said.

"Don't tell you what?"

"Don't tell me you're gonna stay here and run another Hope Haven."

She gave a nervous laugh. "Don't be silly. Mallory House doesn't belong to me."

"Who says?"

The question hung in the air like an overblown balloon, ready to burst at any moment.

. . .

They were a quarter of the way up one leg of the long, horseshoe-shaped driveway when Art let out a long, low whistle. "Holy Toledo. You sure this is the place?"

"I'm sure," Belle said, feeling a thickness in her chest.

Through the leafless trees that dotted the landscape they could plainly see that Mallory House was ablaze with lights, making it look larger and more imposing than ever. Built by Lin's grandfather in the early 1900s, it was Georgian in design with symmetrical wings. Even the outbuildings were lit up.

Belle puzzled over this until she saw the line of parked cars on both sides of the drive leading up to and away from the house. "Good heavens," she said.

"Looks like the kid's got company," Art said.

Belle unbuckled her seat belt and strained forward, one hand on the dash for balance.

"What're you doing? Art asked.

"Looking for Daddy's car."

Art eased up on the gas so they were inching along.

"I don't see it," she said, a note of panic in her voice.

"Take it easy. It's gotta be around here somewhere."

"But what if it isn't? What if they went home?"

“Aw, they wouldn’t do that. Not with you coming.”

She kept looking.

They reached the front of the house. Art applied the brake, intending to let Belle out and find a place to park, but she was gesturing for him to keep going.

“Not here,” she said. “Go around back.”

He shifted gears.

It was a tight squeeze between a Lexus and a Cadillac parked at the side of the house, but he managed to pass through the opening without incident. There, beneath a portico, sat Jesse’s car.

“Oh, thank goodness,” Belle said, expelling a held-in breath. “I would’ve died if they weren’t here.”

“You want I should park here?”Art asked.

“Yes. Pull in next to Daddy’s car.” She leaned back against the seat and fanned her face. “Oh lordy, I can’t believe we made it.”

“You ain’t the only one,” Art said, switching off the ignition. He turned to look at her. “Now what?”

“Now we go in. Just as soon as I collect myself.”

“How long will that take?”

“Forever.”

Fifteen

"Talk about cold," Art said after a few minutes of sitting idle in the cab, "it's like a icebox in here. What're we.gonna do? Sit here and freeze our butts off?"

Belle scooted over to his side and gave him a peck on the cheek. "Thank you for bringing me here, Art. You can be the world's biggest grouch, but you're still my hero."

"Think nothing of it," he said, warmed by her nearness. "You ready yet?"

"No, are you?"

He looked over her head at the house and said, "Let's go."

She led him through the back door and down a passageway until they entered a large, brightly-lit kitchen. Women in all shapes and sizes were bustling about the room. One woman she did not know wore a black uniform with a white apron; the others, wearing tailored suits or dresses, she recognized as members of her mother's church. All of them were busy with some kind of food preparation: peeling off plastic wraps, lifting foil, removing lids, popping dishes into the microwave, retrieving others from the oven. An island in the center of the room served as a depository for the food, which, when ready, was carried through the swinging doors that led into the dining room.

In the midst of all this activity, standing arms akimbo, face screwed into a frown of concentration, stood Edith Weldon.

Belle inclined her head toward Art and whispered, "Follow me."

Hugging a far wall, they had almost made it to a side door when her mother's voice cried out. "Kathleen!" Belle turned to see her mother heading her way, arms outstretched, beaming a smile. "Oh, my precious girl," Edith trilled. "You've come at last."

Belle forced a smile. Not once in her forty years on this earth had her mother called her a "precious girl." It must be for show, she thought, noting that the women had stopped what they doing to watch the scene play out.

Smothered in a crushing embrace and choking on the scent of Edith's lilac talcum powder, it was all Belle could do to utter a single word. "Mother."

Edith held her at arm's length and looked her up and down, the smile quickly disappearing. Leaning in close, she spoke in an undertone. "Well, I never. How come you're wearing such a get-up, Kathleen? I taught you better than this. This is a mourning, not a picnic."

Belle sighed. "I know, Mother. But I've been traveling all day. If you'll let me get my things, I'll change."

Edith clucked her tongue. "Too late for that, Missy, the ladies here done seen you. What took you so long, anyway?"

"Mother, please. Where's Mandy?"

"Last I knew she was heading for the library. Had a passel of her friends with her. Laws, I never saw goings-on. Joking and laughing to beat the band. It's a disgrace is what it is. Don't tell nobody, but I 'spect they been into Lin's liquor. I said to your daddy, I said, Jesse, see if you can't do something about them younguns. You know what he did? He high-tailed it off to the den. Did you ever?"

"Mother, will you do me a favor? Will you please fix Art a plate. If he doesn't–"

"Art?" Edith said, her eyes darting in all directions. "You brought him?"

"No, Mother. He brought me."

"Don't you go getting snippy with me, Missy. I got enough to worry about trying to get this here food on the table. These ladies got big hearts, but they don't know their right hand from their left. I said to Jesse, I said–"

Belle cut her off. "Mother, Art is a diabetic and he needs to eat. If you won't fix him a plate, I'll do it myself."

"You'll do no such thing. I'll fix him a plate, but you keep that man out of my sight, y'hear? Keep him out of everybody's sight. Of all the nerve, bringing your boyfriend to your dead husband's funeral." She let out a huff of air and waddled off, her too-tight rayon skirt riding up on her broad hips and showing the hem of her slip.

Belle let out an audible groan, then looked around for Art. He'd slipped behind the door to which they'd been headed.

"I heard," he said, grimacing.

"Wait here," she said. "As soon as I get your plate I'll take you to Daddy."

"It's a deal," he said.

. . .

From the den, where Jesse and Art were renewing their acquaintance, Belle went in search of Mandy. From what she could gather, the majority of the people who'd come to pay their respects were in the formal rooms at the front of the house. Fortunately, the library was near the far end of the east wing, enabling her to avoid the crowd.

Raucous bursts of laughter punctuated with intermittent shouts came from inside the book-lined room. Dreading what she would find, Belle moved cautiously down the long hall.

Having reached her destination, she peeked around the doorjamb. There, behind the long mahogany bar on the left side of the room, stood her fair-haired child, playing the role of bartender. That didn't surprise her. Lin had taught Mandy how to mix drinks when she was only ten years old. It had amused him to watch her pour, blend, and shake. "This little gal makes the driest martinis this side of the Mississippi," he'd brag to his cronies. As painful as that had been for Belle to watch, this was far worse, for these weren't Lin's friends her daughter was serving, these were Mandy's contemporaries, most of whom were under the legal drinking age.

Belle itched to flee the premises. She'd go get Art. He'd be only too willing to take her to a motel. From there she could call her mother. Tell her she'd fallen ill and thought it best to remove herself from their guests. No sense spreading germs around at a time like this. Her mother would have a fit, of course, but no matter. All that mattered at the moment was avoiding the spectacle that lay beyond the door.

But she didn't flee. She adjusted her clothes, patted her hair in place, then drew herself up to full height. She was the adult here–it was time to act like one. She entered the room.

No one noticed her until she'd almost reached the opposite end of the bar from where Mandy stood. As an aside, someone said, "It's Mrs. Mallory."

She faltered briefly, then kept moving. Though acutely aware of a stirring in the room and the buzz of whispers that seemed to vibrate off the walls, she had eyes only for Mandy, who was preoccupied with whipping up a drink in a blender.

At last Mandy looked up. Not at her mother but at the boy she'd mixed the drink for. His gaze was fixed elsewhere. On Belle.

She rounded the end of the bar, holding onto the brass rail to steady herself. "Sweetheart," she said softly so as not to startle her child.

Mandy turned her way. The girl's eyes lit up for a brief moment, then flickered and dimmed. Tossing her head, she struck a pose, thrusting one hip forward and setting a hand on the other. "Well!" she declared. "Look who's here! If it isn't the black sheep of the family."

"Don't do this, baby," Belle said, her heart in her throat. Where was the little girl who had cried out to her last night?

Turning back to her friends, Mandy clapped her hands together and called, "Everybody! You remember my mother, don't you? It's true she deserted us, but look, she's back. Come to say a final farewell to my father. Let's give her a warm welcome, shall we."

The group stood inert, as though frozen in space.

A sob rose in Belle's throat but she quickly rallied. Moving to stand next to her daughter, she confronted the group, looking from one solemn face to the next, nodding in recognition to the ones she knew, stopping when she got to Lana, Mandy's best friend since childhood.

"It's good to see you, honey," she told the girl.

"It's good to see you, too, Mrs. Mallory," Lana said.

Encouraged by the exchange, Belle addressed the group. "The bar is officially closed. Mandy's grandmother and some other ladies have put out a mountain of food. Please go help yourselves."

"Excuse me, Mother," Mandy said, her voice ringing with sarcasm,"but if you don't mind, this is a private party."

"The party is over, sweetheart. You can join your friends later." She looked at Lana. "Honey? Will you lead the way to the dining room and see that everyone has plenty to eat? Oh, and if anyone decides to leave, please make sure there's a designated driver."

"Sure, Mrs. Mallory." Lana then threw a cautious look at Mandy. "I'll see you in a little while, okay?"

Mandy nodded.

While the group, singly and in pairs, drifted out the door, Belle watched for obvious signs of drunkenness. Either the youths could hold their liquor or they were very good actors. In any case, Lana was a level-headed girl and Belle felt she could trust her to see that her friends made it home okay.

When the last of them had left the room, Belle turned to face her daughter. Though she ached to clasp Mandy to her breast, she held herself back. Having been rebuffed so many times in the past, such a gesture would have to come from Mandy herself.

"Oh, sweetheart ..." she began, her eyes roaming over Mandy's face. She wanted so badly to see those pretty features soften, wanted that icy look of disdain to melt and fade away. But Mandy, so like her father, continued to hold fast to her chilly reserve.

"Well, Mother," she said. "Now that you've got the bar all to yourself, would you like me to fix you a drink? Let's see, if I remember correctly, you prefer vodka on the rocks. We're out of Stoli so this will have to do." She reached for a bottle of Absolut.

Belle inched closer. "I know you're hurting, baby, but please don't do this. All I want is to offer you whatever comfort I can. Please let me. I've missed you so much." Her voice cracked with this last.

"You can save the mushy sentiments, Mother. I'm not in the mood. Do you or do you not want a drink?"

"I do not," Belle said quietly. "I haven't had a drink in over six months. I thought you knew that."

Mandy flicked her a wry glance. "Oh, yes, that's right. You've been cured. I know, I'll drink your drink for you." Using a pair of silver tongs, she proceeded to deposit ice cubes into a tumbler.

Belle gave a great giving-in sigh. "Forgive me for intruding on your grief, sweetheart. I thought you wanted me to come. It seems I was mistaken."

Mandy went on as though she hadn't heard. "Did you know it's supposed to snow tonight?" She poured two fingers of vodka into the glass and added a splash of tonic water.

"Yes, I heard," Belle said, unable to take her eyes off the drink. Oh my God, she could almost taste it. "Is it supposed to be a big snow or a little snow?" she asked, feigning interest.

"They say we could get up to five inches."

"Oh dear," Belle said, the words barely registering. Mandy was stirring the drink with a swizzle stick, and all Belle could think about was how much she wanted it. It would be so smooth going down her throat, not to mention making it easier to deal with her daughter.

Mandy wrapped her hand around the glass, prepared to take a sip. Still watching every move, Belle swallowed and licked her lips. "Don't worry, Mother," Mandy said. "We don't have to bury Daddy.

He's been cremated."

"Good heavens," she said, forgetting about the drink. "I know that's what your father requested, but I didn't think it would be done so soon."

Mandy lifted the glass to her lips, hesitated, then put it down. She gripped the edge of the bar and leaned into it, as though to hold herself up. "I can't believe he's gone," she said in a hoarse whisper. "It was all so sudden. I had lunch with him just last week. He didn't look good and I asked him about it. He said he'd been working long hours on a big case and all he needed was a good night's sleep."

Belle moved closer. She put a hand out and tucked a loose strand of hair behind Mandy's ear. To tell her that she, too, had thought he looked ill when she saw him in New Orleans would only open fresh wounds. Besides, Lin might not have wanted her to know he'd made the trip down there. It wasn't something he would have been proud of. So unless Mandy brought it up, she'd keep it to herself.

Mandy looked at her, then dropped her eyes. "I'm sorry about before, Mother. I'm really glad you're here."

"Me, too, sweetheart."

Mandy made a half turn. Now face to face with her mother, she reached out and fingered the pearls at Belle's neck. "I've always loved these," she said. "Daddy gave them to you, didn't he?"

"Yes," Belle said. "For our tenth anniversary."

Releasing the pearls, Mandy looked up from under moist lashes. "Mom?"

"Yes?"

"You won't ..." She stopped when her chin began to quiver.

Belle tilted her head to one side. "What is it, sweetheart?"

The words tumbled out in a rush. "You won't leave me, will you?" Her face crumbled and a great racking sob tore out of her chest.

Belle couldn't hold back any longer. With a wrench of tenderness she pulled Mandy close, wrapped her arms around her daughter's shoulders and gently rocked her from side to side. "It's all right, baby," she whispered. "We'll work it out. I promise."

Later, after they'd dried their tears and repaired their faces, mother and daughter prepared to join their guests. Although they had six months worth of catching up to do and Belle was eager to get started, it could wait. Right now they had obligations to fulfill

"You go ahead, baby," Belle said. "I'll be there in a minute."

"Where are you going?" Mandy asked.

"To check on Art."

Mandy's eyes widened in disbelief. "*He's* here?"

"Yes."

"Honestly, Mother. I try to be as liberal-minded as the next person, but bringing your lover here was in very poor taste."

"He's not my lover, honey. He's my friend, my very *best* friend, and I want you to be nice to him."

Mandy studied her face as though trying to decide whether to believe her or not. "Where is he?"

"In the den, with your grandfather."

"I want to meet him."

"Now?"

"Yes, now. He *is* the man you're living with, is he not?"

"Living with, not sleeping with." Belle had sent her a change of address shortly after moving in with Art. She'd written four letters since then, always referring to Art as her good friend. As usual, Mandy hadn't responded.

"So you say," Mandy said with a toss of her head.

The two of them made their way to the den, careful to use the labyrinth of rooms at the rear of the house. From the sounds that echoed from the front rooms, the crowd appeared to have increased in size. Would this night never end, Belle wondered. And when it did, where would she wake up in the morning?

The men were huddled over a game table in a corner of the room. Both held a handful of cards. This astonished Belle. Her mother didn't approve of games, especially those played with cards or dice. "It's doing the devil's work," Edith always said.

"What are you two up to?" she asked as she approached.

Jesse jumped up from his chair as though stuck by a cattle prod, his cards falling to the table. Seeing it was his daughter and not his wife, he gave a sheepish grin. "Hi, honey. Art's been teaching me how to play gin rummy. Who you got there?" He peered over the tops of his bifocals to where Mandy was standing. "Hey, sugar, how ya doin'?"

"Okay," Mandy said.

Art laid his cards down and stood up. "Your dad's a fast learner," he said to Belle.

Jesse nodded. "It's a right good game."

"Mother will be delighted to hear it," said Belle.

Jesse looked stricken. "You won't tell her, will you?"

"No, Daddy, I won't tell." How many times had she uttered those same words? Too many to count. She went over and gave him a hug. Then she turned to Art. "Art, I'd like you to meet my daughter, Amanda Jordan Mallory. Mandy, this is Mister Arthur Barkoff."

Art tipped an invisible hat in Mandy's direction. "Hi," he said. "Pleased to meet you."

"My pleasure," Mandy said, assuming a mistress of the manor pose.

Belle gave a light laugh and said, "There now, that wasn't so hard, was it?"

"Whaddaya talking about?" Art asked.

"The two of you being civil to each other."

"Aw, c'mon," Art said, his ears turning red, a sure sign of embarrassment. "Can't you see me'n Jesse are busy?"

"Mister Barkoff," Mandy said. "I'd like to know if you're sleeping with my mother."

Belle gasped. "Mandy!"

"Naw, it's okay," Art said. "Better to get it out in the open, right? No, I ain't sleeping with your mother. I'm not saying I never will, but I got a bum ticker and my blood sugar's all outta whack, so your guess is as good as mine."

"I see," Mandy said.

"Lissen, kid, I'm real sorry about your old man. I never met the guy, but I know he must of loved you. Jeez, you're the spitting image of your mother."

"Thank you," said Mandy, lowering her eyes and relaxing her pose.

"Well," Belle said, "we'll let you gentlemen get back to your game."

"Where're you going?" Art asked.

"To say hello to our guests."

Art shrugged. "Whatever."

"When you come back this way," Jesse said, "how's about bringing me a Co-Cola."

"I'll get it now, Grandpa," said Mandy.

"That's mighty sweet of you, Sugar."

Mandy looked at Art. "Would you like a Coke, Mr. Barkoff?"

"Yeah," he said with a grin, "that'd be nice. I don't know about Jesse, but I could use something to eat. Maybe some nuts or a few pretzels. That is, if you got any."

"I'm sure we do," Mandy said. "I'll bring a variety."

"Hey, thanks," said Art.

"You're welcome."

The men went back to their game.

Pleased with how well the introductions had gone, Belle wanted to gather everyone together for a group hug, but that would be going too far. Instead, she added a little bounce to her step as she followed Mandy out of the room. Maybe they could get through this nightmare after all.

Sixteen

The occupants of Mallory House woke to a rare and beautiful sight. During the night several inches of snow had turned the grounds into a winter wonderland. Ice crystals, glistening like diamonds under a beaming sun, formed intricate patterns on trees and shrubbery. The ornamental cabbages in the central garden looked like giant puffs of cotton; everything else wore a fuzzy blanket of white.

Of the dozens of cars that had lined the drive the night before only four remained–Art's, Jesse's, Lana's and Jerry Thornton's. Except for Lana, who stayed to keep Mandy company, none of the others had planned to spend the night, it just happened, and for the first time in years all of the guest rooms were filled.

Jerry, Lin's partner and longtime friend, had not only been named executor of Lin's will, he had made all of the arrangements for the memorial service to be held, weather permitting, at four o'clock that afternoon. Jerry wanted to be on hand in case anything came up that required his attention. That he and his wife Martha stayed over had comforted Belle greatly. She'd always been fond of Jerry and Martha. They had been particularly solicitous when she lost the twins. Afterwards, when confined to the house because of agoraphobia, Martha had been one of the few people who kept in touch.

Edith used the fear of being snowed in as an excuse to stay over. "What if I get stuck at home?" she had asked. "Who'd take care of you?" Belle knew the truth–Edith was afraid she might miss something. And, as usual, Jesse acceded to his wife's wishes.

With people expected to wake at different times, breakfast was served Continental style. The live-in housekeeper Lin had hired after Belle had decided to stay in New Orleans, a stout woman named Iris Hansen, had laid out fresh fruit, sweet rolls, English muffins, bagels, cream cheese, jams, jellies, hard-boiled eggs, thin slices of baked ham, freshly squeezed orange juice, and coffee. Where, under Edith's supervision, last night's table had been set with the house's finest serving pieces, today Iris had chosen to use the everyday Wedgwood china, Sheffield silver, and Waterford glassware.

Sitting alone in the dining room, trying to reconcile herself to the events of the past twenty-four hours, Belle was on her third cup of coffee when Art wandered in.

"There you are," he said. "Jeez, a guy could get lost in this place."

Belle gave him a sunny smile. "I should have drawn you a map." She gestured toward the sideboard. "Help yourself to some breakfast."

"Where is everybody?" he asked, heading for the food.

"I guess they're still asleep. I've been up since before dawn. I tried to go back to sleep, but my mind wouldn't let me. Have you looked outside?"

"Yeah, how about that? Good thing it didn't snow no more than it did. We mighta gotten stuck here for days."

"Would that be so bad?" she asked quietly.

He craned his neck around to look at her. "You gotta be kidding."

"We can talk about it later."

"Uh-oh. I don't like the sounds of that."

She changed the subject. "Have you been checking your blood sugar?"

"Yeah. So far so good." He brought a plate to the table and sat down in the chair to her right.

Taking inventory of his selections–two bagels, two eggs, several slices of ham and a chunk of cream cheese–she started to chide him, but the thought of sounding like her mother kept her tongue in check.

"This weather must have set some kind of record," she said. "I can't remember it ever snowing this late in the season. It's the end of March, for heaven sakes."

"I didn't think it ever snowed this far south," he said, spreading a linen napkin across his lap.

"It doesn't happen very often. I guess we just got lucky."

"Lucky, ha. I thought I left this stuff behind when I busted outta Jersey." He made a bagel sandwich out of cream cheese and ham.

Watching him bite into it made Belle hungry. All she'd had was a banana and a glass of juice. "Was it really that bad?"

He took another bite of his sandwich, chewed, then swallowed. "You better believe it. Aw, it wasn't so much the snow but what came after. I'd pull up to a curb to pick up a fare and the tires'd throw dirty slush all over 'em. Talk about mad. Like I invented the stuff just to aggravate 'em. It'd get all over the floorboards. I had to carry a bucket of old towels to keep it cleaned up. Then Lil'd holler when I dumped 'em in the wash. You couldn't win."

"I had no idea," Belle said. "You see all these pictures of quaint New England villages covered in snow ... they look so pretty and pure."

"Yeah, it's pretty alright. 'Til it's time to dig out the old snow shovel."

Belle looked past him to the window. "I don't think we'll have to worry about that today. It's already melting."

"Good," Art said, cracking his eggs together as though they were walnuts, then peeling off the shells, flicking bits and pieces from his fingers to his plate.

An image of Lin frowning at them from the head of the table swam through Belle's mind. For twenty years she'd served him the exact same breakfast: a three-minute egg delivered in an antique eggcup, an English muffin, open-faced and toasted till it was light brown around the edges, a dollop of imported strawberry preserves, and a tall glass of tomato juice. With his coffee, which came after his meal, he'd peruse both *The Atlanta-Journal Constitution* and *The Wall Street Journal.* Conversation, no matter how urgent Belle or Mandy thought the subject, was discouraged until he finished. Which was why Belle had preferred to eat in the kitchen. She'd be there now if it weren't for Iris Hansen. Not that Iris Hansen didn't seem accommodating, but Belle didn't want to intrude on the woman's territory.

She'd felt the same way when she first came to Mallory House as a bride. Back then, Lin had a staff of three full-time employees, two of them live-ins. Having been raised in a humble home where she was expected to help with household chores, the preparation of meals and yard work, Belle couldn't adjust to being waited on. She was young when she married–barely twenty–and full of unspent energy. No matter how hard she tried to busy herself with other activities, having servants in the house made her feel completely useless–adrift in a vast sea of rooms.

Lin finally agreed to let the cook go. Later, he gave notice to the live-in maid. It gave Belle great pleasure to prepare the meals and care for the priceless objets d'art Lin's parents and grandparents had collected over the years, until, confined to the house, that's all she did.

And now, though it didn't seem possible, she was back. Not as a resident but as a temporary guest. How temporary remained to be seen.

A stirring next to her caught her attention. It was Art, taking his empty plate to the sideboard and returning with a cup of coffee. "You wanna refill?" he asked.

"No, thanks. I'm coffeed out. I feel like I should be up and doing something, but there's really nothing for me to do."

"I know what you mean," he said. "First thing, when I woke up, I was mapping out my day, y'know? Then I remembered where I was, and it's like I don't have a day. All this sitting around is killing me."

"We could take a walk. You haven't seen the grounds yet. They go on forever and it would be beautiful out there."

"A walk, she says. Like I'm gonna trudge around in the snow with no jacket and no boots."

She started to tell him he could wear something of Lin's then thought better of it.

Another idea occurred to her. "Daddy should be getting up soon. The two of you could ride over to the house. He'll have a jacket you could borrow."

"Now you're talking. A ride sounds good."

"I thought it might."

"Speaking of Jesse, who're all these folks?" he asked, nodding at the series of portraits hanging on the north wall.

"That first painting? Those are Lin's parents. Next to them are his paternal grandparents. Then his maternal grandparents, and finally his great-grandfather on his father's side."

"Huh," Art grunted. "Beats me what any of my grandparents looked like. They died before they could get to America."

"Where was their home?"

"Sicily."

"Sicily. How romantic."

"Ha. That's what you think." His gaze returned to the portraits. "The first one there? The one with his mother in it. She looks like a real lady. Classy, but nice, if you know what I mean."

"You've got a good eye," Belle said. "From all I've heard she was a very kind and gentle soul. Well-loved by everyone she knew. Unfortunately, I never had a chance to meet either of Lin's parents. They died two years before we were married. They were killed in an avalanche."

Art looked at her. "No fooling?"

"No fooling," she said. "They were on a skiing holiday in Switzerland. Gstaad, I think. One morning they went up on the slopes and never came back. The rescue team searched for over a week, but their bodies were never recovered."

"Tough break," Art said.

"Yes, it was tragic. Lin was still grieving when I met him. He said I reminded him of his mother. I think that's why he fell in love with me." Not for the first time she wondered what her marriage would have been like had Lin's parents survived. Would there have even been a marriage? Prior to their engagement, Lin dated debutantes, girls who lived in a world of high society. A world which, to Belle, seemed more like Mars.

"Y'know," Art said, his gaze back on the portrait, "I guess that's why I like looking at her. You two could be sisters. Same kind of classy but nice."

She started to thank him but he went on. "You told me," he said, "but I forget. Who's the stuffed shirt on the end?"

"Oh, that's great-grandfather Mallory. I don't know what kind of man he was, but there's an interesting story behind that portrait. See how he's standing in back of an empty chair? Apparently, during one of the sittings, his wife collapsed and died. Right there in front of him. The artist wanted to finished her part of the portrait from the sketches he'd drawn, but the grandfather told him to leave the chair and paint her out of it. So he did. It makes me wonder if the grandfather had a mistress on the side. Or maybe he and his wife didn't get along and that was his way of getting back at her. I like to think he loved her so much he couldn't bear to be reminded of her. I asked Lin about it, but he didn't know."

"Huh," said Art. "He still looks like a stuffed shirt to me. How'd all these guys make their dough?"

"My, you're just full of questions, aren't you? From what I understand they were involved in a number of enterprises ... land, industry, and the law."

"In other words, they was wheelers and dealers. It figures."

"Why do you say that?"

He made an arching motion with his arms. "You don't get a spread like this by selling peanuts at the fair. I figured they had pieces of lotsa pies, and they needed to know the law to stay outta jail."

Belle laughed. "You're probably right."

"Darn tootin'. I know how these rich guys operate. You hear all kinds of stuff driving a cab. But I gotta give 'em credit. They got it and I don't. 'Course I wouldn't know what to do with it if I did."

"That was my problem."

"Whaddaya mean?"

"I never felt comfortable with all this ... this overabundance. It wasn't the money as much as it was everything that went with it. The constant entertaining and being entertained, the country clubs, the lavish gifts, the drinking, the gossip, the propositions, the affairs ... To my way of thinking, it was so destructive. That's not to say wealthy people don't do wonderful things with their money. A lot of them do, and I'm sure Lin's mother was one of them, but that wasn't Lin's style." She paused, remembering the turmoil of their early years together. "I just wasn't cut out to be a social butterfly. I'm a simple person and I prefer a simple life."

"Like what we got?"

"Exactly."

"So, what're you gonna do about it?"

Unprepared for the question, she turned to him. "Do?"

"Yeah, do." Hunching over the table, he went on. "Lissen, I know you and the kid have been talking. You say you want a simple life, but she ... hell, let's face it, she was born to live this life. So the way I see it, one of you has got a problem."

She let out a long sigh. "You are so right."

Conversation ceased when the sound of Edith's voice radiated from the kitchen. Belle looked at Art and drew an imaginary zipper across her mouth. He gave her a thumbs up. They waited, listening. The voice grew closer.

Art pushed up from the table. He came around to Belle's chair, leaned over and said, "I'll be shooting pool in the rec room." That was where he and Jesse had ended up last night.

"Do you remember the way?"

"I'll find it. That's one good thing about big houses, there's plenty of hideouts."

He'd barely made it into the living room when Edith came barging in from the kitchen. Stopping short when she spied her daughter, she started right in. "I declare, Kathleen, I been looking for you. What'd you do, stay up all night? Your bed don't look slept in."

Belle put on a pleasant face. "Good morning, Mother. Did you sleep well?"

"Did you hear me, Kathleen? Your bed don't look slept in."

"I know, Mother. I slept in the blue room."

"Whatever for? You've got a perfectly good room of your own."

"That's Lin's room, Mother. You may find this hard to understand, but I slept in the blue room because I wanted to." At one time the blue room had been a nursery, ready for the twins who would not live to occupy it.

"Well, I never," Edith huffed. "That man has been a bad influence on you, Kathleen. You never used to talk back to me this way." She marched over to the sideboard, her face screwed into a frown. "You should of woke me up. I said to Jesse, I said, Jesse, how come us to sleep so late. He said he reckoned we were plumb tuckered out. Well, that's no excuse, I said and I got dressed as fast as I could. Then I went to get you up. Imagine my shock when you wasn't there. I'll swan, Kathleen, you could've left me a note. So I hurried on down to the kitchen, fixin' to make flapjacks and bacon, but that Iris woman said not to bother, that she done put breakfast out. Imagine calling this piddling mess breakfast. These eggs are as cold as Job's dead turkey and so's the ham. What in the world are these donutty-looking things?"

"They're bagels, Mother. Would you like me to make you a bagel sandwich?"

"You'll do no such of a thing. I don't care what that woman says. I'm going in there and fix me and your daddy a decent breakfast." With that, she stomped off to the kitchen.

Moments later Jesse came shuffling into the room, eyes on the floor, shoulders drooping.

"Good morning, Daddy," Belle said.

At the sound of her voice, Jesse straightened up. Pushing his bifocals up on the bridge of his nose, he peered over the rims and gave her a broad grin. "Hi there, honey. You're lookin' mighty chipper this morning."

"That's because I'm so glad to see you. Did you sleep all right?"

He shook his head. "Can't say as I did. Your mama's snoring kept me awake half the night. She don't believe me when I tell her she snores. Says I must be dreaming. But I'll tell you, honey, she snores like a rattly old furnace." He looked around the table. "Where's Art?"

"In the recreation room."

Jesse looked confused, as though he didn't know whether to stay and eat or join Art. Belle got up and went to him. She took his arm and led him to the chair at the head of the table. Jesse began to tremble and shake before they could get there. At one point, Belle thought he might stumble and fall. It had only been six months since she left home yet he seemed to have aged twenty years. She wondered when he'd last seen a doctor.

"Sit down, Daddy. Mother's fixing your breakfast, and I'll bring you some juice."

"Thanks, honey." He eased himself into the chair as though his bones ached.

Belle could feel his eyes following her as she went to pour the juice. Presently, he said, "Bring me one of them pears, honey. And one of them eggs and a cinnamon bun."

She looked at him. "Are you sure? Mother's making pancakes and bacon."

"I got room for that too. I didn't eat any supper last night. Too many folks around."

Guilt pricked Belle's conscience. She'd been so intent on having a plate prepared for Art, she hadn't thought to ask if her father had eaten. "Oh, Daddy. I could've brought your supper to the den."

"That's okay, honey. I wasn't all that hungry. All them people made my stomach jumpy."

Her heart went out to him. Everything about Mallory House made her jumpy.

She set a plate and a glass of juice in front of him, then leaned over and put her face up to his. He automatically puckered his lips for her kiss. Straightening, she patted his shoulder and said, "I love you, Daddy."

"I love you too, Sugar. It's good to have you home."

Quick tears welled in her eyes. She blinked them back. If she started crying now she wouldn't be able to stop.

Rather than returning to her chair at the opposite end of the table she took the one to her father's left. By the time she was seated, Jesse had dug his pocketknife out of a back pocket and was slicing the pear into quarters. It relieved her to see that the gnarled hands wielding the knife were strong and steady.

Again, an unbidden image of Lin surfaced. Despite having Edith fawn all over him, he'd never cared for either one of her parents. Had thought they were ignorant crackers. True, they'd both been raised on tenant farms, and true they weren't well educated, but it had pained Belle to know that Lin looked down on them simply because of their upbringing. She could understand why he had little tolerance for Edith, but Jesse had always treated him kindly. Now it seemed fitting that Jesse, old-timey pocketknife in hand, was sitting in Lin's chair.

"Daddy, could you do me a favor after you finish your breakfast?"

"I'll sure try, honey."

"Could you take Art over to the house? He needs to borrow a winter jacket, and maybe a scarf and some gloves."

"Be glad to," Jesse said between mouthfuls of egg. It'd give us something to do." As an afterthought, he said, "You reckon it's safe to drive?"

"You forget Art's a Yankee. He's an old hand at driving on snow and ice."

Jesse looked at her. "That a fact?"

"Yes, sir. He was born and raised in New Jersey. He's only been in New Orleans a few years."

"Well, I'll be dang. He talks like a Yankee but he don't act like one."

Amused, Belle couldn't resist. "How does a Yankee act, Daddy?"

He cackled a laugh and said, "Danged if I know. I don't reckon I ever met one."

They were still chuckling when Edith came bearing a stack of hot cakes.

Jesse sobered instantly, busying himself with buttering his cinnamon bun.

Belle's reaction was just the opposite. The sight of her mother's pinched face and pursed lips, a scolding on the tip of her tongue, caused a fresh burst of giggles.

"Have you no shame?" Edith snapped at her, setting the platter on the table with a thump. "Laughing at a time like this. With all Lin's dead kinfolks watching from the walls. I'll swan, Kathleen, I don't know what's got into you."

Belle muzzled herself by holding her napkin to her mouth. Fighting for control, she breathed in and out, in and out. The napkin smelled like starch. It turned her stomach and she thought she might gag. She tossed the napkin on the table, her giggles dying in her throat.

"I didn't mean any disrespect, Mother," she said. "It's just that you ... well, sometimes you can be so darn funny."

Edith looked at Jesse. "Reckon we ought to call the doctor? I think she needs a shot or something."

"Leave the girl alone, Edith. She's had a terrible shock, is all."

Edith's eyebrows shot up, hung there a moment, then came back down. "Eat your hot cakes, Jesse." She turned and headed back to the kitchen.

As soon as she was out of sight, Belle looked at her father and said, "You were wonderful, Daddy."

"Think so?"

"Oh, yes."

He grinned and said, "Honey, you better pass me them pancakes."

"Did I hear somebody mention pancakes?" Jerry Thornton asked from the doorway. Standing at his side, Martha's face was wreathed in smiles. Both were dressed for the day, Jerry in a charcoal gray suit, Martha in black.

"Hey, there," Jesse said. "Y'all come on in. The bacon will be here directly."

"Good morning," Belle said, rising to meet them.

Martha was the first to reach her. After they embraced, Martha looked her up and down and said, "You look stunning, but tell me the truth. How are you doing?"

"Better, now that you're here."

Jerry came up to them and draped an arm over Belle's shoulders. "You hanging in there, gal?"

"More or less," she said.

"It'll all be over soon. Where's that daughter of yours?"

"I expect she's still in bed. I heard her and Lana talking late into the night. Knowing them, they'll sleep till noon."

He removed his arm from her shoulders. "Well, if she's not up by then, we'll have to wake her. I want to discuss the will before we leave for the service."

Belle's heart leaped to her throat, rendering her speechless.

Martha came to the rescue. "Let's don't talk about that now. Let's enjoy our breakfast. Go fix yourself a plate, Jerry." She gave him a gentle push in the direction of the sideboard. When he was on his way, she looked at Belle and rolled her eyes. "These lawyers never know when to quit."

"I heard that," Jerry said without a backward glance.

"I don't care if you did," Martha retorted.

At the sideboard, he directed his next remark to Belle. "We'll meet in Lin's study at one o'clock. Just the three of us. You, Mandy, and me."

Belle's nod was more like a spastic twitch.

Seventeen

Alone in the house, while the others attended the memorial service, Art had done everything he could think of to keep himself occupied. He'd shot some pool, played a few games of solitaire, and tried to find something worth watching on TV. Failing that, he'd gone out to the cab and checked the oil. From there he'd thought about walking around the grounds. The snow had almost melted and he was curious. From what little he'd seen there was a tennis court, an Olympic-size pool, cabanas, a hot tub, a barn, and two brick buildings that could contain almost anything. In the end he'd decided against it, figuring it'd be just his luck to set off some kind of alarm. All he needed was to have a parade of cop cars screaming up to the house just as Belle was returning. So he'd stuck to the areas he was familiar with, mostly the den and the rec room. He knew there was a library around somewhere, and had wondered if there might be a *Sports Illustrated* he could look at, but he wasn't about to go poking his nose where it didn't belong.

To think he'd actually looked forward to being alone in the house. He'd pictured himself strutting across the miles of Oriental carpets, past the Chippendales, the Hepplewhites, the Queen Annes, trying to get a feel of what it'd be like to be the master of the manor. What a joke. He'd felt dwarfed by the richness of it all–the high ceilings with their fancy carvings, the acres of walls hung with tapestries and oils. With each step he took he seemed to shrink another inch. Worse, every eye in every portrait seemed to watch his every move, as if they were waiting for him to get down on his hands and knees and crawl to the nearest exit.

Now, as he paced back and forth in front of the broad expanse of Palladian windows in the front parlor, he was counting the minutes till Belle got back.

They hadn't had a chance to talk since breakfast. After the reading of the will, they'd run into each other in the hall outside the den. A blind man could see that Belle was in a state of shock. Her face had turned as white as a lily and her eyes had a dull, haunted look. Art had started to give her a hug, ask her if she needed help, but then Edith came marching up. Never mind that her daughter was visibly shaken by something. Did Edith offer a kind word or a soft touch? No sir, not Edith Weldon. Cutting her eyes Art's way, as though to make sure he knew he wasn't invited, she started barking orders about it being past time for Belle to dress for the service.

In all his years, though he'd sometimes been sorely tempted, Art had never slapped a woman, never physically hurt a female in any way, but, to his way of thinking, Edith deserved at least a hard pinch.

That was the only good thing about being alone in the house–he didn't have to worry about Edith popping up on him.

He stopped by one of the windows and looked out. It was almost dark. What was taking them so long? Wasn't a memorial service supposed to be shorter than a real funeral? Maybe they were taking the ashes somewhere. Burying them or flinging them to the winds. A shiver rode up his spine. The very idea of being cremated gave him the creeps. Then again it'd beat being laid out and having people stare at his corpse, murmuring about how good he looked. If he looked so damn good what was he doing lying there?

He resumed pacing, trying to get the image of his dead body out of his mind. He wasn't ready to die. He and Belle were just getting started. Started on what was the question mark.

A blinking light from beyond the windows caused him to stop short. A moment later he recognized a series of headlights flashing on the trees. It had to be Belle and company, he thought, hoping the limo she'd had ridden off in was the first in line.

Now what, he wondered. Should he go up to his room or stay downstairs? As much as he wanted to be there for Belle, he wasn't about to wait at the door. He'd seen enough of Edith's sour face to last him a lifetime, and no telling what shape Mandy would be in. He wanted to make himself scarce yet available.

Spotting two areas behind the bottom of the grand staircase, where the banisters flared out and curved back toward the wall, he crossed to the one on the far side of the coat closet. He didn't think of himself as hiding, he was just staying out of sight. Nevertheless, he tensed at the sound of car doors slamming. Soon, the sound of voices echoed from the foyer.

He needn't have worried about being seen. Without even shedding her coat, Edith rushed off toward the kitchen, no doubt to prepare more food. Mandy and her friend ran up the stairs as fast as their long legs would carry them, and Jesse seemed to be heading for the bathroom in the alcove off the foyer. At the closet, Jerry helped Belle off with her coat and then turned to assist his wife.

Through the frosted pane in the storm door, Art could see a long line of headlights as a steady procession of cars wound their way up the driveway. Knowing he had to make a move but wanting to appear casual, he shoved his hands in his pockets and stepped out from behind the banister.

As though sensing his presence, Belle glanced over her shoulder. Seeing him, she put a sshhh-finger to her lips. Then, excusing herself from Jerry and Martha, she walked his way.

After leading him on a circuitous route down a series of halls, up a back staircase, and down still more halls, they entered a small sitting room. Before he could get his bearings, she threw herself at him, arms around his neck, the side of her face against his throat.

"Oh, Art," she moaned, "it was awful, simply awful."

Holding her close, he could feel her silky curls tickling his chin. Her body was soft and pliant. He breathed her sweet scent deep into his lungs. It smelled like lilies of the valley. He felt a stirring in his groin. Disbelief at such a rare occurrence, especially at a time like this, merged with mortification.

In an effort to hide his tumescence, he loosened his hold and held her at arm's length. "Take it easy," he said, his voice sounding strained. "Just take it easy." He could have been speaking to himself.

She pushed away from him and flung up her hands. "I can't take it easy! No one will let me. This whole thing is a never-ending nightmare."

"You can say that again," he muttered under his breath. Fearing another rush of hormones, he crossed to one of the two love seats and sat down. Patting the cushion next to him, he said, "C'mon. Tell old Art all about it."

"I'm tired of sitting. I've done nothing but sit for the past two days."

She began to move about the room, as though searching for something. Pausing in front of an étagère, she picked up one of the figurines on display and held it up for Art to see. It showed a young boy in a blue romper, one hand stuffed in his pocket, the other holding a teddy bear by its arm. Between his feet sat a red rubber ball. "I've always loved this one," she said. "It's called 'Boy With A Penny.' Isn't he precious?"

"Yeah," Art said, admiring the subtle shading. "Top quality. Dresden?"

"Royal Copenhagen." she said.

"Ah."

She put the boy back and picked up the dog that was sitting next to him. A small white terrier, it had twisted around to bite at a flea on its backside. "When I first came here this was on another shelf," she said. "I moved him next to the boy because I thought they went together. What do you think?"

"You're right. They're a match."

She fingered the dog lovingly and put him back. "Such beautiful things. It's a shame to hide them away up here."

"Yeah, well, let's face it. The joint is full of nice things. It's a regular museum. So, you gonna tell me about the service, or what?"

She turned her back on him, seeming not to have heard.

He pushed up from his seat and went to her. "I know what you need," he said. "You need to lie down and take a nap." He nudged her arm. "C'mon, I'll walk you to your room. Tuck you in."

She gave an irritable twitch with her shoulders. "I don't want to lie down."

He backed off. "Alright, already. Whaddaya want from me?"

She looked at him. "I want you to sit down and listen without interrupting." Her voice softened. "That is, if you want to."

"Why didn't you say so?"

"I just did."

He returned to the love seat. "Okay, I'm sitting."

She stepped to one side of the étagerè and rested her weight on the edge of a lowboy. Settled, she cleared her throat and started talking. "As you know, I'd been dreading the service. Mostly for Mandy's sake but also because I had no idea how I'd react. After all, Lin *was* my husband, the father of my child, and I hadn't shed a single tear. I was afraid I'd be swept away by some sweet memory and start crying, making it harder on Mandy. It turned out neither one of us cried. We were too angry to cry. Instead of a sedate service with people who cared about Lin, there were all these strangers. Even news people were there. Don't ask me why. But there they were, this grubby little man flashing a camera and this birdbrain of a woman who writes for the local paper. Here, Mandy's just lost her father and I'm doing the best I can to be brave and strong for her, and the woman pushes her way through the crowd and sticks a microphone in our face. How were we feeling, she wanted to know. Honestly! How did she think we felt? Happy? I told her to take her cameraman and go home.

"Then we had to practically fight our way into the church. The pews were overflowing with people. More people were standing at the back of the sanctuary and down the side aisles. Still more were milling around outside. If only half of them come to the house we're going to have a mess on our hands. Before we even got to our pew, Jerry used his cell phone to call the security service. He told them to send six extra guards. He thinks some of the people are curiosity seekers, but they could be crooks, ex-cons, or both. Lin once served as a prosecutor. He put a lot of people behind bars. On top of that, crooks could take this as an opportunity to case the house. Lord, if my mother knew any of this she'd faint. She thinks she's serving the cream of society."

She walked to the wing chair across from him and sank into it. "As if that wasn't bad enough, we had to sit and listen to the minister drone on and on about what a saint Lin was, and how the Mallory family had done so much for not only the state of Georgia but for the entire nation. I thought he'd never stop. The man is new to the church and barely knew Lin. I had to bite my tongue to keep from screaming at him.

"Finally it was over, and instead of our friends being able to come up and say hello, we were hustled out a side door, shoved into cars and whisked away." She twisted her hands, a lost look in her eyes. "Art, I don't think I can stand much more of this. I *know* Mandy can't. What are we going to do?"

He'd been listening as hard as he could, but what she'd told him sounded like something out of an old Joan Crawford movie. Crooks, ex-cons, curiosity seekers, flashbulbs going off, a gossip columnist asking stupid questions ... all because some rich guy died. This didn't happen in real life, did it? If Belle said so, it did.

"I think we oughta hit the road."

"But where could we go?"

"Where else? Home."

"I can't do that. I can't leave Mandy."

"We can take her with us."

She stared at him. "Really?"

"Yeah. It'd get her away from all this craziness. Give it time to blow over."

"You wouldn't mind?"

"Hey, she might be a pain in the ass, but she's still just a kid. She's had a helluva shock, losing her dad and all, and now all this mess."

Belle pondered the idea of leaving. "My mother would kill me."

"I doubt it. Without you and the kid, she'd be the center of attention. She'd love every minute of it."

"You're probably right. But what about Daddy."

"Jesse's no dummy. He'd find a way to stay clear."

Her eyes lit up. "Oh, I'd love nothing better than to get out of here. I feel like I'm suffocating."

"Then what're we waiting for? Let's go."

The light in her eyes faded. "It's not that simple. First I have to talk to Mandy. Then I need to discuss it with Jerry. The will was fairly cut-and-dried, but there are a lot of details to clear up."

"So? Can't he straighten it out without you?"

"I suppose so. He did say it would take a couple of months to settle the estate, and he'll have a team working with him."

Art cocked an eyebrow. "What kinda team?"

"Oh, the usual ... legal assistants, accountants, auditors, brokers, bankers ...."

"Thought you said the will was cut-and-dried. Whaddaya need all those guys for?"

"The estate is complicated. It involves a lot of holdings." She closed her eyes and massaged the bridge of her nose.

Though he was curious to know exactly what the will said, he could see she was exhausted. He hunched forward, arms across his legs, hands clasped between his knees. "Lissen," he said, "if you don't wanna talk about this stuff just say so. You think you could sleep now? I could find Jesse and shoot some pool."

She stifled a yawn and opened her eyes. "I'm too tired to sleep."

Art sat back and tried to relax. He was pretty tired himself–and hungry. With any luck Belle would change her mind about taking a snooze and he could sneak downstairs and try to grab something to eat. If nothing else, a cup of coffee would help him stay awake.

Belle started in again. "Oh, Art, I just wish none of this had ever happened. But wishing won't make it go away. Anyway, the most important thing you need to know is that none of this changes anything. Between us, I mean. Our lives will go on the same as before. Maybe not right away, but just as soon as I can get Mandy settled."

Though he had serious doubts about nothing changing, Art kept his thoughts to himself.

"As far as the will goes, Lin set up a sizable trust fund for Mandy and left the rest of the estate to me."

"Huh," Art grunted, not wanting to show his ignorance by admitting he knew nothing about trust funds. His main concern was with Belle's take. How big of an estate were they talking about?

She went on. "I thought he'd leave everything to Mandy. I'd hoped he did. I'd *prayed* he did. I still can't believe he didn't."

"This estate," Art said, resting his palms on the chair arms, "what're we talking about? This place and a coupla mil?"

The unmistakable red blotches of embarrassment bloomed on her cheeks. "Actually, it's more like two-*hundred* million."

Art's eyes bugged out and his jaw dropped open. It took a moment for his features to return to normal. "Holy Toledo," he said. "You talk about Edith fainting if she knew she was feeding a bunch of crooks ..." He swiped a hand across his brow. "One more jolt like that and I'm out like a light."

"Imagine how I felt!" Belle cried. "I went in there thinking Lin had left the estate to Mandy. I couldn't figure out why Jerry even wanted me in there. Other than being her mother, what business was it of mine. After all, Mandy's an intelligent and sensible girl. She's used to having money. She's had money all her life. And then Jerry read the will. It was like he injected me with a gallon of Novocain. He went on and on and I didn't hear a word he said. It was like that time in Jackson, when I had the panic attack. Only this time I didn't have an attack. I went into shock."

Art remembered the time in Jackson all too well. They'd gone up to the state hospital to find Blanche. It was Blanche's birthday and Belle had brought her the special gift she'd bought in Atlanta. When the hospital administrator told them Blanche had never been there, Belle had a bad attack. He'd brought her around by giving her a sip of Mister Vodka. That was the day she'd been referred to Marge. Four days later she entered Hope Haven.

Poor baby, he thought now, as he had then. He wanted to tell her everything would be all right, but this wasn't some quick fix. This even Mister Vodka couldn't smooth over. This was big. Huge. Bigger than anything he'd ever heard of. He'd thought her winning the jackpot in Biloxi was a big deal. Hell's bells, sixty-five grand was chump change compared to this.

"When I finally pulled myself together," she said, "I told Jerry I didn't want it."

What she said didn't register at first. He'd been thinking about the jackpot and how he'd been having her keep track of every cent she spent. He knew all too well how money could get away from you. It was like dollar bills sprouted wings and flew right out of your hand. He'd told her if she wasn't careful she'd end up without a nickel to her name. What a joke.

"You what?" he croaked, his voice gone hoarse.

"You heard me," she said. "Remember when I thought Lin was divorcing me? I didn't want anything from him then, and I certainly don't want anything from him now. Just because he didn't sign the papers doesn't mean we were still married. Well, in a legal sense it does, but as far as I'm concerned we've been estranged for the past nine years and divorced since last fall."

Art put a hand to his chest and held it there. Either he had a bad case of indigestion or his ticker was acting up. "Okay, okay," he said and took a deep breath. "I hear what you're saying. But Belle, baby, you just don't toss a coupla hundred mil down the toilet. Think of all you could do with that dough. Jesus, I can't even count that high."

"Neither can I. Of course Lin didn't make all that on his own. He inherited most of it, and it's not hard cash, it's mostly paper money."

"Whaddaya mean 'paper money?'"

"Oh, stocks and bonds, his half of the firm, some office buildings, a few condos, an interest in a golf course ... things like that."

Art shook his head. "Man, when I said those old guys were wheelers and dealers I wasn't whistling Dixie. But I gotta hand it to old Lin. At least he didn't blow it like some rich punks do. Take your big lottery winners. Blowing all that dough on boats and cars and diamonds and furs. Before you know it it's all gone, everything gets repossessed, and they're back where they started."

"No, Lin didn't blow it," she said. "As a matter of fact, considering the value of the estate, he was quite conservative. I used to think he was extravagant, like when he bought Mandy her car, but now I realize that expense-wise it meant nothing. Still, a girl her age doesn't need to be driving around in a BMW. It's the principle of the thing."

Art grinned. "Maybe so. But you gotta admit it's a damn fine set of wheels."

She smiled for the first time since breakfast. "So is my Tallulah."

They talked a while longer before leaving the room. Parting at the head of the stairs, they agreed to meet later, after Belle talked to Mandy. They'd taken a few steps in opposite directions when Belle turned and said, "Oh, and Art. Please don't breathe a word about the will to my folks. Mother's been trying to worm it out of me, but I don't want her to know what kind of money is involved."

Art gave a puzzled frown. "What will?"

She blew him a kiss and continued down the hall.

• • •

Her rap on Mandy's door went unanswered. She pressed an ear

to the frame and listened. Not a sound could be heard. She tried the doorknob. It turned. She entered the room. "Mandy? Sweetheart?" No response. Maybe she and Lana had gone out for a while, maybe they were downstairs.

Leaving the door ajar, Belle went all the way into the room, surprised to see that everything looked exactly the same. Though she'd only been gone a little over six months it seemed like years, and she'd expected to see a few additions. New photographs, current magazines, something relating to college life.

Her eyes traveled over the French Provincial furniture: the four-poster bed with its layers of silk, the bedside tables with their Tiffany lamps, the vanity table and chair, the secretary, the desk, the bookcase, the bureau, the lingerie chest. In a corner, grouped for conversation, sat matching love seats, side tables and a chaise. Rainbow-hued fabrics lent a dreamy touch and the sweet scent of perfume floated in the air. It wasn't necessary for Belle to look beyond the walk in closet and the dressing room to see the gold fixtures and Italian marble in the bath.

The girls of Hope Haven came to mind. All four bedrooms would fit into this space. There the girls were, with their rickety, pock-marked furniture, lumpy mattresses, squeaky springs, drawers that stuck, scuffed floors, frayed and mismatched fabrics, cracked windows, tiny closets. Yet they thrived among the ruin and clutter. And she had thrived with them, happily.

What would they think of this room? This house? These grounds? Would they be jealous, envious, or awed? Was Mandy truly better off living amid such opulence? Belle supposed she would never know. A quirk of birth had decided it all.

A voice came from the doorway. "What are you doing in here?"

Startled, Belle jumped. "Oh!" she said, gasping a laugh when she saw Mandy. "For a minute I thought you were Gloria."

"Gloria?"

"My roommate at Hope Haven. I wrote you all about her."

"Oh, yes. Gloria," Mandy said, her expression stony. "The former prostitute who turned into Dorothy of *The Wizard of Oz* fame."

Belle winced. "That's not very kind of you, sweetheart. I'm very fond of Gloria. She's a wonderful girl."

"I'm sure she is, Mother. Now, if you don't mind, I'd like a little privacy." She started across the room.

"Wait," Belle said. "Something's wrong. What is it?"

Mandy wheeled around, her face contorted with rage. "Wrong?" she screeched. "What could be wrong? For years you pretended you were suffering from some strange malady. A *nervous condition* that prevented you from leaving the house. Then, for no reason at all, you snuck away without even having the decency to tell Daddy where you were going. Days later you finally got around to calling him. He begged you to come home. Would you listen? No. You moved in with a bunch of drug addicts. So I tried to reason with you. I wrote you about the doctors right here in Atlanta. What did I get in return? A bunch of stupid letters about how great you and all those trashy girls were doing. Finally you were ready to move out of that place. But instead of coming home, you moved in with a cab driver. A man who can't even speak proper English, for God sakes. And now that you're home, who do I remind you of? Saint Gloria. But nothing's wrong, Mother. Nothing at all." She stalked off to the bathroom and slammed the door behind her.

Belle's body had been strung as tight as a guy wire while Mandy lashed out at her. Now she went limp. It was as though all the blood had drained out the soles of her feet. It was out in the open at last. Mandy's sense of abandonment and betrayal.

Too weak and weary to make it to the bed, Belle moved to the chaise and curled up on it. Mandy had to come out of the bathroom sometime.

Eighteen

Belle woke with a start. Aware that someone was watching her but unable to see who, she smoothed her hair back from her face and dug the sleepiness out of her eyes. Her skin prickled with a chill that seemed to sweep across the room. She rubbed her arms to warm them. Then, swinging her legs off the chaise, she prepared to stand up. She froze when she heard Mandy's voice.

"I don't suppose you'd care to tell me why you went to New Orleans in the first place."

Confused and disoriented, Belle looked around the room. Mandy was sitting at the vanity table, looking at her through the mirror. Though her anger seemed to have abated, her expression gave no hint of reconciliation.

"Oh my," Belle said, a hand going to her throat. "I didn't mean to fall asleep. What time is it?"

"Eight-thirty."

"Heavens," said Belle, blinking rapidly. "Have you been sitting there all this time?"

"No. I just came up to see if you were awake."

"Where's Lana?"

"She went home."

"Are the people still here?"

"Yes."

Belle gave a little moan. "Is your grandmother holding up all right?"

"You know Grandma," Mandy said. "She's in her glory."

"Still, she's got to be worn out. Your granddaddy, too."

"Grandpa's with your friend."

"Oh." Reminded of Art and their plans to meet, she hoped he'd at least helped himself to some food. Maybe she should go down and check on him. The thought left her mind when Mandy got up from her chair and crossed to where Belle was sitting.

Mandy sat down in the love seat catty-cornered to the chaise. After crossing her legs, she arranged herself carefully, as though someone might snap her picture. The side split in her skirt showed a length of black-stockinged leg up past her knee. Though lean-limbed her calves were well-defined. She had the legs of a dancer, the carriage of an aristocrat.

Belle wanted a drink of water but was unwilling to say so; it would seem as though she was stalling. Mandy wanted to know why she'd gone to New Orleans and it was time to tell the whole truth. Not that she'd lied when she first left home–she considered Blanche her friend even though they'd never met. After all, they were kindred souls.

If she'd told Lin or Mandy about needing to find Blanche they would have thought she'd gone completely insane–they already thought she was half mad. Besides, Mandy was safely tucked away at college, too busy with her new life to listen to her mother's plan. So Belle had posted a note to Lin on the refrigerator door saying simply that she'd gone to visit an old friend–she didn't say where–and would be home in a few days. She never imagined that New Orleans would soon become her true home.

"Mother," Mandy said with a ring of impatience, "I'm waiting." Belle ran her tongue over her lips to moisten them. If only she had a drink, a tall glass of vodka on the rocks.

"I went to New Orleans to find Blanche DuBois," she said. It was a straightforward answer, she thought, but Mandy looked puzzled. "The lady Tennessee Williams wrote about in his play," she added as clarification.

Mandy wrinkled her brow. "I never heard of her."

Stunned, Belle's eyes widened. "But how can that be? Surely your English courses covered the plays of Tennessee Williams. He was one of America's greatest playwrights, if not the greatest. The play I'm referring to is *A Streetcar Named Desire.* It first appeared on Broadway. The original movie version won four Academy Awards."

"We studied the classics, Mother. Shakespeare and Chaucer and Swift, to name a few."

"My word," Belle said. "I had no idea your studies were so limited."

Mandy bristled. "I'm not majoring in American literature, Mother. In case you've forgotten, I'm going to be an attorney. Like my father." She emphasized this last.

"I know that, sweetheart, but ... well, I guess things have changed since I was in school."

Mandy's silence spoke for her.

"Oh dear," Belle said. "This makes it harder for me to explain my connection to Blanche and why I felt compelled to find her. But first, despite what you said earlier about me faking my illness, I think you know that's not true. Each time I couldn't attend one of your dance recitals I wanted to lie down and die. And I'll never get over not being able to watch you graduate ... oh, I missed so much, so very much. And the worst of it was, no one knew what was wrong with me. The doctor said it was nerves, but I thought I must be crazy. No one in her right mind would be afraid to go out of her own house. But I was ... deathly afraid. Whenever I tried, and I did try–many times–I became paralyzed. Oh, if only someone had recognized my symptoms." She paused, remembering.

"It wasn't until I went to New Orleans and met Marge that I found out I was suffering from agoraphobia. And because she said she could help me learn how to live a normal life if I stayed and went into treatment, I didn't think I had a choice. What would you have done?"

Instead of answering, Mandy stood up. "I'm going to get a glass of iced tea. Would you like some?"

"I would love some tea."

During Mandy's absence, Belle used the bathroom, washed her hands and splashed cold water on her face. She didn't think about what she'd said or what she still wanted to say–it would come to her as she went along.

Rather than returning to the chaise, she chose to sit in the love seat opposite the one Mandy had sat in.

By the time Mandy handed her a glass of tea she felt refreshed and fairly composed, ready to carry on.

"Thank you," she said.

"You're welcome."Again, Mandy carefully arranged herself. She took a sip of her tea then set the glass on the table to her left. In the time it took her to do this, Belle had gulped her tea down as though dying of thirst. The empty glass sat on the floor near her feet.

"While I was downstairs," Mandy said, "I looked up agoraphobia. The dictionary said it's an abnormal fear of open spaces. I took that to mean a fear of being out in the country. What has that got to do with you being afraid to leave the house? And if you were that afraid, how did you get to New Orleans?"

"Oh, I wish Marge was here," Belle said. "I tried to explain it in my letters, but I guess I didn't do a very good job. Bear with me, sweetheart, and I'll try again." She paused, collecting her thoughts. "'Open spaces' actually means outside of your safe place, which in my case was here in this house. My first panic attack happened in the supermarket, my second in the post office, my third on the street near the dry cleaners... three completely different yet familiar places, places I went to all the time. It was very scary to think it could happen anywhere at any time. But I had a life to lead. I had responsibilities, obligations to fulfill, so I forced myself to go out. Then it happened again, and again. I'd lost all control. It was like this ugly demon had taken over my body. I kept fighting it; I kept telling myself I could do it. But then, after I wrecked the car and your father took away my driver's license, I gave up hope. It wasn't until years later, when I started drinking vodka, that I worked up the courage to try again. And when I finally made it through the front door and out into the sunshine ... oh, baby, I felt like I could spread my wings and fly. It was a miracle. The demon within me had died. Or so I thought. That's when I decided to go to New Orleans and search for Blanche. If it hadn't been for Mister Vodka, I never would have made it."

"Mister Vodka?"

"I used to carry vodka in an empty Scope bottle. I named the bottle Mister Vodka. He was very dear to me."

Mandy arched a brow. "So you were drunk when you went to New Orleans."

"No. I was stone-cold sober. You see, I'd gotten to the point where I didn't have to actually drink the vodka, I just had to have the bottle with me. As long as I knew Mister Vodka was within reach, I could make it through the door. That's not to say the attacks stopped. I still had them every now and then, but they weren't as bad. Even more important, I knew I'd live through them. But depending on vodka or anything else isn't normal. I had to learn how to depend on myself. And of course I had to give up Mister Vodka when I entered Hope Haven. It's a drug-free environment, you know."

"Mother, do you have any idea how that sounds?"

"It may sound crazy, but it's true."

"I see," Mandy said, skepticism written all over her face.

"Do you?" Belle asked. "Do you understand that my leaving had nothing to do with you? You were at Agnes Scott, caught up in the whirlwind of college life. It had nothing to do with your father, either. You know what his schedule was like. When he wasn't at the office, he was on the golf course or at the club. To tell you the truth, I didn't think he'd even notice I was gone. Besides, I only planned to stay away for a few days. What harm could that do?

"My plans changed when I went to see if Blanche was a patient at the state hospital in Jackson. I had a very bad attack during a meeting with the administrator. It was a bad attack, and the next thing I knew I was in Marge's office, listening to her explain what was wrong with me. Imagine, if you can, how incredible it was to finally find someone who not only knew what was wrong with me but who knew how to treat it. I couldn't leave her, sweetheart, I just couldn't."

"All right," Mandy said. "I'll grant you that much. But what is this Blanche person to you? Why was it so important that you go all the way to New Orleans to see her?"

Belle sighed. "What is Blanche to me? I think of her as a sister sufferer. I suppose it's because of our mutual sense of isolation. Our feelings of hopelessness. I'd lost the twins, and then, because of the attacks, I'd lost my ability to function. Blanche had lost her young husband, her parents, her teaching job, the family home ... all she had left in the world was her sister Stella and a steamer trunk full of clothes. So she went to New Orleans to stay with Stella until she could get back on her feet. The problem was, Stella was married to an insensitive brute. Stanley harassed Blanche unmercifully. He accused her of all kinds of things, and, when that didn't drive her away, he talked Stella into having Blanche committed to an insane asylum. That was easy to do back in those days. Of course there's a lot more to the story, but the point is, I felt compelled to find her. I wanted her to know that someone understood her losses, that someone cared about her. I still feel that way. I'm still searching. I *will* find her."

In the silence that followed, Mandy gave a spare, tight shake of her head. Her lips parted then closed. Turning her eyes on her glass of tea she seemed to consider whether she wanted a drink. Declining, she lifted the hair off the back of her neck and let it drop so it flowed around her shoulders. Then she shifted ever so slightly in her seat, careful not to disturb the folds in her clothes.

"This therapist of yours," she said. "This Marge person. Does she know about Blanche?"

"Yes. Unfortunately, she thinks Blanche is nothing more than a fictional character. That's all the more reason I need to find her. To prove to Marge that Blanche really exists."

"I see," Mandy said. "Well, Mother, if I were you I'd see another therapist. We could ask Jerry to research the psychiatrists in this area. Find one that could deal with your problem."

"But I don't have a problem, sweetheart. I haven't had an attack in over four months. And I haven't had a drink since last September."

"That's not the kind of problem I'm talking about. I'm talking about you moving in with that man instead of coming home where you belong. I'm talking about you searching for someone who may or may not exist. It seems you may have a problem coping with reality."

Belle felt a flash of anger but was quick to contain it. This was the first serious discussion she and Mandy had ever had, though God knows she had tried to talk to her many times. If they were to keep the lines of communication open she had to maintain control of her emotions. Even though she acted like an adult, Mandy was still a child, a pampered child at that. She talked about reality, but she had no idea what the real world was like, the world outside her social circle. Also, she could not possibly know how hard her mother had worked to conquer her fears.

"Sweetheart," she said, "I'm not going to debate Blanche's existence with you. You'll just have to take my word for it. As for coming back here after I left Hope Haven ... I have a whole new life in New Orleans. I have the best friends a person could ever have. Most exciting of all, I have a career. I'm actually making money with my mural painting business. It's a heady feeling to be able to pay my own way. And I like living with Art. For the first time ever, I'm sharing a home with someone on an equal basis. You can't imagine how liberating that is. Please try to understand."

Mandy regarded her cooly. "I've never understood you, Mother. We're different, you and I. We always have been."

Belle lowered her eyes. Sad to say, it was true. Once upon a time, when Mandy was little, they had been so very close. They had played games, had tea parties, painted pretty pictures, read story books, made jewelry out of beads, baked cakes and cookies ... all of the things little girls like to do. At about the age of ten, Belle had noticed a shift in her daughter's attitude. She became aloof, sarcastic, totally lacking in emotion. Belle had thought it was a stage she'd grow out of, puberty at its worst, but that never happened.

Mandy went on. "And from the sounds of it, we always will be."

"But it doesn't have to be that way!" Belle cried. "I want you to go back with me. You could transfer to Loyola. You'd love New Orleans. You could get an apartment in the Garden District. Have your friends down anytime you wanted to. It's so beautiful there, so lush, and there's so much to see and do. We could really get to know each other. We could–" She stopped herself. "You don't want to go with me, do you?"

"No, Mother. This is my home. All of my friends are here, and I'm all settled at Agnes Scott. It's the perfect school for me, and I'm close enough to be able to spend weekends here at the house. That reminds me ... I'm leaving for Costa Rica tomorrow. Lana's parents have a place down there. We'll stay a few days and then we'll go back to school."

Belle's eyes roamed over her daughter's flawless face. "Where is the little girl who cried out to me over the phone?"

Mandy gave a light laugh and tossed her head. "That girl got caught in a moment of weakness."

"Is that what you call it? Weakness? I'd call it something else. I'd call it an honest show of emotion."

For a brief moment Mandy lost her composure. Eyes glinting with anger, she spat out the words. "My father had just died, Mother. He meant everything to me, *everything*."

Why was it, Belle wondered, that the parent who gave the least was often loved the most? "I know, sweetheart, I know."

"So," Mandy said," what are we going to do about all this? Are you going to sell the house? Should I start packing my things?"

"Of course not," Belle said, shocked that she would think such a thing. "You heard what I told Jerry. I don't want the house or anything else. This property belongs to you. As for the rest of the estate ... that's one of the things I wanted to talk to you about. It's too soon to discuss the details, but I'd like to set up a charitable foundation. What do you think?"

Mandy was quick to respond. "Daddy wouldn't like that. You know he didn't approve of giving to charities. He thought the administrators were paid much more than they were worth."

Belle nodded, remembering Lin's stand on the subject. "Our foundation would be different. We'd set certain standards. But we don't have to discuss it now. It will be a while before the will is probated. In the meantime, you can be thinking about it."

Mandy eyed her suspiciously. "Are you really going to give it all away?"

"Absolutely. You're set for life and I don't want it. I've got a nice little nest egg and I–oh, that reminds me. Did I tell you about winning the jackpot in Biloxi? No, I don't believe I did. Well, that was so exciting. What happened was ...." She launched into the story as though telling it to an old friend she hadn't seen in a while. Maybe, when Mandy was older, that's what they could become–dear friends.

. . .

The following morning, at Belle's request, everyone sat down to breakfast together. Jerry and Martha had gone home the previous night, so it was just the five of them: Edith, Jesse, Mandy, Art, and Belle. Iris Hansen had prepared an egg and sausage casserole, Edith had made blueberry muffins, and Belle had set out an assortment of fruit. As they passed the dishes, the conversation consisted of polite chit-chat, mostly about yesterday's unusual weather and the warming trend predicted for today. They could be strangers, seated at one end of a community table at a country inn.

Until the talk turned personal.

"I'll swan, Kathleen," Edith said, "I don't know why y'all have to go running off today. You just got here. Seems like you can't wait to get clear of here."

"We have jobs, Mother."

"Humph," Edith grunted. "That's the silliest thing I ever heard. What's a person with all the money in the world want with a job?"

"Self-respect, Mother."

"If you had any respect you wouldn't go running off like this. You'd stay here and see to it that Mandy goes back to school instead of flying off to some God-forsaken country in the middle of nowhere."

Belle glanced in her daughter's direction. Mandy was looking down at her grapefruit, barely concealing the smirk on her face.

"Mandy's quite capable of making her own decisions, Mother," Belle said. "Personally, I think it'll do her a world of good to get away for a while. Neither one of us has any interest in being an object of curiosity."

Edith set her fork on her plate. Wagging a finger at Belle, she said, "Don't you use that tone with me, Missy." She reined in her finger and put her hand on the table. "What's that mean, anyway? *Object of curiosity*?"

"It means that half the people here last night were trying to get a look at how rich folks live. They were also helping themselves to some fine food and drinks, thanks to you and your church ladies."

"Well, I never!" Edith said. "Did you hear that Jesse? Your very own flesh and blood is saying I catered to a bunch of busybodies."

"Please, Mother, that's not what I said. You couldn't know who was who. You did a wonderful job, didn't she, Mandy?"

Mandy looked up from her grapefruit. "You and the church ladies outdid yourselves, Grandma. All my friends were talking about how lucky I was to have a grandmother like you."

Edith preened. "Well, it's nice to know someone appreciates me. I never worked so hard in all my born days. After we got in bed last night, I said to Jesse, I said, Jesse, I'm plumb tuckered out. You best take me home tomorrow. I won't be worth a plug nickel if'n I don't get me some rest."

A thought sprang into Belle's head. "I have an idea," she said. "Why don't you and Daddy go down to Florida for a week or two. Get away from it all and just relax and do nothing."

Edith looked at her as though she'd grown another head. "I do declare, Kathleen, you come up with the most peculiar notions." She turned to Jesse. "Did you hear what your daughter said?"

"Yep, I heard," Jesse said. "Sounds like a right good idea."

"Jesse Weldon, have you lost your mind? I've got circle meeting on Tuesday, the box supper on Wednesday, and the bake sale next Saturday. Who you think is going to take charge of things if I was to run off to sun myself?"

"What if you was to drop dead, Edith? Like Lin did. I reckon the ladies would just have to manage without you."

A collective gasp came from the three women. Whether from the reference to Lin's sudden death or from the shock of hearing Jesse talk back, only the women knew. But to the portraits on the wall it looked like business as usual. Belle took a bite of egg casserole, Mandy dug another wedge out of her grapefruit, Art buttered a muffin, Edith stirred her coffee, and Jesse sat deep in thought.

Presently, he said, "Well, it's the durn truth. None of us knows when our time's coming so we ought to shed clear of all the nonsense. That church roof ain't gonna cave in if you're not there to hold it up, Edith. I say we oughta go. I've always wanted to see that Epcot Center, and with the way my eyes are failing, if we don't hurry up you're gonna be leading a blind man around."

While waiting for Edith's reaction, four pairs of eyes cast surreptitious glances her way. They were not the eyes on the wall.

"What about that Universal Studio they got down there?" she said. "And that Sea World. I've heard tell they got a real whale that does tricks. And dolphins that'll eat right out of your hand. Have you ever?" She marveled at the thought. "I reckon we could get us a motel room somewhere close by. That way we wouldn't have to drive all over creation. What do you think, Kathleen? Reckon we could get a place with a kitchenette? We could eat most of our meals in the room.

It'd save us a whole bundle of money."

Belle could hardly contain herself. Except for a disastrous trip to St. Augustine when she was eight years old, she couldn't remember her parents ever taking a vacation. "Hang the money, Mother. We'll make reservations at the finest hotel down there. If you don't feel up to going out to eat, you can order room service. We'll also hire a driver to chauffeur you around. There's no sense in Daddy trying to find his way. Oh, you'll have the time of your lives. My treat."

Edith sniffed her nose and looked at Jesse. "Listen to Miss Money Bags. She just can't wait to start spending her inheritance. It's a crime is what it is." Her narrowed eyes shifted to Belle. "You ought to be ashamed of yourself. That money could be put to better use than throwing it away on fancy hotels and folderol such as that."

Much to Belle's surprise, Mandy rushed to her defense. "That's not fair, Grandma. Mother's not going to spend her inheritance. She's got her own money. Money she's earned as an artist, and money she won in a jackpot."

It was all Belle could do to sit still. She wanted to jump up and shout hallelujah. She wanted to run to the other side of the table and hug Mandy's neck. Her daughter had called her an artist. What's more, she'd sounded proud when she said it. Oh yes, there was hope for them yet.

"What's she talking about?" Edith wanted to know. "What jackpot?"

Belle turned to Art. "Do you mind? You tell it so well."

Art shrugged. "Why not. Okay, here's the skinny. After we hit a brick wall in Laurel–that's in Mississippi–we headed down to Biloxi. I'm thinking ..."

Content to listen, Belle sat back and relaxed. But not before mouthing her thanks to Mandy and exchanging conspiratorial grins with her.

Nineteen

"Oh, it's so good to be home," Belle said, sliding into her chair at the kitchen table. "It seems like we've been gone a year." Before her sat a bowl of cheese grits, a glass of tomato juice and a cup of black coffee.

"You can say that again," Art said, digging into his bowl of cereal.

She laughed. "I already did. Several times, starting last night." She scooped up a spoonful of grits. Sunlight streamed through the window over the sink, throwing golden stripes across the middle of the table and down a length of linoleum. The thermometer outside the back door read sixty-seven degrees. A high of eighty, with no rain on the horizon, was predicted. Perfect porch weather, she thought, picturing the two of them whiling away an hour or two in the rocking chairs.

Art swallowed his last bite of cereal and pushed the empty bowl aside. "Y'know," he said, "for all the dough they spent on that castle you'd think they'd have a decent mattress. My back is killing me. One wrong move and I'm on the floor. Don't even think about trying to pick me up."

Belle could sympathize. She ached all over. She'd thought it was from tension, but maybe it had been the mattress. It had been too soft, like sleeping on a pile of downy feathers. Last night, when she'd finally climbed in her bed here at Art's, the mattress felt like a board. She supposed her bones needed time to readjust.

"The long drive home didn't help," she said. "I thought we'd never get here." First she'd had a meeting with Jerry at his office in downtown Atlanta. From there she and Art had gone to Hartsfield International Airport to see Mandy and Lana off to Costa Rica. Thank goodness Art had had the foresight to pack the cab before they left Stone Mountain. Otherwise, they would have had to return to Mallory House for their luggage. As it was, they left town from Hartsfield soon after the girls were airborne. Even so, they didn't make it home until a little after two in the morning.

"All I gotta say is, the easy life ain't for me. My butt aches from sitting so much."

"My mind aches," Belle said. "I honestly think mental stress takes a far greater toll on a person than physical stress. I can stand on a platform and paint all day long and not feel a bit tired, but put me in a room with my mother and in three minutes I'm exhausted."

"She's something alright. Old Jesse put her in her place though. Do you think they'll go to Florida?"

"Oh, yes. Daddy's determined. Martha said she'd have her travel agent make all the arrangements. I just hope Mother loosens up enough to enjoy it."

"Don't bet on it."

"If Daddy keeps standing up to her she won't have much choice. I was so proud of him. He looked downright perky when they left the house."

"Yeah, and the kid didn't do too bad neither."

"Oh, I know. Did you hear her call me an artist? I almost fell out of my chair."

"Yeah, I heard. The kid's okay. Full of herself, but when push comes to shove she's okay."

"It's funny," Belle mused aloud, "if Lin hadn't died chances are we would never have talked things out. Well, maybe never is too strong a word, but it might never have happened. Not that I'm glad Lin died, mind you. It's just strange how things work out. When the twins died it drove Lin and me apart, yet when he died it helped bring me and Mandy together. Of course we've still got a ways to go, but at least we got a start."

"Wish I could say the same about my kids," Art said.

She reached across the table and covered his hand with hers. "You will, Art. You just have to have faith."

"It ain't easy," he said.

She withdrew her hand. "Well, maybe our next trip should be up to New Jersey."

"No way. They wanna see me they can come down here."

"Now you're talking," she cheered.

"Me and my big mouth."

"*Au contraire*," she said. "It shows that you're thinking about it. And that's all I have to say on the subject. For now."

"That's what I'm afraid of."

Her eyes lit on the prescription bottles he kept on the table, one to control his blood pressure, the other for diabetes. "Don't forget to take your pills."

"Bossy broad," he muttered. He uncapped the first bottle, tapped out two pills, popped them in his mouth and swallowed them down with water. He repeated the process with the other bottle.

"Good boy," she said. "Shouldn't you be seeing the doctor soon?"

He held up a hand. "Don't start."

"Alright, already," she mimicked and took another bite of grits.

"What're you gonna do today?" he asked.

She blotted her lips with a napkin. "Well, first I'm going to call my folks and let them know we made it back in one piece. Then I'll call Mammy Daisy and tell her the same thing. Then, if Marge is back, I'll call her. And then I'll unpack." She'd been too tired to do it when they got home. "After that I was hoping we could sit on the porch and watch the world go by."

"You ain't going to work?"

"It's Saturday, remember? Besides, I'll be lucky to make it through the day without a nap. How about you?"

"I'm thinking I'll wash the cab. Maybe give her a wax job. It all depends."

"On what?"

"On my back."

"Is it that bad?"

"You better believe it. Feels like my spine's ready to crack wide open."

"Oh dear. Do you have any liniment I could rub on it?"

"Naw, that stuff burns my skin."

"How about a heating pad?"

"Forget about it. I should've kept my mouth shut."

"No secrets, remember?"

"Talk about secrets ... you never did tell me if you feel guilty about Lin dying like that."

The question took her by surprise. Where had it come from? "Guilty? Why would I feel guilty?"

He shrugged. "The guy comes down here. He tries to get you to go home with him. You won't. The next thing you know he drops dead."

Disbelief flooded her face. "Are you saying my refusal to go with him caused him to have a heart attack?"

"No, that ain't what I'm saying. But you gotta admit it coulda had something to do with it."

Offended by the assumption, she spoke in clipped tones. "I hardly think so. Anyone who looked at him could tell he was not a well man. He had deep hollows around his eyes and they were red and puffy. His skin looked dried out, like it was parched or something, and it had a sickly yellowish cast to it. I even remarked on it. He didn't come right out and say so, but he intimated that he was not in the best of health. Of course I could tell that by looking at him."

"Yeah, well, did'ya ever think he knew he was gonna die and he wanted you to be with him?"

"What are you implying? That I should have gone with him?"

He gave another shrug.

She got up from her chair and stood glaring down on him. "Art Barkoff, how could you? And I thought I knew you. I thought you were my friend. My best friend in the whole world." She started to walk off.

"Hold on a minute," he said. "Here's another question for you. Does the kid know about him coming down here?"

"I don't think so. At one point I thought about telling her, but then I decided against it. We had so many other things to talk about. Why do you ask?"

"No reason," he said. "Just wondering."

She returned to her chair and sank into it, all the steam from her anger gone in a puff. If Mandy had known about her father's trip to New Orleans and Belle's refusal to accompany him home, it could explain why she'd been so hostile that first night in the library. Then again, if she'd known she would have been more than hostile, she would have made–more like screamed–terrible accusations.

"I'm certain she doesn't know," Belle said. "And as far as I'm concerned, she doesn't need to know. It's useless information. As for me contributing to Lin's death because I wouldn't go home with him, you can think what you like. But I don't believe it for one minute."

"Okay, okay, I was just asking in case you was worried about it."

"Well I'm not. Sad and sorry, yes, but not worried or guilty."

"Forget I mentioned it," Art said.

"I already have." She picked up her spoon and attacked her grits.

Art watched her gobble the stuff down. How she could stand to eat the same boring foods day after day he didn't know. Left up to him he'd have bacon and eggs, ham and biscuits, or pancakes every morning. This rabbit food left him as empty as he started. That was one good thing about Edith. The woman knew the way to a man's stomach. So did Mammy Daisy. Not Belle. She worried too much about calories and cholesterol and all that crap. He knew he was supposed to watch his diet, but this was ridiculous.

"Y'know what I'm craving?" he asked.

"What?"

"A muffuletta. Whaddaya say I pick some stuff up at Central Grocery and we eat lunch at Washington Square."

"Oh my," she said. "That sounds tempting."

"C'mon. It won't kill me to eat half a sandwich and a few mushrooms."

"Well," she said, dragging the word out. "I don't suppose it would hurt. It's a fine day for a picnic, and I haven't been to the park in ages."

"Then it's all set. I'll pick up the grub and meet you there at twelve sharp."

"Meet me? Where are you going?"

"I decided to have the cab detailed. That is if my regular guy can work it in. You can take Tallulah for a spin." He got a kick out of her naming the car. He'd bought the Checker new in 1971 and had never thought of giving her a name.

"Tallulah will have to wait," she said. "It's too pretty a day to drive. I'd rather walk. And instead of calling Mammy, I'll stop by Hope Haven on my way."

"See if she can spare a coupla cookies for our dessert." He pushed up from the table. "Oh, and Belle ... what I said about Lin ... I was just making sure you didn't have no regrets. You get my drift? About moving in with me instead of going back."

She regarded him solemnly. "No regrets."

"Okay, then. See you later."

"Be careful of your back."

He was nearing the door when she called to him. "Hey! Look at this mess you left me with! Do I look like a maid or something?"

He gave her a backhanded wave and kept going. A second later she could hear him whistling.

"Brat!" she hollered and laughed.

• • •

She had unpacked her clothes and was putting her suitcase in the hall storage closet when a knock sounded at the door. The knock was followed by a man's voice. "Hallo! You in there, Art?"

Unaccustomed to having anyone drop by, much less a man, and wondering whether or not to answer, Belle tiptoed to a spot where she could see out but the person couldn't see her. She was surprised to see not one but two men standing on the porch, their gazes fixed on something in the side yard. Tallulah, perhaps.

From where she stood, she guessed the men to be in their sixties. The one wearing a blue work shirt, khaki pants, and loafers had a head full of wiry smoke-gray hair. He was slim and well over six-feet. The other man had a bald pate with wispy tufts of brown over his ears. Portly and about five-nine, he was wearing Army fatigues and combat boots. After deciding they looked perfectly harmless, Belle went to the door.

"Hello," she said through the screen. "Can I help you?"

They turned as one, looked at her, looked at each other, then back at her. Their eyes glinted with mischief when the one with the hair said, "You don't look a bit like Art."

"Not a bit," echoed the baldheaded one.

They laughed, showing what looked to be identical rows of pearly white teeth.

"Thank goodness for that," she said. "My name is Belle Reve. I live here now."

At that, the two men inclined their heads toward one another and whispered loud enough for her to hear. "She must be the one."

"A perfect doll."

"Precious."

"Lucky Art."

Then they faced Belle. "I'm James," said the one with the hair.

"And I'm Henry."

"We're your neighbors."

"The ones who helped Art furnish the house."

Belle, who hadn't known what to make of them, gave them a big smile. "Oh, I've been wanting to meet you," she gushed. "You do such beautiful work. I can't wait to see your shop." She opened the door. "Come in, come in. I have a fresh pot of coffee. Please join me."

"We'd be honored," said James.

"We've been dying to meet you too," said Henry with a little bow.

On the way to the kitchen, with Belle in the lead, the men stopped in the den and proceeded to carry on a conversation as though she weren't there.

"That's where he wants to put the chest," James said.

"Hmmm," said Henry, eyeing the spot. "He needs the elephant table to go next to it."

"No, no, no. The elephant would look gauche there. Too close to the bookcase."

"Hmmm, maybe you're right. Too bad he doesn't have room for the spinet."

"Maybe the spinning wheel."

"No, no, no. Too Americana."

"His kitchen's Americana."

"Who wants a spinning wheel in his kitchen?"

"It'd be unique. A conversation piece."

"Hmmm, maybe if we set a slop jar next to it. Give it that homey feel."

"Art's aYankee. He wouldn't know what a slop jar is."

Henry chuckled into his hand. "And we won't tell him."

"You devil."

"We'll tell him it's a spittoon," Henry said and laughed out loud.

Belle, who'd lingered in the doorway to the kitchen, giggled.

The men's heads turned her way. Both looked abashed. "Please forgive us," said James. "We've been terribly impolite."

"Terribly," Henry agreed.

"Oh," said Belle with a wave of her hand. "I love hearing you talk. I think it's fascinating."

They flashed their pearly whites. "That's because you're an artist.

Art has told us all about your marvelous murals. Is the offer of coffee still open?"

"Of course." She preceded them into the kitchen.

Because they seemed like refined gentlemen, she retrieved Art's best cups and saucers from a top shelf. Coffee mugs with Havoline emblazoned on them simply would not do. She also set out the matching creamer and sugar bowl, spoons, and napkins. As an afterthought, she placed some dried figs on a dish.

"These are the only sweets I have," she said, setting the dish on the table. We just returned from Atlanta and I haven't had time to shop."

"That's quite all right," James said.

"What were you doing in Atlanta?" asked Henry.

"Attending a funeral."

"Oh, we're sorry to hear that."

"Very sorry."

"A close relative?"

"No, my ex-husband." She settled in the chair across from them. "Actually, he was still my husband, but I didn't know that. I thought he'd signed the divorce papers last fall, but as things turned out, he didn't. So instead of being a divorcée, I'm a widow. Anyway, my daughter Mandy–she's nineteen–was devastated, and my parents were there, and it was all very stressful."

"We can imagine," James said with a glance at Henry.

"Stressful indeed," said Henry.

A strained silence fell over the room, as though none of them knew what to say next.

Belle sat perfectly still, gazing fixedly at the figs. Henry and James toyed with their spoons, each waiting for the other one to change the subject.

At last James gave a polite cough and said, "So, you're a Georgia peach."

"And a beautiful peach at that," said Henry, beaming a smile.

A blush colored Belle's cheeks. "You're too kind."

She looked from one to the other, studying their features. Though they shared certain mannerisms they didn't bear the slightest resemblance to one another. James had deep-set brown eyes, a long patrician nose, and a pointed jaw with a cleft in its center. Henry's bluish-green eyes were round and expressive. He had a pug nose and a square jaw.

"Art told me you were brothers," she said, "but you don't look a bit alike."

"Art's mistaken," James said with a laugh. "We're not brothers."

"We're lovers."

"Oh, then that explains it."

"Explains what?" James asked.

"Do tell," Henry said, sitting forward in his seat, all ears.

"Why you don't look alike. Not that all brothers do. Oh, I remember when I was little. At Christmastime, people would ask me what I wanted Santa Claus to bring me, and I always told them I wanted a big brother. And every year I'd be crushed when I didn't get one. It would have been so nice to have someone to look out for me. You know, to chase the bullies away ... that sort of thing."

"No one looked out for you?" asked James.

"Not a single soul?" Henry said.

"No, not really. Not when it counted, like on the way to and from school and on the playground. There was this one boy who liked to scare me. He'd hide behind a tree or a fence and then jump out and make these horrible faces. I'd try my best to avoid him. I'd go out of my way to get to school, but somehow he always knew where I was."

"Did you tell on him?"

"I would hope so."

"Oh, no," she said. "That would have made it worse. I just kept trying to dodge him. My father did his best to look out for me, but he couldn't be everywhere. Besides, he had to be careful because my mother was jealous. She thought I loved him more than I loved her, which I did, but I tried not to show it. Does that make any sense?"

"Yes," James said

"Perfect sense," said Henry

She went on. "I was what they used to call a change-of-life baby. My mother was forty-two when she had me. She stayed in the house almost the entire nine months because she was so ashamed of being pregnant. Isn't that sad? Nowadays women in their fifties are having babies. Heavens, I read about a woman in her sixties."

"Perish the thought," said James.

"Amen," said Henry.

"Well, I don't have to worry about that. I had a hysterectomy years ago. I was heartbroken, of course, but I've gotten over it."

"That's good."

"And you have a daughter," Henry reminded.

"Yes, I have a daughter." She started to tell them about Mandy's plans to become a lawyer, but caught herself. "Goodness," she said. "I haven't let you get a word in edgewise. You'd think I'd be tired of talking. It seems like that's all I've done for the past three days. Sitting and talking. Now it's your turn. Tell me where you're from."

"Henry's from all over the world," James said. "His father was a master sergeant, and Henry's a retired paratrooper. He's been in New Orleans–" he looked at Henry. "What? Eleven years now?"

"Eleven years in June."

"I thought that was about right." He looked at Belle. "I was born and raised in Mobile. Worked on oil rigs most of my life."

"Very dangerous work," added Henry, as though being a paratrooper wasn't.

"My," she said. "Such interesting backgrounds. How did you meet?"

As usual, James was the first to reply. "We met about eight years ago at an estate sale." He smiled at Henry and looked back at Belle. "Neither one of us had ever had a home of our own until we moved here. We'd always rented, so we were just starting to buy furniture."

Henry took up where James left off. "We kept bidding against each other, which showed how much we liked the same things."

"It also drove the prices up," James interjected. "Until we realized we liked each other more than we liked antiques."

"Here, here," said Henry, chuckling and nudging James with a shoulder.

James nudged him back and went on. "Since mine was the larger of our two houses, we decided to sell Henry's place and he moved in with me"

"Thus combining our collections," added Henry.

"But instead of quitting, we kept going to sales."

"And auctions and flea markets."

"And one thing led to another."

Belle clapped her hands together and said, "It must have been fate. You two meeting at the sale."

"Something like that."

"How did you meet Art?" Henry asked.

"Oh my, that's a long story. Are you sure you want to hear it?"

"We'd be delighted."

"Do tell."

"Well, I'll try to be brief. I came here last September. I took the train all the way from Atlanta. It was the first time I'd ever been anywhere by myself and it was very scary. But, as you can see, I made it. I'd planned to take the streetcar named Desire, transfer to the one called Cemeteries, and get off at Elysian Fields. But then Mister Walkie-Talkie–he was the security guard at the train station–told me the only streetcar left was the one on St. Charles. Well, that threw me into a tizzy. The guard said I should take a cab. So I looked them over and decided on the shiny yellow Checker. And guess who it belonged to."

"Art!" they chorused.

"Exactly. So he took me to the Kowalskis' house, at six-thirty-two Elysian Fields, but when I got there the house belonged to a group of lawyers. It was pitch dark out and I was very tired. I'd hoped to spend the night with Stella and Stanley, but what with the lawyers and everything I had no idea where they were. They could've died for all I knew. Well, you can imagine how panicky I felt. Here I was in a .

strange town with no place to stay. I hadn't eaten all day and I was starving. But I'm happy to say Art came to my rescue and we've been best friends ever since."

"Aha."

"Bully for Art."

"I don't know what would have become of me if it hadn't been for him. He's my hero. The big brother I never had."

"Did you ever find–who was it? Stanley?"

"Stanley and Stella," Henry corrected.

"No, sad to say, I didn't. They seem to have disappeared off the face of the earth. Blanche, too. She's the one I actually came to see. We've looked everywhere and we still can't find her."

Both pairs of eyebrows went up. "Blanche?"

"Yes. Blanche DuBois."

"Long live Blanche!" James cried.

"Here, here!" cheered Henry.

A wild fluttering began in the pit of Belle's stomach. "Do you know Blanche?" she asked, eyes wide with hope.

"We don't actually *know* her," said James.

"We know *of* her," said Henry.

Belle folded her hands over her chest. "Oh, I can't tell you how happy that makes me. Most of the people I talk to about Blanche look at me like I'm some kind of nut."

"We don't think you're nuts."

"Not at all."

"Thank you. That really means a lot to me. Especially after what Mandy said. She's never even heard of Blanche and–oh, never mind." She noticed that their cups were empty. "Dear me, I've just rattled on and on. Would you care for more coffee?

"We'd love some."

"Please," said Henry.

She took their cups to the sink, emptied the dregs, rinsed them out, and poured refills. Her own cup still sat on the table, the untouched coffee gone cold.

Returning to her seat, she said, "Oh, I'm so glad you're here. I've been wanting to talk to you about a clock for Art. It's a surprise, a belated thank you gift for taking me to Mississippi. I'd like an old one that chimes on the quarter hour. What would you recommend?"

"That would depend on your price range," James said.

"And where you plan to put it," Henry added.

"Well, I can't afford anything too expensive. Would three-hundred dollars buy a nice clock? I thought I'd leave where to put it up to you two."

The men each set an elbow on the table, braced the corresponding jaw with a hand and, without saying a word, studied each other as though transmitting signals through brain waves. Several moments later, each gave a nod as though sealing a deal. They sat up straight and looked at her. Again, James was the first to speak.

"We'll hang the banjo clock above the new chest."

"He'll love it," said Henry.

Belle had never heard of a banjo clock, but it had to be special if James and Henry liked it.

"Would you like us to hang it now?"

"We could set the chest up as well. It's ready to be delivered."

"Oh, goodie," she said, tingling with excitement. "Could I help?"

"Most certainly," said James.

"We'd be delighted," said Henry.

"By the way," James said, standing. "What were you doing in Mississippi?"

"Looking for Blanche."

"Long live Blanche!"

"Here, here!"

She gave them her special smile.

The three of them filed out of the house. When they reached the front walkway, James came to a stop. He looked at Belle and said, "We have a confession to make."

"Yes, we do," said Henry.

"We came calling to ask about the woody."

"Is it yours?"

At first she didn't know what they were talking about and then it dawned on her. "Oh, you mean Tallulah. Yes, she's mine. Do you like her?"

"We adore her. Very classy."

"*Tres* chic."

"Thank you," she said, bursting with pride. "Would you like to go for a ride?"

"We'd love it," said James.

"Wheeeee," said Henry, rubbing his palms together. "What fun."

Belle said, "I'll get the keys." She whirled around and headed back into the house. What a glorious day, she thought, and it had only just begun.

· · ·

What Art couldn't get out of his head was how aroused he'd gotten when he held Belle after the memorial service. There had been times in the past months when he'd had a trouble catching his breath or he'd felt a tightening in his gut. He'd wanted to press his lips to hers, have her run her fingers through his hair, hold his head in both her hands and pull him tighter. He'd wanted to go on holding her till doomsday, but his privates had never stood at attention. He'd thought those days were gone forever.

Sure, he'd had fantasies about her, especially since she'd moved in. He'd have to be deaf, dumb and blind not to. He'd dreamed she was lying next to him in bed, curled up against him spoon-fashion. They'd be wide awake, content to just lie there and do nothing but snuggle. He'd wondered what she looked like without her clothes on. Sometimes, when he heard the water running in the shower, he pictured her standing there naked, soaping herself all over, rubbing the suds away. He didn't dwell on it, just had these fleeting thoughts. Chalked it up to wishful thinking.

But now, after what happened in Georgia, it worried him. What would happen the next time he held her? And he would hold her. Of that he was sure. What was he supposed to do when she needed a hug? Push her away? Turn his back on her?

Take this morning. He'd gotten turned on just by looking at her. She'd been sitting there, all rosy and sweet-smelling after her shower, her hair still damp, dressed in the yellow sweater and the tan pants that showed off her curves. She hadn't even looked at him in any special way; she'd been jabbering away like she usually did, and he'd gotten a sudden urge to pick her up, aching back and all, and carry her off to bed. So what did he do about it? He'd turned mean. Brought up all that stuff about Lin dropping dead. As if she'd killed him. As if any of it was her fault. Then he'd walked out on her, leaving her with his mess to clean up.

What was happening to him? Why all of a sudden? Maybe the pills he was taking were making him horny. Maybe he was having what they called a mid-life crisis. Maybe he was lapsing into his second childhood–the teen years. All he knew was he had to get hold of himself. Either that or ask her to marry him.

Whoa! Where'd that come from? He was already married, for crissakes, and once was enough.

Even if he wasn't married he couldn't marry Belle. Not now. She'd think he was marrying her for her money.

Wait a minute. What money? She was gonna give it all away. At first he'd thought that was a crazy idea, but the more he thought about it the more relieved he was. And it had nothing to do with him thinking about marrying her. That kind of money was too heavy a load–it'd scare her to death. Him, too. She'd be thinking about it, worrying about it, getting ulcers over it. She'd have vultures circling around, wanting a piece of her hide. She might even be kidnapped! She wouldn't be able to go out of the house without somebody pestering her. They'd have to build a fortress to keep the scavengers out. What kind of life would that be? Not worth a damn. She'd probably start having those attacks again. Yeah, he had to hand it to her; she'd been smart to dump it in Jerry's lap. Let him and the team worry about it.

Which led him back to his original problem and what to do about it. Maybe he should talk to Marge. Not about his condition, but whether or not she thought Belle would marry him–*if* he asked her. But first he'd better think about getting a divorce. Man oh man, life sure could get complicated.

Suddenly aware of his surroundings, he saw that the shop's waiting room had emptied out. He looked at the clock on the wall across from the black vinyl couch. Eleven-fourteen. Sammy would be taking his lunch break at eleven-thirty, which meant he should be about finished with the cab. He hadn't planned on getting her detailed–she wasn't due till next fall–he'd just wanted an excuse to get out of the house.

Conscious of his back, he eased himself to the edge of the couch, twisted around so he could brace his hands against the arm, then slowly pushed himself up. Despite his caution, it hurt like hell. It also took a moment for him to stand up straight. Maybe a heating pad wasn't such a bad idea. Better yet, maybe Belle would give him a massage.

Twenty

Still in high spirits from her visit with James and Henry, Belle skipped up the steps to Hope Haven's front door. Swinging it wide without bothering to knock, she called, "Yoo hoo! Anybody home?"

Mammy Daisy answered from the back of the house. "That you, sugar!"

"Yes, ma'am!" Belle said, advancing toward the kitchen.

She met up with Mammy near the end of the front hall. After a warm embrace, Mammy put a partially floured hand to her cheek and patted it tenderly. "Child, you is a sight for sore eyes. Thank you, Lord," she said, casting a glance heavenward. "I been so worried. We all been worried. 'Fraid you wouldn't come back."

"I missed you, too," Belle said. "And you needn't have worried about me coming back. This is my home, and you're my Mammy." She gave her another hug.

A frown clouded Mammy's face. Averting her eyes from Belle's gaze, she gathered the hem of her apron and examined it as though searching for loose threads. By the time she turned the fabric loose and looked up, she'd put on a brave face. "Come sit and tell me all about it."

Belle saw straight through her. "Something's wrong, I can feel it in my bones. What is it?"

"I gots to get off my feet," Mammy said. She shuffled off, her ever-present terry cloth slippers slapping at her heels.

Belle was comforted by the mouth-watering aromas that drifted from the kitchen. Nothing could be too wrong, she thought, else Mammy would've been too upset to cook. Sniffing the air, she detected something sweet, something tangy, and the unmistakable scent of roasting meat. She tried to guess what it was. A pork loin rubbed with a clove of garlic, she decided. No one, not her mother or any of the church ladies, could cook pork like Mammy. It came out so tender you could cut it with a fork, and though she'd tried to duplicate it she'd never succeeded.

"Mmmm, that smells so good," she said, settling in her old chair cater-cornered to Mammy's.

"Child, you is always sayin' that."

Belle reached over and chucked her under the chin. "That's because it's true. Now, tell me what's wrong."

Mammy pulled a long face. "We gots troubles, sugar. They's talkin' 'bout closing this here house down."

The news was so unexpected it took a moment for Belle to process it. "This house?" she said. "Who's talking about closing it?"

"Them mental health folks. They come down from Jackson. Been snoopin' around, askin' questions. Ask to see a sample of my menus and such as that. I don't have no menus, I told 'em, I just cooks the food my girls like. They asked did I have a budget and what'd I do 'bout petty cash. They even asked how many baths did the girls take and did we burn lights all night. Foolish mess like that. Said somethin' about money bein' cut and they was fixin' to get rid of waste. I didn't say nothin' to y'all 'cause I don't know nothin'. Wish Marge was here. Her mama's gettin' worser and worser. Don't know when she'll be back. But I been prayin' on it. I been prayin' real hard."

"Well," said Belle. Never in her wildest dreams did she imagine Hope Haven could cease to exist. As far as she was concerned, it was a permanent fixture, like the statue of Andrew Jackson at Jackson Square. She shuddered to think what would have become of her, the other girls, and all those who came before them, had Hope Haven not been here. That anyone could consider closing it down was inconceivable.

"We can't let that happen," she said.

A glimmer of hope appeared in Mammy's dark eyes. "You gonna try an' stop 'em?"

"I most certainly am. But first I've got to find out who they are. Did they give you their names?"

"They was two men and one woman. Didn't none of 'em tell me who they was."

That infuriated Belle. How dare they come in here and snoop around, asking all sorts of questions, silly questions at that, without identifying themselves. Who did they think they were? Didn't they know Mammy Daisy was a colleague and not a maid. Even if she was a maid she deserved the courtesy of an introduction.

"You said they came down from Jackson."

"That's what the lady said."

"Believe me, Mammy, she was no lady."

The remark went over Mammy's head. "What is we goin' to do if they close us down?"

"They're not going to close us down," Belle said, her mind reeling.

"What you gonna do?"

"I'm not sure, but I'll think of something."

"I be countin' on you, sugar," Mammy said. "You an' the Lord."

Belle laughed. "Well, between the two of us we ought to be able to make things right. I'm going to find out who those people are, and then I'm going to find out why they came here. In the meantime, try not to think about it."

"I'll do my best, sugar," Mammy said.

"Good. Now, tell me about the girls. Does Gloria have a new roommate yet? Has Darleen been by? Does Janette still like her job?

Have you heard from Boots? What about Fran? And Gracie and Millie. Oh, I feel so out of touch."

"Slow down, sugar." Mammy said. "You be talkin' so fast I can't keep up. 'Sides, I wanna hear about you. How'd that daughter treat you? How's your folks doin'?"

Knowing she wouldn't get any news until she gave a full report, Belle launched into a condensed version of her stay at Mallory House. While she talked, Mammy made all the appropriate noises and gestures. With the girls out and about, it was the first time the two of them had been alone in the house since the day Belle entered Hope Haven as a resident. That she might never have met and come to love Mammy and the girls was impossible to contemplate. The important thing was she had, and, if she had her way, so would all the women who were yet to come.

• • •

Standing at the northwest gate to Washington Square, Belle could not believe her eyes. Always before, when she'd visited the park, it had been mostly deserted. Thinking back on the past six months she could recall having seen only one stranger, an older man wearing a hat decorated with fishing lures, and he was merely passing through. She and Marge had held a therapy session here once, over there on the bench she'd claimed as her own. Once or twice she'd met Art here. But most of the time she'd been alone with her thoughts. She'd done some of her best thinking here.

And because she could sit and gaze across the street at the dusty rose house on the corner of Royal and Elysian Fields–the house where Stella and Stanley had lived and where Blanche had come to stay–she'd felt closer to Blanche. Had actually felt her presence. But now everything had changed. And it had taken place in just a few short weeks.

While she'd been preoccupied with work and adjusting to life with Art, someone had turned the park into a neighborhood gathering place suitable for all ages. A playground for the children had been added. It was equipped with swings and slides, a jungle gym, sandbox and a twirl-a-whirl. Diagonally across from the play area and shaded by a red and white striped canopy was a meeting place for adults.

The trees and shrubs looked newly trimmed, the flower beds were free of weeds; the benches, the gas lamps, and the wrought iron fence and four corner gates that enclosed the park wore fresh coats of black paint. And the grass looked greener and thicker than ever before. In the past, Belle had picked up the trash that had blown in from the street or been dropped by pedestrians taking a shortcut through the park. Today, not a speck of litter could be seen.

Overall, the park looked brand new, as if it had sprung up overnight, and, although she was happy for the neighborhood, she felt a deep sense of regret. Blanche no longer lingered here. Belle could feel it in her bones–the spirit of Washington Square had moved on.

Too downhearted to sit in her usual spot near Elysian Fields, the bench where she imagined Blanche had sat to ponder her future, Belle sought an isolated place on the Frenchmen Street side of the park. Perhaps there she could quiet her mind while waiting for Art.

On the way she noticed a sign affixed to a wooden stake set into the ground amid a bed of Ligustrum and daylilies. Curious, she moved close enough to read what it said: "This Area Maintained Thanks To The Gay & Lesbian Building Association." Below the words someone had drawn a round-headed figure with a smiley face and upraised arms. Belle had no idea what the drawing and the rainbow colors symbolized, but the sign helped to lighten her mood.

Once seated, she took a good look around. On the far side of the park, several young women were supervising a group of children on the playground. A lone male stood apart from them, helping a small child climb the ladder to the top of a slide. High-pitched squeals and laughter, interrupted by an occasional shout, floated back to her. In another area of the park, two older women wearing straw sun hats sat with their heads together, their hands in constant motion as they chatted. About twenty yards from the women a young couple in tank tops and shorts lay facing one another on a plaid blanket. While she watched, the girl raised up, leaned over her companion, said something in his ear and then nuzzled him.

Belle felt her heart expanding as she took it all in. It had been selfish of her to want the park all to herself–selfish to want to keep Blanche's spirit there. Now, thanks to the gays and lesbians involved, it was being put to its intended use. What good was a park that didn't bring pleasure to people wanting to enjoy some kind of outdoor activity? Just an empty block of greenery which might as well be a cement parking lot.

Before she had time to gather her thoughts, she heard footsteps crunching behind her. She glanced over her shoulder and saw Art carrying the familiar paper bags that contained their lunch. He was walking slowly and stiffly, trying unsuccessfully to hide the pain he was in. When he drew close enough she stood up and greeted him with a quick kiss.

"Your back is worse," she stated flatly. "When are you going to do something about it?"

"Don't start with me," he grumbled, setting the bags on the bench.

She gave an exasperated sigh. "Why are you so stubborn?"

"Why are you such a nosy broad?"

She shook her head. "I give up."

"That's my girl," he said. "Let's eat."

They settled on the bench with the bags between them. "Well," she said, "since I'm not allowed to nag you about your back, tell me if you notice anything different."

He looked her over from head to toe and ventured a guess. "You done something to your hair?"

"No, silly. It's the park."

He took a look around. "How 'bout that. If I didn't know better I'd think I was in the wrong place."

"That's how I felt. At first it saddened me to see all the changes, but now I'm getting used to it."

"What's to be sad about? It looks pretty good to me."

"It's Blanche. She's not here anymore."

"Aw, she's around here somewhere."

"No. I'm afraid she's gone for good." Hot tears burned her eyes. "I may as well give up on her."

"Hey," he said, "whaddaya talking about? You said you'd never give up on finding her, remember?"

She blinked away her tears. "I know what I said. But it's getting harder and harder to keep my hopes up. Especially now that her essence has left Washington Square. Maybe it's a sign. Maybe I'm not supposed to find her. Maybe I should leave well enough alone." Fresh tears threatened.

"Aw, c'mon," Art said, "you'll feel better after you eat. I got the mushrooms and a stuffed artichoke to go with the muffuletta."

She eyed the oil-stained bags, inhaling their delicious aroma when she sniffed her runny nose. Unable to resist the hunger pangs that gnawed at her she dug into the bags. After arranging the containers and the plastic cutlery as though they were dining at home, she tucked one paper napkin under her chin and laid another across her lap.

"Next time we'll bring a blanket and have a real picnic," she said.

"The ants'll get us."

"They don't seem to be bothered by ants," she said, nodding in the direction of the couple on the plaid blanket.

He looked that way. "That's 'cause they got other things on their mind."

Her tone took on a wistful note. "It looks like true love."

"Huh," he snorted. "Looks more like true lust to me."

"Oh, you old poop. Where's your sense of romance?"

"It's damn sure not out here in the park."

The couple were now locked in a steamy embrace, their hands groping various body parts. "Oh dear," she said. "I spoke too soon."

"Don't look at 'em," he advised.

"I won't," she said, taking a peek to see what they were up to.

Turning her attention back to the food, she picked up her half of the muffuletta. In between bites, she popped mushrooms in her mouth and skinned the meat off artichoke leaves with her teeth. Art did likewise. As always, the servings were tasty, plentiful and filling.

It truly was a perfect day for being in the park. Overhead, a few cotton candy clouds drifted through an azure sky. Nearby, a pair of squirrels were playing tag in an oak tree. Up and down the trunk they went, jumping from branch to branch and from limb to limb. The cheep-cheep-cheep of baby birds came from an azalea bush pregnant with buds. Blackbirds, pigeons, robins, wrens and sparrows dotted the grounds, hopping from spot to spot in search of food. Though tempted, Belle knew better than to offer a crust of bread. Unless she had a whole bagful of crumbs the weaker birds wouldn't get a fair share. It was too disappointing to watch a sparrow peck at a piece of bread only to have a greedy blue jay or a thrush swoop down and snatch it away from him. She contented herself with watching them forage for worms, grubs and berries.

"That hit the spot," Art said, balling up the butcher paper the sandwich had been wrapped in. He leaned back, spread his arms across the top of the bench, turned his face to the sun and closed his eyes, a peaceful expression on his face.

It pleased Belle to see him looking so relaxed. "You deserved a break from your diet," she said. "But I'm giving you fair warning. We're eating light tonight."

"Never mind tonight," he said, opening his eyes and craning his neck to look at her. "Where're the cookies?"

"Oh no," she said, remembering the container of banana pudding Mammy had fixed for them, which happened to be Art's favorite dessert. "I forgot."

"She forgot," he said out of the corner of his mouth. "The one thing I ask her to do and she forgets."

"I had a very busy morning." It was a lame excuse, but she wasn't quite ready to tell him she'd been distracted by Mammy's revelations about Hope Haven.

"Yeah? Doing what?"

"Visiting with James and Henry."

"No kidding? How come?"

"They came down to see Tallulah and I took them for a ride."

"Huh. They finish the chest yet?"

It was all she could do to keep a straight face. The chest and the banjo clock were ready and waiting for him to get home. "I didn't think to ask,"she said.

"Those bums," he said. "They shoulda finished it by now."

"They may have," she said. "We were busy talking about other things. They've led such fascinating lives, and I told them all about our trips to Mississippi and to Georgia."

"That musta been some ride. Where'd you go? Baton Rouge?"

"Oh, we didn't talk in the car. Well, we did, but not about our lives. We had coffee in the kitchen. I wished I'd had some muffins to offer them, but the best I could do was serve those old figs. Anyway, we had the nicest visit. We really got to know each other."

She didn't notice that Art's peaceful expression had turned into a scowl. "You invited 'em in," he said in a voice filled with disbelief.

"Of course. They're our neighbors."

"Yeah, but they're guys," he said with the emphasis on *guys*.

"What difference does that make?"

"Jesus, do I have to spell it out for you?"

"I have no idea what you're talking about."

"For crissakes," he said, his voice rising. "I'm talking 'bout you being alone in the house with two guys you don't even know."

"What on earth is wrong with that? You know them, and now I know them, too."

"Yeah, but the point is you didn't know 'em when you invited 'em in."

"I knew they were perfect gentlemen."

"What? You look in your crystal ball?"

"Don't be silly. I could just tell, that's all. And I was right."

"So why'n't you invite the whole damn neighborhood in? There's guys all over the place."

"Maybe next time I will. Maybe I'll have a party and serve tea and crumpets."

"Like hell you will. I can see the headlines now: 'Heiress Gets Raped By Perfect Gentlemen.'"

"Is that what you're worried about? That they'd be attracted to me?"

"Hey, you catch on fast. 'Course I'm worried. In case you haven't noticed, you're a beautiful woman with a dynamite shape. Any guy on the planet would have the hots for you."

"Not James or Henry," she said quietly.

"Oh yeah? Says who?"

"Says me. They're homosexuals, Art."

He flicked a wrist in dismissal. "Get outta here. They're brothers."

"No, you misunderstood. James and Henry are lovers, not brothers. They met at an estate sale nine years ago."

"What! They're a coupla fags?"

She winced. "That's not a nice word, Art. I wish you wouldn't use it."

"Pardon me all to hell. You like queers or fairies better?"

"I don't understand why you're acting like this."

"'Cause it ain't natural, that's why. An' I ain't gonna have nothing more to do with 'em."

"You liked them well enough when you thought they were brothers. They're very talented men who happen to have excellent taste. Besides, they didn't choose to be gay. They didn't sit down one day and say, 'Gee, I think I'll love men instead of women.' They were born that way."

"You believe that garbage?"

"It's not garbage. I've read a lot about it. It has to do with chromosomes. Some babies carry an extra number of the opposite genders' hormones. Of course there are good apples and bad apples in every bushel, just like with heterosexuals. But James and Henry are lovely men, and I'll be terribly disappointed if you're mean to them."

He ran a hand through his hair. "Jesus, I can't get over it. James and Henry. You can't trust nobody these days."

They sat silently staring out at nothing in particular.

Belle berated herself for telling him. Because of her she'd ruined a perfectly good relationship between the three men. She should have known Art would be homophobic. Whether from his religious background, personal experience, simple disgust, disdain or fear, she didn't know, but it was not up to her to try to change his mind. That was something he'd have to do for himself. She just wished she could take it all back–have him believe James and Henry were brothers.

"Hormones, eh?" he said with a sideways look.

She nodded. "That's what the geneticists say."

"Who're they?"

"Scientists who specialize in how we're affected by our genes."

"How do you know all this stuff?"

"Soon after I entered Hope Haven I heard the girls using language I didn't understand. Back then I was too embarrassed to ask what those words meant, so I asked Marge. She explained the terms and gave me some medical journals to read."

"Marge, eh?" he said. "So they're like freaks of nature?"

"Well, I wouldn't call anyone a freak. That's another ugly word. I'd call it an *accident* of nature."

He opened his mouth then shut it. After ruminating a while longer, he said, "Okay, here's what I'm gonna do." He paused. "I'm gonna forget you told me. Far as James and Henry go, s'long as they don't start hitting on me everything'll be hunky-dorey."

"Thank goodness," she said, breathing a sigh of relief.

A thought occurred to her. "I wonder if James and Henry are part of the team that fixed up the park."

Art looked at her. "Now whaddaya talking about?"

"That sign over there. It says the gay and lesbian business association are responsible for taking care the park."

"Jesus, they're everywhere." He looked all around, his eyes wary, as if expecting to see an army of angry hedge-trimmers marching his way.

"C'mon," he said to Belle, "let's get outta here."

"But I haven't told you what's going on at Hope Haven. It seems–"

He held up a hand. "Hold it. Don't tell me nothing I don't wanna hear."

"You may not want to hear it, but I have to tell you anyway. The mental health department is thinking of closing the house down."

"Aw, jeez. Why would they wanna do that?"

That's all it took. She was off and running on the subject.

Twenty-one

Belle had thought the banjo clock would sound like the musical instrument when it chimed. It not only didn't sound like a banjo it didn't look like a banjo. Made in the early 1800's, it was an elongated wooden affair with a golden eagle perched on top and a carved box engraved with a pastoral scene at the bottom. Roman numerals circled the dial, dainty filigreed hands told the time.

James and Henry could not have made a better choice. Hanging above the newly refurbished chest it immediately caught the eye. If Art had had any lingering doubts about continuing his friendship with the men, they'd been dispelled the moment he set eyes on the new additions. Naturally he'd made a fuss over Belle spending her money on him, but she'd expected that. Thankfully, he didn't protest too loud or too long.

While Art stretched out to rest his back, she drove Tallulah to the mental health center. It was within walking distance, but by mid-afternoon, especially after such a big lunch, she felt drained of energy.

At the center, Connie, the receptionist, confided more information than anyone else was willing to give her, and that still wasn't much. Hope Haven, along with most other social service programs, was funded by a federal grant and dispersed through the state mental health system. Funds had been slashed; therefore, certain programs would either be cut to the bone or eliminated. At this point, no one knew which programs would be affected, but office gossip had it that Hope Haven would be at the top of the list.

The efficacy of treating substance abusers had always been a source of controversy among the hierarchy at the local, state, and federal levels. Some thought it a vital component of mental health services, others thought it a waste of money.

Careful to not divulge any information of her own, Belle left the center with a plan. Rather than wait to see if Hope Haven lost its funding, she would take matters into her own hands. Whether Mandy approved or not, Hope Haven, or a facsimile, was about to become a private enterprise under the stewardship of the soon-to-be-established charitable foundation.

No more scrimping on decent furnishings, no more ragged linens, no more chipped dishes, no more longing for a van to transport residents to and from rehab, AA and NA meetings, doctor's appointments and so on. It would be oh so nice for them to be able to go out for a simple Sunday drive. There was so much to see and do in and around New Orleans, and the girls of Hope Haven had seen little more than the seamier side of town. A van would open up whole new worlds: museums, art galleries, the aquarium, the zoo ....

The more she thought about it the more excited she got. The foundation would buy a new house. According to Connie, the present location had been leased from a private owner who had repeatedly refused to make needed repairs. Water leaks and insufficient wiring were not only wasteful and inconvenient, they also posed a danger. Besides, the house was too small for eight women, nine counting Mammy Daisy. They needed larger bedrooms, more bathrooms, a wider stairwell, a recreation room, a modern kitchen. The list grew longer and longer.

While they were at it, they could buy another piece of property and turn it into a boardinghouse for those who completed the program and had no home to go back to. Like Janette, who was having to live in a boardinghouse clear across town. Because of the location, she had to take two buses and walk more than half a mile to get to work; never mind how long it took her to visit Mammy and the girls.

After winning the jackpot, Belle had dreamed of buying such a property. She'd even picked out a name for the boardinghouse–Belle's Place. But first taxes had taken a big chunk of the money and then she'd found out what properties in the area sold for. Now things were different–God bless Lin's soul.

. . .

Art was lying on his right side, his hand tucked up under his cheek. Belle could tell by the rise and fall of his chest that he was fast asleep. Though she was bursting to tell him all about her plan she knew he needed his rest. They could discuss it later, out on the porch.

Her heart swelled as she gazed down on him. Yes, he was prejudiced against those he didn't understand, and yes he could be grumpy and stubborn, but he was a kind and generous man. A man who took time to listen, a man who was open-minded enough to change his views and admit he'd made a mistake even when it irked him to do so. No matter his faults and foibles, she adored him.

As she leaned against the doorjamb, watching him sleep, her shoulders began to sag and her eyelids started to droop. Exhaustion overwhelmed her and she felt herself drifting ... drifting ...

Jerking awake, she knew she should go to her room and lie down, but the distance seemed too great. Unable to resist, she tiptoed to the far side of Art's bed, kicked off her shoes and eased herself onto the mattress. Stretching out on her right side, she slid her left hand to within an inch of Art's back and left it there, wanting to touch him but afraid such a move would wake him.

This was nice, she thought. Lying here together like this. Being this close to Art made her feel safe and secure, even if he was facing away from her. It made her want to slip under the covers and snuggle close.

Gazing at his broad shoulders and down the long length of him, she remembered the couple in the park. A warm tingly sensation started in the pit of her stomach. How wonderful to be in love. How glorious to be swept away in a passionate embrace. Would she ever feel that breathless sense of joy again? Was it too late for her and Art?

How silly she'd been to be fearful of moving in with him. Fearful his nearness might awaken her sexuality. Fearful she would long for him to make love to her only to have him reject her. Like Lin had.

It had comforted her greatly when Art told her she needn't fear any advances from him. That his heart trouble, his high blood pressure, and now his diabetes had destroyed his sex drive. But now she found herself hoping he was wrong. After all they'd been through together she wanted to express her emotions in a more demonstrative way. She wanted to feel as close to him as two people could get. In essence, she wanted to make love to him.

• • •

Art stirred from a dream about Belle dancing in the park. Instead of clothes, her body was encased in blue feathers. As she twirled around and around, her bare arms flung out like wings, a cloud of yellow butterflies circled above her head like a halo. It reminded Art of the night they celebrated her fortieth birthday at Pat O'Brien's. The entertainers that night–two female singers who played dual pianos–had coaxed Belle to join them on the stage so they could lead the audience in a rousing rendition of the birthday song. Standing there in the golden glow of the spotlight she'd looked like a shimmering angel sent down from heaven. The image had played in Art's mind for a long time, had kept him company on many a dark and lonely night during her months of treatment.

Hoping to fall back to sleep and pick up where the dream left off, he made a half turn onto his back. When his left arm made contact with a solid object, his eyes popped open and his head came up off the pillow. Before he could look to see what the thing was, a spasm of pain radiated all the way from his spine to the back of his skull. It took his breath away and clouded his vision. Fearing another spasm, he eased his head back onto the pillow and lay flat and still. Whatever was lying next to him didn't seem to be going anywhere.

When the pain started to subside, he closed his eyes and tried to relax. With any luck he'd be able to call up the image of Belle dancing in the park.

As he lay there waiting to sink back into the dream, he thought he heard someone breathing. No, it sounded more like purring. Like a kitten purring. Yeah, he bet that was it–Belle had found herself a kitten somewhere. That would explain the purring sound and the soft thing his arm had brushed against.

Belle had told him she'd always wanted a cat, but first her mother and then Mallory wouldn't let her have one. According to them, pets of any kind were too much trouble. Art wasn't crazy about cats–he was a dog man–but he wasn't about to deny Belle anything.

Curious as to what kind of cat it was, he opened his eyes and carefully turned his head. What the hell? It wasn't a cat or a dog either. It looked like a human. He blinked several times in rapid succession and looked again. Damned if it wasn't Belle.

What was she doing in his bed? Had she read his mind? Knew he was dreaming about her? Knew he wanted her to lie beside him? Whatever the reason, he sure wasn't going to wake her up. Despite his aching back, he smiled with utter contentment. This was far better than any dream.

Jeez, he thought as he gazed at her, she looked so young and innocent. So vulnerable. And that could be a big problem. She was too damn trusting for her own good. She'd take up with anybody. Like that pimp, Tyrone.

Last fall, when Belle was still new in town, they'd been taking a walk through the Quarter. On St. Peter Street, she'd stopped to point out the house where that playwright guy, that Tennessee Williams, used to live. While she was telling him about the play the guy wrote about Blanche, who should come out of the building's front door but this black dude wearing an orange leather get-up, lots of gold chains, and boots trimmed with ostrich feathers. Art had tried his best to steer her away from the guy, but no, not Belle; instead she'd struck up a conversation. Turned out the dude lived in the same building as the playwright, so she got all excited. Asked him did he know anybody who might've known Tennessee. The dude didn't and finally they'd parted and gone on their way, but not before the guy found out where she lived.

Next thing Art knew the dude was at Hope Haven with two fat cat buddies of his wanting Belle to paint nudes on the walls of their apartment. If Art had been there he would've slammed the door in their faces. Not Belle. She'd invited them into the foyer and explained ever so politely why she had to decline. It wasn't because she didn't want the job, she told them, it was because she had no experience painting nudes. If it hadn't been for Mammy Daisy showing them the door, she probably would have sat them down in the parlor and told them her life story. Which just went to prove she was an easy mark for any Tom, Dick or Harry that came along.

Now that she was a rich widow he had even more to worry about. One hint of her net worth and every scumbag in town would be knocking on the door. Knowing her, she'd start passing out hundred dollar bills like they were gum drops. He had to give her credit, though. She'd had enough sense to turn the money down. Well, not down exactly, but at least it was going into some kind of foundation and not into her bank account. He didn't care if Jerry and his team skimmed a little off the top or not, just as long as Belle didn't have to handle it.

Funny how hopes and dreams changed as a person aged. Back when he was a kid in Newark, holding down a legit job after school and running numbers on the side, he'd wanted nothing more than to be filthy rich. He'd see the cats cruising the streets in their Cadillacs and their Lincoln Continentals. Dressed in their silk suits, silk shirts and flashy ties, diamond rings on their pinkies, smoking Havanas, they'd stop for a shave and a shine every day of the week. Twice a week they'd get their hair trimmed and their nails buffed. And the women ... the women flocked around them like they were movie stars straight out of Hollywood. He never knew how they earned their dough, he just knew they carried fat rolls of bills in their pockets. And he wanted to grow up to be just like them.

When he finally wised up and saw them for the crooks, punks and losers they were, he still wanted to be rich. But more than that he wanted respect. Self-respect, the respect of his family and friends, the respect of a good woman. So he'd stopped running numbers and started driving a hearse. Mostly he picked up dead bodies from hospitals and delivered them to his uncle Vinnie's funeral home. When he wasn't driving the hearse he drove a delivery truck for Manny's Meat Market. Instead of spending every dime he made he started saving his dough.

Ten years later he and Lil celebrated six years of marriage. After a two-year hitch in Viet-damn-Nam, he bought a cab–the 1971 Checker he still drove–and they put a down payment on a house. They had two kids, a boy and a girl, both of them born with all their fingers and toes. He paid his bills on time, mowed his lawn, went to mass on a regular basis, coached Little League. Along the way, he'd earned a moderate degree of respect. But he still wanted to be rich. Rich enough to pay cash instead of buying on credit, rich enough to buy Lil a new car–it didn't have to be a Cadillac, they'd be happy with a Ford or a Chevy–and rich enough to fly his family out to California on vacation. Visit Disneyland and Knott's Berry Farm.

By the time he turned forty he began to suspect he'd never strike it rich. Truth was, he was stuck in a rut–driving the cab twelve hours a day six days a week, putting up with a whole lot of bullshit from his fares, and spending his off hours at baseball games, the track, or down at Tony's Bar, a neighborhood joint where all his buddies hung out. The closest he came to taking Lil and the kids to California was a week at the Jersey shore.

Lil was into the family scene, sisters and brothers, nephews and nieces all over town, someone always in trouble. And his own kids were showing signs of rebellion: Artie staying out till all hours, bringing home failing grades, playing his music loud enough to crack glass. Sandy ... well, he hated to admit it but any fool could see she was either already sleeping around or the biggest tease in town. And nothing he did or didn't do made a damn bit of difference.

Things went from bad to worse: Artie into drugs in a big way, with Lil supporting his habit by slipping him Art's hard-earned dough every time Artie promised to get his act together, and Sandy marrying and then divorcing every loser who got her pregnant–she had three kids, each with a different surname. Oh, Art had failed bigtime. He'd failed his family; he'd failed to get rich. What's more, no one showed him any respect, least of all himself.

What to do? Clear out of Jersey and make a fresh start, he'd suggested, and Lil had agreed wholeheartedly. Who knew? Maybe they'd still strike it rich. Maybe he could regain his self-respect.

For five years they told everyone they were going to make a move–clear out of Jersey and start over somewhere else. That's all they talked about, where they'd go, what they'd do. After a while people started to say it would never happen, that it was all talk and no action. No, they'd answer, they were going just as soon as the latest crisis had passed.

Finally they got a breather. Artie had checked into a drug rehab program and Sandy was sharing an apartment with another single mom. As for the rest of the family, they seemed to be holding their own. A couple of nephews were in the slammer, and their mothers –Lil's sisters–needed consoling, but the kids would be out soon. Before they could be picked up again for another misdemeanor or, God forbid, a felony, he and Lil decided to drive down to New Orleans to look things over. Why did they pick New Orleans over somewhere in Florida, where most Jerseyites went? Because, being a tourist town, Art figured business would be good and Lil wanted to sit on a verandah and sip mint juleps.

Okay, so nothing had worked out as planned. Soon after he bought the house on Esplanade, Lil moved back to New Jersey for good and, coincidentally or not, Artie went AWOL from rehab and Sandy's roommate moved out. He, Art, was still supporting everyone's habits, he still hadn't struck it rich, and his sense of self-respect had fallen below zero.

Did he care that he wasn't rich? Hell no. One thing he'd noticed about rich guys–at least the ones who took his cab–was that they were never satisfied. They were always scheming and dreaming about how to get richer. He had enough troubles without worrying about how to make more dough.

Financially speaking, he hadn't done too bad for himself. He didn't owe anybody anything, and he sent Lil seven hundred and fifty bucks a month, two hundred of which went to Sandy and her kids. If one of the kids was sick and Sandy needed extra, he sent it. If he was rich they'd be wanting the moon, and what would they do with it? Blow it.

A person needed a reason to get up in the morning. That was the trouble with his family. Lil was an able-bodied woman of fifty, fully capable of supporting herself, but to hear her tell it she'd end up a bag lady if he cut her off. Same went for Sandy. Like Belle said, Sandy, being a single mother of three, would probably be eligible for some kind of job training. If not, she could sign up at the state employment office for job placement. Two of the kids were in school now and the youngest could be put in day care. He'd told her as much the last time she called. She said she'd think about it. Knowing her, she forgot it the second she hung up. As long as she knew his check was on the way, why bother?

Art knew he wasn't doing anybody any favors by continuing to bail them out, but he didn't know what to do about it. None of them listened to a word he said. As for showing him any sign of respect, forget about it.

Belle had told him to never give up on his kids. This summer, as soon as the grandkids got out of school, he'd asked Sandy to bring them down for a visit. They could take the train. The kids would love it. Belle could line up an appointment with Marge. Introduce her to

Sandy and let Marge do her thing. If she could talk Belle into entering Hope Haven for six months, anything was possible.

As for Artie ... since neither he nor Lil had been able to get through to him, maybe if Sandy went back to school or got a job she could encourage her brother to do the same. If one sibling could dig her way out of a hole it might give the other one hope. The girls of Hope Haven had had it worse than his kids and they were making out all right. With that thought in mind he shoved the family into a corner of his mind.

Belle was still purring like a kitten. God, how he loved her. She was the one bright spot in his life. If it hadn't been for her picking his cab out of the queue at the depot he probably would've died of loneliness.

The funny thing was, he didn't know he was lonely until he met her and got caught up in her search for Blanche. What a wild ride it had been! Sure, they'd hit a few potholes now and then, but the road had been smooth more often than not. Nothing like that other life he'd led.

Talk about rags to riches. Belle had been raised in a simple home by ordinary people, if you could call Edith ordinary. From that beginning, she'd married into a world of wealth. Did being rich make her happy? No. It was the guy she fell in love with, not his money. But the guy's lifestyle and later his neglect had ended up making her miserable. So ill and miserable she'd had to build a new life for herself. And just when she was hitting her stride, enjoying life for the first time in years, bingo! she's rich again, richer than Midas. Did the news make her any happier than she already was? No. Now she has to make sure the money is put to good use, and both of them have to make sure word of her inheritance doesn't leak out. Truth is, she'd be better off without it. He knew he would.

Belle opened her eyes. She didn't flinch, twitch, jump, or jerk when she saw him. She just laid there watching him watch her as if it were the most natural thing in the world.

"Hi," she said.

"Hi, yourself."

"How long have you been awake?"

"Maybe fifteen minutes."

"That long?"

"Yeah."

"Does your back feel any better?"

"So long as I'm lying here it does. No telling what it'll feel like when I get up."

"Then don't get up."

"I won't if you don't."

She smiled. "It's a deal. Think you can go back to sleep?"

"Naw. But it feels good to lie here."

"It does, doesn't it. We should do this more often."

"How's about tonight?"

"Do you mean it?"

"Sure, why not. But I gotta warn you. I been having romantic ideas."

"You have?"

"Yeah. Who'd'a thought?"

"Maybe it was seeing the couple in the park."

"Naw, I started having 'em before that."

"Really?"

"Yeah. Like I said, you're a beautiful woman with a dynamite shape."

"What if I was ugly? What if I had a big wart on my nose with long black hairs sticking out of it?"

"I'd still think you was beautiful."

"I'll bet you say that to all the girls."

"How'd you know? Mammy Daisy tell you I been hitting on her?"

She giggled. The laugh caught in her throat when the telephone rang.

"Don't answer it," he said.

"But what if it's Mandy? What if it's Lil or Sandy?"

"They'll call back."

She rolled onto her left side and pushed up from the bed. "Stay put," she said. "I'll be right back."

He groaned.

True to her word she returned within minutes, but he could tell by the look on her face that the mood had been shattered. No more talk of romance, no chance of a soul-satisfying kiss.

"It was Janette," she said, perching on the side of the bed. "She needs me tomorrow for a couple of hours."

"For what?"

She gave him a serious look and said, "She gave me permission to tell you, but you've got to promise never to repeat this to anyone."

"Hey, you know me better'n that."

"Janette has a child in foster care. A little four-year-old girl named Amber. Janette was supposed to have a year after she left Hope Haven to prove she could be a fit mother. In the meantime, she's had supervised visitation rights. Now Amber's foster parents want to adopt her, and Janette's social worker has been putting the pressure on her to sign the papers. Tomorrow, instead of her visitation being in the church downtown, where it's usually held, it's going to be at the foster parents' house in Metairie. I guess the social worker wants Janette to see what kind of home Amber would have. Anyway, Janette needs a ride over there and she asked me to take her."

"Jeez," said Art. "One of my nieces had the same thing happen to her, only her kid was a boy. Ended up with the kid's grandma–one of Lil's sisters–raising him."

"How has it worked out?"

"Okay, I guess. What about Janette's mother? She around?"

"The last time Janette heard from her mother she was living in Colorado. She doesn't even know she has a grandchild. Janette wants to keep it that way."

"How come?"

"Let's just say, Janette's mother wasn't a very good role model. She was what they call a camp follower. Still is, I imagine. Anyway, Janette ran away from home at fourteen to get away from it all. Sad to say she ended up running into a worse situation. But the important thing is she's worked hard to straighten out her life, and she's doing a good job. I'm afraid this whole thing with Amber is going to knock her legs out from under her."

"I hear you," Art said. "Seems to me that social worker oughta live up to her part of the bargain. She trying to do Janette in, or what?"

Belle looked at him. "That's a good question. Maybe I should ask her."

"It couldn't hurt."

A smile lit Belle's face as she twisted around and came toward him on her hands and knees. Crouching next to him, she said, "Turn over. I'm going to give you the best massage you've ever had."

"Uh-oh," he said, grinning. "You're just asking for trouble."

"I know," she murmured.

• • •

Slow, tender and languorous defined their lovemaking. There was no rushing, no grasping, no mad clutching. They had all the time in the world to explore each other's bodies and awaken the embers thought long dead.

Never mind Art's aching back–he never gave it a thought.

Although Belle was self-conscious at first, she quickly became overwhelmed by desire.

Their clothes came off a piece at a time. No ripping or tugging, just a lazy peeling of layers. Once naked, they stroked one another. Their kisses were soft, long and deep. She fingered the mat of hair on his chest. He caressed her breasts and fondled her nipples. They shied away from their lower parts until the need became excruciating.

The banjo clock chimed the hour; birdsong floated through the window screen; traffic rumbled in the distance, yet inside the snug cocoon of their bed the only sounds that mattered were their murmurings, their occasional gasps for breath, the beating of their hearts.

When they came together at last it was as though they'd been born for the moment. Their previous lives had been nothing more than a prelude–a dress rehearsal for their true birth. That they weren't joined by a piece of paper pronouncing them man and wife was inconsequential. What they shared transcended mere formality. If it were possible they would stay locked together forever.

When the phone rang again they let it ring. Moments like this came once in a lifetime. The outside world could wait.

Twenty-two

Art couldn't stop smiling. Not only had his ultimate dream come true, but there wasn't a man alive who wouldn't envy his performance. Yes sir, he still had what it took–and then some. They'd made love in bed, they'd made love in the shower, and then they'd gone back to bed for more. He'd told Belle that he was the *lovor* and she was the *lovee.* And he'd been so right.

He knew he had a bad case of the 'big head,' as his old school chums called someone who bragged on himself, but he couldn't help it. Any fool would be damn proud of himself, and he was a fool in love.

Then again, maybe he was having some kind of delusion. It had been so long since he'd had sex, maybe he wasn't as good a lover as he thought he was. Maybe Belle was just faking it, her orgasms in particular. If that was true, all he could say was she was one helluva actress. So far as he knew, Belle had never lied to him, and in his book faking was the same as lying. So he was back where he started–damn proud of himself.

'Course he had to admit he'd had a little bit of help in the lover department. With skin as soft and smooth as velvet, a pin-up girl's body, and a scent like roses–she even tasted good–she made making love to her easy.

What was the name of that old song? "So Easy To Love?" That was Belle. God, how he adored her!

Instead of sitting here on the porch, waiting for her to bring him whatever she was fixing for supper, he wanted to strut up and down the street singing: "I'm in love, I'm in love, I'm in love, I'm in love, I'm in love with a wonderful girl!"

He glanced over his shoulder at the front door, hoping to see a sign of Belle's shadow. He saw nothing but a pale strip of light thrown by one of the lamps. What was keeping her? He'd offered his help in the kitchen, but when he couldn't keep his hands off her, she'd shooed him out of the room.

And now the damn the phone was ringing. If it was one of the girls they'd keep her yakking half the night. He knew it was selfish but he didn't want to share her with anyone–he wanted her all to himself.

Since that was impossible, he leaned back in his chair and closed his eyes. He would relive every moment of their afternoon, from the time he found her in his bed.

Moments later he dropped off to sleep. The contented smile he'd been smiling never left his face.

. . .

Belle set a loaded tray on the wicker table between the two rocking chairs. She leaned over Art whispered in his ear. "Wake up, sleepyhead. You need to get some food in your tummy." She gave him a peck on the lips.

Before she could stand upright, Art reached out, grabbed her hips, and tried to pull her onto his lap. "C'mere, you gorgeous girl. I gotta have some more of those kisses."

She laughed and slapped at his hands. "Not until you eat your soup. We'll save the kisses for dessert."

"Okay," he said, releasing her, "you win. What kinda soup?"

Belle moved to her chair and sat down. “Vegetable. Now eat.”

“Bossy broad,” he muttered.

“Sex maniac,” she muttered back.

Art flashed her a wicked grin. “You got that right.”

She put a hand to her mouth in an attempt to smother the giggles. When she withdrew her hand, a giggle escaped. “Please don’t make me laugh,” she said. “Our soup is getting cold.”

“Alright already.” He hunched over the tray, crumbled crackers into his soup and picked up the bowl and a spoon. After swallowing a mouthful, he said, “Y’know, I been craving a pastrami on rye, but this tastes pretty darn good.”

“And it’s good for you. Besides, we don’t have any pastrami, so finish your soup.”

They ate the rest of their meal in silence. When their bowls were empty, Belle stacked the dishes on the tray and carried it back to the kitchen.

Art was ready for her as soon as she returned. “Time for dessert,” he said, trying to catch hold of her.

Evading his hands, she sidestepped to her chair and sat down. “Not quite yet. I’ve heard some sad news.”

“Don’t tell me someone died ‘cause I don’t wanna hear it.”

“I’m afraid you have to. Marge’s mother died.”

“Aw, jeez,”Art said. It was hard to believe anything bad could happen when he was sitting on top of the world. But that’s the breaks, he said to himself. Bad news seemed to lurk around every corner. “I hate to hear that.”

“Me, too,” Belle said. “Mammy called while I fixing supper. She’s also the one who called earlier. Anyway, she said Marge sounded so weak and tired she could hardly hear her. Poor Marge, she must be totally exhausted. She’s been taking care of her mother for weeks now. The mental strain, along with the physical strain, must have been awful.”

“Yeah, that’s gotta be rough. I like Marge. She can be a pain in the ass, but she sure knows her stuff.”

"Well," Belle said with a sigh. "I don't have to tell you how I feel about her. I've really missed her."

"Yeah, but hey, you've done alright by yourself. When Marge hears about all you been through ... Lin dying and the kid and everything, she's gonna be real proud of you."

"Yes, but just remember I got through it because I had you."

"You've still got me, kiddo. Fact, you're stuck with me whether you like it or not."

"I not only like it, I love it."

"That's my girl," he said, smiling a proud smile.

When Belle's gaze shifted past his head and a frown lined her brow, his smile dissolved. "You thinking about Marge?"

"Yes. The visitation is tomorrow night from seven until ten, and the funeral is set for Monday morning at eleven. Both services will be held in Livonia, Marge's hometown. It's not far from Baton Rouge." She looked at him. "I have something else to tell you. Promise you won't get mad at me?"

"*Me* mad at *you*? The love of my life. The sexiest girl on the planet. You gotta be kidding."

"Stop," she said, putting a hand palm-side out, "you're going to make me laugh and this is serious."

"Hey, I'm only telling the truth. But okay, I'll be serious. What'd you do now?"

"I told Mammy we'd take her and the girls to the visitation, which means we'll have to take both cars."

"You telling me I don't get to drive up there with you?"

"I'm afraid not."

"Aw, jeez. Why'd you go and do that?"

"Because they don't have any other way to get there and we can't all fit in one car. And don't forget, I've got that date with Janette tomorrow from two till four. So instead of taking her back to the boardinghouse, I'll bring her home with me. Then we can drive both cars over to Hope Haven and pick the others up."

He winked at her. "Tell you what. Let's go back to bed and forget the whole thing."

"That would be lovely. But ...."

"Yeah, there's always a *but*. You're gonna tell me we gotta think of Marge."

"Yes, we do. We've got the rest of our lives to think about us."

He rocked forward in his chair, pushed himself up and held out a hand to her. "Yeah, well, we're wasting time. We better get started."

She smiled at him. "What about your back?"

"That massage you gave me cured it right up."

She took his hand and they went inside.

Later on they moved her things into Art's room.

• • •

On the following day, as they were preparing to leave Hope Haven for Livonia, the girls started arguing over who would ride in which car. Since there were an even number of passengers, it was decided they would take turns going up and coming back. On the way up, Mammy would sit in Tallulah's front seat with Belle while Fran and Janette rode in back. That left Gloria, Millie and Gracie to ride with Art. The other girls, Darleen and Boots, hadn't been notified because they couldn't be reached. A message had been left on Boots's mother's answering machine, but as yet the call hadn't been returned. Every effort to reach Darleen through Roger's cell phone had been blocked by a busy signal. No one was overly concerned about Darleen–she'd been good about reporting in since Roger's route had changed, but it didn't bode well for Boots. She hadn't been heard from since she left Hope Haven, and that had been weeks ago.

Finally they were on their way to Livonia with Art leading the way. Belle tried to concentrate on keeping up with him, but her mind kept wandering back to Janette's visit with Amber. She had wanted to talk to Mammy about it, but they hadn't had a moment alone together, and now she couldn't mention it because Fran was present. More than once Belle had tried to talk Janette into telling the other girls about Amber. Keeping her daughter a deep, dark secret–no matter the circumstances– was unhealthy, she'd thought, but Janette wouldn't hear of it.

"You don't know these girls like I do," she'd said. "I don't trust any of them."

"How can you say that?" Belle asked. "They love you. They're your family."

Janette's reply was always the same. "Your family, maybe, but not mine. Sooner or later one of them would throw it up to me. I'm not taking any chances."

Belle had given up. Janette had made it clear why it was so hard for her to trust anyone. Everyone the girl had ever loved, especially her mother and Amber's father, had let her down. As for her own father, Janette didn't even know who he was. Just one of the countless men who passed through her mother's life.

The visitation with Amber had not gone well. Belle had dropped Janette off in front of the foster parents' house, a neat clapboard bungalow with a fenced-in backyard and lots of trees. Up and down the street children were outside playing: riding bikes, aiming a ball at a basketball hoop, jumping rope, playing hopscotch. Two blocks before they reached the foster parents' house they'd seen more children gathered at an elementary school's playground.

Belle had wanted to go inside the house with Janette–she'd been most eager to meet Amber at last–but that wasn't allowed, so she'd spent the time browsing through an independent bookstore at a nearby strip mall. Back at the house a few minutes before four o'clock, she'd hoped Amber would walk her mother out to the car, but out came Janette by herself, wearing a long face.

They'd driven several miles before Janette uttered a word. "I told them I wanted to meet back at the church next time. The only reason they had me come all the way out here was to show off. You should see Amber's room. She's got ballerinas everywhere. On the walls, the curtains, the bedspread, music boxes. She's got enough toys for ten kids and her closet's stuffed with clothes. All these fancy dresses with ruffles and lace. I've got to get her out of there. They're spoiling her rotten and she's too damn happy." She turned to Belle. "How in the hell am I supposed to compete with that?"

Belle's eyes flickered between Janette and the road. "You're not. You're her mother and you love her. Oh, honey, you've got to hang on. I'm calling your social worker first thing in the morning. She's got to stop tormenting you like this."

Janette slumped in her seat. "It won't do any good," she said.

"You don't know that. Maybe this is her way of reassuring you, showing you that Amber is in good hands and you don't have to worry about her."

"Wrong. It's her way of showing me I'll never be good enough."

"But you are good enough! You just need more time. No one expects you to provide Amber with a home overnight."

"I'll never be able to give her what they can. She'd hate me for taking her away from all that."

"Kids adjust faster than you think," Belle said. "She doesn't need a roomful of toys and fancy dresses, she needs your love and attention."

"I hope you're right."

Me, too, Belle had thought to herself.

Now, as she cast an eye at Janette through the rearview mirror and heard her complaining to Fran about her job at the dental clinic and how demanding her boss was, she had a sinking feeling she'd said all the wrong things. Under the best of circumstances, parenting was the hardest job in the world. Was Janette capable of being a responsible parent when she herself was still growing up? Serious doubts crept into Belle's mind. Perhaps Amber would be better off being raised by her foster parents. They'd had a lot of experience with children and they appeared to provide a loving and stable home, a combination that would nourish Amber in ways Janette, never having lived in such an environment herself, couldn't possibly fathom. Whatever the outcome, someone was bound to get hurt. Belle could only hope it wasn't Amber.

Belle looked ahead at the shiny Checker cab and was comforted by the sight of Art in the driver's seat. She would share her concerns with him later, after they returned from Livonia.

. . .

The funeral home was a sprawling brick building on the outskirts of town. Art circled the parking lot twice before finding two open spaces side by side. Playing the gentleman, he opened the doors for the girls, helped them out of the cab, and then came around to Belle, who stood waiting for him. While Mammy and the girls adjusted their clothes and gathered the flowers they'd brought, he draped an arm over Belle's shoulders, leaned down and kissed her. The nearness of him took her breath away and she was having very unfuneral-like thoughts.

"I saw that," Gloria said, sauntering up to them.

"So?" Art said. "I missed her."

Gloria laughed. "I could tell."

"Come on, children," Mammy called as she neared the carved-oak double doors. She was carrying a potted hydrangea wrapped in lavender foil and tied with a net bow. "Y'all behave, y'hear?"

"Yes, ma'am," sang the chorus as they moved forward, some carrying baskets of spring flowers, others empty-handed, all dressed in what they considered their best, which, due to Belle's influence, consisted mostly of vintage fashions found at flea markets. Though a few of the outfits, like the black slinky satin pants and see-through black lace top Gracie had chosen to wear, and the puff-sleeved pink organdy that made Fran look like a ten-year-old on Easter Sunday, would no doubt raise a few eyebrows, they wouldn't faze the one person who mattered, Marge. Belle herself was wearing the classic Chanel suit in a teal blue linen that she'd found in Biloxi. With it, she wore her pearls and black patent pumps. Art wore his standard brown worsted suit, pale yellow shirt and striped tie. If nothing else, they made for an interesting group.

They marched inside single file with Belle and Art taking up the rear. Gloria, who was fourth in line, kept glancing back at them with a knowing look. At one point Belle made a face at her. Gloria laughed and wiggled her butt.

"The brat knows," Belle told Art in an undertone.

Art put a hand on her fanny and said. "I don't care if the whole world knows."

Belle pushed his hand away and hissed, "You maniac."

They played slap and grab all the way through the people-filled foyer and down the people-filled halls. Two other visitations were taking place and they wandered a while before finding the room assigned to Marilee Hobart, Marge's mother. It was in the last hall they traversed. Stationed at the entrance, a tall man in a gloomy black suit introduced himself as a representative of the funeral home. He promptly relieved Mammy of the potted hydrangea, disappeared for a moment, then came back for the baskets of flowers. After everyone had signed the guest register, the group of eight joined a long line of mostly adults waiting to get inside the room.

Belle noticed that several of the girls kept looking around with wide-eyed expressions of wonder. It occurred to her that this might be their first time in a funeral home. She knew it was their first time to go anywhere en masse. That made her more determined than ever to find transportation for the household. Art didn't know it yet but he was going van-shopping again. This time they would bypass used car lots–this time they would look at brand new models.

Gloria was staring at her with that same know-it-all grin. Because the line was barely moving, Belle inclined her head toward Art and said, "I'm going to the powder room."

"Hurry back," he said, giving her rear another pat.

Sidling up to Gloria, Belle yanked on the girl's sleeve and said, "Come with me." With Gloria in tow, she headed off in search of the ladies' restroom.

The lounge adjoining the lavatory was outfitted with white vanity tables topped with three-way mirrors, a sofa upholstered in a deep red velvet, two wing chairs covered in damask, and a three-legged table bearing a sparkling crystal lamp. An arrangement of multi-colored snapdragons sat atop a marble pedestal table, perfuming the air with their sweet fragrance.

Two elderly ladies sat before mirrors. One lady was powdering her face, the other was patting her hair in place. On one of the wing chairs sat a young woman, presumably a mother, retying a ribbon in a little girl's hair. The child was holding a single red rose, twirling it around and around by its stem. Once again, Belle was reminded of Amber. Would Janette put ribbons in her hair?

Belle pulled Gloria into a far corner of the room. Pressing an index finger against the girl's chest, she spoke in a near-whisper. "I want you to stop giving us those silly looks. It's terribly embarrassing, and this is not the time or the place."

Her eyes twinkling with mischief, Gloria replied in a normal tone. "You finally did it, didn't you?"

"Sshhh," Belle hissed and looked behind her to see if anyone had heard. Satisfied that no one had, she turned back to Gloria. "You know what you need? You need a good spanking."

Gloria waggled her eyebrows. "Is that what Art did? Did he spank you? How kinky."

"Gloria, I'm warning you."

"Oh, don't be so coy. I won't tell anyone. How was it?"

"None of your business," Belle said through gritted teeth.

"I knew it!" Gloria crowed in triumph.

Thoroughly exasperated, Belle clapped a hand over the girl's mouth. She knew she was smearing Gloria's lipstick and getting it on her hand as well, but she didn't care. "I'm not letting go until you promise to be good," she said.

With speech impossible, Gloria made guttural noises from deep in her throat.

"Stop that," Belle said, keeping her hand firmly in place. "In case you've forgotten, we're in a funeral home. You're supposed to show respect for the dead."

Gloria added gestures to still more noises. Deciding to trust her, Belle removed her hand.

"The dead can't hear us," Gloria said.

"Yes, but the living can," said Belle, threatening her with the hand.

"There's nobody here but you and me." Gloria said. "See for yourself."

Belle glanced over her shoulder and saw that it was true. The little girl and the women were gone.

"Now you can tell me all about it," Gloria said. "When, where and how many times."

Ignoring her, Belle walked toward the lavatory to wash the lipstick off her hand.

Gloria tagged behind her. "Okay, so don't tell me. But I'll bet it was great. You're glowing like a hundred-watt bulb and Art's sniffing after you like a bear after a honey pot."

Belle continued to pretend she wasn't there. She turned on the faucet, ran her hands under the water, and squeezed liquid soap onto her hands. Taking her time, she washed and dried her hands, then applied a dab of lotion provided by the funeral home. Next she examined her face in the mirror, turning this way and that, studying her reflection from all angles. Gloria was right–she was glowing.

Having brushed her hair and reapplied her lipstick, Gloria was fast on Belle's heels as she headed back to the lounge. "I'm sorry I poked fun at you," she said. "Please don't be mad at me. I won't do it again. Honest."

Without looking at her, Belle said, "Apology accepted." Then, unable to keep it in another moment, she whirled around and faced Gloria with a radiant smile. "Art and I are crazy in love. We're so happy we can hardly stand it."

"Woo hoo!" Gloria cried. "Whoops, sorry," she said before Belle could shush her.

Belle went on in a rush, wanting to get it all out before someone came in. "He's asked me to marry him. Can you believe it? Of course he has to get a divorce first, but he says that shouldn't be a problem. A lot of Catholics are getting divorced these days. Not that that's a good thing, mind you, but it wouldn't be like he and Lil were the first. But whatever happens, he wants us to spend the rest of our lives together. Oh, and to think I was afraid to fall in love with him. I was so afraid he'd reject me. And all that time he was waiting for me to make the first move. Lord, I still can't believe it."

Gloria grabbed her in a hug and the two of them bounced up and down. "Oh, Belle, I'm so happy for you."

A sudden dizzy spell made Belle's head spin. She blanched and put her arms out for balance. "Oh, dear. I think I'm going to faint."

"Oh God," Gloria said, "you're as white as a ghost. Here, lean on me." She slipped an arm around Belle's waist and helped her to a chair. "Put your head between your knees and do your breathing thing."

Belle did as she was told and soon the dizzy spell began to pass.

Standing by, Gloria set her hands on her hips and said, "Don't tell me you're pregnant."

Belle's head came up with a jerk, causing her to see double. "No," she moaned. "I can't be."

"Why not?" Gloria wanted to know.

Still bleary-eyed, Belle tried to think but her mind was filled with fuzz. "It's not possible," she said. But for the life of her she couldn't think why.

"Did you use protection?" Gloria asked.

"No."

"Then it's possible."

At last it came to her. "No, it isn't. I've had a hysterectomy."

Disappointment etched Gloria's face. "Damn. I was hoping for a baby."

"I think Art and I are past the baby-raising stage, thank you. We'll just have to wait on you."

"Ha. I'm not having any kids."

"We'll see about that."

"Let's drop it, okay? Let's talk about you and Art. You have no idea how much I've wanted the two of you to get together. Art's been crazy about you since day one. I thought you'd never wake up. But you finally did and I couldn't be more thrilled. You make the perfect couple. Even if he can be an old grump."

Belle laughed.

A middle-aged woman came through the door. When she saw the two of them laughing, she pulled her shoulders back, looked down her nose and marched on by, clearly expressing her displeasure.

"Excuse us," Belle said to the woman's backside. "We were just leaving."

Linking arms and giggling like school girls, the two of them made their exit.

"You been gone too damn long," Art grumbled when Belle finally joined him. "What was that all about anyway?"

"You know Gloria," she said. "It took a while to straighten her out."

"About what? Us?"

"Of course."

He grinned and slid the hand at the small of her back toward her fanny. "That's my girl."

She swatted his hand and turned to face him. "What am I going to do with you?"

"Guess."

. . .

Inside the visiting room and nearing the head of the line, Belle was shocked at Marge's appearance. The weeks of caring for her dying mother had taken a heavy toll. Never one to care about the latest fashion or style in dress, Marge had also eschewed all forms of makeup and had kept her hair cropped at chin length. Still, she'd always looked neat and healthy. Now she looked positively gaunt and disheveled. Her plain black nylon dress was two sizes too big, her nylons bagged at her ankles, her uncut hair hung loose and stringy, and dark puffy bags circled her eyes.

Though she wanted to weep, Belle managed to remain dry-eyed when her turn finally came. Afraid of cracking a rib if she hugged Marge too tight, she held her loosely. "My heart bleeds for you, Marge," she murmured.

"Thank you for coming," Marge said. "It was good of you and Art to bring Mammy and the girls."

Belle's eyes roamed over her ravaged face. "Is there anything I can do for you? Anything at all?"

"Tell me how you're getting along," Marge said.

Belle mustered a smile. It was typical of Marge to think of others instead of herself. "I'm doing just fine."

"I heard your ex died and you went back to Georgia. You must be tired of funerals by now."

"I see Mammy has kept you posted. Did she tell you Mandy and I are friends now?"

Marge nodded. "She did. I'm glad some good came out of it."

"Yes." Belle said. "And I expect more good to follow."

Marge put a hand on her shoulder. "I'm very fond of you, you know. I'm going to miss you."

Belle felt like a fist was squeezing the air out of her lungs. "Does that mean you're not coming back to the center?"

"I don't know. I doubt it. Things are changing, and not for the better."

Belle suspected she was talking about the cut in funding. She wanted to tell her everything would be all right, that given time things would change for the better, but of course she couldn't. Not even Marge could know about the foundation.

"You'll never be rid of me, Marge," she said. "I owe you my life." She choked back a sob.

Art gave her arm a little squeeze and stepped up to take his turn.

Twenty-three

On the Wednesday following the trip to Livonia, Belle stood on her platform trying to concentrate on the new mural. All was ready: paint, brushes, cloths and sponges laid out in neat rows, other utensils within reach; smock and bandana protecting her clothes and hair.

Go ahead, she told herself, put the brush to the wall and start stroking. Once you get into the rhythm the paint will start to flow. She'd prepped the wall on Monday and Tuesday. Now it was time to start on the background.

She stood there for another ten minutes, squinting hard at the blank space before her, eyes watering from the effort of trying to envision the scene, neck and shoulder muscles burning with tension. Finally she laid her brush across the top of the nearest paint can and climbed off the platform.

Standing back at a critical distance, she surveyed the wall from top to bottom and side to side. It wasn't that large, a mere eight by ten-foot portion of the Cliffords' den. With the sun streaming through the windows at her back, the light was excellent. And because the Cliffords had moved the furniture to the center of the room, she had plenty of space in which to work. Not wanting to distract her, the Cliffords themselves were staying out of the way.

Retirees in their seventies, the missus was puttering about in the kitchen and the mister was out in his workshop, where he spent most of his time. Today he was rewiring a lamp for a friend. The house was perfectly quiet: no radio, no TV, no chiming clocks, no jangling phone, no pets. All in all, the conditions were ideal. So what was the problem? Had her creative juices dried up?

Yes, she had a lot on her mind, but in the past her art had been the perfect antidote. She could forget the outside world by losing herself in the scene she was painting. In this case the Cliffords had provided several photographs to help put her where she needed to be. Taken from across the street, the pictures showed different angles of the restaurant they'd owned and operated for thirty-seven years.

Located on North Claiborne, it had been a typical mom and pop operation with an old brick facade, a large plate glass window, a sign proclaiming Cliffords Diner, and a small parking lot on one side.

Regular customers knew the breakfast menu by heart. The daily luncheon specials were posted on a chalkboard. Though the restaurant didn't open until six o'clock in the morning, the Cliffords always arrived at four to begin preparations for the day's selections. Mrs. Clifford's biscuits, country ham, grits and red eye gravy were popular throughout the region. Although they closed for business at three in the afternoon, clean up and paperwork took several more hours–fifteen hour days with Sundays as their only day off. In all those years neither one of them had taken a single sick day. Nor had they taken a vacation.

Belle's admiration for them had soared when she heard their story. The Sidneys, the neighbors next door to Hope Haven, had told her the Cliffords were nice people. She hadn't imagined just how nice until she met them. They'd gone out of their way to accommodate her every need.

When she repeated their story to Art, he couldn't believe it.

"Jeez," he'd said, "and I thought I'd worked long hours."

An interior shot of the restaurant showed red vinyl booths against one wall and a lunch counter with bolted-down stools along the other.

In between sat six square tables with seating for four. But it was an exterior scene the Cliffords wanted on their wall. They wanted a reminder of their life's work in a bygone era. The restaurant, as well as a shoe store, a liquor store and a barber shop, had been razed to make way for a home building supply center.

And now here she stood, seemingly unable to provide them with the scene that would enrich their lives with pleasant memories. If only she could block out the rest of the world.

Words from the Serenity Prayer came to mind. *Accept the things you cannot change.* No matter how bitterly disappointed they were, she and Art would have to accept the fact that Lil refused to give him a divorce.

"I know what it is," he'd said shortly after making the call. "It's the monthly check. She's afraid I'm gonna cut her off."

"Tell her you'll put it in writing," Belle had suggested. "That way she'd know she could take you to court if you reneged."

"I already did. It didn't make no difference."

And that was that.

Legally, Art could try for an annulment. He'd talked to a priest and was told he had a solid case. For one thing, Lil had denied him sex since she'd learned she was pregnant with Sandy. That was over twenty-two years ago. For another, Lil had deserted him. She'd pack her bags and gone back to New Jersey a year ago. Moreover, she had no intention of returning. That in itself was cause enough. But Art didn't want to air their private life in public. He didn't care what people said about him, but he didn't want every friend and relative from Newark to Brooklyn whispering about Lil behind her back. What they said about Sandy and Artie was bad enough. He didn't love Lil, but she was the mother of his children.

Having been gossiped about herself, Belle understood all too well. Yes, it would be lovely to get married. They'd talked about having an outdoor wedding in Washington Square, a small affair with a reception at their house afterwards. But all their talk had been for naught. Now they must accept the thing they could not change–Lil's mind.

She walked over to the window and looked out on the day. Poor Art, she thought. He'd taken the news much harder than she had. She'd done her best to cheer him up, but he remained in the doldrums. That was one reason she'd been eager to get started on this job. She'd wanted to get out of the house and give him time to brood. She knew he'd snap out of it eventually and life would go on. It was just a matter of time.

Then there was the matter of Amber's pending adoption. Belle had reached Janette's social worker on Monday. It had disturbed her greatly to hear the reasoning behind the woman's motives to bring the case to an end, and the sooner the better. Put simply, her assessment of Janette's relationship with Amber contained nothing but negatives. Not only had Janette arrived late to several of the recent visitations, on one occasion she had failed to show up at all. As if that wasn't troubling enough, when Janette was with her daughter the interaction between them was strained at best. Janette didn't seem to know what to say to her daughter, and when Amber talked she didn't appear to listen. Hugs were tentative and declarations of love rang hollow. Perhaps Janette was still suffering huge amounts of guilt for her earlier neglect of Amber; perhaps she was afraid to get too close for fear of losing her entirely, or perhaps she simply didn't want to be there. Whatever the cause, when the two of them were together, Amber kept asking the supervisor of the visit if it was time to go home.

Belle had not discussed the conversation with Janette, she had not talked to her at all. That Janette had not called suggested she already knew the social worker's report would be unfavorable. All Belle could do at this point was hope Janette made the right decision, which, after taking everything into consideration, would be to sign the adoption papers.

Another matter that required patience was the establishment of the charitable foundation. As the executor of the estate, Jerry Thornton had told her to put off shopping for suitable properties to house a facsimile of Hope Haven–never mind a boardinghouse. It would be at least two months before all of the paperwork was in order. He could advance her funds within reason, he said, but he advised her to wait. Of course she had her jackpot winnings, but using her personal funds would lead to complications, according to Jerry.

As for buying a van, that was also on hold, and for more reasons than money. Innocent questions put to Mammy Daisy on the ride to Livonia led to the news that Mammy didn't know how to drive. What's more, she didn't care to learn. Further questioning revealed that of the girls in residence, only Millie and Gracie possessed valid driver's licenses–the others' had either been revoked or were nonexistent. Given that Millie was attending classes at odd hours, Gracie, in her position as unofficial assistant housemother, was the logical choice, but Art, after hearing of her driving record, nixed the idea due to high insurance costs. What they needed was a dependable and insurable driver–someone who could be available when needed, someone who liked females and liked going places.

Belle turned away from the window. Dwelling on a myriad of problems wasn't getting her anywhere. She took another look at the blank wall, then wandered toward the kitchen. Maybe hearing more stories about the restaurant would inspire her.

She paused on the threshold and looked around. Mrs. Clifford was standing across the room, her back to the doorway and her hands in the sink. The sound of water sloshing in the sink indicated she was washing something.

"Hello," Belle said. "Mind if I come in?"

Pulling her hands out of the sink, Mrs. Clifford made a half turn. She seemed surprised, as though she'd forgotten Belle was in the house. Drops of water fell from the tips of her fingers to the linoleum floor as she studied the person in the doorway.

"Well, now," she said, recognition appearing to dawn. "How you doin', shug?"

"Not too well, I'm afraid," Belle said, moving into the room. "I can't seem to get started. That's never happened to me before."

"Well, you sit right there in that chair and I'll get you some lemonade." She dried her hands on her apron and went to the refrigerator. A tiny, bird-like woman, her movements were practiced and quick.

"I been washing collards," she said. "Never could figure out how they collect so much dirt. Takes four rinsings to get 'em clean enough to cook. You like collards? Do, I'll fix you some to take on home."

"That would be lovely," Belle said, thinking the greens might help to improve Art's mood. He'd never heard of collards until Mammy Daisy served them, and then he'd loved them. Mustard greens and poke sallet, too.

She took a swallow of the lemonade Mrs. Clifford handed her. "Yum," she said, "this tastes extra good. Just what I needed, thanks."

Mrs. Clifford gave a toothless grin, causing her jaw to collapse in on itself. "It's my secret recipe," she confided, "but I'll tell you if you promise not to tell nobody."

"Cross my heart and hope to die," Belle said, making the sign of the cross on her chest with an index finger.

"I add a big pinch of brown sugar," Mrs. Clifford said with a mischievous gleam in her eye.

"Well," Belle said. "I'll have to try that the next time."

"Make sure the sugar's fresh. Don't use none that's gone hard in the box. Now, you sit right there and talk to me." Mrs. Clifford went back to the sink. "Help yourself to the lemonade whenever you get thirsty."

"Thanks, I will." She took another swallow then set the glass on the oilcloth-covered table. "Mrs. Clifford, I was wondering ... have you and the mister lived here all your lives?"

"No'um. We was raised up in Kosciusko, Mississippi. Didn't move here till after the war."

"Is Kosciusko anywhere near Laurel?"

"I reckon we're a hundred miles from Laurel. You got folks up there?"

"Sort of."

Mrs. Clifford gave her a peculiar look. "What sort of people are they?"

"People I care about. People I've been searching for but can't find. Two sisters, to be more specific. Blanche DuBois and Stella Kowalski. They were raised on a plantation called Belle Reve, the same name as mine. Stella left Laurel to marry Stanley, and Blanche stayed behind. She taught school, high school English. Then her life fell apart and she came here to stay with Stella."

"You don't say," Mrs. Clifford said. She pulled the plug in the sink. While the water gurgled down the drain, she looked back at Belle. "Seems like I heard of them two."

"You have?" Belle said, her skin beginning to tingle.

"Lemme think a minute. Mebbe it'll come to me."

Belle strained forward in her seat, willing the woman to remember.

"Seen 'em on the TV," Mrs. Clifford said. "They was in some movie or other. Reckon they're the same folks you're looking for?"

Belle bounced up from her chair with an explosion of breath. "Oh, I'm sure of it," she said, rushing across the room to stand next to Mrs. Clifford. "You see, a very famous playwright named Tennessee Williams ..."

She babbled on and on, all about the original production of the play in New York and the subsequent movies featuring various actors in the lead roles. How the story was based on real people and real events, and how it always ended the same way, with Blanche being taken away to a mental institution. How she and Art had gone to the state hospitals in Mandeville and Jackson, how they'd gone to Laurel only to find the town closed down for the mayor's funeral, and how she'd questioned countless people–all to no avail.

By the time she finished, Mrs. Clifford's collard greens, seasoned with a slab of fatback, were simmering on the stove and she was chopping cabbage for cole slaw. Now that Belle had stopped talking, she stopped chopping. She looked at Belle and said, "You say they lived here in town? Right around the corner?" The Cliffords lived on

Marigny, two blocks from Stanley's old house.

"Yes. On the corner of Elysian Fields and Royal. Back in the days after the war, when you and Mister Clifford moved here, it was a dilapidated old place with a rickety staircase leading to the upstairs apartment. But now ... now it's painted a dusty rose and it has dark gray shutters and a canopy over the front door. I don't know if Stanley fixed it up before he sold it, or if it was the lawyers who bought it. It really doesn't matter; I just wish I knew where he and Stella went."

"I must'a seen the house a million times and never looked at it," Mrs. Clifford said. "You know how it is. Me and Carlus, we'd get in the car of a morning and we wouldn't come home till late. Many's the time we didn't see daylight 'ceptin through the diner's window."

"I understand," Belle said, feeling a crush of disappointment. "But oh how I wish you could tell me you knew them. If only I could find just one person in this city who had actually laid eyes on one of them. I don't care if it was only Stanley, I'd still give that person a big hug."

"Well, I'll take a hug, but I only seen 'em on the TV."

"That's good enough," Belle said, folding the spare woman in her arms and giving her a little squeeze. "It felt good just to talk about them. In fact, I think I'm ready to go to work. For real, this time."

. . .

"Guess what?" Belle exclaimed the minute she stepped onto the porch.

Art, who'd been waiting for her in his rocking chair, looked up from the evening paper. "What?"

"Oh, Art, you are not going to believe it," she crowed, her eyes as bright as hundred-watt bulbs. "I stopped by Washington Square on my way home and the most wonderful thing happened. Oh my goodness ... even I can't believe it." She paused and patted her chest as though out of breath. Then she flung her arms upwards and cried to the heavens: "Blanche is still there! "

Art folded the paper and laid it on the table. "Whaddaya talking about?"

"I'm talking about Blanche. Remember when we ate lunch in the park? Remember how fresh and spiffy everything looked? And I was so sad because I thought Blanche had moved on?"

Art gave a stiff nod.

"Well, I'm happy to say I was mistaken. I sat on my bench today, just like I used to do, and within minutes I could feel her presence. It was like her spirit seeped through the soles of my feet and all the way up to my heart. It made me feel warm and fuzzy all over. Then the most exciting thing ever happened. I actually saw her! Honest to God. There was a kind of silvery glow shimmering before my eyes. And it wasn't a dream or a hallucination, I swear I saw her essence floating in the air. Isn't that just too marvelous for words?"

"Yeah," said Art, "it's terrific. So what else is new? What's in the bag you got there? Stanley's shrunken head?"

Belle stuck out her tongue at him. "Oh, don't be such an old grump," she said. "I refuse to let you bring me down from my cloud." She waltzed over to him and proceeded to swing the bag back and forth in front of his nose. "Does this smell like Stanley?"

"You're just full of it, ain't ya?" he said, a tiny grin tugging at the corners of his mouth.

"Go ahead," she said. "Guess what's really in here."

He leaned forward and took a whiff of the bag. "Some kinda greens, some chicken, and some bread."

"Give that man a cigar!" she cheered. "It's collards, corn bread, fried chicken wings, and slaw." She snatched the bag out of his reach and hid it behind her back. "But it's bad for your health, so I'll just have to eat it all."

"Like hell," he said, halfway rising out of his chair.

"Well," she said, "I might give you a piece of corn bread ... if you can catch me." She made a dash for the door and raced inside the house.

Art chased after her. She led him through the living room, the den, the kitchen, down the hall, and into the bedroom, where she dropped the bag on the dresser and collapsed on the bed.

By the time Art climbed up beside her she was engulfed in a fit of giggles. He wrestled her onto her back, swung a leg over her middle, and pinned her arms above her head.

"Gotcha" he said, lowering his face to hers.

She jerked her head to one side, successfully avoiding his kiss. "Not until you tell me you're happy I communed with Blanche," she said.

"I'm happy," he said.

"About what?" she demanded.

"About you and Blanche."

"What about me and Blanche?"

"You know. That you got together again."

"Well," she said, considering his declaration. "I suppose that will have to do." Then, tickling his sides, she said, "Kiss me, you old poop, before I change my mind."

He did as he was told.

. . .

Later, as they lay entwined in each other's arms, the bed sheet pulled up to their bare chests, Art said, "Y'know, I been thinking ... and I decided to try cutting Lil off starting now. See what she does when the monthly checks dry up."

"Oh dear," Belle said. "Do you really think you ought to do that?"

"Why not? It's not like I owe her or anything. She's the one left me, not the other way around. We don't have nothing like a legal separation. I been sending the dough 'cause I thought she needed it. But then I look at you going to work every day and I'm thinking, hey, why can't Lil get off her duff and get a job. And that goes for Sandy. Why should I keep sending them my hard-earned money so they can sit around drinking coffee, watching their soap operas and game shows, and visiting family. It don't make sense."

Belle didn't know what to say. When she was married to Lin he wouldn't hear of her getting a job. For better or worse, he wanted her to stay at home. How different their lives might have been had she gone to work or at least had volunteered her services. She might never have become afflicted with agoraphobia, might never have taken up with Mister Vodka.

"Apparently they've become very dependent on you," she said, an inane statement if ever she heard one.

"Yeah," Art said. "And it's all my fault. But that don't mean I can't do nothing about it. Or that I shouldn't do nothing. The more I think about it the more I think it's the right thing to do. And I ain't doing it out of spite. I been thinking about this a long time. You with me on this, or what?"

Not knowing what to say, Belle stalled for time."How are you going to tell her? Are you going to call her or write her a letter?"

"For sure I ain't calling her. She'd start hollering bloody murder. I'm gonna write her a letter. Try to get it down just right. Will you lend me a hand?"

"Gee, do you think that's wise?"

"Sure, why not. I don't want you to write the damn thing, I just want you to look it over. Dot all the i's and cross all the t's."

"That I can do."

"Great. We'll work on it after supper. But first ..." He raised up on one elbow and cupped a hand over her breast. "First, I got a little business to tend to."

. . .

"Who's this?" a snarly voice asked the moment Belle answered the phone.

"Who are you calling?" Belle said, certain the party had the wrong number.

"You the reason Art wants a divorce?"

Perplexed, Belle held the receiver away from her ear and looked at it, as though it might show her who was at the other end of the line.

She knew the caller was a woman because of the voice. Then it came to her. The woman must be Lil.

So soon, Belle thought, mentally calculating the number of days since Art mailed the letter. Today was Saturday. They'd mailed the letter on Thursday. And to think people complained about the postal service!

"This is Belle Reve speaking," she said into the mouthpiece. "Art's not here right now, but I'll be glad to take a message."

"When's he gonna be back?" the woman snapped

"In about an hour. Would you like me to have him call you? Is this Lil?"

"Your darn tootin' it's Lil. Who else knows about him wanting a divorce?"

"Well, ah, I, uh ..."

"Spit it out, girlie. You put him up to this, didn't you? I've a good mind to come down there and give you what for."

"Oh, that would be wonderful," Belle gushed. "You coming down, I mean. I've been wanting to meet you. And I'm dying to meet Sandy and the boys. In fact, Art's planning to have them down this summer, after the boys get out of school. Of course, we'd love to have you too. There's this charming little hotel not far from here. I stayed there when I first came to New Orleans. They serve the best breakfasts–Eggs Benedict, French toast with these little sausage links, poached eggs with crispy strips of bacon ... yum, it makes my mouth water just to think about it."

When Belle heard nothing but a prolonged silence she thought Lil had hung up. "Hello?" she said. "Are you still there?"

Lil came back on the line. "Girlie, are you for real?"

Belle gave a light laugh. "You know, back when I lived at Hope Haven, the girls used to ask me the same thing."

"What's Hope Haven? Some kind of cloister?"

"Not exactly. It's a halfway house for female drug addicts."

"And you lived there?"

"That's right. It was my home-sweet-home for six months. Then

I moved in with Art."

"You're living with Art?"

"Yes, ma'am. It's such a pretty house, a little doll house, really. You should see how he fixed it up. You'd be real proud of it. It looks ever so much better than when you were here."

"How do you know what it looked like?"

"I've seen pictures. It's a shame you didn't like the house. It really had a lot of potential, and Art knew just what to do with it. He's got these friends named James and Henry? Well, they live down the street, and they've practically decorated the whole house. Art bought a few pieces on his own, but James and Henry's have an interior design business. They buy antiques that have been neglected and then they restore them. You should see their work. It's exquisite."

"How old are you, girlie?" Lil asked.

"Oh, please call me Belle. I'm forty. I'll be forty-one in September. I have the same birthday as Blanche. I don't know what year she was born, but I think she'll be seventy-four. She could be older than that, though. I think she fibbed about her age."

"She living there too?"

"Blanche? Oh my, how I wish she was. But no, Blanche is the lady I came to New Orleans to see–I used to live in Georgia, but this is my home now. The trouble is, I can't find her. Do you know I still have her birthday gift from last year? It's a red satin kimono, exactly like the one she wore when she stayed at Stella and Stanley's. Stella's her sister."

"Then how come you don't ask Stella where Blanche is?"

Belle sighed. "Believe me, I'd love nothing better. But Stella and Stanley moved and no one seems to know where they went."

"Who's the oldest? Blanche or Stella?"

"Blanche."

"Have you tried looking in the nursing homes?"

Belle froze in place. "What did you say?"

"I said, have you tried looking in nursing homes."

"That's what I thought you said."

"Well? Have you?"

"Why no. No, I haven't."

"Huh," Lil snorted. "That's the first place I would've looked."

The idea made Belle feel stupid and excited at the same time, stupid for not thinking of it herself and excited by the thought of a new search.

"Oh my lord, Lil, you are a true genius. I can't imagine why I didn't think of that. It's such a logical place to look. Oh my, I can't wait to get started. And I can't thank you enough."

"Think nothing of it," Lil said. "Tell Art to call me."

Just as Belle opened her mouth, another gush of words on the tip of her tongue, she heard a click.

"Hello? Hello?" she said.

Nothing.

She hung up the phone, flung out her arms and began twirling around the room. Lil had opened up a whole new world of possibilities. It was as if Blanche herself was telling her where to look for her. First her spirit had appeared in the park, and now this. Oh lordy, she could hardly wait to tell Art.

Twenty-four

“Goodness,” Belle said, “I had no idea there were so many nursing homes.” Seated in her rocker on the porch, she turned another yellow page in the telephone book and scanned the list. “It’ll take me forever to contact all of them, and a lot of them are outside the city limits. Blanche could be most anywhere.”

“Or nowhere,” Art muttered to himself. He was still put out with Lil and her big mouth. Because of Lil’s brainy idea, Belle thought she was the greatest thing since sliced bread. Hell, he could’ve told her to look in nursing homes, but, talk about depressing. All they needed for a cheerful evening was Belle coming back from some old folks’ home with her head hanging down to her knees ‘cause she didn’t find Blanche and it was all so sad. “Oh, those poor, pitiful souls,” he could hear her saying.

“Please don’t be so negative, Art. I have a feeling this is my last hope.”

“Hey, wait a minute. What about going back to Laurel? We were gonna check that out again.”

“You heard what the people in Laurel said. None of them had ever heard of Blanche.”

“That don’t mean she’s not there. Maybe she’s doing a Greta

Garbo routine."

"Then why would her spirit be lingering in the park? No, I'm convinced she's around here somewhere."

He shrugged. "Suit yourself. Just don't expect me to start running you all over town."

"Don't worry," she said. "Tallulah will take me wherever I need to go, thank you. And I'm not going anywhere until I talk to someone in the know. I'm hoping they'll have some sort of central listing for patients in nursing homes. I'll talk to Mrs. Bardet at the courthouse. She'll know who I should contact."

"Don't count on it."

Belle closed the telephone book and put it on the porch floor. She scooched around in her chair until she found her spot and then she started rocking to and fro. "When are you going to call Lil back?"

"Never. She wants to talk to me she can do it on her own dime."

"My, but we're in a sour mood tonight."

"I was in a good mood till I got home," he muttered under his breath.

"I heard that," she said. "Does that mean you've grown tired of me already?"

He looked at her, saw the worried look on her face–that beautiful face with the creamy skin, those big blue eyes, that pert little nose, and those kissable lips–and his heart did a little flip-flop.

"You know what your problem is?" he said.

"What?"

"You're too damn nice."

She gave a nervous laugh. "Am I supposed to take that as a compliment?"

"Take it whatever way you want."

"Then I'll take it as a compliment. But I think you meant it as an insult."

"See what I mean?" Art said. "You always look on the bright side. The glass is always half full."

She stopped rocking. "What's wrong with that?"

"It ain't natural."

"It is to me," she said quietly.

"Tell me about it," he said. "Nobody but you would make friends with the woman who won't give me a divorce. It's like you've taken her side or something."

"Ah, so that's what's bothering you.."

"Damn straight. I'm wanting us to get married in the worse way and you go bouncing along like it's no big deal that we can't."

"It isn't that big of a deal. We don't need a piece of paper to live together like man and wife. We're already doing that. Besides, if I'm friends with Lil, maybe she'll end up liking me so much she'll want to make me happy. Which means she might change her mind about the divorce."

"Fat chance," said Art, slumping further down in his seat.

"Okay, here's what I think we should do. Let's see, it's the third of April, so we'll give Lil two months. If she doesn't change her mind by the middle of June, we'll have a mock wedding. We'll invite everyone we know and have a ceremony in the park. Washington Square is gorgeous in June–so many flowers in bloom ...birds and butterflies everywhere. We could call the ceremony a ... oh, I know–we'll call it a celebration of love. It would be the next best thing to getting married. We could even take a trip afterwards. Just like a real honeymoon. What do you think?"

Art thought it over and had to admit it wasn't such a bad idea. A real wedding would be better, but, hey, at least this way everyone would know they were a couple. And when you came right down to it, even if they were to get married for real, the Catholic church wouldn't recognize them as man and wife. That was Lil's main objection. As far as the Church was concerned the two of them–him and Lil–were stuck with each other till doomsday. Or until one of them died. With his luck it'd be him.

He pushed the thought away and went back to what Belle said. What appealed to him about her idea was having a plan and a time frame to go on. Either way it worked out, divorce or no divorce, they would still get to take a trip. He could do without the ceremony in the park, but knowing it'd mean a lot to Belle he'd go along with it. He might even buy a new suit. And maybe one of those dressy shirts with French cuffs.

"Sounds good to me," he said, sitting up straight and ready to talk about hitting the road. "So, where you wanna go? California?"

"You and your precious California," she said with a laugh. "But if that's your number one choice then that's where we'll go."

"Now you're talking."

They spent the next hour or so discussing their plans. How they would drive out west and stop and see the sights along the way. They would take the southern route going and the mid-western route coming back.

When it came time to go inside and get ready for bed, Belle said, "I hate to bring this up, Art, but you need to call Lil back before it gets too late."

"Aw, jeez," he said, expelling a groan. "Why'd you have to go and spoil everything?"

"Because if you don't call her she'll think I forgot to tell you, and I don't want her to be mad at me."

"She ain't gonna be mad at you, she's gonna know I don't wanna talk to her."

"No, she'll think it's all my fault."

"For cryin' out loud," he said, getting up from his chair. "You beat all I ever seen." The screen door slammed behind him as he disappeared inside the house.

. . .

The first words out of Lil's mouth were: "How'd you find out? Sandy tell you?"

"Tell me what?" Art asked, already bored with the conversation. It was always the same with Lil; they went around and around and never got anywhere.

"About my job."

The shock of her statement made Art's ears ring. "You got a job?"

"You didn't know?"

"Would I be asking if I did?"

"Oh," Lil said. "I thought that's why you stopped the checks."

"I told you why. I told you in the letter. Didn't you read it?"

"Yeah, but that doesn't mean you were telling the truth."

"C'mon, Lil, I don't have all night. What about the job?"

"Promise you won't laugh."

"What could be funny about you getting a job? You're blowing my mind."

"I'm a Wal-Mart greeter."

"What's that?"

"What's a Wal-Mart or what's a greeter?"

"Whaddaya think I am, stupid? A greeter."

"I greet people as they come in the store. Answer their questions and make sure they're not carrying anything in or out that needs checking."

"How about that," Art said, still in a state of shock.

"And you know what?" Lil asked.

"What?"

"The boss says I'm doing a really good job. If I keep it up, he says he'll put me on as a security guard. I'll get to wear a uniform and everything."

"Yeah? Hey, that's great. That's really great. Congratulations."

"Thanks." Art could picture the self-satisfied grin on her face. "I don't know what I'd do without this job," she said. "I had to get out of the house. Sandy and the kids were driving me nuts."

"I hear ya. Sandy's the one needs a job."

"That's what I keep telling her. Maybe one of these days she'll wake up and smell the you-know-what. Oh, and soon's Artie heard the news, here he comes with his hand out."

Art's heart skipped a beat at the mention of his son. "How's he doing?"

"Same old same old," she said.

"Y'know, they got halfway houses up there. Too bad he don't check himself into one. You should see the girls that're in the one Belle lived in. They're doing great."

"Yeah, I met Belle. That is, I talked to her on the phone. She the reason you want a divorce?"

"As a matter of fact, she is."

"Well, I'm sorry to disappoint you, Art, but you're gonna have to wait till I drop dead."

"That ain't funny, Lil. Nobody's wanting you to drop dead."

"I wouldn't bet on it."

"You can take it to the bank," Art said.

"Speaking of banks," Lil said, "now that I'm making my own money I've opened a savings account. And I'll tell you one thing, Artie's not getting a dime of it."

"That figures," Art said. "You'll give him my dough but you're not about to part with any of yours."

Lil cackled a witch's laugh. "That's 'cause your money was easy to come by."

"Not anymore."

"No, not anymore. And Art, I gotta tell you, I been expecting it. So's Sandy. It's a wonder you paid out as long as you did."

"Now you tell me."

"You know what they say, there's one born every minute. Well, I got first shift tomorrow so I gotta get to bed. See you around, Art."

"Right," he said, disappointed that they couldn't talk a while longer. He couldn't remember the last time they'd had a decent conversation. If he could keep it going, maybe they could've figure out a way to help their kids.

"Hey, Art," Lil said. "You still there?"

"Yeah, I'm here."

"I just wanted to say thanks."

Art shook his head to clear it. Had he heard right? Lil had never thanked him for anything–she'd been too full of gripes and blame. He gulped a breath of air and said, "You're welcome." Then, because he was suddenly ill at ease, he said, "Well, it's been nice talking to you, Lil. Keep in touch, okay?"

"Not to worry," she said. "We still got kids in common, y'know."

"Yeah, I know. Take it easy, y'hear?"

"I don't believe it," Lil said . "Art Barkoff with a Southern accent. *Ciao* for now, pal."

He hung up the phone and stood staring at it for several seconds, halfway expecting Lil to call back and shout April Fool! Here he'd been sweating it out over cutting her off, and she'd not only seen it coming she'd gone out and gotten a job. Yes sir, she'd played him like the sap he was. But he couldn't fault her for that. So she'd pulled one over on him, so what. At least his conscience was clear.

He could hear Belle running bath water into the tub. Itching to scrub her back, he headed that way.

. . .

The next few weeks flew by in a flurry of activity. The month of April had been ripped off the calendar. Before they knew it June would be here.

A change in Belle's routine occurred after she talked to a lady at the Office of Community Services. There was no such thing as a central listing for seniors in residential facilities, the lady said. If Belle really wanted to find her friend, she would have to visit all the approved sites. So every Tuesday like clockwork she took off work a few hours early and, with a city map laid across Tallulah's passenger seat, set out to find Blanche.

The places she visited encompassed nursing homes, senior centers, assisted living complexes and retirement communities. Because they were spread across a wide range of territory, she tried to be systematic in her approach, choosing a locale and then tracking down all the facilities in that area. Despite her best intentions, she found herself lingering at one place or another; sometimes spending an entire afternoon.

Contrary to Art's dire predictions that the visits would make her sad, she actually enjoyed the outings. Always on the lookout for those residents who were desperately lonely, it made her feel good to provide a little comfort. Some wanted to be read to, some wanted simple conversation, some wanted nothing more than a *hello*, some wanted a touch. She was particularly drawn to the little old ladies, none of whom, unfortunately, bore the name of Blanche. But she never got discouraged.

Tuesdays were popular days for bingo games at residential and community centers alike. Conducted by volunteers, Belle always joined in. Her favorite job was helping the visually impaired locate the numbers on their bingo cards. On the weekends she had fun shopping for prizes, which she handed out whether there was a bingo game or not. Jewelry, especially bright beaded necklaces and earrings, went over well with the ladies; the men liked pocket knives and eye-catching key chains.

Another change took place when Marge returned to the mental health center to resume her work as a therapist. Before she left, Belle was still living at Hope Haven, her departure having been postponed. At that time she'd been scheduled to see Marge three times a week, but those plans went by the wayside when Marge's mother took ill.

Not long after Marge took sick leave to care for her mother, Lin had come to town. And, as things turned out, Belle had been forced to take control of her life without Marge's guidance. Because she'd done "such a splendid job," according to Marge, further treatment was considered unnecessary. They would remain friends, however, seeing one another when time allowed.

On one occasion, when they met for lunch in Washington Square, Marge confided that she was thinking of going into private practice. Uncertain about Hope Haven's future–*if* Hope Haven even had a future–and unhappy with the state's political wrangling over funds, she wanted out of the system. Whatever she did, she planned to stay in New Orleans. It was a good thing, Belle thought. Marge didn't know it yet, but once the foundation was up and running, she would be offered a job.

Marge provided more relief when she managed to track Boots down. A conversation with Boots' mother led to a conference call placed by Marge to Boots' residence. The call was made on a sunny Sunday afternoon from the staff lounge at the mental health center, with Belle and Hope Haven's finest in attendance.

The news from Boots had its highs and lows, but it was far better than expected. Her homecoming had not gone well, Boots said, because her mother treated her like a child. She'd laid down more rules than Hope Haven had, and she'd checked up on her constantly, even as she slept, Boots imagined. So she'd left her mother's home and moved in with a friend until she had saved enough money to rent her own place. It wasn't much, she said, just a small, furnished trailer, but it felt good to be on her own. More than anything else, she was excited about her weight loss. Always on the far side of plump, she'd lost twenty-two pounds despite working in a donut shop.

After apologizing for not staying in touch and promising to do better in the future, Boots said a tearful goodbye. The women then traipsed across the street to Hope Haven for coffee and strawberry shortcake.

Another major source of relief had nothing to do with Marge. Belle received the phone call on the last Saturday in April. She and Art had just finished lunch and he'd gone outside to change Tallulah's oil.

"Hi," Janette said. "I just wanted you to know I cancelled tomorrow's visitation."

Belle felt a niggling of alarm. "Why? Are you ill?"

Janette hesitated. "Not exactly. I don't have the flu or anything, but I must be mentally ill. I've decided to sign the papers."

"Oh, Janette ... are you sure?"

"I'm ninety-nine percent sure." She heaved and sigh and went on. "That's good enough for me."

"Oh, sweetie," Belle said. "I can't tell you how–"

Janette cut her off. “Listen, Belle, I don’t want this to turn into an emotional binge. I’ve had my cry and now I just want to get it over with. Let’s face it, I’ve been kidding myself all along. Thinking I could give Amber a home ... wanting nothing more than for us to be together. It was all a crazy pipe dream. Hell, I’m barely getting by on my own. All I need is to get tied down with a kid. Besides, what do I know about kids? But never mind all that. I just wanted you to know. I’ll be okay, so don’t worry about me.”

Belle gave a mirthless laugh.“You know I will, but I’ll try not to worry myself sick. Janette, honey, you are the bravest person I know. Now you take good care of yourself, and remember I’m always here for you. I love you, baby doll.”

“Thanks, Belle. I love you, too.”

. . .

“Wait till you hear this.” Gloria said without preamble.

“What?” Belle asked. It was a good thing Art was outside tinkering with the Checker, she thought. The seemingly endless phone calls from the girls on Saturdays tended to annoy him. Especially since this was also her day to call Mandy and her parents.

“I’ve got a new roommate,” Gloria said.

“Oh? How do you feel about that?”

“I’m pissed. Oops, sorry ... I mean I’m upset. After all, Millie and Gracie have each had a room all to themselves ever since Darleen and Janette left. Besides, Mammy knew how I felt about not wanting anyone to take your place unless it was absolutely necessary. So what does she do? She gives me the new girl. I came home from class yesterday and surprise, surprise. I would’ve called you last night, but this is the first chance I’ve had. You’d think Mammy could’ve given me some kind of warning.”

“Maybe she was as surprised as you were.”

“Mammy surprised? Not hardly. Marge tells her everything in advance and you know it.”

"Well? How is it working out?"

"Okay, I guess. Her name is, get this, Latessiah. Why do black people give their kids names nobody can spell? What's the matter with Mary or Ann or just plain Jane?"

Belle had to laugh. "Spelling never was your strong suit."

"Ha ha. Very funny."

"Oh no," Belle said, sobering fast. "I just thought of something. Has she said anything about the mural?"

"No, why?"

"What if she doesn't like it? What if she wants to paint over it?"

"That'll be the day," Gloria said. "If she says one nasty word about the mural she's out of here, I don't care what Mammy says. It's me or her. If Mammy chooses her, I'll come live with you."

The very thought sent a chill up Belle's spine. She loved the girl dearly, and in his own way Art loved her too, but he'd have a fit and a half if she moved in with them.

"Now, Gloria, be nice."

"Nice, my as–foot. That mural's off limits. I wish I could take it with me when I move out."

Even though Gloria couldn't see her, Belle nodded. "That's exactly how I felt."

"So when are you going to get around to painting one on your wall? Art's been wanting one in the worst way."

"I know," Belle said, feeling a pang of guilt. Her rule about not painting in someone else's bedroom no longer applied because now it was her room, too. "Maybe I'll get started on it after I finish my current job."

"Which is?"

She'd done two other murals since she finished the Cliffords' diner–one a Mississippi River scene, and one of a courtyard filled with tropical foliage. The latter had a pond with a frog sitting on a lily pad and a parrot perched in a banana tree.

"This one is a bayou scene," she told Gloria. "It's got cypress trees, hanging moss, alligators, nutrias, and all kinds of wading birds.

I'm having fun with it. It reminds me of the day Art and I went on that boat tour of the swamps and bayous out near Westwego."

"Sounds neat," said Gloria.

"It is, if I do say so myself. But back to you moving out. You're not planning on it any time soon, are you?" Somehow she had to dispel Gloria's notion of moving in with them. Besides, she'd been hoping Gloria would stay put until the foundation had purchased a suitable property for a boardinghouse. That way, Gloria could move right in.

"Not real soon," Gloria said. "I have to stay here till the end of next quarter. Then if my grades are good enough, which I'm sure they will be, Shirley–you know, my rehab counselor–she said she'll help me find a part-time job. Then as soon as I get enough money together I'll move in with Janette. I just wish that place she lives in wasn't so far away."

"Well," Belle said, tingling with excitement, "maybe a good fairy will open up a place on this side of town."

"She'd better hurry up."

"How do you know it'll be a she?"

"All good fairies are women, silly."

. . .

Gloria called back the next day. "Just thought you'd want to know ... Latessiah likes the mural. Thinks it's way cool."

"Thank goodness," said Belle.

"Oh, and guess what. She knows Darleen. Back when they were turning tricks, she and Darleen used to work the same corner."

Belle sighed. "I could have gone a lifetime without knowing that, thank you."

Gloria laughed and said, "Gotta go. Me and Latessiah have a hot Monopoly game going. 'Bye."

. . .

Belle saw the house on the first Tuesday in May. She'd been driving down Esplanade, on her way home from an assisted living facility in Gretna. She was four blocks up and on the opposite side of the street from Art's–she still thought of the creole cottage as Art's.

The first thing that caught Belle's eye was the name on the For Sale sign planted in the front yard. Though she only caught the barest of glimpses, the name Stanley jumped out at her. Thinking it could be *her* Stanley, Stella's husband Stanley Kowalski, Belle mashed her foot against the brake. Screeching to a stop, she saw the last name–Johns. Stanley Johns. It was then that she realized what she'd done and where she was–stopped in the middle of the street. Had a car–worse, a bus–been behind her, Tallulah would be crushed metal by now. With her heart thudding against her chest, she ever-so-carefully pulled the car over to the curb and switched off the ignition. A delayed reaction to her near-miss caused icy prickles of gooseflesh to crawl over her flesh.

When her skin warmed and her heartbeat returned to normal, she climbed out of the car. Painted the yellow of an early spring morning, the house–it looked like a mansion–had a silver tin roof and sparkling white trim. Large front porches supported by massive square posts extended out from both the first and second levels. A narrow wrought iron balcony ran the width of the third level. Shutters flanked multi-paned windows, matching bay windows and single casements. At the rear of the second level, jalousied windows enclosed what appeared to be a sun porch. Since there were no obvious signs of life either in or outside the house, Belle took her time walking around the property. The longer she looked the more excited she got. If she'd had a cellular phone she would have called Stanley Johns right then and there. As it was, she finally climbed intoTallulah and headed for home.

At precisely seven o'clock that night, she and Art met Stanley Johns at the property. The three of them hit it off immediately. A jovial, down-to-earth man, Stanley had a head full of prematurely white hair. Dressed in blue jeans and a red T-shirt, he'd ridden a

Harley to the house. He'd not only brought the plat, a copy of the deed and all the specs on the house, but a verbal history as well.

The three-story mansion–it truly was a mansion–had undergone several transformations over the years. Originally a single family dwelling for one of the town's wealthiest men, it had been converted into apartments after the man's death. Later, a new owner turned it into a small hotel. Eventually, due to poor management, the property fell into disrepair and was put on the auction block. Two men, self-described life partners, won the bid and set about fixing it up with the intention of reopening the hotel. They had the new roof installed and the exterior painted. They'd just gotten started on the interior when one of the men was diagnosed with AIDS. They then put the property on the market, and here it was, just waiting for Belle to notice–except she had to be careful to not show a personal interest or hint at what the property might be used for. As far as Stanley Johns was concerned, she and Art were looking at it as a possible investment for a lawyer friend in Atlanta. Which Belle didn't consider to be an outright lie. Jerry Thornton was a lawyer and he lived in Atlanta.

The interior was indeed in disrepair: rusted-out plumbing, buckling linoleum, cracked window-panes, torn screens, peeling wallpaper, mold buildup, stained ceilings ... the list went on and on. But, oh, there were so many rooms and so much potential. Art saw it, too, just as he'd seen the possibilities at his creole cottage. It was all Belle could do to keep from bouncing up and down. But she and Art managed to remain noncommital. They thanked Stanley for the tour and told him they would be in touch.

Later, at home, they discussed the prospects at length. "I think we should combine the two." Belle said. "The house–excuse me, the mansion–is way too big for a halfway house. And since we're only going to have six boarders at a time, it's too big for a boardinghouse. If we divide the house into two sections, we could have both under the same roof."

"Not a bad idea," Art said. "It'd be a lot easier, not to mention cheaper." He thumped the side of his head with a hand. "What am I saying? Here I am talking cheap to a zillionaire."

"Hush," she said. "We're not going to mention that, remember?"

"How could I forget."

"By the way, did you happen to count the number of bedrooms?"

"I thought you did."

She laughed a merry laugh and said, "Well, I guess we'll just have to go back to the house."

"Fine by me," Art said. "I wanna take a look at the pipes, see if all the toilets flush and stuff like that."

Belle laughed. "Be my guest."

• • •

They met Stanley Johns the following morning at ten o'clock. This time he brought a diagram of the house, complete with square footage. They spent over two hours going from room to room, making notes of needed repairs as they went.

Even with their notes and a copy of the diagram, they wanted yet another look later that afternoon. When Stanley heard, he said, "I figured as much. The key's under the mat at the back door. Be sure to lock up when you leave."

That night they celebrated by having a sumptuous dinner and a bottle of wine at K-Paul's. Though an offer to purchase the property had yet to be made, in her heart and in her mind Belle already thought of the house as hers.

Twenty-five

The invitations read:

Please join us for a Celebration of Love.
Where: Washington Square.
When: On June 29 of this year.
Time: Five o'clock.
Reception immediately following the ceremony.
Location: The Sunshine House on Esplanade.
No gifts, please. Your presence is gift enough.

On the chance that Lil wouldn't change her mind at the last minute, the invitations were sent out two weeks prior to the big event. If by some miracle Lil did decide to grant Art a divorce, and if time allowed, they could surprise their guests with a real wedding. If not, they could make it official after they returned from their trip. They might even decide to get married on their way out west. According to Art, Las Vegas had more wedding chapels than casinos.

The days leading up to the twenty-ninth flew by in a whirlwind of activity. Besides working at their respective jobs and planning the celebration ceremony and the reception afterwards, it fell to Belle to pack for their trip. In an effort to stay out of her way when she started raiding the closets, Art tried to make himself scarce. He'd warned her to pack light, that the cab's trunk wasn't a boxcar and they needed to save room for all their souvenirs. Thinking it'd look great in the den, Art wanted a cigar store Indian for himself. 'Course he couldn't fit one of those six-or-seven-footers in the cab, he'd have to settle for a smaller one, but he wanted one all the same. And he knew Belle would buy a ton of stuff for Mammy and all the girls.

He could care less about what clothes to take. Some underwear, socks, a couple pairs of pants in addition to the ones he'd wear, a few extra shirts, and a jacket in case it got cold in the mountains. When their stuff got dirty they could always find a Laundromat somewhere or wash things out in a sink.

Did Belle listen? Not a chance. She was bound and determined to take enough clothes for every conceivable occasion. And what with the season's changeable weather, she wanted to prepare for hot, cold, and everything in-between.

As the twenty-ninth neared and she still hadn't packed, Art made the mistake of popping in on her one day as she rifled through their clothes. She'd pull a dress or a pair of slacks out of the closet, look the item over, then put it back. Eventually, she went through every article of clothing they owned, including what they had stacked in drawers. Nothing suited her, everything looked dull and shabby.

"So buy yourself some new duds," Art suggested.

"We can't afford it," she said. "The trip itself will cost a fortune."

He gaped at her. "I'm not believing what you just said. Hell, if you wanted to you could buy every department store in town. But that's beside the point. I already told you I got the trip covered, and I got more than enough to spring for some new duds."

"Thank you, Art, but no thank you. I will not have you spending all your money. As long as we're comfortable I don't suppose it really matters what we look like. Chances are we won't see anyone we know, and, like you said, we can find a Laundromat when our clothes get dirty." With that, she went back to the closet.

"Right," said Art. Knowing she didn't believe a word she'd just said, he hightailed it out of there.

. . .

By the twenty-eighth day of June, the eve of the celebration in the park, the suitcases remained empty. What's more, it started raining along about dusk.

To get her mind off the rain and back onto packing, Belle started grabbing clothes out of the closet and piling them on the bed. It would be so much easier to choose what to take once it was all spread out before her. Before long the pile grew into a hill and then a small mountain. Undaunted when a few items slipped to the floor, she kept adding more piles.

Finally she worked her way to the back of the closet and the fancy dresses she rarely wore. It was then that she made a shocking discovery. She'd been so distracted by other matters she hadn't given a single thought to what she'd wear to tomorrow's ceremony!

Overcome by all the things she'd failed to do, and after she'd worked so hard, she covered her face with her hands and burst into tears.

. . .

When the rain started blowing in the direction of the porch, Art pushed up from his rocker and headed into the house, grumbling to himself as he went. The last thing he wanted to do was get in Belle's way. She'd been acting crazy for days: talking to herself, popping up from the couch or the dinner table to go do something and then forgetting what it was, jumping with fright whenever she noticed him in the room with her, filing her fingernails every other day ... weird stuff like that. He was afraid all the nuttiness was going to bring on one of those attacks, the kind that kept her trapped in the house. What did Marge call it? Agoraphobia? All he knew was if Belle had one of those things no way could she make the ceremony tomorrow. And no way could she make the trip to California.

Don't think about it, he told himself as he settled in the den. What would help make time pass was some action on TV. He picked up the remote and started surfing the channels, keeping the sound turned off so as not to disturb Belle. All he could find on ESPN was a basketball game. Just his luck, he thought–he was a baseball kind of guy. To Art, most basketball players were overgrown and overpaid brats. He surfed awhile longer. Desperate to find something worth watching, he put down the remote and picked up this week's *TV Guide.* He got more and more discouraged as he flipped the pages. A good movie was coming up on TMC in about an hour, but for now he was stuck with the game.

Because he kept the sound on mute, every now and then he could hear Belle slamming around in the bedroom. He wished she'd hurry up and finish packing so they could watch the movie together. It was an old Alfred Hitchcock classic, *Rear Window.* Jimmy Stewart was one of Art's favorite actors, and Grace Kelly was easy on the eyes.

His head snapped to one side when he thought he heard a cry. Maybe it was a stray cat wanting in from the rain. All they needed right now was to get stuck with a cat right before they left town. He got up and went to the screened door, peered through the gloom and saw nothing but fog and rain. Relieved, he headed back to the den. On the way he paused at the door to the bedrooms. Sure enough, he heard a muffled cry. It had to be coming from Belle.

Barging into their room, he found Belle sprawled on top of a pile of clothes. "Hey, hey, what'sa matter?" He crawled on top of the bed and hovered over her.

Turning her face to him, chin quivering, she said, "Oh, Art, we can't go through with it. You need to start calling people right away." Tears streamed from her cheeks to the stack of sweaters under her head.

Art's heart gave a lurch. "Did'ya have one of them attacks?" He held his breath while waiting for an answer.

"No!" she wailed.

His held-in breath exploded into the air. "Then whaddaya talking about?"

"The ceremony. We have to postpone it."

"Aw, c'mon, Belle. Whatever's eating you can't be that bad."

"Oh but it is," she wailed. "I don't have a thing to wear!"

. . .

It was still raining at daylight the next morning and forecasters were predicting scattered showers for the rest of the day and well into the night. At nine o'clock on the dot, the banjo clock starting chiming and the phone starting ringing. First one and then another of the invited guests called, all wanting to know what they planned to do. Art wanted to move the ceremony indoors. Belle wouldn't hear of it. Absolutely not, she said. Come rain or come shine, they would gather in the park. Why else had umbrellas been invented?

The sun peeked out around ten past three. The phone had long since stopped ringing. Apparently people had resigned themselves to braving the elements regardless of the weather.

Dressed and ready to go since noon, Art had gone out to the porch at least a dozen times to look up at the sky. When not on the porch, he was either watching the weather channel on TV or pacing the floor.

Belle let him be, knowing it would be futile to try and stop him. Besides, she still had to get dressed. The suitcases had been packed at long last. After last night's crying spell, Art had talked her into taking a long, hot bath–he'd even scrubbed her back. Afterwards, as he gently dried her off with a downy towel, they'd both become aroused. The heat they generated had led them to Belle's old bed, since their own was still laden with clothes. After making sweet love they'd cuddled for a while and then drifted off to sleep.

Relaxed and refreshed when they woke from their nap, instead of shooing Art out of the room, Belle had asked him to help her pack. Wonder of all wonders, not a word of protest had come out of her mouth when he'd made short work of it, and they were soon back in their uncluttered bed. Had anyone asked what was in their suitcases, Belle couldn't have told them. By then she didn't really care. Her mind had returned to the fancy dresses.

Earlier today, full of renewed energy, she'd cleaned the house, washed her hair, painted her nails with clear polish, and bathed. Now all she had to do was put on her makeup and clothes.

Deciding what to wear had been a form of mental torture, worse even than trying to decide what to pack. What she really wanted to do was wear four dresses, one on top of the other, because they all fitted the occasion so perfectly. They were vintage dresses from the '40s, the very ones she'd brought to New Orleans to impress Blanche–to transport Blanche back to a time when her life still held promise.

It had taken an entire summer to collect the dresses. The hats had taken even longer. She knew Art would prefer that her hats stayed in their boxes, but today she was going to wear one anyway–the high frothy cream-colored creation she'd worn the day they went up to Jackson. The cluster of artificial violets that had been stitched to one side had somehow gotten squashed so she'd replaced the flowers with a heart-shaped broach made up of seed pearls rimmed in gold. That was the lovely thing about hats–you could add all kinds of doodads to dress them up or down. She would take the hat off before the reception, but, no matter what Art said, she was wearing it during the ceremony in honor of Blanche.

Men were so lucky, Belle thought, not for the first time. All Art did was shower, shave, run a comb through his hair, put on his shirt, socks, shoes, tie and suit, and he was ready to go. Thank goodness he'd bought a new suit. She hadn't wanted to say anything, but she'd been afraid he'd wear his rumply old brown thing. Instead, he'd surprised her by going out and buying a navy blue pinstripe, a white dress shirt with French cuffs, and a good-looking navy print tie with tiny maroon squares and white dots. He'd even bought a pair of cufflinks: heavy bands of gold that had been twisted to resemble Turk's-head. When she asked if they were symbolic of anything, he'd said no, he just liked the looks of them. She liked the looks of him–he looked scrumptious.

The dress she finally selected was the pale yellow lace over a matching rayon slip. It had a scalloped neckline, loose elbow-length sleeves, and a skirt with an uneven hem that hit her shins in front and her ankles in back. It was old-fashioned yet elegant, and it made her feel like a fairy princess. With it, she wore her last good pair of seamed stockings–not that anyone would notice with her long skirt covering the seams–, her cream-colored sling pumps, and her strand of pearls and matching earrings.

At last she presented herself for inspection. "How do I look?"

"Like an angel," Art said, his eyes moistening as he gazed at her.

She retrieved her hat from the top of the chest and put it on. "How do I look now?"

"Like an angel with a hat. C'mere, I could use a hug. I could use more than that but we don't have time." He opened his arms to her and, giggling, she went to him.

Standing back, she straightened his boutonniere, a single white rose, and gave it a little pat for good measure.

"Jeez," he said. "I almost forgot." She watched while he went to the kitchen and got something out of the refrigerator. He must have hidden it well, for she was surprised when she saw it.

"Gardenias!" she cried. It was a nosegay with white satin streamers. "Oh, they smell so delicious I could eat them."

"Don't even thing about it," Art said.

She burbled on, "They remind me of my birthday last year. Remember? You brought me a gardenia corsage and we had dinner at The Court of Two Sisters. That was the night I met the wizard."

"Yeah," Art said. Truth was, he'd forgotten about the wizard. "Wonder whatever happened to that bum."

"Arthur Barkoff, shame on you. He was no bum, he was a mystic."

"Mystic schmystic, let's go. We're gonna be late."

She glanced at the clock. "Oh dear, you're right."

The sun disappeared and it started to drizzle just as they were leaving the house. As if on cue, the phone rang. Ignoring it, Belle plucked her umbrella from the stand beside the door and crossed over the threshold to the porch. With a backward glance at Art, she said, "Tell whoever it is that I'm not home." She glided to the edge of the porch. Before descending the steps, she pressed the button on her fancy floral-printed parasol and up it sprang, like a bunch of flowers pulled from a magician's hat. And off she went, the nosegay in one hand, the parasol in the other, looking every inch the princess.

Ignoring the phone, Art caught up with her when she was halfway down the block. "What're you, nuts? Come back and get in the car. You're gonna get soaked."

"*Au contraire*," she chirped gaily. Without breaking stride, she continued on her merry way. "Somewhere beyond all those clouds it's a perfectly splendid day."

"Yeah, right," Art groused, popping open a black umbrella and holding it over his head. Despite feeling like a fool on parade, he kept pace with her the rest of the way. At least the drizzle kept the flies out of his face.

As they entered the park from the Frenchmen Street gate, the sun reappeared for a fraction of a second and then slipped behind a cloud. Having arrived in various vehicles, the guests had already assembled in the designated area on the Elysian Fields side of the park. Because of the inclement weather, no doubt, the rest of the park was deserted, which suited Belle just fine. It reminded her of the old days, the days when she felt Blanche's presence most keenly.

A few umbrellas could be spotted among the crowd, but most heads were exposed to the elements, which at that moment consisted of a hazy mist. A cheer rang out as Belle and Art approached. Flash bulbs began to pop and a few of the girls ran to meet them. Hugs, kisses, and compliments were bandied about–words like *gorgeous, beautiful, happy, handsome*, and *lovely.*

Except for Boots, all of Hope Haven's finest were in attendance, including Latessiah and the newest girl Tameka. Tameka was still going through the usual period of adjustment, acting like she hated the world and everyone in it, but today she looked bright and cheerful in her multi-colored African garb, a long silk robe with gold satin trim, a matching turban, and large loop earrings.

Mammy and the girls had ridden to the park in a sleek new Dodge Grand Caravan, driven by none other than Marge. The same anonymous donor who'd purchased the van had also bought the house where the reception would be held. Though it was still undergoing renovation, the front rooms and the kitchen were far enough along for everyone to move about without fear of tripping over loose boards or wires. They were using the occasion to celebrate the birth of *The Sunshine House*, a soon-to-be completed halfway house and boardinghouse.

Ideas for naming the house had been a major topic of conversation for weeks. In the end, all it took was a simple exchange between Belle and Gloria: "That coat of yellow paint makes the house look like a ray of sunshine," Belle had said, to which Gloria replied, "It sure does." Thus, *The Sunshine House* was born.

Mammy Daisy and Marge would have preferred to name the house after the donor, but they had no idea who he or she was. And though they pestered the firm that handled the closing to reveal their benefactor's identity, the lawyers stood firm. Thus, the name of the person responsible for their good fortune remained a much talked about mystery

The two women who would be in charge of the house and its residents were keeping a close eye on the renovations, expecially when it came to their private quarters. As the director-therapist of the new program, Marge would have an office on the first floor, a meeting room for group therapy sessions on the second floor, and a suite consisting of a bedroom, a sitting room and a bathroom on the third floor. Mammy's domain would be centrally located on the first floor–the kitchen, dining room, pantry, and a suite similar to Marge's.

Marge was so excited about her new job that she'd gained weight and taken a sudden interest in her appearance. She'd even gone to a beauty salon and had her hair styled. The only thing that bothered her was not knowing who her boss was. The funds for the operation of the house and hers and Mammy's salaries would be distributed by a group of local attorneys through another firm they knew nothing about, not even where it was located. She'd been assured there was no need to worry about a budget cut– the charitable foundation in question had enough funds to last several lifetimes. Still ... she allowed as how it would be odd to not have a boss to report to.

In addition to a new kitchen, new laundry facilities, new bathroom fixtures, new flooring, crown molding and baseboards, every square inch of the house needed cosmetic work. Lastly, the house needed furnishing, which was where James and Henry would lend their expertise. What with everyone eager to work on it, *The Sunshine House* was scheduled to have its grand opening well before Hope Haven closed its doors for the last time. The decision to eliminate the halfway house had been announced the first day of June, and the closing would take place on September 30.

Though everything was falling into place exactly as Belle hoped it would, none of the arrangements had been simple. The hardest part was keeping her involvement a secret. While the others discussed goals and plans and decorating ideas, she'd done little more than offer an occasional comment, If she hadn't been able to talk openly to Art she would have gone mad. Maybe someday, when she was an old lady in one of the nursing homes she visited, she would reveal the truth. Until then she would, as Art would say, keep her lips zipped.

Continuing to scan the crowd, she was pleased to see that Darleen and Roger had made it into town. Roger's route had changed once again–from Dallas to Kansas City and back–and they'd driven out of their way to be here. It was heartwarming to see them looking so healthy and vibrant, and it was obvious they were still very much in love.

It was also good to see Janette looking so well. Instead of wearing a worried frown or an angry scowl, her features were relaxed, face open, eyes alive with possibilities. The change in her demeanor had come about a few weeks after she signed the adoption papers. It was as though she'd turned into a whole different person, a carefree twenty-one-year-old with her whole life stretched out ahead of her.

Standing next to Mammy and the girls were James and Henry. Belle was delighted to see that they'd worn their tuxedos. Because it wasn't a formal affair, they'd asked her beforehand if she would mind. Silly question, she'd laughingly told them.

The Sidneys, the Cliffords, the Bardets, the Joyces, the Alstons, the Barrilleauxs and the Greens–all friends and customers of Belle's–were also present. So was Stanley Johns, the realtor. Connie, the receptionist at the mental health center, and six AA members rounded out the group.

Because this wasn't an official ceremony, Edith and Jesse had declined the invitation. It was too hot and humid to travel all that way, Edith said. But they'd sent their love and best wishes. Ever since their holiday in Florida, Edith had been much easier to get along with, and Jesse seemed happy puttering in his garden. Bitten by the travel bug, they planned to tour New England in the fall, be among the thousands of leaf peepers that descended on the area every year.

Mandy couldn't make it because she was spending the summer in Paris. She could have flown in for the weekend, but because Belle and Art were leaving on their trip tomorrow, they wouldn't have had enough time together. Since her father's death, Mandy was having second thoughts about her career choice. In truth she'd only wanted to become an attorney to please Lin. Now that he was gone and Jerry Thornton had taken over the firm, she was thinking more along the lines of fashion design. The idea thrilled Belle no end. What with her own interest in fashion, it gave them something to talk about. Mandy was most eager to see her vintage clothing collection. Which meant she'd have to come to New Orleans. Belle could hardly wait.

Sandy and the boys were postponing their visit until she saved enough vacation days. She had almost completed an apprenticeship in the ad department of a company that published a weekly tour guide. The two older boys were currently away at camp and the toddler was being cared for by a great-aunt. To say that Art was proud of his daughter was an understatement.

As for Artie ... they still held out hope.

Since their conversation back in March, Lil had called every now and then, mostly to see if Belle had found Blanche. Why she was so interested struck Belle as curious, but she liked hearing from her.

No, she always told Lil, she hadn't found Blanche. Not that she hadn't tried. She'd visited more residential facilities than she could count, including group homes run by individuals. At the rate she was going it would take her the rest of the year to cover the general area. Meanwhile, residents moved on, went home, or died, and new ones took their place. No matter, she planned to keep searching.

"Gather around everybody!" Marge called to the group. "It's time to begin."

Presiding over the service with a borrowed book of devotions, Marge took her place on a patch of newly-mown grass and beckoned Art and Belle to come stand before her.

Too late Belle thought to warn her that the wet grass would stain her pretty linen pumps.

Art, who hadn't left her side, took her hand in his and the two of them stepped forward.

A rustling could be heard as the guests arranged themselves behind the pair. Just as everyone was settled and the service was about to start, Gloria cried, "Look!"

All eyes followed her gaze. The arc of a rainbow spread its pastel colors across the horizon. A chorus of "Ahhhh's" rose up. Belle thought it a good omen–Blanche would be joining them soon.

Though the sun played peek-a-boo during the service, the rain held off. Washington Square had turned into a sparkling wonderland of various hues. Dewdrops glistened like diamonds, flowers perfumed the air, birds sounded their mating calls, and squirrels skipped over the grounds.

Passersby would have thought they were witnessing a marriage ceremony. They would have been almost correct. Except for substituting *man and woman* for *husband and wife*, the vows spoken used much of the same language. Rings were exchanged, blessings were given, and a pronouncement was made. A slow, tender kiss sealed their pledge.

Hugs and handshakes, hearty salutations, whoops and bursts of laughter followed. The girls had even thought to bring small bags of bird seed, handfuls of which they tossed at the ducking couple. More flash bulbs popped, and then it was on to the reception. But not before Belle flung her nosegay to the group at large and Darleen caught it.

As the guests quickly dispersed, Belle lingered behind. Standing perfectly still, her eyes roamed over the landscape, looking for a sign of Blanche. *Come to me*, *dear heart,* she mentally pleaded.

A strange hush fell over the park. The air seemed to grow thicker, the birds went mute, and the squirrels hid in their burrows. A filmy scrim of gray cloud blocked the rays of the sun. It was unnaturally quiet, as though time had stopped. The back of Belle's neck and her shoulders burned with tension.

"What're you waiting for?" Art asked, shattering the stillness.

Startled out of her wits, Belle gasped and jumped at the same time. Her pulse quickened and irregular heartbeats pounded in her ears. Breathing through her mouth, she sucked great gulps of air into her seemingly depleted lungs.

"What's the matter with you?" Art asked. "You having one of them whatchamacallits, them attacks?"

She whirled on him then, eyes flashing anger. "Don't say another word," she hissed. "I'm waiting for Blanche."

Art pulled an imaginary zipper across his lips. Then, heaving a sigh, he looked for a bench. Might as well make himself comfortable, he thought, loosening his tie and unbuttoning the top two buttons on his shirt.

He settled on a bench not five feet from where Belle stood frozen like a statue. It was then he realized how tired he was. The last few days had worn him down to a nub. Trying to keep up with Belle was like trying to qualify–never mind trying to win–at Indy. You had to keep one eye on the road ahead while the other eye watched both flanks. Right at that moment he was bringing up the rear. Maybe a few winks would help restore his reflexes. Some zzzzz's sure couldn't hurt. This waiting for Blanche business could take a while. He closed his eyes and let his head fall to one side.

With peace restored, Belle's eyes darted from place to place like a frantic bird searching for a spot to land. Where oh where in the world was she? Had Art scared her away? Oh, please, please, don't let it be so.

Ah! There she was! Just to the left of the wooden sign at the near end of the roundabout, the sign that read: WASHINGTON SQUARE.

It was some distance away, and the sun had slipped out from under the clouds, making her blink and squint against its brilliance, but there was no mistaking the beam of shimmering silver light. It had to be–it *was*–Blanche's spirit.

Keeping her eyes fixed on the light, she clasped her hands and held them over her heart. *Oh, my dearest Blanche, I cannot thank you enough for coming. Of course I'd rather see the real you. Is that possible?*

As if in answer to her mental transmission, a gentle breeze blew in her direction. It was Blanche sending a message back to her. *Please continue your search. I'm waiting for you.*

The breeze blew stronger, lifting the brim of Belle's hat. She began to shiver, whether from excitement or a sudden drop in temperature she did not know–she focused solely on Blanche.

Tell me where you are, she telegraphed. *I have to know where to find you.*

Instead of revealing her location, the message Belle heard went like this: *When you find me, we'll sit down together on your favorite bench right here in Washington Square. I'll tell you everything that's happened to me. That's what you want, isn't it?*

"Yes, oh yes," Belle murmured out loud, quick tears of happiness filling her eyes. "But I have to know where to find you. I've looked everywhere."

I have to go now, Blanche whispered on the wind. *Promise you'll keep searching.*

"I promise," Belle said, crossing her heart with an index finger. When the light began to dim, she grew panicky. Reaching out with both hands, as though to grab hold of the spirit form, she said, "Wait! You haven't told me where you are."

The sun slid behind a cloud and the beam of shimmering silver light dissolved into space.

Belle drew her hands back and wrapped her arms around her middle. Even though she knew Blanche had given enough of herself for one day, she would wait for the light to reappear. She had to know if her imagination had been playing tricks on her, if the beam was truly Blanche's spirit or merely a reflection thrown by the sun.

Reality slowly crept into her thoughts as she stood silently waiting. She remembered Art and how badly she'd treated him. How could she have gotten so angry at him? And on their almost wedding day! All he'd done was ask a simple question, for heaven's sakes. She loved him dearly, a hundred times more than she loved Blanche.

Where was he, anyway? She looked around, fearing he'd walked off and left her. But there he was, sound asleep on a bench. Seeing him like that, so sweet and innocent, make her feel even worse. Oh, the poor dear. She had a lot of making up to do.

Then came an image of the group of friends waiting at the house. Lord! Could she behave any more selfishly? She'd all but forsaken everyone she cared for and who cared for her because of a woman she'd never even met.

Feeling a crush of guilt on both accounts, she walked over to where Art was sleeping. With a wrench of tenderness she lifted a hand from his lap and held it to her breast. That's all it took. Art's eyes popped open and a grin split his face in two.

"Thank you for being you," she said and gave him her special smile. "I'm ready to go now."

"That's my girl," Art said, pushing up from the bench. He took her in his arms and gave her a proper kiss.

Laughing and holding hands like children, they headed out of the park. Art didn't ask if she'd seen Blanche and Belle didn't tell. She also didn't look back to see if the light had reappeared. From now on she would keep her priorities in order. First came Art, then Mandy and her parents, followed by Mammy, Marge, Gloria, Janette, and the rest of the girls, her friends, Blanche, and finally her mural-painting business, 'Scenes by Belle.' As for The Sunshine House and the charitable foundation, she'd do whatever was necessary to keep both enterprises going and leave the actual management to the perfectly capable people already in place.

. . .

"Don't you wish we'd brought the car?" Art said as they made their way up Esplanade on foot. "All the food'll be gone by the time we get there."

Belle's feet were killing her but she was not about to admit it. She'd been wearing paint-splattered sneakers for so long, she'd forgotten what real shoes felt like. "You could have ridden in the van with the girls," she said, teasing.

"Ha," he snorted. "That'll be the day."

"Be grateful it's not raining. Oh, I'm so glad it didn't start up again during the ceremony. The heavens smiled down on us the whole time." Along with Blanche, she said to herself. "And the rainbow added a lovely touch."

"Yeah, I just hope the heaven's are still smiling when we're up in the air tomorrow."

She looked at him. "You're worried about flying, aren't you?"

"Damn right," he said. He'd never flown in an airplane and he was already queasy at the thought. "It don't seem natural for something that big and heavy to take off into the wild blue yonder."

She came to a sudden stop in the middle of the sidewalk. "I've had a brainstorm," she said. "Let's cash in our tickets and take the train."

He wrinkled his brow. "Train? What train?"

"The Amtrak train that goes to California. I think it's the same one I took down here from Atlanta, The Sunset Limited. We could get a sleeper and everything. Oh, it'd be so romantic. I just love trains."

Art warmed to the idea in a matter of seconds. What he'd really wanted to do was drive out west so they could stop and see the sights along the way. But with everything that was going on these days a road trip would take too long. So they'd planned to fly out to L.A. and rent a car. But if they could get there by train, so much the better. It would only take a coupla extra days and they could still rent a car when they got there.

"Sounds good to me," he said.

"Do you mean it?"

"Sure I mean it. That way we can still see some of the country. Take our time. No muss, no fuss."

"Exactly."

"So what're we waiting for? Let's go check it out."

"Go home, you mean?"

"Where else?"

"But what about the reception?"

"It can wait. So they'll think we stopped off for a quickie, so what. It'll give 'em something to talk about."

"You're terrible," she said, giggling. Then she hiked up her skirt, held it above her knees and went sprinting up the block, her aching feet forgotten.

By the time they reached the party some of the guests–the AA members and four of the couples–had already departed; the rest were standing around quietly talking. The festivities started up in earnest once the happy couple breezed in.

As soon as the news about their train trip was delivered, they headed for the food. Long wooden planks set on sawhorses served as tables for party sandwiches, spinach balls, crab puffs, sausage balls, cheese logs, crackers and chips, a variety of dips, mixed nuts, mints, and a platter of raw vegetables and relishes. Coolers held iced soft drinks and juices and Mrs. Clifford had brought a jug of her special lemonade.

In the middle of a card table sat a three-layer cake. Vanilla frosting over chocolate fudge, Mammy declared. Instead of featuring a bride and groom, someone had stuck two miniature dolls on top. The dolls bore a remarkable resemblance to Barbie and Ken.

"Gloria did it," Janette announced, hooting with glee.

"That figures," said Art, grinning at the girl he used to call Punk.

Both touched and amused, Belle blew Gloria a kiss. "Thanks for the keepsakes, sweetie. We'll treasure them always." Gloria returned the blown kiss.

Still more flash bulbs erupted off when Belle, with Art's hand holding hers steady, cut the cake. A shoving match broke out among the girls when they tried to line up for a slice. It was all in fun, however, and even Mammy chuckled at the girls' antics. It was easy to see that Lateeshia and Tameka had joined the family.

The party started breaking up around nine o'clock. First the Sidneys and the Cliffords left, then Stanley Johns, Connie, the Alstons, and finally Marge and Mammy and their rowdy band of charges. Since James and Henry had volunteered for cleanup duty, they stayed behind. Not in any hurry to get started, they sipped from glasses of white grape juice while Belle and Art nursed glasses of lemonade.

After giving the men last minute instructions on watering the plants and collecting the mail while they were gone, Belle said, "Oh, and if you have any spare time, please try to drop by one of my nursing homes. It doesn't matter which one, but try to make it on a Tuesday. That's when the folks usually play bingo and the staff could use your help."

"It would be our pleasure," said James.

"Indubitably," said Henry.

"Who knows," James said, "we may find that special someone."

Belle knew exactly who that 'special someone' might be. Like Lil, James and Henry seemed overly interested in her search for Blanche. Sometimes she thought they were teasing her, but she always tried to be good-natured about it.

"Well," she said, half-joking,"if you find her, tell her to stay put until I get back."

At that, both James and Henry raised their glasses in a toast. "Long live Blanche!"

"Here, here!" cried Belle, thinking: If they only knew.

Praise for *Searching for Blanche*

"Once in a while, angels appear among us. How else can one explain this book's main character, an endearing, troubled woman who calls herself Belle Reve, after the plantation in *A Streetcar Named Desire.*

"Spurred by a traumatic loss, Belle quashes her paralyzing agoraphobia (fear of leaving home) just long enough to reach New Orleans, where she searches for Tennessee Williams's characters, especially Blanche DuBois, with whom she identifies. Like Blanche, Belle relies on the kindness of strangers and finds it in cabbie Art Barkoff.

"As the two journey the streets of New Orleans and beyond, Belle's sweet innocence bewitches a calloused cab dispatcher, a streetwise panderer, a con artist, and even staff members of a psychiatric hospital.

"When Belle seeks treatment for her anxiety disorder, she ends up at a halfway house, where she transforms a bevy of fallen girls with her own essential goodness. The real question, though, is can Belle save herself?

"Through Belle Reve, Alabama author Mary Kay Remick has written the story Blanche DuBois deserved, one in which her gentle nature is not vilified and abused, but rather rewarded and valued. If people like Stanley Kowalski allowed vulnerability to appeal to their best rather than base instincts, then angels like Belle might reside among us more often."

Nancy Dorman-Hickson, *Southern Living*

Praise for *Sweet and Sour*

"... a delightful romp through the Deep South when cousins, Nickel "Nicky" Summers and Penny "Perfect," come together to seek revenge on a snake-handling preacher. You'll laugh till you cry."

Dot Senn, *The Oak Ridger*

"Alabama author, Mary Kay Remick, has brought us yet another rich landscape populated with characters so real you can almost reach out and touch them. *Sweet and Sour* will make you laugh, cry, and leave you wanting more."

Dixie Huthmaker, author of *Inside the Salt Shaker*

"This novel is rich in setting, characterization and plot ... kept me turning the pages to see what would happen next! ... I was fascinated with the wise use of detail that made each scene come alive. What a great read!"

Dr. Betty Roe, textbook author and educator

Printed in the United States
16230LVS00002B/49-306

9 780966 712834